THE
FINAL ACT
OF JULIETTE
WILLOUGHBY

ALSO BY ELLERY LLOYD

The Club
People Like Her

THE
FINAL ACT OF
JULIETTE
WILLOUGHBY

A NOVEL

ELLERY LLOYD

HARPER

An Imprint of HarperCollins*Publishers*

THE FINAL ACT OF JULIETTE WILLOUGHBY. Copyright © 2024 by Ellery Lloyd Ltd. All rights reserved. Printed in the United States of America. No part of this book may be used or reproduced in any manner whatsoever without written permission except in the case of brief quotations embodied in critical articles and reviews. For information, address HarperCollins Publishers, 195 Broadway, New York, NY 10007.

HarperCollins books may be purchased for educational, business, or sales promotional use. For information, please email the Special Markets Department at SPsales@harpercollins.com.

FIRST EDITION

Library of Congress Cataloging-in-Publication Data has been applied for.

ISBN 978-0-06-332300-1

24 25 26 27 28 LBC 5 4 3 2 1

AUTHOR'S NOTE

With the exception of the fictional Juliette Willoughby, Oskar Erlich, and Austen Willoughby, all the artists mentioned or who appear in this novel are genuine historical figures.

THE FINAL ACT
OF JULIETTE
WILLOUGHBY

CAROLINE, DUBAI, THE PRESENT DAY

It is time to begin.

I am standing at a podium in front of a painting in an art gallery in Dubai. It is not a large painting—30 inches by 21 inches, to be precise. It is not a very large gallery—we are in the biggest of its three rooms, a white-painted space about the size of a school classroom. Arranged in front of me are several rows of folding chairs, occupied by reporters. I have already been introduced to a writer from the *Telegraph* and the *Gulf News* podcast team. A group of press photographers are clicking away, flashguns strobing. At the back are two TV crews, one from a local Arabic station, one from BBC News.

Beside me at the podium is the owner of the gallery, the organizer of this press conference, Patrick Lambert.

"Dr. Caroline Cooper," Patrick is saying, "is a Fellow of Pembroke College and professor of modern art at the University of Cambridge, specializing in the Surrealist movement in the 1930s, with a focus on Surrealist art by women, in particular the British painter Juliette Willoughby."

Patrick lists my publications, highlighting my 1998 biography of Juliette, the first ever written and still—he reminds everyone—the definitive account of the artist's life, work, and untimely death. He also mentions how long he and I have known each other. One or two audience members smile knowingly.

The painting on the wall behind us is entitled *Self-Portrait as Sphinx*. It was painted by Juliette—then twenty-one years old—in the winter of 1937–38, and was first displayed at the era-defining International Surrealist Exhibition in Paris in 1938. For decades it was lost, believed destroyed. Last night it was sold, right here, for £42 million.

"Thank you, Patrick," I say as he takes a seat in the front row. He gives me a wink. I stifle a smile back.

I have been asked to keep my speech short: just five minutes in which to explain Surrealism, its historical context and underlying philosophy. To convey why this artwork matters, why I believe it to be genuine, and why I am prepared to stake my professional reputation on that opinion. To tell the story of the artist and this painting, and how it was lost, and how it was found again—twice.

It is a story that begins one wet autumn morning in Cambridge in 1991, at our first dissertation supervision with Alice Long, with the conversation that set Patrick and me on a path that would eventually lead us to Juliette's lost masterpiece.

It is a story that begins one winter evening in Paris in 1937, when a runaway British heiress embarked, in the cold and cramped Montmartre studio she shared with her famous artist lover, on one of the most remarkable paintings of its era.

It is also, I suppose, the story of Patrick and me. How we fell in love. How a painting brought us together, drove us apart, and now seems to have united us once more.

Of everything I have to say, I am aware that thirty seconds at most will make it onto TV, a sentence or two into the newspapers. The headlines will be all about the sum the painting sold for, and who bought it.

What I really want to tell everyone in this room is: *Look at it*. Look at *her*, I almost said. Because it is *her* you notice first. The work's dominant central figure. Her wild auburn mane. Her ice-blue eyes. Her expression: defiant, fearless. Then you notice her breasts are bare. Then you notice there are six of them, arranged like the teats on a cat. Then you notice she has a cat's legs too, a cat's haunches, tortoiseshell-patterned. Sharp claws. And you start to wonder what it might mean, to depict yourself as a Sphinx. As *this* Sphinx.

Only up close can you truly appreciate the painting's vast intricacy, the people and creatures arranged around the central Sphinx, all intent on their individual tasks, seemingly unaware of one another, in a setting that is part overgrown English country garden, part junglescape. Each new group you notice inviting reflection on the story that together they might tell, your initial bewilderment perhaps fading, perhaps deepening, as patterns and echoes emerge and new mysteries present themselves.

The mystery that the journalists in this room are interested in, of course, is a far simpler one: how can this impossible painting exist at all? The answer is that I am not sure. All I can confidently state is my belief in its authenticity, which means we need to reconsider everything we thought we knew about Juliette Willoughby, her life, and her work.

As it turns out, in the end, I don't have time to say any of that. I have just wished everyone a good afternoon when there is a commotion at the doorway—three latecomers have loudly barged in, asking the same question repeatedly in Arabic. Someone turns to shush them. I am just about to point out that there are still some empty seats at the front when I notice they are in uniform: khaki shirts and trousers tucked into shiny black boots, with angled gold-badged berets. A gallery assistant points out Patrick and they make their way in our direction. I am still—somewhat distractedly—talking about the painting. Patrick, frowning, is out of his chair and advancing to meet the men. The photographers are snapping away, the TV cameras are rolling.

Capturing for posterity and a global audience Patrick Lambert's arrest for murder.

PART I

THE JOURNAL

What do you consider the essential encounter of your life? To what extent did this encounter seem to you, and does it seem to you now, to be fortuitous or foreordained?

—ANDRÉ BRETON, *Mad Love*
(1937, TRANS. MARY ANN CAWS)

CHAPTER 1

PATRICK, CAMBRIDGE, 1991

Oh bloody hell. That was my first thought as I plowed through an axle-deep puddle and turned onto Elm Lane, making out through my windshield a bedraggled figure, her blond hair hanging in dripping ringlets down her back. This was going to be awkward.

It was Caroline Cooper.

There seemed little doubt we were headed for the same place—why else would she be wandering up a windswept street on the outskirts of Cambridge on a weekday morning? My director of studies had mentioned that these final-year dissertation supervisions would be taking place *à deux*. He said he hoped that would not be a problem and I reassured him it would not be, vaguely hoping my supervision partner would be attractive, female. I should also have hoped for someone with whom I had not already slept.

She was standing at the end of a driveway, peering up it, presumably looking for a house number. I slowed the MG to a crawl. Even rain-soaked, she was stunning. I checked my own appearance in the rearview mirror. Caroline Cooper. What were the chances of that?

She and I had slept together twice, back at the very beginning of our first year. Once after a party, then again a few weeks later, having tipsily bumped into each other at a college dance. The first time was in her room, with its fairy lights around the mirror and Frida Kahlo poster on the wall. I recalled the narrowness of her bed, waking up in the night desperate for a pee but not wanting to disturb her or break the moment's spell, our legs entangled, her head on my chest.

The second time, we had meandered back to my room holding

hands, stopping now and then to kiss in a doorway. Half that night we stayed up talking, drinking cheap white wine from chipped mugs and smoking out the window, surveying the moonlit quad below. Talking about Cambridge, her first impressions of it. Discussing art and artists. I told her stories about my father, about boarding school. It was obvious we were attracted to each other. It also felt like we were really connecting, as if this was the start of something very exciting indeed.

What happened next was . . . nothing. I left a note in her college cubbyhole. No reply. I kept an eye out for her in lectures. She began arriving just before they started and sitting on the opposite side of the lecture hall, then slipping off quickly at the end.

I turned that second night over and over in my mind, trying to pinpoint what I'd done wrong. Was it something I had said? I probably was a bit of a show-off in those days, keen to make an impression, establish myself as a bit of a Cambridge character. Driving around town in my silly sports car. Playing up to the public schoolboy thing, the floppy hair, the posh accent . . .

It quickly became obvious what while I may have felt a spark between us, Caroline had not. When we passed in the Art History Department corridors or she accidentally sat opposite me in the library, I received only the faintest of acknowledgments. Once or twice, I caught her crossing the street to avoid me. After a while, no matter how much you like someone, you have no choice but to take the hint.

I tapped the horn lightly and Caroline looked up. She recognized my car, of course—how many students tooled around Cambridge in a red MG convertible?—and forced an unconvincing smile. I pulled over and rolled the window down. It was not a situation in which we could just both ignore each other, after all.

"I suspect we're looking for the same place," I said.

"I think this is it," she replied. "Number thirty-two?"

"That was the address Dr. Bailey gave me."

The house certainly looked the part. Let's put it this way: either an academic lived here or the place was derelict. Slates were missing from the roof. The downstairs curtains were drawn. Something shrubby was sprouting from a sagging gutter. Caroline pressed the doorbell. Nothing happened.

"Are you sure you . . . ?" I asked.

She invited me to try for myself. It was unclear if the buzzer was even connected to anything. Tentatively at first, then again more firmly, I knocked. Caroline took a step back to peer up at the first-floor windows.

"There are no lights on," she pointed out. "Do you think she's forgotten?"

"Maybe. She must be getting on a bit, after all. Have you ever heard of her, this Alice Long?"

I had not, although the university library did list three books by her—one on Man Ray, one on Brassaï, and another on the history of photojournalism. She had been a press photographer herself, for *Time* and *Vogue*, according to the author bio in the last of these, published in 1980. Even a decade ago, Alice Long had looked quite old in her author's headshot.

"Maybe she can't hear us," I said. "Do you think I should go around and shout over the back fence?"

"For God's sake," Caroline muttered behind me. "Who is this person, anyway? She isn't part of the faculty. She isn't affiliated with a college. Why is she supervising final-year dissertations? I might complain. This project is an important part of our degree, you know."

I could understand Caroline's anxiety. Even in the first year, she had been clear about how seriously she took her subject, what her end goal was: a life of scholarship, teaching, writing. I could easily see her as a cool young academic, inspiring her students, probably while wearing a leather jacket and red lipstick. Like a dickhead, trying to impress her, I had detailed my own career plans: a first-class degree, a job at Sotheby's, my own Mayfair gallery by the age of thirty. I must have sounded obscenely entitled and overconfident, but in my defense, I *was* eighteen. I said a lot of things out loud in those days that I have since learned to keep to myself.

Still, the bottom line was this: if we had been stuck with a dud supervisor and it impacted badly on our final-degree result, we could both kiss our respective dreams goodbye.

From the other side of the door, a bolt was pulled back with a screech. It was another few minutes before the door finally opened—in the meantime much fiddling with other locks could be heard.

"Hello there," I said loudly, I hoped reassuringly. "It's Patrick and Caroline. We're History of Art students. From the university."

The face in the doorway was wrinkled and sallow, topped with a tangle of white hair. Alice Long was wearing a brown pleated dress, gray knee-length socks, and a suspicious frown. She looked even older than I had been expecting.

"You're late," she said sternly.

"Sorry," I told her. "We have been knocking for a while . . ."

As I stepped into the hallway, I checked my hair in a foxed little wall mirror. Alice Long shuffled off, disappearing through an open door, obviously expecting us to follow her. In the gloom, I was vaguely aware of a Persian rug underfoot, dirt-darkened, threadbare. Framed black-and-white photographs hung on the wall, a thick layer of dust obscuring their subjects.

I let Caroline go ahead of me and when she reached the end of the corridor I saw her stiffen.

"Please," Alice Long said, indicating a very small sofa—a large armchair, really—with high sides. "Sit."

She settled on a wooden chair next to a table piled with books. Caroline and I sat gingerly on the sofa, trying to avoid touching each other. The room's net curtains were drawn, its main source of light an unshaded bulb hanging from a wire.

"So, Patrick," said Alice Long without preamble. "You're interested in Surrealism, are you?"

"*Very* interested," I said firmly, leaning forward to emphasize this, eager to make a good impression. "What fascinates me is the way Surrealist art fearlessly explores the inner workings of the mind. Its rejection of conformity and willingness to embrace the mythical and dreamlike. All those haunting, seemingly random scenes and images that seem to spring direct from the subconscious."

Alice Long smiled faintly, eyeing me intently.

"People always go on about Dalí and Magritte," I continued, "but the painter who really encapsulates the movement for me is Oskar Erlich."

This was clearly not something she had expected me to say. She raised a slightly surprised eyebrow and gestured for me to continue.

"Anyway, I want to focus my dissertation on the 1938 International Surrealist Exhibition in Paris, their last great show before the war. It was a huge media event, all the artists associated with the movement showing: Erlich, Picasso, Man Ray, Miró . . ."

Alice Long made a little gesture with her hand as if to say, *I know all this*.

"I intend to explore the way the exhibition was organized," I continued. "The manner in which it was publicized, its cultural impact."

She greeted this with a thoughtful frown. "You have a potentially interesting topic there. The argument will need development, though," she said.

"Oh, definitely," I said, a little crushed. *Potentially* interesting? Potentially *interesting*?

Alice Long then pivoted in her chair to ask Caroline what she was working on. Caroline cleared her throat, brought out her notebook, and started to read. It quickly became clear that she had done a lot more preparation than I had. She intended to explore Sphinxes in Surrealist art, she explained. She had notes on the different types of Sphinx (royal and monstrous, Greek and Egyptian), male and female, winged and unwinged. She made the point that we use the Greek word *Sphinx*—masculine, I interjected, pleased with myself—to describe interchangeably what were actually distinct and unrelated creatures in Greek and Egyptian mythology. She ended by saying something like: "And that's as far as I have got, Sphinx-wise."

Alice Long—engaged, enthusiastic, a lot livelier than when I had been talking—asked her which particular works she would write about. Caroline mentioned Max Ernst's *Une Semaine de bonté*, Dalí's *Three Sphinxes of Bikini*, Leonor Fini's *Little Hermit Sphinx* . . .

"What about Juliette Willoughby's *Self-Portrait as Sphinx?*" asked Alice Long.

"Oh yes, of course," said Caroline, although with a trace of hesitation in her voice.

If that was a line of inquiry Caroline was interested in pursuing, Alice Long continued, she should examine the Willoughby Bequest. "It's a collection of Egyptological materials formerly in the possession of the Willoughby family deposited at the Museum of Archaeology and Anthropology, here in Cambridge," she explained, in response to Caroline's confused frown. Caroline wrote this down and as she did so glanced at me meaningfully. I offered her in return the facial equivalent of a hapless shrug.

Juliette Willoughby? The Willoughby Bequest? Was Alice Long being serious? Like most people with an interest in the Surrealists, I knew only two things about Juliette Willoughby, the most obvious being that she had been Oskar Erlich's lover. All his biographies recounted their love story and its tragic ending.

This had to be some sort of test. If it was not, then I really did think we were going to have to talk seriously to our respective directors of studies about this supervisor they had assigned us. From the look on Caroline's face, she was thinking the same thing. I raised my hand.

"Mr. Lambert?" Alice Long said curtly.

"Isn't there a bit of a problem, for anyone planning to write about Juliette Willoughby?" I asked. Because there was only one other thing everyone knew about the artist and her work. *"Her paintings don't exist."* I continued. "None of them. Everything she produced at art school was lost when she left England for Paris in 1936. *Self-Portrait as Sphinx*, the only thing she ever exhibited publicly, is listed in the catalogue of the 1938 Surrealist Exhibition and described in a couple of reviews, but that's it. Not a single photograph of it survives, none of her sketches or studies, and the painting itself was destroyed in a fire in Paris in 1938."

The same unexplained fire that killed both Juliet Willoughby and Oskar Erlich.

CAROLINE, CAMBRIDGE, 1991

Philophobia. That's the technical term for it. A fear of falling in love. A *chronic* fear of falling in love. I didn't know it even had a name back then, but thanks to Patrick Lambert, I knew its symptoms well enough: panic attacks, dizziness, nausea, a feeling that your throat is closing up and you are about to pass out. Every time you think about someone, or how much you like them.

The first time I met Patrick, I was instantly smitten. The dark curls, the hooded green eyes, the lopsided grin that poked a dimple in one cheek. He was funny, smart. Unlike a lot of the boys I had met at Cambridge, when he asked you a question, he genuinely listened to your answer.

The second time we slept together, we were both quite drunk. We kissed on the dance floor. We kissed on the quad. We kissed in his room, unable to keep our hands off each other, then sat, sheets wrapped around our naked bodies, talking and laughing for hours. He told me how it felt being sent off to boarding school at the age of seven, suddenly surrounded by larger, louder, more confident boys and desperately missing home. I listened intently, deftly deflecting his questions about my own childhood.

"Hey, I really like you," he said at one point, casually cool, bumping bare shoulders affectionately.

"I really like you too," I said back truthfully, although even then I could feel my spine stiffening, my stomach tightening. Because how many times had I heard from my grandmother about what a brilliant, joyful girl my mother had been, growing up. About her painting, her drawing, all the competitions she had won. All the friends she had, all the hopes and ambitions, before she met my father. How many times had I promised myself I would never allow anyone to stand between me and what I wanted to achieve? No matter how much I liked them. No matter how tousled their hair, how appealing their dimple.

Perhaps I could have handled things better, tried to explain all this to Patrick. But where would I have begun? How could I have explained something that I could not yet put a name to?

Even now, it is hard to describe the roil of emotions, the hot surges of embarrassment and alarm, of horror and happiness, that I felt when Patrick pulled up outside Alice Long's house and it dawned on me we would be meeting like this all year. I spent quite a lot of that first hour-long supervision trying to work out if I could politely decline a lift back into town. Then we got outside and saw the weather.

The drizzle had turned into a downpour. Patrick was standing a step ahead of me on the porch, trying unsuccessfully to angle his umbrella so it sheltered us both from the rain.

"Can I offer you a ride?" he asked.

"Um, well . . ." I hesitated, aware of how long I'd had to wait for a bus out here.

"On a count of three, then," said Patrick. We ran to the car in attempted lockstep under the umbrella, his bag bumping between us.

I had never been in a sports car before and was unprepared for the intimacy of the experience. How close to each other we were sitting. The way that every time he changed gear, his hand brushed my knee. Just like in the supervision, I tried not to think about the last time we had been this physically proximate.

By the time we approached the center of town, the rain was even worse, bouncing off the car windows, hammering on the roof. When we stopped at a set of traffic lights, Patrick turned and fixed me with a serious look. "So what do you make of Alice Long, then?"

"Well, she's certainly . . . unusual."

"That's an understatement."

"I also think she's kind of . . . amazing? All that stuff she was saying about Juliette Willoughby?"

There had been moments over the last three years, in lectures, in seminars, when it felt like my whole world was being tilted slightly on its axis. When things I had unquestioningly accepted my whole life suddenly came apart to reveal their constituent components and they all fitted together, or else disintegrated entirely. When the thing that everyone took for granted turned out to be not the end of the discussion but the start of a much more important one. Had Juliette's masterpiece been lost? Maybe so, Alice Long had conceded. But what does it *mean* to say *lost*? Lost why? By whom? Are you happy—her bright eyes burned into mine as she asked—to simply accept that? Her *Self-Portrait as Sphinx* was personally selected for the exhibition by André Breton—the pope of Surrealism himself, the movement's great theorist and propagandist. Contemporary reviewers compared her talent to that of Salvador Dalí and Max Ernst, Alice Long reminded us. Why not reexamine those reviews, the letters and diaries of Juliette's Paris circle? There must be mention of her work somewhere. *Lost? Pfft,* Alice Long exclaimed. *Lots of things in the world are only lost because no one has bothered to look for them.*

It sounded like a challenge. It sounded like a life's work. It made me think of my own mother and her dreams of becoming an artist, and all the overlooked, underappreciated women like her over the centuries.

Patrick did not seem to have found all this quite as inspiring as I did.

The windshield wipers swept back and forth, squeaking. He mused in silence for some minutes. "Lots of Oskar Erlich's work was lost in that fire too, you know," he said defensively.

"Exactly Alice Long's point! Lots of his work was lost but lots survives, because he spent pretty much his entire career being celebrated and collected and written about in books that barely mention Juliette, let alone the fact that she was an artist in her own right."

The light turned green and we sped off, Patrick careering through a massive puddle and soaking from head to toe a student in an orange raincoat. In the rearview mirror I could see him shaking himself down, staring after us. I turned in my seat to mouth an apology.

"Here we are," said Patrick, flicking the indicator too late as he swerved over to the other side of the road. "The Museum of Archaeology and Anthropology."

It was time to lay my cards on the table. "Patrick, had you ever heard of it before, this Willoughby Bequest? Have you any idea what Alice Long thinks I'm going to find there?"

He smiled. "I do know a little about it," he said. One of his hands was resting loosely atop the steering wheel. The other was on the stick, ready to shift his car into gear. "Have you ever read anything about Juliette's family and their history?"

"Not much. I know the Willoughbys were well-off. Her father, Cyril, was an MP, wasn't he?"

"And a collector of Egyptian artifacts. He filled an entire wing of his house with them. Quite an eccentric, by all accounts, and a bit of a recluse in his later years. He's buried at Longhurst Hall, the family estate, in a mausoleum he commissioned, supposedly a scale model of the Pyramid of Djoser in Saqqara, the oldest known pyramid in Egypt."

"So Alice Long wants me to explore if there is a personal angle to Juliette's interest in Sphinxes?"

"I'd imagine so, and in that case this Willoughby Bequest would certainly be a good place to start. When Juliette's father died, Longhurst Hall and his collection all went to his youngest brother, Austen, Juliette's uncle. Who kept the house but off-loaded the Egyptian stuff to the University of Cambridge."

"And that's how it ended up here?" I gestured out the window to the looming redbrick building that Patrick's car was currently double-parked outside, hazard lights flashing.

"Exactly. As it happens, my dad was at Cambridge with Austen's son Philip. And I was at school with *his* son, Harry."

Of course you were, I thought. It was still astonishing to me, after three years as a student here, how frequently and how casually people like Patrick would slip this sort of thing into conversation. That his father had been at Cambridge with Juliette Willoughby's cousin. That Patrick had been at school with his son. Like my friend Athena Galanis, who halfway through a Picasso lecture had told me she was pretty sure her father had at one point owned the painting in the slide. Like the boy in a second year tutorial whose uncle turned out to have written the definitive work on the week's topic (Flemish Mannerism in the Early Sixteenth Century). It was a small world and it felt very distant from the one I grew up in.

"The thing is," Patrick continued, "even Philip and Harry can't quite explain what happened. Because the family never even tried to sell what Cyril spent decades accumulating, although it was worth a fortune. They just gave it all away. Which, if you knew the Willoughbys and what they're like about money . . ."

Someone trying to squeeze their car past us down the street honked their horn. "Okay, okay! Keep your wig on," Patrick muttered over his shoulder. He returned his attention to me.

"The rumor is that the Willoughbys wanted to get rid of all that stuff because—well, they have had a lot of bad luck, that family. Odd and unfortunate things have happened in that house."

"Patrick, are you seriously trying to tell me they believed the collection was cursed?" I asked.

He shrugged stagily. I opened the car door and climbed out.

Patrick rolled down the window and rested his elbow on the frame. "I guess all I am saying is"—he dropped into a parody of a horror movie voice, adding a little creak and echo to his words—"*be careful, Caroline!*"

He grinned and winked, then revved the engine and sped away, and with a slight tingle of apprehension—and a lurch of the stomach—and perhaps just a touch of annoyance I realized just how attractive I still found Patrick Lambert.

FIVE HOURS LATER, MY excitement about working on Juliette Willoughby, and much of my enthusiasm about working with Alice Long, was wearing off. The library was airless and silent. Through the windows, the gloom of an autumn afternoon was deepening rapidly to night.

As far as I could see, the Willoughby Bequest was a mess. The first thing the librarian—an elderly woman with striking blue eyes and a somewhat suspicious manner—had asked me was which part exactly I wanted to view. I must have looked blank. She explained that the bequest was divided into three parts: the artifacts, some of which were on display in the museum upstairs; the many papyri (very fragile, not accessible without special permission); and the seventy-two boxes of unsorted general material, unlabeled, undated. Assuming this was where anything relevant to Juliette and her interest in Sphinxes would be, I asked for this unsorted ephemera first.

It was possible this had been a mistake.

The boxes seemed to contain the entire contents of Cyril Willoughby's study. Old letters. Handwritten notebooks full of hieroglyphs. Notepaper from Shepheard's Hotel in Cairo. One by one, the librarian brought these boxes up from the bowels of the building. One by one, I combed through them, trying to give the appearance of someone who knew what they were looking for. She explained that a new archivist, a PhD student, had been hired to put it all into some sort of order. His name was Sam Fadel and if I had any questions I should look him up.

After five hours and nineteen boxes, I was getting increasingly frustrated with the whole process. Promising myself that if I managed to sift through them all I could at least tell Alice Long I'd done my best, I began lifting the next battered manila carton's contents out item by item and placing them on the table. More letters, invoices. More notebooks. Then a tattered envelope caught my attention, *M et Mme Cyril Willoughby* written in looping script on the front. It was heavier than I had been expecting, when I picked it up, and much more intriguing than anything else I had yet come across.

Easing the envelope open carefully with my thumb, I tipped it and out slithered a thin gold chain—a necklace, with a pendant attached. The pendant was beaten gold, oval-shaped, about two inches long, etched on one side with an elaborately stylized representation of an eye: a long, curving line to represent an eyebrow, a line sweeping back from the eye's rear corner, terminating in a curl.

I could also feel the outlines of two book-like objects inside the envelope. One had a grainy texture, and I shimmied this out first. It was a navy blue British passport, the royal coat of arms embossed on the front. Handwritten, in block letters, in the little lozenge-shaped window at the bottom, was "Miss Juliette Willoughby."

I let the passport fall open, and from the photograph page the most extraordinary face stared back at me—wide-awake, icy eyes; thick, arched eyebrows; a full mouth set in a hard line; a young woman with a dusting of freckles. Juliette's wild tumble of curls filled almost the entire frame. I turned the pages and found Juliette's signature and two stamps, one for Rome (1935), one for Paris (1936). It was a stark reminder that she had been a real, living person, just like me. That with this in her hand, she might have imagined traveling all around the world, and instead . . .

Hands quivering, I placed the passport on the desk and slid from the envelope a fragile-looking notebook, its unlined pages filled (as I discovered when cautiously I opened it) not just with dated diary entries but sketches and studies. Charcoal drawings of a Sphinx, the artist's fingers dragged across the page to contour the creature's eyes, lips, mane. Intricate pencil compositions, the same characters over and over placed in different scenes. Interspersed between these, passages of text in spidery, barely legible cursive handwriting. On the back pages there were daubs of color, each with a number and a scribbled comment next to it.

On the flyleaf, in fountain pen, someone had written the initials "J. W." and an address in Paris.

I traced the letters with a finger. Their curves. Their swirls.

J. W.

Juliette Willoughby.

I turned the pages carefully, terrified that the brittle paper would crack or crumble, until I came to the first entry. It began: *11th November 1937—It is almost midnight. I am writing this in bed. . . .*

First Entry

Thursday, 11th November—It is almost midnight. I am writing this in bed. The night is cold and I am tucked up under every blanket in the place, my toes like little lumps of ice in Oskar's thick woolen socks. I am saving the last of the firewood for the morning, and there is just a very faint glow from the embers in the stove, the occasional clink as they settle.

This *appartement* that Oskar and I rent is on the top floor of a five-story building. Once it must have been rather grand. Now it is terribly shabby. Every so often you come up the stairs to find another chunk of the cornicing has come off, another strut from the banisters is missing. In the summer, ours is the hottest room in the whole place, in winter the coldest. There is running water in the kitchenette, when the pipes have not frozen. The bedroom and our studio are one space, not especially large, divided by a canvas curtain, made of the same fabric Oskar stretches over wooden struts and primes for us to paint on.

Apart from the bed (iron, ancient, unbelievably heavy), two wooden chairs and a small round table are the only furniture. There is no carpet. There is a little potbelly stove you have to be careful not to brush up against. There is a single flushing toilet (one sits with one's knees right up against the door) at the end of the corridor. Our windows overlook a courtyard, from which at all hours the sounds of the rest of the house rise. A dog is barking. A woman is shouting. On the walls are paintings, ours and gifts from our friends, as well as photographs I have taken of Paris and people we know, on the little Leica camera that Oskar gave me for my birthday.

It all feels a very long way from Longhurst. From the world of my childhood.

We have been happy here in Paris, Oskar and I. Deliriously happy, at times, and yet . . . Do truly happy people keep diaries? I wonder. To whom am I really trying to explain myself, on these pages?

I should write something about Oskar.

I first met Oskar Erlich at a party at the New Burlington Galleries to celebrate the opening of the first International Surrealist Exhibition in London. It was June 11, 1936. He was standing in front of one of his own paintings, *The Young Girl's Dream*—a red-haired waif in a diaphanous dress, back to the viewer, her pale thin face and enigmatic expression reflected in an ornate mirror. He was surrounded by men with notebooks, women in hats, all fawning, asking him to explain Surrealism, what it meant to be a Surrealist. I was loitering by the doorway, hoping no one too boring or awful would talk to me, waiting for the friend who had invited me to come back from the loo.

Then Oskar and I locked eyes.

Oskar always says he will never forget the way I met his gaze and returned it, the unhesitating confidence with which I crossed the room to introduce myself. "Hello," I said, offering him my hand to shake. "My name is Juliette Willoughby and I'm an artist."

I may have sounded bold, but inside I was trembling. All around the room I could see—or thought I could see—people staring at me, exchanging looks, wondering who I was, how I had the nerve to just walk up and present myself to the star of the evening like that. It is a question I have since asked myself. It probably helped that I could see from his paintings that Oskar had a type and I was it.

All that evening, Oskar and I talked—my friend rather put out about that, flouncing off back to our lodgings eventually—and the next day we met again, at a little coffee stand in St James's Park. As we walked around the fountain and examined the art for sale on the railings, he told me about his early years in Düsseldorf, his student days in Paris, the rows he had with his parents about his decision to give up his medical studies and become a great painter. I told him about my life in London, my classes at the Slade, the disappointment I felt in my teachers.

How heroic, how foolish it all appears, written down. Gambling our whole lives on an instant of intense connection, two people noticing each other across a room and feeling an affinity. Making a decision that would transform the course of both our lives after having known each other for less than twenty-four hours. The strangest thing of all being that it did not seem strange when he asked me at the end of that day if I would consider returning with him to Paris.

And live where? I asked him. And live with me, he said. And do what? I asked him. He smiled a little to himself, as if the answer was obvious, and then he said: paint. It should have sounded ludicrous, felt absurd. Instead, in the moment, what would have felt absurd would have been to refuse.

I was under no illusions about how my father would react to all this. It was clear the break must be sudden and final. There would be no wedding in the little chapel at Longhurst, no party in the gardens by the lake. There would be no forgiveness, no reconciliation. To have fallen in love with an artist, that would have been bad enough. To have fallen in love with a foreign artist, a German? Unthinkable. Especially when that artist was more than twice my age and still married to somebody else.

They must have no warning, I told Oskar. Nothing but a letter to let them know I was safe, that I was in love, that they should not try to find me, and they would never see or hear from me again.

I left my farewell note with a friend, not telling her what was in it, asking her to post it in a day or two's time. It was goodbye to my old life, and good riddance.

I threw all my sketchbooks, all the canvases propped against my bedroom wall, all the awful, lifeless work I had produced at the Slade into the bins at the back of the building. I packed my paints and brushes—expensively replenished on regular trips to an art shop in Covent Garden with my uncle Austen—a very few things to wear, and my passport, acquired for that dull and disappointing field trip to Rome to troop around the Vatican galleries. Then I left my lodgings and took the underground alone to Charing Cross station, and vanished.

It is hard to believe that it has been more than a year since I first arrived here in Paris. Sometimes my dreams of that passage are so vivid it feels as if, were I to open my eyes, I would find myself back at the station, so crowded, so cacophonous. On that train, every carriage crammed, or anxiously searching at the other end for the right boat. Hearing the click of the cabin door behind us, as the reality of what we were doing suddenly hit me.

We woke early, Oskar and I, and went up on deck to watch in the dawn for the first glimpse of France. As we had agreed, we did not acknowledge each other in the line to have our passports stamped. There was some part of me not just anxious but convinced someone was going to stop us. The police? A private detective? My father himself? I was not quite sure.

It was late afternoon, the city a smear of lights through a grimy window, as the boat-train began to slow and we neared the Gare du Nord. From time to time, I made a point of conspicuously twiddling on my finger the phony wedding ring Oskar had bought me from a pawn shop in Holborn.

Paris! I could not believe it, really. It all felt too easy. It was almost dismaying to imagine that this freedom had always been mine to reach out and grasp.

"You see?" Oskar had asked me, the glow from a streetlamp falling through the taxi window and illuminating the curve of his mouth, "I told you it would be fine." I smiled back, returning the squeeze of his hand. I tried not to imagine my father's fury, my mother's bewilderment, attempting to maintain the self-belief I had felt in the moment I met Oskar. I wondered if it had occurred to him that I might still be a virgin, that this would be the first time I had ever spent the night in bed with a man.

I was intensely conscious that this was just one of the many things Oskar did not know about me yet.

CHAPTER 2

PATRICK, CAMBRIDGE, 1991

The day after our first supervision with Alice Long, I returned to my college room from a morning lecture to find a note under my door. My father had called and someone had jotted down a message from him: he was passing through town today on his way back from East Anglia and would be waiting to meet me for lunch at Browns at one o'clock. I checked my wristwatch. It was 12:45.

This was very much par for the course with Dad. Turning up unannounced. Expecting me to drop whatever plans I might have and meet him.

As a child, I idolized my father. He was handsome. He was stylish (the cars, the tailored blazers, the monogrammed silver hip flask: *Q. M.* for Quentin Lambert). He was conspicuously charming, with a considered opinion about everything (wine, art, London restaurants). He was also, it turned out, a deeply unreliable serial philanderer.

As we were being shown to our seats, Dad immediately started flirting with the waitress, trying to upgrade our table. I sighed inwardly. It was one of the things I had told Caroline about my father, his obsession with always trying to get a window table, a better table, the best table. A performance I had to endure every time we dined together. A chance to demonstrate his powers of persuasion. A way of drawing attention to himself.

We ended up—the two of us—at a six-seat table by the window, looking out on Trumpington Street.

Once we were settled and had ordered our drinks, the first thing he asked about was the car. Running okay, was she? I was taking good care of her, he hoped. *Like a dream*, I told him. *Waxing her every week*. It was a big symbol of my relationship with my father, that car. He'd bought it the day I received my Cambridge acceptance letter. On one hand, it had been an extravagantly generous gesture, one I suspected he could not really afford. On the other hand, it was also a massive pain in the backside. Finding somewhere safe to park it. Never knowing on cold mornings if it would start. Having a car at all in a place where I was never more than a ten-minute walk from anywhere else I wanted to be. When I had tried to explain all this to Caroline, she had asked me why I did not just sell it. She had a point. She also did not know my father.

The next thing Dad asked was how my studies were going. He wanted to know all about my dissertation, my supervisor. Although I had not mentioned this to Alice Long, it was actually my father—an art dealer himself—who had first got me interested in the Surrealists, when he took me to the Oskar Erlich retrospective in London a few years back, and who had suggested the 1938 Paris Surrealist Exhibition might provide an interesting topic for a dissertation. He had also encouraged me to think about my chosen topic in career terms, as a chance to establish myself as the expert in some corner of art history no one else seemed very interested in.

Over our starters, Dad explained why he'd been in East Anglia (a house clearance just beyond Norwich—he was there to value things on behalf of the family, make sure nothing valuable accidentally got sold for a song, or if it did, that it was to him). He had popped into Longhurst on the way back to see Philip Willoughby. There were a few things at the house that Philip had wanted him to value. He had, as usual, stayed in the Green Room, the bedroom he always stayed in at Longhurst, and which by some weird tradition Harry's mother also now always put me in. This was the sort of thing that delighted Dad, and that he was always trying to shoehorn into conversation.

They were pretty formulaic, these catch-ups of ours. He asked about Mum, I asked about his latest girlfriend (these were of quite a specific type, usually, divorced blondes who drove convertibles and owned boutiques in the Cotswolds). He would tell a work-related story in which he was right about something and everyone else wrong and then (a glass of wine in) grill me on whether I was making the most of Cambridge, moving in the right circles, meeting the right sort of people.

He had, once or twice, actually used that phrase *the right circles*. "Do you mean posh people, Dad?" I had asked him. "Or do you just mean rich people?"

"I mean the kind of people who can give you a leg up in life," he had replied. "Especially if you are serious about getting into my line of work. People who own art, people who buy it."

As we were waiting for our mains to arrive, he asked if I had been invited to Harry Willoughby's twenty-first, at Longhurst.

Every time we met, Dad asked me about Harry. Not about any of my new friends here, whose names he stubbornly refused to remember. Always it was Harry he wanted to know about. If we saw much of each other. If we were still close. If he had a girlfriend. No, was always the answer to this last question, because never have I met anyone in my life more focused on their future political career than Harry, anyone who showed less interest in romantic entanglements of any kind. It sometimes felt that the only reason Harry even had friends was because he thought it was the sort of thing a future prime minister ought to have.

"Of course I've been invited," I said. It would have been embarrassing had I not, given how long I had known Harry, the connection between our fathers, the fact that we were in the same college.

It was not until the end of our meal that Dad revealed he had a favor to ask. Over dessert, I told him I was popping down to London the next week to look up some things in the Witt Library at the Courtauld Institute—Alice Long had suggested that their extensive holdings of exhibition catalogue clippings might hold something useful on the 1938 Surrealist Exhibition.

"The Witt?" he said. That was handy. There were a couple of paintings that Philip Willoughby was planning to sell and had asked him to establish the provenance of—who had owned them when, who had bought them where, the sort of paper trail that played such an important part in establishing a painting's authenticity.

With its archive of millions of photographs, reproductions, and clippings documenting the work of tens of thousands of artists, the Witt Library was as valuable a resource for art dealers as it was for scholars—once you had gotten used to its somewhat complicated filing system. The thing that was especially helpful for my father's purposes being that among the library's holdings are thousands of pictures taken by the Witt's own librarians, who from the 1920s until the 1970s were periodically sent around to the great houses of England with cameras to record their art collections. To Cliveden. To Longleat. To Longhurst.

Which meant there was one simple, surefire way of establishing that a painting had been in the possession of the Willoughbys when the Witt's librarians visited with their cameras in 1961. The downside being that someone had to go through all those green fabric-covered folders of hundreds of unsorted grainy black-and-white photographs and find the ones of the specific paintings in question.

Would I mind, if I was down at the Witt, my father asked, just checking a few things for him? He would make a note of what he wanted me to look for, the names of the paintings, the dates.

"Of course," I heard myself saying.

"There might be some cash in it for you," he added.

"Fine," I said. "Sure. Since I'm down there anyway."

It would have been churlish to refuse. He had done a lot for me, after all. He was the one who was paying for lunch. Who had paid my school fees, even when the business was not going well. I had been given a lot of chances in life that he had not. I did not ever want to seem ungrateful. It probably would not take me more than a couple of hours.

Still, it would have been nice if just once in a while, my dad dropped in on me without warning like this and did not have a favor to ask.

As I was walking Dad back to his car, two abreast on a pavement carpeted with wet leaves, he asked if I was excited about that evening.

"This evening?" I asked, as if I did not know what he was referring to.

"Your investiture," he replied, grinning, practically nudging me in the ribs. "The Osiris Society."

Ah yes. Two things I had been attempting *not* to think about, as it happened.

For almost as long as I could remember, Dad had been going on about the Osiris Society. Their famous dinners. Their legendary antics. How important it was, *when* I went to Cambridge (never *if*), that I was asked to join. For the seal of social approval. For the ridiculous pinkie ring.

It being the first Thursday of the month, it was also the first dinner of Michaelmas term, when new members were invested. There only ever being thirteen at any one time, this was considered something of an honor. When I had showed Dad the embossed invitation, signed by Harry as society president, it was a little tragic how excited he was.

"I'm not sure," I told him, "whether it's really *my thing*."

He asked me what I was talking about.

One did not turn down an opportunity like this, he told me. If I really did not understand the potential professional advantages for someone planning a career as an art dealer in making these kinds of contacts, perhaps I should consider a different way of making a living. He probably did have a point.

I had once, as a snotty teenager, made an offhand remark about his never having been made a member, despite his *great friend* Philip being president when they were students. How that must have stung. How that must have rankled. Because at the end of the day, I observed—coldly, unkindly, annoyed with him about something, aiming to wound— despite all his sucking up, despite all his efforts at self-reinvention, none of those people were ever really going to forget, were they, that he was just a grammar school lad from South London who had grown up in a council flat?

He did not speak to me for a month.

"Are you nervous about the investiture?" he asked.

The truth was, I was dreading it. I had spent my whole time at Cambridge consciously avoiding the kind of boozy, boorish evening I was letting myself in for tonight. To make matters worse, Harry's cousin Freddie—a practical joker, and like Harry a member of Osiris ever since their very first term at Cambridge—had been trying to make me as anxious as possible. Dropping hints about what it would involve. Like a cross between a rugby club initiation and joining the Masons, was how I had always imagined it. As it turned out, it was going to be far worse than that.

A week earlier Harry had told me what I was expected to procure for the ceremony. He had said to meet him in a pub around the corner from college, and I had arrived to find half the society at a table next to the fireplace, Osiris signet rings glinting as they sank their drinks. Freddie Talbot. Ivo Strang. Benjy Taylor. Arno von Westernhagen. Eric Lam. Handsome Hugo de Hauteville—Hugo de *Hot*ville, some of the girls called him. All of them the sort of boys my father was so keen for me to associate with: rich, ambitious, well-connected. Absurdly so, in some cases. Arno von Westernhagen—tall, tanned, a keen skier, an even more enthusiastic rugby player—was an actual German count. He had gone to school in England but spent summers at his family castle—the *schloss*—in Bavaria.

I offered to buy a round and, when they all nodded thanks, prayed I had enough cash for eleven pints of lager and a Diet Coke with ice and lemon. This last item was for Arno von Westernhagen, who was not currently drinking, on medical advice, following a rugby head injury a few weeks earlier. "I was out cold for *ten minutes*," I could hear him explaining to Hugo and Benjy. "I went out for a few pints with the rest of the team that night and had a fucking *seizure*. The doctor told me no booze for six months."

Harry followed me to the bar and handed me an envelope.

"What's this?" I asked him.

"Instructions," he said.

I went to open it, but he shook his head and told me to wait until I got home. So I finished my beer, made my excuses, and slipped off to fumble the envelope open. On the piece of paper inside, in Harry's weirdly childish writing, were three words. Freddie was outside smoking with Eric Lam and Arno von Westernhagen as I left. He glanced down at the note in my hand.

"Bring an animal?" I said incredulously. "What does it mean, bring an animal? A live animal? A dead animal? What kind of animal?"

"That's up to you, Patrick. We've all had to do it. What was yours, Ivo? A pheasant?" Freddie said, smirking.

Ivo nodded. "Got my dad to send it in the post."

"Arno, you brought a rabbit, if I remember correctly," said Freddie, clearly enjoying himself.

Arno confirmed this. He seemed to be smoking twice as much as usual now that he could not drink—he stubbed out one cigarette in a shower of orange sparks and immediately lit another.

"Fur and all," he added. "I had to buy it frozen from a place that does pet food for snakes."

Everyone seemed to be laughing, but I genuinely couldn't tell if Freddie was joking.

"We didn't make this shit up. It's all in the rules. It's been the same investiture ceremony since the society was founded." He shrugged.

I gave him a long, hard look.

"And what am I going to have to do with it, this animal?"

Freddie's smile just widened.

"Can't tell you that, I'm afraid, Patrick."

"Why not? The rules again?"

Freddie shook his head. "Oh no, nothing in the rules about that. I just don't want to spoil the surprise."

CAROLINE, CAMBRIDGE, 1991

Right up till closing time I had stayed, reading Juliette's journal, so intent on the pages in front of me that I didn't notice the library emptying out. Eventually, the only ones left in the building were me and the librarian and someone pushing a mop around.

It was a vertiginous, rabbit-holey feeling, reading those diary entries.

Juliette's story. In her *own* words. In her handwriting (beautiful but extremely hard to decipher), with her illustrations in the margins or sometimes taking up a page to themselves. Ink splotches from a fountain pen elaborated into drifting clouds, watercolor waves and landscapes in outline, deft charcoal sketches of the objects, places, and people she was describing. Had it really been sitting right here all these years, at the bottom of a cardboard box?

If I was not finished with what I was looking at, the librarian gently reminded me, I could put the box to one side and continue with its contents when they reopened at 9:00 a.m. I looked up at the clock on the wall—it was five to seven. The cleaner had finished mopping now and begun turning lights off.

In the middle of a fitful night's sleep, I did experience a brief moment of panic. What if I went back the next day and the box was gone? What if I opened it and the journal was missing?

At ten to nine the next day, I was waiting outside the library, clutching my notepad. Without a break all morning, I laboriously transcribed, frowning over crossed-out phrases, indecipherable words. Eventually, I reached the end of that long first entry, winning a hard-fought battle with Juliette's inky swoops. In the lobby of the library was a pay phone. From it, I called my friend Athena to ask if she could meet me for lunch in our college hall. I needed to speak to someone about all this. I was also starving.

In some ways we were an unlikely pair, Athena Galanis and I. If we hadn't been put in neighboring rooms in our first year, I probably would have been too intimidated even to talk to her. She was confident. She was clever. She was gorgeous, with a beauty people felt compelled to comment on the moment she left a room (tall and slender, with long, dark hair and enormous green eyes). It was only as I got to know her better—we first spoke properly when she asked to borrow my lecture notes, having missed a lecture for a family wedding on a private Greek island—I realized how funny she was too.

Athena was unlike anyone I'd ever met, and yet somehow, incrementally, over the course of that first year, she became my best friend. She was certainly the only person here I had told anything about my family, my childhood—although even with her there were lots of things I left out. Athena, in contrast, was full of stories about her dad (a

Dubai-based Greek Cypriot businessman) and her mother, his second wife, Mila, a former model and Miss Russia runner-up.

Athena's phone—she had moved out of college at the end of the first year, into a house her father bought her in central Cambridge—rang for a long time before she answered. When eventually, groggily, she did so, it was clear I had woken her up. I checked my watch. It was midday.

"Caroline! I am *so* glad you called," she squealed when she realized it was me. "Because rumor has it you were spotted yesterday cruising through town in Patrick Lambert's red sports car . . ."

"We had a supervision together. He offered me a lift afterward. It was raining," I explained, trying to ignore the way that even the mention of Patrick's name made me feel.

I could hear a soft chortle at the other end of the line. "You know he still fancies you, right?"

It was not the first time Athena had aired this theory—based as far as I could tell on nothing more than having seen him looking at me ("with those soulful eyes of his") across a lecture hall.

As usual, because just the thought of having to explain how I felt about relationships—and why—could threaten to bring on familiar throat-tightening symptoms of panic, I swerved the subject. I wasn't calling about Patrick, I said. This was something much more important. She agreed to meet me in twenty minutes. As ever, despite having only just rolled out of bed, she looked immaculate when I arrived at the college dining hall. On the long oak table in front of her was a plate of cucumber onto which she was shaking a snowstorm of salt, her lunch most days. She greeted me with an expectant expression as I unraveled my scarf and sat down.

I talked her through the last twenty-four hours as swiftly as I could. Alice Long. The Willoughby Bequest. The passport and the necklace and the journal. Telling someone else about it for the first time made it all feel both more real and more strange, somehow.

"My God, Caroline, this is incredible," Athena kept saying, eyes wide. "*So* exciting."

"That's not all," I told her. I took my notepad out and read her my transcription of the final paragraph of the first journal entry.

Athena put her fork down. She was looking at me seriously. "Go on, then," she said. "What are these secrets, the things she has not told Oskar about herself? What happens next?"

"I don't know," I admitted. "I've only read the first entry so far."

Athena rolled her eyes in frustration. "So let's read on, right now."

"We can't. There is only one copy of that journal in the whole world," I explained. "It's not something they are going to let anyone photocopy or borrow."

"I'd just have taken it," Athena said. "I'd have liberated the lot. Are you seriously going to copy the whole thing out by hand?"

"Of course!" I said. If that was what it took, I mentally added, suddenly aware of the scale of the task ahead of me. This was precisely the kind of discovery which Alice Long had been talking about. The kind which put forgotten female artists back on the map. The kind which shed new light on women we thought we knew. The kind—and I must admit this thought had also occurred to me—which launched academic careers.

"What I don't understand," said Athena, "is how any of that stuff got there in the first place."

"I'm meeting the archivist to ask exactly that, at two o'clock," I said. I was also planning to go first to the History of Art library to borrow Walter Loftus's classic, definitive biography of Oskar Erlich.

"Well, well, well," a familiar voice boomed from across the hall.

We both looked up. Freddie Talbot.

He barreled over with his lunch tray, dropped down onto the bench, and pecked Athena swiftly on the cheek without ever quite breaking eye contact with me.

"Caroline," he said, a little curtly.

"Freddie," I replied, without warmth.

I had never understood Athena's relationship with Freddie, her on-off boyfriend—although I'd never heard *him* use that word—of the past two years.

On paper at least, I suppose they were well-matched. Athena was charming, intelligent, gorgeous. She spoke at least five languages fluently—Greek with her father and half siblings, Russian with her mother, the French and Arabic she had picked up from her Lebanese nanny, and English at her international school. Freddie, a final-year vet student, was tall, well-built, and every bit as good-looking as she was, with a mop of sandy hair, freckles, an oddly appealing sports-flattened nose, and a strong jaw. He rowed for his college. He played rugby for the university.

He was also a complete arsehole. The kind of person you are never quite sure is going to acknowledge having met you before. Useless at making plans, or at least remembering them. Rude. Deliberately boorish. A liability when drunk, with a well-known habit of suddenly climbing up things: fountains, scaffolding, stationary Sainsbury's trucks. The kind of twat who deliberately sets off fire alarms.

Pretty much their entire relationship, it seemed to me, was conducted between the hours of 11:00 p.m. (college bar kicking-out time) and whenever he skulked back from Athena's room to his. More than once he had staggered in after some boozy dinner with his equally awful friends just to throw up in her sink and pass out. Every so often, he would publicly hook up with another girl in a nightclub, and there would follow weeks of recriminations and crying.

Whenever I had tried to talk to Athena about their relationship, she had made it clear that the situation was complicated, that Freddie was complicated, that I would not understand. Occasionally she would also drop unsubtle hints about their sex life. How passionate it was, how intense.

Something I had not noticed about Freddie before, or at least really registered, was the signet ring on his pinkie. Seeing me glance at it, he swiftly moved his hand under the table.

"Freddie," I said, "can I ask about your ring?"

"My ring?" His expression, the tone of his voice, sought to suggest he had not even really been aware he was wearing a ring.

"Can I see it?"

Freddie hesitated. Eventually, Athena nudged him. Reluctantly, he brought his hand out from under the table and held it up for me. The ring had the same design on it as Juliette Willoughby's necklace. The same elaborate eye design, exactly.

"Well, go on," said Athena, nudging him again. "Tell her what it is."

Freddie said nothing.

"It's an Osiris ring," explained Athena. "It means Freddie is a member of the Osiris Society."

"The Osiris Society? What's that?" I asked.

"It's nothing," said Freddie, with a scowl at Athena.

"It's a drinking society," said Athena, smiling back at him. "A *secret* drinking society."

"It's a dining society," Freddie corrected, his scowl deepening. "We have dinners four times a term. There's nothing secret about it."

Having finished his lunch and pushed his plate away, Freddie wiped his mouth with the back of his hand and checked his watch.

"Christ," he said. "I'd better go. Got something to pick up from the vet school at one thirty." Then with another peck on Athena's cheek— and a little glance around to see if anyone had noticed—he was gone, leaving us his empty plate and tray to clear.

THE HISTORY OF ART library is on Scroope Terrace, a ten-minute walk from my college. I was approaching it when I heard the banging. Unable for a moment to tell which direction it was coming from, I finally spotted a dark blue car, parked facing in my direction—in the front were two men, the passenger screaming at the driver, so furious he was repeatedly punching the ceiling of the car, bouncing red-faced in his seat like Rumpelstiltskin. The driver was just sitting there, staring straight ahead, flinching occasionally. Then the angry man abruptly stopped yelling and took three attempts to get out of the car—kicking the door open so hard it swung closed on him again, catching the sleeve of his gray tracksuit on something and then storming off past me, muttering to himself, a man in his forties with glints of silver in his close-cropped hair.

Only as I got closer and I saw who was sitting in the driver's seat did I realize whose car it was: Freddie's. I was about to walk over, tap on the window, and check that he was okay when he started the car, swerved out into the traffic, and screeched off.

The strangest thing of all was his expression, one I had never seen on his face before. Freddie Talbot looked genuinely scared.

"The Fire"—an extract from *Oskar Erlich: Man and Painter,* by Walter Loftus (London: Faber & Faber, 1982)

The fire that killed Oskar Erlich and Juliette Willoughby broke out just after midnight on February 25, 1938.

It was the concierge of their apartment building, M. Robert Durand, who first raised the alarm. Awoken (he would later recall) by a knock at his door, he opened it to investigate, found no one there, smelled smoke, and looked up to see an orange flickering behind the curtains of Oskar and Juliette's fourth-floor apartment. By the time he had brought his wife to look, the curtains were on fire.

If there was a silver lining to the tragedy, it is that the apartment Oskar and Juliette shared was on the very top floor of the building. Thanks to the timely intervention of M. Durand and his wife, the lower floors were evacuated swiftly, the building's inhabitants ushered into the courtyard, where they huddled on one side of it to watch in horror. There was no chance of rescuing either Oskar or Juliette.

Multiple neighbors later reported having seen Oskar return to the apartment at around ten that evening, seemingly a little tipsy. Whistling his way down the street, across the courtyard, up the stairs. Others recalled hearing raised voices from the apartment—a man and a woman, speaking loudly, in English—at around the same time. It would appear that the fire broke out a few hours later, when both Oskar and Juliette were sleeping.

The most likely cause of the blaze was a spark escaping from the stove, or a flammable item placed on top of it combusting in the heat. Given the typical contents of an artist's studio—paper, canvas, tins of paints, bottles of white spirit—it is hardly surprising the fire spread as swiftly as it did.

According to eyewitness reports, M. Durand repeatedly tried to climb the stairs, calling Oskar and Juliette's names, attempting a rescue. The third and final time he was forced back by the heat and smoke the sleeve of his shirt was smoldering. It took almost three hours to extinguish the blaze, innumerable gallons of water.

Word spread to the bars of Montparnasse, and the building's inhabitants, mostly in pajamas with coats thrown over them, found themselves joined by Juliette and Oskar's friends and contemporaries. Artists and models. Waiters and taxi drivers. All silently gathered to watch as the flames licked the sky, hoping perhaps for some unexpected miracle. For the apartment to have actually been empty, for the lovers to come arm in arm around the corner, alive and unharmed.

The word the official report used for the condition of the two bodies found on what remained of the iron bedstead was *carbonisés*. Two blackened skeletons fused by the heat of the room in which they died in a permanent embrace. Juliette's body was identified by the gold pendant she wore around her neck, Oskar's by his steel wristwatch.

It is said that someone in the crowd—a fellow artist? a hopeful buyer?—inquired, as the soot-blackened firefighters washed themselves down at the pump in the courtyard, if any of the paintings in the apartment had survived. There was an exchange of looks between the men at the pump, scrubbing hands that would nevertheless remain gray for days, a headshake, then the eventual answer: *Non, tout a brûlé.*

All the work, finished and unfinished, that once hung on the walls would have been the first to go. The paint. The canvas. The frames. All of it popping and hissing, cracking and sizzling, exploding into flames as the curtains danced in the updraft.

As one of the most brilliant artists of the era died at the age of forty-six in the arms of his beautiful young lover.

CHAPTER 3

CAROLINE, CAMBRIDGE, 1991

Sam Fadel, the PhD student tasked with cataloging the materials in the Willoughby Bequest, was tall, nervous-looking, and clearly only a few years older than me. He had a habit of poking his glasses up his nose for emphasis at the end of each sentence, an air of selecting every word precisely before he spoke. His voice was soft, his accent American—although his parents were both from Cairo, he explained, he had grown up in the States, majoring in ancient history as an undergraduate at NYU before moving to Cambridge. Like most PhD students I'd encountered, he seemed terribly kind, terribly earnest. He was obviously delighted to find someone he could talk to about his work.

We met for tea in the café on the ground floor of the Arch and Anth museum, where I explained my dissertation topic. He listened thoughtfully. There was an extraordinary amount of material, as I had probably gathered, he said. Not just the papers I had looked at yesterday but a whole room in the basement here was lined with shelves, dusty glass cases, crates, and boxes. He offered to show me around.

"What was it that Cyril actually collected?" I asked as Sam scanned us through a STAFF ONLY door.

"Mummies, funerary items, canopic jars. Lots of papyri. Many wealthy Europeans back then made a hobby of buying those items—legally or illegally—some of which the Egyptian government has been trying to repatriate for decades. But Cyril took collecting to an extreme—he was the sole heir of his father's railway fortune, so money was no object."

As he spoke, Sam led me down a flight of stairs and through a green-painted metal door. He pulled the string to turn the lights on, illuminating, after a couple of flickers, a very large room.

"All of these wooden drawers"—Sam indicated row after row of them, filling a wall from floor to ceiling—"contain Cyril's papyri. He began to acquire them as a Cambridge undergraduate in the early 1900s and he was still amassing them right up until his death in 1952. My job here is to make sure all of this is correctly ordered and labeled." He gave a wan smile.

I asked him if I could see one of the papyri. "Of course," he said, carefully opening a folder to reveal a plastic sheath which encased a ragged little rectangle with three columns of hieroglyphics on it: a bird, an eye, three parallel waves.

"This is well over two thousand years old. From a tomb near Thebes."

"What does it say? Some sort of curse?" I asked, half joking. Sam pulled a face.

"Actually," he said, a note of weariness in his voice, "the idea of the ancient Egyptian curse is a Victorian invention, an orientalist fantasy from colonial times, later amplified by Hollywood. If anything, this is the exact opposite of a curse: it's a blessing. This is a fragment of a funerary text—it would have been buried with a body, tucked into the bandages during the mummification—a scroll with sacred formulae on it, words of power and protection to help the deceased navigate the afterlife."

"Sacred formulae? Like prayers?"

"Or spells. Invocations of assistance from the gods. This fragment, for instance, is addressed to the goddess Aukert, and means something like 'open to me the enclosed place, and grant me pleasant roads upon which to travel.' It is all quite practical stuff they are asking for, mostly. Which gives a fascinating insight into what they thought the afterlife was actually going to be like."

"Which was?"

"More of the same, basically. Which is probably also why they thought they'd need so much stuff."

Fascinating as all this was, it was the mystery of the journal I wanted Sam's help getting to the bottom of.

IN WALTER LOFTUS'S BIOGRAPHY of Erlich, Juliette remained a cipher, simply Oskar's young lover, her artistic ambitions a footnote to his achievements. I may only have deciphered her first diary entry so far, but it was clear Juliette's journal covered the period she had spent working on her great lost masterpiece, *Self-Portrait as Sphinx*, those final, fiercely creative months of her tragically curtailed life. Ringing in my head as I read—or tried to read—Juliette's handwriting was Alice Long's insistence that it was the duty of scholarship to correct decades of contempt and forgetfulness and neglect. That was the opportunity this journal had handed me, that was the task which faced me, and it was hard not to think there was a reason for that.

How I wished, holding the thing, turning its pages, I still had something like it of my mother's, one of the sketchbooks I watched her fill with exquisite, intricate drawings and watercolors when I was little. Some of my most treasured childhood memories are of waking up at night and slipping downstairs to find her at the kitchen table, illustrating one of the extraordinary stories she would make up for me at bedtime. Her transfixed expression. The way in which these projects seemed to transport her, to make everything else a little more bearable.

It was really in tribute to my mother I chose to study art history—if I could draw or paint or felt I had the imagination to write stories, I am sure I would have done that instead. It was the thought of how proud she'd be that had pushed me to work hard enough to get here and which made me want to take advantage of the opportunities I had now. My hope was that I was living up to her idea of what was possible in life, even if she was not around to see it.

Just like Juliette Willoughby, my mother had spent her last days immersed in her art and looking to the future, with no idea of the brutal suddenness of the fate that awaited her.

Sam asked me which box the diary was in and brought it down from the shelf. "My gosh," he said as we opened it. The envelope was tucked upright, exactly as I had left it. Gently, I slipped the pendant out and held it up to the light.

"Ah, well, this, you see, is a *wedjat* eye." He crossed the room, pulled a leather case from the shelf, placed it on a table, and unclipped the lid. Inside were stones of varying sizes and colors, pinned onto a pale blue velvet pad, all identical in shape to the locket from the envelope.

"Cyril had rather a lot of these, as it happens," Sam said.

"What were they for?" I asked.

"They symbolize the healing eye of the god Horus and were mounted in amulets worn to project the wearer from harm."

My first thought was that it did not seem to have worked in Juliette's case.

Next, I passed him the diary. He opened it very slightly, just wide enough to see the initials on the first page. I showed him the passport.

"There are two things I don't understand," I said. "First of all, how these things could have survived the fire."

He scratched his head, thought for a moment. "They're all items of value—perhaps they were stored in something that helped shield them from the flames."

This sounded plausible.

"The other thing I don't understand," I continued, "is how they all ended up here."

Sam was checking the outside of the box for any clue. He found none. "If I had to guess," he said eventually, "perhaps these were all the identifiable personal items that survived that blaze, and the authorities sent them back to England, to the family. And they ended up in her father's study, and got bundled in with the rest of his papers when they were given to the university. Something I *would* note about the bequest: it does not appear that any care was taken sifting through it, before it was donated. It was just thrown into boxes like they couldn't get it out of the house quick enough."

As he was walking me back to the entrance of the building, one more question occurred to me.

"The *wedjat* eye," I said. "It isn't just on Juliette's necklace I have seen it recently. Have you ever heard of the Osiris Society? They have the exact same symbol on the signet rings they wear."

He nodded. "They're a dining society, which basically—as I'm sure you know—means a drinking society. All male. All public school. A bunch of posh guys dressing up in white tie, eating roast beef and getting absolutely"—he shifted into an attempt at a British accent here—"*hammered.*"

He smiled and pretended to shudder. It did sound awful, I thought. A roomful of braying Freddies.

"But why is it named after an Egyptian god? And why do they wear *wedjat* eyes?"

"Because like a lot of these societies, it has evolved over time. When it was first founded, it was a club for undergraduates with an interest in Egyptology to read each other scholarly papers and play show-and-tell with their latest ancient acquisition. I guess the only things that have stayed the same are the name, the building, and the fact that the president of the society has always been a Willoughby, when one happens to be studying at Cambridge."

"A Willoughby?"

Now I was really confused. Sam and I were standing back in the lobby of the building now. He smiled again. "Oh yes. That's how I happen to know so much about it. The Osiris Society was founded in 1901 by Cyril Willoughby."

PATRICK, CAMBRIDGE, 1991

Freddie sauntered around the corner half an hour later than we'd arranged to meet, five minutes before we were due at the Osiris clubhouse. I was loitering in front of the Round Church, smoking my seventh cigarette in a row, in a vain attempt to steady my nerves. He handed over a black sports bag and watched as I reluctantly removed five crisp tens from my wallet.

"We agreed to a hundred, didn't we?" he said.

"No, Freddie, we agreed to fifty," I corrected him.

With impressive speed and a licked thumb, he double-checked my counting and stuffed the cash into his pocket. I told myself I should be grateful. When I had woken up that morning, I still had no clue how I was going to procure an animal for tonight's investiture, uncertain whether I was really going to go through with this. In my dream I had just been telling the whole Osiris Society to go fuck themselves.

It was a sharp rat-tat-tat on the door that woke me. I expected it to be one of the college cleaners, come to empty my wastepaper basket. Instead, I found Freddie leaning against the banister, arms folded, looking even more pleased with himself than usual. He raised one amused eyebrow at my paisley silk dressing gown, another gift from my father. "Morning, Patrick. Just wanted to check if you're ready for tonight."

"What do you mean, ready?" I asked him.

"You know exactly what I mean," he said. "Because I'm going to the vet school today, so if you're not I can help."

"That's very generous of you, Freddie."

He told me how much it was going to cost. I thought this over for a moment or two before I reluctantly nodded. We discussed where and when we would meet.

This had better all be worth it, Dad, I thought.

The bag Freddie gave me was surprisingly light. I could not bring myself to inspect its contents. "What is it?" I asked him.

"Cat," he said.

"A *dead* cat?"

"It bloody well should be—it's been on ice in the vet school for the past month."

It was a three-minute walk from the Round Church to our destination. When we reached it, Freddie took the steps two at a time ahead of me, unlocking the front door with an almost comically large barrel key on a great jangling ring of them, and inviting me inside.

"Time for a quick drink before we start, if you want one."

I nodded and followed him down the corridor.

One of a terrace of brick-fronted Victorian houses in central Cambridge, the Osiris clubhouse was distinguished from the outside only by a small brass plaque. Inside, things got weirder. Freddie led me through to a living room with a battered Chesterfield sofa and a few threadbare club chairs. Vibes-wise, it was reminiscent of the sixth-form bar at a boarding school, the major difference being that in a glass case in the corner was a mummy—a shabby, haunted-looking thing, its wrappings brown and crumbling. I decided not to think too much about the fact that it had once been an actual person.

Freddie opened a drinks cabinet and pulled out a bottle of whiskey, poured two glasses, and sank his in one. I did the same, regretting it as soon as it hit my already uneasy stomach.

"Coats through here," he said, leading me to a small cloakroom with a little loo next to it. Freddie ducked in to the loo first, to straighten his tie, as he put it. "Little sharpener on the corner of the sink for you," he told me with a wink, on his way out.

For almost as long as I had known him, Freddie had been the go-to guy when anybody wanted drugs. At school it was hash and weed. Now it was pills, speed, and coke, with Freddie disappearing every so often off to London or Bristol for supplies.

"It's almost time, Lambert," he announced when I reappeared, gesturing toward the stairs.

On the first floor of the building, things got a little more glamorous. The curving staircase was lined with paintings of former Osiris presidents all the way back to Cyril himself. I spotted Harry's father, Philip, about halfway up. At the top, there was a long corridor of dark wood paneling, hung with brass sconces and old framed lithographs (a prospect of Alexandria, a view of one of the temples at Karnak).

Off the corridor was a series of doors.

"Take a look around," Freddie said. "I'm going to check if they're ready for you."

My father's son at heart, I couldn't help having a snoop. The first door I tried was locked. The second opened into a room lined with glass cases, each containing pots, jars, wooden carvings of ships and animals, fragments of painted plaster that looked to have been chipped off the walls of tombs. There was a stone sarcophagus in one corner. My God, I thought. If this was the sort of stuff that Cyril had filled Longhurst with, it was no wonder Juliette was interested in Sphinxes. It must have been like growing up in the British Museum.

Freddie was waiting for me when I emerged into the corridor. "They're ready for you," he said. "Don't forget your bag."

When I entered the dining room, everyone was already seated. I spotted Harry, Freddie, Arno, Benjy, Eric, Hugo. Others I knew too but less well: Douglas Burn, Toby Gough. The only light was coming from silver candelabras placed at intervals down the length of the dining table. Freddie took his place at one end, and, still holding my bag, I sat at the head. All of us were in white tie—mine inherited from my father (tight across the shoulders, short in the leg). No one spoke. No one made eye contact. I don't think I had ever seen any of them looking as stern or serious as they did now. *What the hell have I let myself in for?* I wondered, with alarm.

I was beginning to think that line of coke downstairs might have been a mistake too.

In front of me was a cone of incense, spewing smoke into the air, and an enameled silver platter. Next to the platter was a leather-bound notebook. Leaning forward, feeling very conscious of being the person in the room that everyone was looking at, I picked up the notebook and opened it. My heart sank. "This is all in Greek," I said.

"Ancient Egyptian, actually," said Harry. "Transcribed phonetically into Greek, by my great-uncle Cyril."

"You must remember some of your Greek from school, Lambert, a clever scholarship boy like you," Freddie added with a snicker.

Ga ba ka, baba ka, I silently read to myself. *Ka ka ra ra phee ko ko.*

"What about this?" I asked, pointing to the bag.

"Take it out and put it on the platter," Freddie instructed me.

I reached inside my bag and gingerly pulled out a small, damp ball of fur. A kitten, dark and soft, eyes closed, cold. I swallowed the urge to retch and gently placed it on the platter, silently apologizing to it for whatever I was about to do.

"And I'm supposed to read all of this?" I said, lifting up the notebook.

Nobody answered.

"What is it?" I asked.

"It's an ancient incantation," Harry told me.

Still none of the faces around the table was showing even a hint of a smile. I flicked through the pages. I cleared my throat, ran a dry tongue over my lips, and began to read. Around the table people shifted and settled in their seats. After a while, as I chanted by candlelight those syllables I could enunciate but did not understand, I began to sink into something of a trance, everyone else in the room seeming to grow further away the more absorbed I grew in my task.

Ta ta ra ke re ko re.

Harry indicated to me with a gesture that I should raise the platter above my head, continuing to read the pages on the table in front of me. I did so, feeling increasingly ridiculous.

When I first heard the sound, I told myself I was imagining things. That it was nerves, exacerbated by the whiskey and cocaine. Then I heard it again. A scratching noise, above my head. I tried to ignore it, but then the weight of the platter shifted. It must have been my imagination, I told myself, my aching arms twitching. Then from above me there came a low, quiet mewl. I stopped reading for a second. There was another mewl, louder this time, distinctly animal in origin.

"*Jesus* fucking *Christ.*"

The kitten, eyes open, clearly very much alive, leapt from the platter and attached itself to the front of my shirt. I could feel its claws puncturing my skin through the cotton, scratching my chest. I could see them hooking into and shredding the satin of my lapels. It seemed to be heading for my face. With a yelp I jumped backward, sending the silverware clattering to the floor, knocking my chair over with the backs of my knees. The kitten jumped, skittered along the table, gave a little cry, and zipped off.

"Jesus fucking *Christ*," I said again, looking up at everyone. Wondering if they had seen what I had just seen. It was only then that they all burst out laughing, with a laughter that was all the more raucous for having been bottled up so long.

"*Ra ra fa so la ti do*," said Hugo.

"*Ta ta ra ke re ko re*," chuckled Benjy. "Bit rusty on your pronunciation there, I have to say."

"Your fucking face!" said Freddie.

Arno cornered the kitten, scooped it up, and began stroking it.

"It wasn't dead?" I said. The entire room was howling with laughter.

"Did you actually think you had developed magical powers, Lambert? That the *ritual* was working? My God, you did, didn't you?" Freddie hooted.

"It was fucking sedated, wasn't it, you vet student cunt," I hissed, my heart still pounding. "You absolute . . ."

"Just a little ketamine," said Freddie. "A perfectly harmless tranquilizer. Let me know if you ever want to try some yourself . . ."

Toby Gough asked if it was time to get pissed yet. Hugo passed me a glass of red wine and Arno eyed it jealously as I gulped, so fast it stung my nostrils. Ivo poured me another. Eric Lam had the kitten in his arms now and was petting it.

Harry patted me on the back and handed me a gold signet ring and a key. "You've earned those," he told me.

On the far side of the room, I could hear Freddie doing an impression of me, and laughing.

Ga ba ka, baba ka. Ka ka ra ra phee ko ko.

They had always loved a practical joke, the Willoughbys. Oh yes, the Willoughbys had always loved a prank.

Second Entry

Sunday, 21st November—The task of the artist, Oskar once told me, is to abolish coincidence.

Well, here is a coincidence to puzzle over.

There was an English-language newspaper—the *Times*—in the café last night. When Oskar and the others sat down, he noticed it on the table and pocketed it to bring home for me. And there it was, on page seven. A picture of Longhurst, from the back lawn, my parents standing on the terrace. My heart stopped. Then with great relief I saw the headline was something about a charity fete. I could just imagine it. My mother spinning the tombola, my father bellowing the numbers. The story was nothing to do with me. I was not mentioned at all. Thank God for that.

I have always suspected that the most upsetting aspect of my disappearance, as far as my parents were concerned, would be the prospect of the newspapers picking up the story. A professional embarrassment for my father, a social one for my mother. Another scandal on top of all the tragedies and horrors of the past few years. As time passed, I wondered how they were explaining to their friends, their circle, my prolonged absence, my nonappearance at family events. Were they still keeping up the pretense that I was in London? Was I now one of those topics which people learned to avoid by how icily my parents reacted when it was brought up? As ever with my parents, it was easier to imagine what they might be saying to other people than what they might actually be feeling themselves.

It was not until later that another thought struck me. Mostly, when you see a *Times* in Paris, it is the day before yesterday's. How did a London newspaper find its way into that particular café, onto Oskar and his friends' usual table, to catch Oskar's eye, the very same day it was published, on the exact anniversary of when he and I first arrived in Paris?

Perhaps, Oskar suggests, it was a practical joke. But whose? I keep asking him. He shrugs. One of his friends'? Perhaps. I can imagine how pleased some of them would be with themselves for having discovered who my family is, how wealthy, how prominent. How funny they might find it. That the strange, solemn little English girl with her camera around her neck, who can make a single cassis last a whole evening, and who would rather walk an hour than pay for a taxi, has a politician father who collects Egyptian antiquities and a grandfather who was one of the richest men in England.

I have always hated practical jokes, I told him.

It would be almost impossible to express how tedious I found it at Longhurst whenever we had guests. The apple-pie beds. The unscrewed salt cellars. The way my grandfather and father would delight in mis-introducing people at dinner. The cruelty, the reliance on an unspoken imbalance of power, had always turned my stomach.

Would Oskar ask his friends tonight, I pleaded, if one had left the newspaper there as a joke? "Of course," he said, unconvincingly, on his way out the door, clearly bored of the topic. It was three in the morning when the sound of his key in the lock woke me up. I listened to him grapple his boots off, splash water on his face, grope his way to bed. I moved over to make space.

"Did you ask them?" I murmured. "About the newspaper?"

An irritated grunt was my answer.

The thought troubling me was this: what if it was a signal, from my father? Meaning: I know where you are. Meaning: you are under observation. Meaning: I shall not allow myself to be embarrassed by you. Meaning: watch your step.

Oskar was already snoring, flat out on his back.

It is not possible they know I am here, I told myself in the dark. I could be anywhere, with anyone, doing anything. When people take pictures of Oskar, I am careful never to be in them. *Jules*, he calls me, never Juliette.

I fell asleep anxious, listening to the clunk of the pipes in the wall. I awoke much calmer, in a room flooded with sunlight. It was a fine morning, so I went out to pick up some things—eggs, saucisson, a bottle of *vin ordinaire*—from the little market in the square around the corner. It was as I was walking back along the rue Jolivet that I realized I was being followed.

My first thought was: Oh God, not this again. Not all this again.

For months after we arrived in Paris, Oskar's wife had trailed us everywhere. Even after he had told her he wanted a divorce, moved all his things out. Even after it was clear he was in love with me. Somehow, she seemed to believe that if she stalked us, pale and miserable, simply stood there, never confronting us, just staring, he would change his mind and take her back.

It did unsettle me, at first. To look up from dinner and find her at the restaurant window. To be leaving someone's apartment late at night after drinks or an evening of intense discussion with Oskar's friends to find her in a doorway across the street, watching. Arriving to meet people in a café to see she was already sitting there, waiting.

I did feel sorry for Maria. I could also not imagine anything more likely to burn off any guilt Oskar did feel for her, curdle any lingering affection for her. Making herself look ridiculous was one thing. Making *him* look ridiculous in front of his friends and fellow artists? Unforgivable. The only response was to ignore her, Oskar said, to refuse to treat the whole thing seriously. Just once he had lost his temper with her, crossed the street to remonstrate, began making threats about what he would do if she did not leave us alone. It was the first time I had ever encountered that side of him. The way his face contorted, the little flecks of spit flying from his mouth, the wildly waving arms, the strong sense that this was someone no longer in control of himself, a million miles from the kind and playful Oskar I knew. Maria had not flinched. She just stood there, staring impassively. At him. At me.

It did sometimes worry me, what could be going on in her head. What dreams of revenge might be brewing. I have seen what a person with a broken heart is capable of, I would tell him. I have watched the way someone can lash out at a world they believe has wronged them. Oskar always laughed at me. He insisted that if we ignored Maria, she would eventually grow bored. And after a while, she did seem to.

Now it was all starting up again. Well, I simmered, catching a glimpse out of the corner of my eye of the shadow creeping along the street after me, feeling my pulse quicken, I had spent enough time feeling sorry for Maria and now I was angry. Now she had to go away and leave us alone. Rarely, I think, have I been so full of rage, so ready for a confrontation.

I turned and the street was empty.

There is a reason I am writing all this down in my journal and not telling Oskar.

One of the side effects of having spent time in a lunatic asylum is that it sometimes feels like everyone who knows about that is continually on the lookout for signs you are going mad again. Sometimes at parties, when you hear what someone is saying and you reply with a non sequitur, you catch a little glance they give you, a little puzzled frown. Sometimes in a café, you laugh at something too loudly, and the person you are with flinches.

Nor is it always easy to convince even those closest to you that you are sane.

I dream of it often, that hospital. Those months of indescribable boredom and horror. For at least the first week I was convinced that any minute the doctors would realize there had been a terrible mistake, tell me I was free to go. Then it finally sunk in that there had been no mistake and I no longer had any idea how many days I had even been there, or what day it was, the only way to measure the passing of time those horrible, painful injections.

They kept asking me, the doctors, if I knew why I was there, if I could remember the things I had been saying. The terrible things I had been shouting in the street. I could see now how revolting, how absurd they were now, couldn't I? Of course they are revolting, I kept saying. Of course they are absurd. But I did not invent them. I am not the mad one.

Each time I said it, I could feel their frustration. And I could feel how easy it would be to agree with them, knowing that in agreeing lay my only hope of freedom.

It was not easy, telling all this to Oskar. Knowing, during those first few exhilarating weeks in Paris—meeting his friends, discovering his world—that there was something so huge he did not know about me, something I had kept from him that might change how he felt about me so drastically. Because as much as Oskar and his friends might talk about madness, and praise the art of the mad, that is something quite different from realizing the woman with whom you are in love has only recently been released from a madhouse. And because if I told him half the things I was locked up for saying, I am sure he would think me quite mad too.

CHAPTER 4

PATRICK, CAMBRIDGE, 1991

When I first noticed Athena Galanis approaching, outside the department after our lecture, I assumed she was going to ask me for a cigarette.

"Hi, Patrick," she said. "What are you up to tonight?"

The question threw me a little, to be honest. I knew about her and Freddie, and I knew she was friends with Caroline, but Athena and I had been studying the same subject for almost three years now and this was the first time she had actually spoken to me. I was a bit surprised she even knew my name.

"I'm having a dinner party," she told me, even before I had answered her question. "You should come."

"I would love to," I said. "But actually I have plans already . . ."

Had Freddie put her up to this? Was it a joke, and if I said yes was there going to be some sort of punch line? Since my Osiris investiture, I had been dreading word somehow getting out about that cat business—one of the reasons I had not yet worn my pinkie ring in public. Athena asked what my plans were. I told her I was having dinner with Harry Willoughby.

"Harry! I know Harry. I love Harry. Bring Harry!"

"I can certainly ask him," I said.

"Tell him I insist," she said. "Tell him Freddie will be there. My place—you know where I live, don't you?—tonight, seven o'clock."

I did know where she lived, as it happened. It was something of a joke in our year that Athena's father had bought her a house three doors down from the Art History Department building and yet she still managed to be late to every lecture she attended.

When I went to his room to tell him, Harry seemed as bemused by our invitation as I was. "I've only met her once for about ten minutes," he said. "She and Freddie had a blazing row at the bar, and she stormed off."

"Well, she was very keen on us coming," I told him. "She also said to tell you Freddie will be there."

He made a face. Despite their being cousins, and both members of Osiris, I was never quite sure how much Harry actually *liked* Freddie. They were certainly very different characters—even as a child, Harry had been the serious cousin, the straitlaced one, conscious always that he was the one who would inherit the big house and the responsibility that came with it. Nor was there much physical resemblance between them. Freddie was confident, attractive, with razor cheekbones and a carefully maintained six-pack. Harry had a round, shiny face with pink cheeks, eyelashes so blond they were almost white, and hair that at twenty was already starting to thin in places.

"So what do you think?" I asked.

Harry—a classics student—rested on his chest the Loeb edition of Horace he had been reading on his bed and looked at me. "Do you want to go?"

"I wouldn't mind seeing what her place is like," I said with a shrug.

"Ghastly, I expect," he said. They could be very snobbish, he and Freddie, especially about people they suspected of having more money than they did. "But I suppose anything is better than college food."

As IT TURNED OUT, the house was exquisite—the color scheme elegantly understated, the lighting soft, the carpets so deep your feet sank in them almost to the ankle. It was also even bigger than it looked from the street. Athena led us through a vast shiny kitchen to the dining room—an enormous glass box sticking out of the back of the house. There were two people already sitting at the table. One of them was

Giles Pemberton, another art historian: blond, gay, a little tweedy, a self-conscious connoisseur of things. He was wearing a bow tie and swirling the glass of red wine he was holding up to a candle—the first person our age I had ever seen do this not as a joke. The other person at the table was Caroline. She looked just as surprised to see me as I was to see her.

Two other places had been set, presumably for Freddie and Athena, but there was no sign of Freddie yet. I remarked on the lovely smells coming from the kitchen as Athena made sure everybody who did not know each other was introduced—placing rather a lot of emphasis on Harry's surname. This made little impression on Giles but gave Caroline a little start.

"Oh!" she said. "I'm writing a dissertation chapter on the painter Juliette Willoughby."

Harry smiled politely.

"Not just that," said Athena. "Tell them, Caroline."

Caroline gave her a look. She gave Caroline a look back.

"She's found a journal," said Athena. "Juliette's diary, with sketches. From her time in Paris."

"In the Willoughby Bequest?" I said.

Caroline nodded. A timer went off in the kitchen. Athena excused herself and hurried off.

Harry looked confused. "I thought that was all Egyptological papers. There is some research student—Sam something—working on it, trying to get it all into order. Every so often he writes to my father with some question about Uncle Cyril or the collection that none of us have the first clue how to answer."

"Mostly it *is* Egyptological material. That's what makes this so strange," said Caroline.

"What kind of journal is it?" I asked, leaning in across the table, intrigued.

"I'm still in the process of transcribing it, but it's very personal. I'm not sure she ever intended for anyone else to read it." She turned to Harry. "For instance, I hope you don't mind me asking, but do you know anything about her having been in a mental institution?"

Harry thought about this. "No, but perhaps that's why we don't really talk about her much in the family. I can imagine some of my relatives being a bit funny about something like that. My grandfather Austen, on the other hand . . ."

"You're related to Austen Willoughby?" said Giles, evidently both amused and excited by this information.

Harry confirmed this. Giles clapped his hands.

Caroline asked somewhat apologetically who Austen Willoughby was.

"*Austen Willoughby* was the most successful canine portraitist of his era," said Giles, half turning in his chair to face her. "A Fellow of the Royal Academy of Arts. A genius, really. When it came to painting rich people's dogs, anyway."

Caroline was clearly unsure if she was being teased. She was not. Austen Willoughby had inherited Longhurst Hall when his brother Cyril died, and the place was still full of his paintings. Thoughtful spaniels. Plucky terriers. Noble setters. It was the expressions in the eyes of the dogs he painted for which he was most celebrated, his ability to capture an individual canine's character. As far as I could tell, both Harry and his father were entirely sincere in their admiration for his work. As far as it suited him, so was my dad.

No doubt the fact it still sold well helped. One of my strongest memories from childhood visits to Longhurst was leaving in our car with one of Austen's bubble-wrapped paintings in my lap, something my father was selling on Philip's behalf. Since there were many collectors around the world and a seemingly endless supply at the house— extraordinarily formulaic, absolutely consistent in style—it was a steady source of commission for my father and much-needed income for Philip. Even as a child I had a sense of how much it cost to keep a country pile like that going, the never-ending nature of the task.

"If you'd like to see them, do drop in sometime," Harry was telling Giles. "Similarly, Caroline, if ever you'd like to visit the house where Juliette grew up, we'd be delighted to have you. In fact, it's my birthday party next weekend. You should come. You should both come. The whole family will be there, Caroline—maybe someone will remember Juliette. Patrick can give you a lift."

"Absolutely, I'd love to," she said, perhaps a little too quickly, obviously delighted. Giles said the same.

"Is that really alright about the lift?" she asked me.

"Of course," I said, very pleased by this development, in fact.

Giles and Harry were already discussing trains and timing.

"I can't wait to see Alice Long's reaction when you tell her about the journal," I said to Caroline, perhaps just a little jealous of her discovery, in no doubt who was going to be the star of our next supervision. "Is there anything in there about the 1938 Surrealist Exhibition that might be helpful for my project?"

"There might be, but I haven't gotten to it yet," Caroline said. "It's been slow going—it's her handwriting that's the problem. There are five long entries, and I have only managed to get through two of them. I am starting to speed up a bit—I can distinguish her *e*'s and her *l*'s now, most of the time—but it's not something you can skim."

Her expression darkened. She leaned in closer to me, our shoulders almost touching. I could smell her perfume.

"There is one thing in what I have read so far that I can't get out of my head," she said, her voice lowered. "Juliette writes about how Oskar's wife used to follow them, harass them. She sounds genuinely worried about what Maria might be capable of. And what with the fire . . ."

She paused, watching my face as this sunk in.

"I don't want to jump to conclusions," said Caroline, "but there is something nagging at me, about the night Juliette and Oskar died. The knocking?"

I gave her a puzzled look.

"In his biography of Oskar Erlich, Walter Loftus mentions that someone knocked on the concierge's door and woke him up, which was how he saw the apartment was on fire, which meant he could raise the alarm, get the other residents out."

Her eyes were shining in the candlelight as she waited for the penny to drop.

"You're saying you aren't convinced the fire was an accident, and Oskar's wife might have been the one who started it?"

"I think it's a possibility. Juliette seemed to think Maria might be capable of something like that. Which also makes me wonder if Juliette sent her journal to Longhurst just in case something happened."

Caroline fell briefly, thoughtfully, silent. I followed her gaze. It was resting on Harry's signet ring, which he was absentmindedly fiddling with. "I'm also hoping the journal might explain why Juliette painted herself as a Sphinx, and how that's linked to her father's interest in Egyptology."

Athena appeared with plates piled high with meze, muttering something about not wanting them to get cold as she topped up our glasses. There was still no sign of Freddie. As the evening wore on, Athena spent ever longer periods in the kitchen, and each time she returned I expected her to bring the next course, but instead she arrived with more wine. No one seemed to know if we were waiting for Freddie, nor could we work out quite why we were there. Caroline had been invited the night before. Giles revealed that he had only been asked that afternoon.

By the time Athena served the mains, there were eight empty wine bottles and it was nearly midnight. I retain a vague impression of lamb. The dessert was cold. Ice cream, I think? There was brandy afterward, I'm fairly certain. Still no Freddie. By tacit consensus, his absence went unremarked upon.

Caroline asked how my dissertation was going, and I told her—with a bit of a grimace—that I was planning to drive down to London the next day to visit the Witt. I was not much looking forward to slogging through the archives on my dad's behalf, especially not with the hangover I was expecting.

As we were all leaving at around one a.m., Athena gave me a very firm hug and whispered something in my ear I did not catch. Harry and Giles wobbled off on their bikes, and I offered to walk Caroline back to her college.

It was a bright, cloudless night, everything sharply silvered, a hint of frost in the air. Both quite drunk, we found it difficult to stay two abreast on the pavement without bumping into each other. We brushed hands a few times and every time we did so, I felt an electric shock of hope. Then somehow I found her hand warm in mine.

We reached her college. Without saying anything, we kept walking. By now I could feel a distinct tingle in the base of my spine. The moon was full, the shadows long on the empty street in front of Trinity. From somewhere nearby came a peal of laughter. Caroline squeezed my hand. I squeezed hers back. We both looked up at the same time and locked glances momentarily and smiled. It felt a lot like the night we first met.

As we neared my college, I had mentally started to compose a casual invitation upstairs for a nightcap when suddenly she stopped. Still holding my hand, without breaking eye contact, she took a couple of steps backward, pulling me into a doorway, half disappearing into the shadows. Our faces were now so close we were practically kissing already. Then we *were* kissing, and her hands were on my shoulders. One of my hands was on the small of her back. Her legs were pressing against mine.

Then Caroline pulled away from me, ran her hands through her hair, and gave me a slightly sheepish smile. "Patrick," she said. "Let's go to your room."

CAROLINE, CAMBRIDGE, 1991

"Well that was . . . unexpected," Patrick said, as we lay there in the dark, my head on his chest, sheets tangled at our feet.

I laughed, reaching around on the floor for a blanket to cover myself. "For everyone apart from Athena, I think."

He took a moment to process this. "You mean the whole evening . . . ?"

"Was my best friend playing Cupid, yes," I said, laughing.

The instant Patrick walked into that dining room, I had realized it was a setup. That Athena—despite all my attempts to convey to her the complexity of my feelings about Patrick, despite all the times I had tried to explain to her the intensity of my anxieties around relationships generally—had taken it upon herself to matchmake. I was not sure if I felt annoyed about this or amused. Athena had always been so easy to read, at least to me (except when it came to Freddie, whose appeal was eternally baffling). Apparently the same could not be said the other way round.

Then again, I had often felt that Athena's brain was not wired quite like other people's—the directness of the way she approached things, perhaps to do with the way she had been brought up, an assumption that if she wanted something enough she would always get it.

It was a little irritating to think she would claim credit for all this, and yet as Patrick and I stood in that doorway, his lips pressed against mine, never before had I been so certain about what I wanted to happen next. Never in a moment like that had I felt so in control of my anxiety, so confident that if a wave of panic did start rising, I could face it down.

We giggled all the way up the stairs. We kissed in the corridor outside his room. There was a clash of teeth, more laughter. Then we were on his bed. His body on mine. My body on his.

It was only afterward, lying there, that I started to feel that familiar anxiety simmer. I sat up, asked Patrick for a glass of water. He passed me a mug, with a grin. "Even if it was Athena's doing," he said, "I'm really glad this happened. I really hope that maybe this time around . . ."

I tried to keep my breathing steady, to stop my throat from constricting. "Maybe," I said. "I think, perhaps . . . it's just that . . . it's not that I don't like you. There's just quite a lot of stuff I'm working through. Family stuff. Complicated stuff. I'm sure I'll tell you about it one day, but for the moment we are going to need to take things very slowly, okay?"

"Of course," he said. "We can take things at whatever pace you want. Just know that I like you—I don't think I ever stopped liking you—and I can be patient." He thought to himself for a minute and frowned—or pretended to. "Although I *was* going to ask you if you wanted to come to the Witt Library with me tomorrow. But if you think that would be too . . ."

"That sounds great," I said, with genuine enthusiasm.

Then somehow, we were kissing again, urgently. But even as we melted into each other, at the back of my mind was the knowledge that if I wanted this to be more than a three-night stand, I would have to find a way to open up to him. To try to explain why Juliette Willoughby's journal spoke to me so personally. To explain that I could remember exactly how it felt, that sense of constant anxiety she described, of always being on guard, never knowing if you were being too paranoid or not paranoid enough.

I was ten years old when my mother finally left my father. She must have spent years building up the courage to do it, months working out the practicalities, weeks waiting for the perfect moment to run. I understood implicitly that I would not be going back to that school or seeing my friends again. That we would be in a new place, a new city. That this was the last time I would ever see our house. I was allowed one bag and had half an hour to pack, and all that time she was standing by the window, watching for his car, terrified he would return early from work.

He had always said that if she ever tried to leave, if she ever tried to take me away from him, he would find her and he would kill her.

PATRICK'S VISION, I THINK, had been for us to cruise up to London in the MG with the roof down, stopping somewhere for a pub lunch in the sunshine. When we woke up it was raining. We got to the car and found it would not start. He was touchingly apologetic about this as we waited for a lull in the rain and then made a dash for the train station. All the way to King's Cross, Freddie Talbot was our main topic of discussion.

It was a relief to learn that Patrick was as uncharmed by him as I was. His not turning up for dinner the night before was typical, I explained.

As was Athena's reaction to it, the realization visibly dawning on her that Freddie was either not going to show or would be wasted if he did come.

"There are good reasons *why* he is the way he is, though," Patrick commented. "Because my dad is friends with Philip Willoughby, I spent a lot of time at Longhurst as a kid, hanging out with Harry. Often Freddie would be there too. I remember playing hide-and-seek for hours. Freddie would always win—you'd spend ages looking for him and there he would be, stretched out on a rafter."

I tried to imagine them, three little boys with the run of a great big country house—the very house that Juliette grew up in. Perhaps I should have been more surprised than I was to discover that Freddie was Harry's cousin—when I had first arrived in Cambridge I would have thought it almost as bizarre a coincidence as the discovery that they were both related to Juliette. Now, though, it just further underlined the interconnectedness of the circles into which I had stumbled.

"Why was Freddie at Longhurst so much—did he live there too?" I asked.

"Not exactly," Patrick said. "Most of the time he was at boarding school, but he'd stay during holidays when Arabella—his mother—didn't want him. She'd be in Monaco on someone's yacht, or in Spain on honeymoon, or doing yoga up a mountain. She moved to South Africa with husband number five when Freddie started secondary school, but I don't think he's been over there once."

"That must have been unsettling for him," I said.

"He certainly never liked to talk about it. If you really wanted to annoy Freddie, asking him where Arabella was would always do it. Not that upsetting Freddie was ever really something you wanted to do, because he's always had a mean streak. To freak Harry and me out, he used to tell us about all the creepy stuff Cyril kept in the house—the mummies, the old scrolls. He also had this Usborne *World of the Unknown* book of unsolved mysteries with the story of Longhurst's Missing Maid—this servant who disappeared there back in the 1930s. He always claimed that the room I'd been given to sleep in had been hers, and he would tell us about various family members who had *definitely* seen her ghost. Which, aged eight, you laugh about when you're all together, but come bedtime I'd sleep sitting up, back to the wall, with all the lights on."

Patrick paused. "The thing that really explains Freddie, though, the root of all that bitterness, is that technically Longhurst should be his."

"I'm sorry?"

"Juliette's father, Cyril, was the oldest of three brothers, but he never had a son. So when he died, Longhurst should have passed sideways to the second-eldest brother. That's where it gets peculiar. Freddie's grandfather Osbert was the next in line. Harry's grandfather Austen was the youngest. It skipped a brother: the house, the inheritance, all of it."

"Why?"

"Not sure," Patrick said. "Harry says he doesn't know and neither does Freddie. My dad thinks it was to do with Freddie's grandfather being a drinker, that Cyril was worried he'd piss the lot away. But I would imagine it does rankle with Freddie."

What none of that explained, I said, was what I had seen the other day, the peculiar incident in the car, Freddie being screamed at. Patrick said he was not sure what that could have been about either, or who had been screaming at him.

"The thing about Freddie is, he's always had a peculiar talent for pissing people off."

THE WOMAN BEHIND THE Witt Library's front desk explained it would take me a little time to get a reader's card. Patrick asked if I would mind if he went ahead of me to start on the task his father had set him.

"Of course not," I said. It sounded like he had a lot of photographs to leaf through.

Frustratingly, in contrast, my search for material on Juliette Willoughby yielded slim pickings. Predictably for an artist with no extant art, her name was not listed in the library catalogue at all. Instead, I contented myself with leafing through the files for work by other Surrealists featuring Sphinxes. I was sifting through a box full to bursting of photographs of Salvador Dalí's paintings when Patrick's face appeared over the top of my carrel. He was grinning.

"Did you find the paintings you were looking for?" I asked.

He shook his head. He was still grinning.

"What is it?"

"I've made a bit of a discovery. Come with me."

A box was open on Patrick's desk. It was labeled Longhurst Hall, 1961.

"What is it?" I asked.

He pulled out a chair and invited me to sit. "This is one of those boxes of photographs I told you about," he said. "The ones my dad asked me to go through."

He indicated the picture at the top of the pile. It showed a painting of a sad-eyed bloodhound, the background incomplete, the work unfinished, the painting unsigned. The photograph was old and of poor quality, black-and-white. He shifted it across to a different pile. Under it was a photograph of a painting of a wolfhound, nose to the ground, clearly undertaken by the same hand. Patrick added that photograph to the other pile too, revealing the one underneath.

"What do you make of that?" he asked me.

"It can't be," I said.

The photograph—frustratingly fuzzy, annoyingly monochrome— was centered on a single female figure. I could feel Patrick watching my reaction. It was her. The young woman from the passport photograph. Juliette Willoughby.

On her face was an expression of bold challenge. Around her neck was a familiar pendant, which she was pointing at with an index finger. Her paws—this figure was from the waist down feline—were crossed on a rock in front of her. Around the central figure, infuriatingly hard to make out, were other scenes. A pale girl with dark hair. A hooded figure in a boat.

"It can't be. Nothing in that apartment survived the fire," I said, shaking my head. "Everyone knows that. You said it yourself."

"What about the journal, what about the passport you found, the locket?" said Patrick. "*They* clearly survived the fire. They somehow found their way to Longhurst."

"It's impossible," I said.

Patrick shook his head. "It's *Self-Portrait as Sphinx*," he said.

Third Entry

Monday, 13th December—I sometimes wonder how history will remember us, Oskar and me.

For days he has been tinkering with *Three Figures in a Landscape*, the enormous, overwhelming painting in oils he has been working on for as long as I have known him, agonizing over, wrestling with.

All morning, Oskar has been bouncing over to the front window to peer out, expectantly. This being a Monday, the concierge's wife was mopping the stairs and landings, and every time her mop collided with the baseboard he would start, convinced it was a knock at the door. Every time Oskar passed the mirror he would run a hand through his hair, straighten his tie—gestures that made him look rather like a nervous maître d' waiting for opening hour.

He checked his watch. He picked up the paper and stared at it. He checked his watch again. Finally, with a grating sound, we heard the big wooden street door opening. Voices, one of them the concierge's wife, the other the man we were waiting for: André Breton. The acknowledged leader of the Surrealist movement, certainly its most celebrated theorist and spokesperson. The man whose opinion Oskar respects more than that of anyone else in the world.

I have always found him a bit pompous, if I am honest.

There are some celebrated people who seem at all times very conscious of that fact. My father, the MP, is one of them. Breton is another. The first time Oskar brought me to a Surrealist meeting—at the Promenade de Vénus café, where they all used to gather at five thirty every day except Sunday—the first thing I thought about Breton was: he speaks like he is expecting someone to write it down. He was certainly more than happy to pose for my photos, self-consciously holding thoughtful, photogenic poses—elbow on the marble table, or smoking and gazing out the window.

The reason Oskar was so nervous about this visit was that Breton was here to decide which—if any—of Oskar's paintings is worthy of inclusion in the upcoming International Surrealist Exhibition.

It took him a long time to climb the stairs. Finally came the knock at the door, Oskar literally leaping across the room to open it. As usual, Breton was almost comically courteous, formal, greeting me with a little bow, a polite question in French about how I was.

"Very well indeed," I answered, in my best schoolgirl French. "*Très bien, merci.*"

"And this is what you have been working on?" Breton asked Oskar, again in French. Taking up an entire wall of the studio, the one with the best light, was Oskar's near-complete masterpiece.

Breton lingered in front of it for a while. In some ways it must have been familiar already, given how many nights Oskar spent describing it to him, all the preliminary studies he had seen. He gave a satisfied grunt. He awarded it a little approving nod of the head.

Then something else caught his eye.

"*Mais cette peinture,*" said Breton, eyes widening. "*C'est incroyable!*" I glanced at Oskar's face, to see his expression. His eyes did not meet mine. His smile looked stiff, frozen. Breton took several quick steps across the room, clapping his hands together as he did so, an almost girlish gesture. "*Vraiment Surréaliste!*" He turned to smile, first at Oskar and then at me. Why had Oskar not said anything to him about *this* piece he was working on, he asked playfully. Of course this must be in the exhibition.

Oskar did not answer. It seemed he was incapable of speech. I returned Breton's smile but found myself temporarily unable to reply either. Because it was not one of Oskar's paintings that had caught Breton's attention.

It was my *Self-Portrait as Sphinx*.

I suppose it should have been no surprise that it would appeal to Breton. After all, the piece had started life as an experiment in automatic drawing at his apartment, all of us sitting there in silence with our paper in front of us, very serious, trying not to let our conscious minds interfere with what our pencils were producing. It was only when I was finished that I understood what I had drawn.

"Are you alright?" Oskar had asked. "Is something wrong?"

I had told Oskar by then about my time in the asylum. What I had not been able to bring myself to admit was exactly *why* I had been committed, the accusations I had been flinging around. Symptoms of my illness, was how doctors told me to think of them. Sick products of a hysterical mind. "Think of your father," they kept telling me. "Think of his reputation." That was the message, day in, day out, for months.

I had promised that if I was released, I would never say those things again. I understood this was something on which my freedom was conditional. Even now, when I think of writing my darker suspicions down in this journal, my fingers flinch from the task.

What I never promised was that I would not draw or paint them.

CHAPTER 5

PATRICK, CAMBRIDGE, 1991

Our second supervision with Alice Long was scheduled for ten the following morning, although when she opened the door she showed no sign of having been expecting us. For a moment, it was unclear if she even remembered who we were.

"Well, you'd better come in then," she said, eventually.

Caroline waited until we were all in the living room and Alice was sitting down before she told her about the journal. Where she had found it. What it contained. Juliette's words. Her drawings. On the back page, she had realized after some research, were Juliette's color notes, where she had daubed different shades, perhaps keeping it on hand as she was painting to remind herself of their exact composition. Alice leaned forward in her chair to listen. She let out little gasps—of delight, of surprise, of amazement. Her eyes were bright.

"This was in among the papers in the Willoughby Bequest?"

Caroline said yes. Along with Juliette's passport and pendant. "What I was hoping you might be able to help me with is how they got there."

"I have no idea, I am afraid," Alice said. Caroline and I exchanged a look, and she gave me an almost imperceptible nod.

"There's something else," I said. "We don't think the journal is all that survived the fire."

Alice tilted her head, raised an eyebrow. "And what would make you think that?"

"Did you know *Self-Portrait as Sphinx* was withdrawn from the International Surrealist Exhibition?" I asked her. "That Juliette only allowed it to be shown for a single night?"

"Of course I do," said Alice, a touch sharply. "That's well-documented. After the opening night of the exhibition, she decided that she did not want the painting on public view, and that it was no longer for sale. That's why it was in their apartment when the fire broke out. That's why it was destroyed."

"But what if it wasn't?" said Caroline. "What if it survived?"

As I explained about the photograph we had found at the Witt, Alice Long let out a few coughs and splutters of surprise and—I was pathetically pleased to see, given her obvious disdain the first time we met—a nod of what looked like grudging admiration.

I did feel bad that she was the first person with whom we had shared our discoveries, and not my father. Given his connection to the Willoughbys, to Longhurst, given he was the reason we had stumbled across the photograph of the painting in the first place. Should I have told him? Probably. Somehow, though, this felt like something Caroline and I were meant to do together—or to put it another way, what I did not want was for him to swoop in and grab all the credit.

As with most people in his profession, one of the dreams that had kept my father crisscrossing the country from auction house to estate sale all these years, that had him thumbing through typewritten auction catalogues in bed every night, was the dream of stumbling across a valuable work that no one had correctly identified. A sleeper. Unlike most people in his profession, he had actually already stumbled across one, once.

When I was about a year old, when money had never been tighter, he convinced himself he had found the painting that was going to make his fortune, change our lives. What he believed to be a small early Madonna by Raphael that had spent a century hanging in a country house outside Norwich, then ended up in a general sale of its contents. It was in bad condition, varnish thick and darkened. Someone had overpainted an arm (at a jarringly peculiar angle) to cover up damage to the canvas. Nevertheless, my father said, he *knew*.

It required a lot of expensive restoration that he would need to cover the cost of. He would have to spend months in the archives establishing a convincing provenance, and then it would have to be authenticated by an authority on the artist—he asked his former college tutor, an acknowledged Raphael expert. Dad brought the painting up to the professor's rooms himself, the murk of decades removed, the original colors glowing from the canvas. The expert scratched his chin, peered first at one corner of the painting then another through his glasses (Dad did a very convincing impression of this). His verdict was— School of Raphael. Probably undertaken by a follower, a decade or so after the master's death. A very nice piece, impressive in its way, but no Raphael. He even estimated what it might be expected to fetch at auction: about ten thousand pounds (when Dad sold it, it achieved just over eight, and he recouped only a fraction of his costs).

As they were walking to Dad's car, the professor—apologetic, friendly—had mentioned that he was working on a new edition of his own authoritative book on Raphael. Dad wished him luck. To my father's surprise, when the revised book was published, the professor's opinion had for some reason changed and the painting Dad had shown him was included among the canon of works by the master himself. The next time the Madonna came up for auction, three years later, it sold for fifteen million. There were many ways my dad told this story. Wry. Rueful. Self-pitying. Furious. I must have heard it in every variation at least a hundred times.

He had been robbed of that sleeper. There was no way, if I dropped even the slightest hint at what Caroline and I had found, he would not try to somehow claim this one for himself.

"What I don't see," Alice said, sounding genuinely confused, "is how it could have got there. Juliette's painting. To Longhurst."

I said we could not yet answer that either. The main thing was that, in the Witt Library, there was concrete evidence that the painting had been at Longhurst in 1961. It might still be there.

"I suppose there is really only one way of testing that theory," said Alice thoughtfully.

I told her that Caroline and I would actually be at Longhurst for a party over the weekend, that Harry Willoughby, her uncle's grandson, was at university with us, and turning twenty-one.

"And there's something else," Caroline said, clearing her throat. "I think I know why she painted herself as a Sphinx. Look here, at this photocopy of the photograph we found at the Witt."

Caroline took it out of her bag and passed it to Alice, who then brought the paper back and forth toward her eyes, adjusting her glasses and blinking. "Well, well, well," she said. "Well, well, well."

It was frustrating that the grainy black-and-white picture was not of high enough quality to allow the viewer to piece together what was happening in the inset scenes surrounding the central figure. The photocopy made it all even less decipherable. I pointed out to Alice where it was just about possible to make out what was being depicted. In the bottom left corner, a pale figure, female, young-looking, with hair floating upward. There was a boat of some kind down in the bottom right, with a hooded figure standing in it, crossing a dark river. Above all this, over a tangled treescape, hung the moon.

There was one detail, though, that Caroline had fixated on. "See there?" she said. "Wings, folded against her back. Juliette painted a self-portrait of herself as a *winged* Sphinx."

"Aha." Alice turned to me. "Meaning, Mr. Lambert?"

"A winged Sphinx is a Greek—as opposed to an Egyptian—Sphinx."

"The difference being?" Alice asked.

"An Egyptian Sphinx guards a tomb," said Caroline. "A Greek Sphinx is a Sphinx with a riddle. That's why she painted herself as one. That's what the wings are telling us. She's telling us this is a painting with a secret in it. A mystery for us to solve."

CAROLINE, CAMBRIDGE, 1991

I was looking through one of Patrick's drawers for a paracetamol, the morning we were due to drive up together to Longhurst for Harry's party, when I found his Osiris ring.

"Patrick," I said, "can I ask about this?"

He did seem a bit embarrassed. "Look, I *have* been meaning to mention it. It probably does seem weird, my wanting to join something like that. The thing is, it means a lot to my father . . ."

"You're a member of Osiris. The drinking society founded by Juliette's father. And despite everything, you never mentioned it?"

"I've been to *one* dinner. I've literally been inside their building once."

I asked him to describe it for me. He did so.

"You have to get me in," I told him.

"I can't," said Patrick. "It's not allowed. No guests. Definitely no female guests. No exceptions."

"Oh come on," I said. "If there's stuff in there that belonged to Cyril, that ended up in the possession of the Osiris Society rather than going into the Willoughby Bequest, there might be something which will shed light on how the journal and the painting ended up where they did . . ."

He breathed a deep sigh. He ran his hands over his face. He checked the time. "Okay, given that everyone should be heading up to Harry's party, this might be our only opportunity."

Half an hour later we were pulling up outside the building.

"Let me go first, okay?" he said. "Just to make sure the coast is clear. If anyone is around, I'll tell them I'm looking for a dinner jacket for tonight."

"Got it," I said with a nod. He did actually need a dinner jacket, as it happened. When he'd brought the one he had been planning to wear out of its garment bag the previous evening, it turned out to have had its satin lapels shredded by a cat.

"A cat?" I'd asked.

"Long story," Patrick told me.

I watched him walk up the street, take the stairs, tap on the door, and—when no one answered—bring a key out from his pocket and unlock it. He stepped through swiftly and left it slightly ajar. I counted to ten and climbed out of the car and followed him.

It was a little like stepping back in time, stepping into that house. Pulling the door closed behind me, I turned to confront an interior that it was easy to imagine had not changed much in a hundred years. The dim light falling through the stained glass over the front door. The brass umbrella stand. The checkerboard tiled floors.

There was a bowl of cat food and a water dish at the foot of the stairs. From the gloom at the end of the corridor, I heard a distant meow and glimpsed something dark darting across the hallway.

"Most of the Egyptian stuff is on the first floor, I think," Patrick told me.

Halfway up the stairs something creaked and both of us froze. What would they do, the Osiris boys, if they caught us here, I wondered. From the sounds of it, at the very least, Patrick would be out of the club.

All the doors on the first-floor corridor were shut, so we began trying their handles. The first one Patrick turned did not open, so he moved on to another. The first door I tried, the large brass knob did not budge at all. I turned around and tried the door directly opposite. This time, it gave. I tried not to flinch as it squeaked.

I stepped inside a room illuminated only by the light creeping in around the edges of its heavy velvet curtains, giving a vague sense of glass cases lining the walls. The gilded frames of the paintings on the walls were visible, but it was too dark to see the paintings themselves. Dust motes hung in the air. I made my way over to the curtains and parted them slightly.

"Good God," I said aloud.

In one corner was a whole case of *wedjat* eyes. Opposite it, another full of jade scarabs of varying sizes. Next to that was a trio of painted limestone busts. It was hard not to feel like this should all be in a museum. It was easy to see why the Egyptian authorities might want some of this stuff back.

Each glass case rested on a waist-high wooden cabinet with drawers. Gently, carefully, I tried one of these. It slid open to reveal a carefully arranged selection of papyri under glass.

I closed the first drawer and opened a second. For a moment, I genuinely could not quite take in what I was looking at. In the drawer was a single long strip of papyrus, its edges cracked and flaking. Clearly, at some point it had been ripped in half. The portion that survived showed the lower half of a robed figure, standing in a boat, steering it across the river. The boat itself—high in the prow and stern—was identical to that in the murky old photograph of Juliette's painting. The boat bobbed confidently amid stylized waves, their color astonishingly fresh and bright. If it was of a similar age to the papyri Sam showed me in the Willoughby Bequest, I was nevertheless looking at something thousands of years old.

I was leaning in to get a closer look when a door I had not seen, on the far side of the room from the door I had come in through, suddenly swung open. I froze.

From the door emerged Freddie, with something under his arm. What was he doing here? He was not supposed to be in Cambridge. He had told Athena he would be driving up to the party at Longhurst from a friend's place in London and that was why he could not give her a lift.

Quietly closing the door through which he had entered, Freddie locked it with a key which he then returned to his back pocket. He had not seen me yet, but if he turned his head just a little to the right, he was bound to.

He double-checked the door. He patted the key in his pocket. He turned to cross the room. Something, a creak of floorboards from another room, a change in the atmosphere, gave him pause. He stood where he was. He looked like he was listening for something.

I had been holding my breath for almost a minute, squeezing into the shadows. I closed my eyes. When I opened them again, Freddie had crossed the room and was closing the door behind him. Finally, with a gasp, I let out the breath I was holding.

From the downstairs hallway, I could hear voices—Freddie's, Patrick's. Then I heard the front door slam. A few minutes later, Patrick appeared.

"Are you in here?" he asked loudly.

"Over in the corner."

"No sign of a dinner jacket anywhere. I'll have to pick one up on the way," said Patrick. "Freddie was here. He came sneaking down the stairs and gave me the fright of my life. He didn't see you, did he?"

I shook my head. It had been a close call, though. Even now my heart was thumping.

Patrick asked me if I had found anything of interest. "Yes. I don't know what it means yet, but it must mean something. Remember that boat in the photograph of Juliette's painting?" I said, beckoning him over to the open drawer in front of me, the one with the papyrus in it. "Well, look at this . . ."

WE WERE HALFWAY TO Longhurst before Patrick revealed that the place we would be stopping off to pick up a replacement dinner jacket was his mother's house. That I would be meeting her for the first time. The plan had been to get to Longhurst early, so that Patrick could help Harry set up, and therefore I was dressed for comfort—hoodie, jeans, sneakers—rather than elegance. It was midday—were we expected to have lunch with her? Should I have brought flowers, a present? I tried to ignore the rising panic in my chest.

I had only the vaguest idea of what Mary, Patrick's mother, was going to be like. I knew he had lived with her when he was home from school for the holidays. That after the divorce from Patrick's father, she had trained as a paralegal. That she had a partner, Steve, someone Patrick always spoke of with mild disdain. He had made it very clear that Steve was her boyfriend, not his stepdad.

The house was not at all what I had been expecting. It was in Suffolk, and I suppose I had been imagining something charmingly rustic—a cottage, maybe, or a farmhouse. To my surprise, it was in a row of houses, in a village that reminded me of my grandmother's. The same sort of redbrick two-story 1930s semidetached houses, with about the same amount of front garden, the same red tiled roofs. The same sorts of cars in the driveways.

The MG was definitely an anomaly.

I remembered various self-deprecating things Patrick had told me about himself as a teenager—the smoking jacket he affected at home for a while, the hours he spent in the bath reading Proust and Wilde and *L'Uomo Vogue*—and found myself rapidly recontextualizing them.

"Well, here we are," he said, as we turned onto a sloped cement driveway. "Don't forget to take your shoes off. My mother is very particular about her cream carpets."

It is surprisingly tricky to extricate oneself with dignity from a sports car parked on a slope. By the time I had done so, the front door of the house had opened, and Patrick's mother was bustling out to greet us and to tell Patrick off for being late. She had sandwiches. Did we want sandwiches?

"It's fine, honestly," said Patrick. "We don't need anything. We had breakfast. We were thinking about stopping at a pub for lunch. It's going to be a big dinner tonight. Unless you want anything, Caroline?"

I said I did not unless she had gone to the bother of making it. Which is how, as Patrick and his mother searched his bedroom, I found myself sitting alone on the living room sofa with a large plate of crustless smoked salmon sandwiches in front of me.

"It was definitely *here*," I could hear Patrick saying, through the ceiling.

On the mantelpiece sat school photos of Patrick at different ages. Patrick and his mother and Steve on vacation somewhere, Spain, perhaps, Patrick with a center part and wearing an enormous white T-shirt and baggy swim trunks.

"Well, I don't know where it is, then," Patrick's mother was saying, with audible frustration. "What would *Steve* want with your dinner jacket?" I heard her ask a moment later.

They could not all be for me, these sandwiches. There were enough to feed a cricket team.

Eventually, Patrick reappeared with a jacket under his arm and announced we were leaving.

"It was nice to meet you, Caroline," his mother said, as she was showing us out. "I'm sorry we didn't get more of a chance to chat. Hopefully we'll see each other again soon."

Her smile was hesitant, tentative—she was evidently unsure if I was just a friend, or a girlfriend. To be honest, so was I. It was a week since the dinner party. He had slept over in my room twice. I had slept in his room three times. If we had not quite worked up the courage to put a name on what was happening, it was pretty clear *something* was. Without consulting me, when Harry had asked if we would want one bedroom or two at Longhurst, Patrick had said we would share.

Every time I had seen Athena recently, she had been smug about how things had turned out. It was okay, I reassured myself. Patrick was a nice guy. We were having fun. It was not when I was with Patrick but when I was not that my anxiety spiked.

"I hope you two have fun this weekend," Patrick's mum said. "Do you know Norfolk at all?"

I said not really. She asked me where I had grown up, a question I always dreaded. "Oh, all over the place," I told her. "Bedford for a bit, then London, and then Cherry Hinton, near Cambridge."

"Oh, lovely," she said. "Is that where your parents live?"

"My grandmother does," I said. "My parents aren't actually around anymore."

This was both technically true and a bit less stark than the full story.

Somehow, as we drove off, I found myself with three or four full sandwiches, elaborately wrapped in paper napkins, on my lap.

"Sorry about that," said Patrick. "I mean about your parents. I didn't know. I would have warned her. I hope she didn't upset you."

"It didn't upset me," I said, trying to reassure him.

Something in my tone must have warned him this was nevertheless not something I wanted to discuss further. Not here. Not now. Not yet. We drove in silence for a while.

"Oh, by the way," said Patrick. "I dug out something that might interest you."

He reached around and produced a book. Published by Usborne, one of those big illustrated kids' books from the 1980s: *The World of the Unknown: Unsolved Mysteries*. On the cover there was a picture of a UFO and a cowled apparition. I gave Patrick a puzzled look.

"You remember me telling you about Longhurst's Missing Maid? The story Freddie used to read to scare us, about that girl who vanished there in the 1930s? That's the book. It's all in there, photographs and everything. Of the house, the maid, the newspaper headlines."

I flicked through until I landed on the pages. One of the headlines read: "Is the Missing Maid a Victim of the Willoughby Curse?"

Patrick glanced over, the car swerving slightly. "I think it was around then that the idea of a family curse started to circulate. Probably not a good idea to bring it all up this weekend, though. They can be a bit funny about that stuff."

"I can imagine," I said, knowing all too well what it felt like to have to come to terms with tragedy and sorrow in public.

HE FOUND US. MY father found us.

After all those months in hiding, in hostels, in different women's refuges. Checking up and down the street for him every time we stepped out the front door. Being woken up in the middle of the night by a car outside and wondering if that was him. Unable even to tell my grandmother where we were, so as not to put her in danger of threats or violence.

I can still remember how it felt to finally have our own little flat. To know this was a place we could speak as loudly as we wanted, laugh as loudly as we wanted. Where we did not have to be always thinking three moves ahead to avoid upsetting my father. Where we were not always waiting for his mood to crack abruptly. Where I could spill a glass of water without expecting a sharp slap around the back of the head. Where the walls and the doors were not full of dents—foot-shaped, fist-shaped, head-shaped.

I think she thought he would give up looking for us eventually. That all his talk of tracking us down and making her pay if she ever left him was just performative, like so many of his promises. It turned out she was wrong.

A friend of his gave us away, it emerged at the trial. Someone who had spotted my mother and me, coming out of the library, and had casually mentioned it at the pub. That is something I will never understand. That decision. In a world in which to take no action would incur no consequences, where keeping your mouth shut would cost you nothing, why speak?

Another question I will never have an answer to is what would have happened to me if I'd been there when he came knocking. Would he have killed me too? I expect so. At the trial, he said a red mist descended. His actual words. *A red mist*. He had just come for a conversation, he said. He had been drinking, he admitted.

She had embarrassed him. That is the only explanation I can come up with. I was sure that if he had thought about it for just five minutes he would have seen he did not want us back. God knows having a kid around the house had driven him up the wall. The problem, the burr under the saddle, was the loss of face. Going from being the man with the pretty wife to the man whose wife had left him.

If I seem awkward, if I freeze a bit, when people ask where I grew up, or about my parents, that's why. Because, like Juliette, I know there are some things it is impossible to describe.

Because when I was thirteen years old, my father strangled my mother to death with enough force to fracture multiple vertebrae in her neck, and then left her there for me to find on the kitchen floor. And then gathered up her sketchbooks and put them on the barbecue in the garden and burned the lot, so I have not one single thing my mother ever wrote or drew to remember her by.

Then he left and spent the rest of the evening laughing and drinking with his friends in the pub.

PART II

THE PAINTING

*I remember not long ago hearing Picasso and
Gertrude Stein talking about various things
that had happened at that time, one of them
said but all that could not have happened in
that one year, oh said the other, my dear you
forget we were young then and we did a great
deal in a year.*

—GERTRUDE STEIN, *The Autobiography
of Alice B. Toklas* (1933)

CHAPTER 6

PATRICK, DUBAI, THE PRESENT DAY

I am trying to think when I have been this scared before. Never, I think, is the answer.

I didn't really quite grasp that I'd been arrested until I was walked out of the gallery and into the waiting police car.

All the way to the station, I kept asking what the issue was and getting no answer. A scratched Perspex divider separated where I was sitting from the front seat. One officer squinted through the dusty windshield; the other stared out of the passenger window as we drove to the station compound. The whole time, playing on an ever-escalating loop in my head, were all the horror stories I had heard about people who had found themselves on the wrong side of the legal system here. The tourists jailed for public lewdness. The friend of a friend who got into a drunken argument with the security guard at a hotel brunch. The married man who kissed his husband in a nightclub. The sexual assault victim, here on holiday, who made the mistake of reporting the incident to the police.

It would be hard to explain to someone who has not lived in this country, the permanent low buzz of expat paranoia, a paranoia that is not quite paranoia, because things can go wrong here, even for people like me. And when they do go wrong, they can go very wrong, very fast.

It is a city of two sides, Dubai: the shiny side and the other side. I can pinpoint the exact moment today when I passed from one into the other. As we walked in through the entrance of the police station, with its polished floors, its glossy posters and framed mission statements, it was still possible to believe that I was here simply to assist the police with their inquiries about something. No one said anything about giving up my phone. As if it was just a formality, I was told they would need to take my fingerprints and a mugshot.

Then we go through a door and suddenly we are on the *other* side: a corridor painted a drab green, the overhead lights humming and flickering, acrid disinfectant not quite covering other smells. I am directed into a room and told to sit.

After what feels like a very long wait, the door opens. I shiver, unsure whether it's the apprehension or the air-conditioning. Two men enter. Both take a seat. One man's face is heavily lined, with pockmarked cheeks. The other man is younger, slimmer, with rimless glasses.

It is the younger guy I find myself addressing.

"I'm very sorry, but I still don't really understand why I am here," I tell him, smiling in what I hope is an ingratiating manner, consciously playing the amiable befuddled Englishman. "Is this something to do with money? I know how seriously you take debt here—if I am overdrawn or have missed a payment for something, it is just a temporary misunderstanding. If you let me call my bank, I can very quickly clear things up . . ."

The older man says something to the younger, gruffly. The younger translates.

"This has nothing to do with your empty bank account or your credit card debt, Mr. Lambert."

"Is it something to do with the painting, then, Officer?"

The painting I have just sold had not, after all, made its way to Dubai through quite the correct channels. In fact, it came in Harry's suitcase on an economy Emirates flight. It could be that this is a customs duty thing. Or perhaps was it something to do with the sale of the painting and how it had been conducted? There were lowball offers I had politely declined, and it was not unheard-of for a disgruntled collector to make some sort of spurious accusation . . .

"*He* is the officer," the younger man says, indicating his unsmiling colleague. "I am just the translator."

My throat is dry. I ask for a glass of water. They exchange words. The younger man turns to me with a smile.

"Of course you can have something to drink. But first it is important we clarify a few things."

"Of course," I say. "Ask me anything you like."

For some reason, he keeps asking me about Harry Willoughby, how I know him, how long I have known him. He asks me why I think it was to me that Harry came to sell this painting, this *Self-Portrait as Sphinx*. I explain again about the relationship between my father and Harry's father, the length of my and Harry's friendship. They ask about the terms on which I had agreed to sell the painting, whether I thought they were fair. They ask when I last spoke to or contacted Harry. Had I thought it strange he was not at the press conference?

A little strange, I say. A bit rude, perhaps. I had left several messages, asking where he was.

"Is all this about Harry?" I ask. "Is Harry in trouble?"

Only then do they tell me that Harry is dead, that Harry has been murdered.

Only then does it dawn on me the reason I am here is that they think I killed him.

CHAPTER 7

CAROLINE, LONGHURST, 1991

"Welcome to Longhurst," said Patrick as we turned in at the wrought iron front gate and rumbled up an oak-flanked driveway. So this was it. The house where Juliette had grown up. The house the photograph at the Witt suggested her painting had somehow found its way back to.

Patrick followed my gaze to a huddle of ripped yurts in a distant field. "That's Philip Willoughby's doing," he explained. "One of his many attempts to monetize the estate. Those are from the failed opera festival, I think. The truth is, Philip has had rather more misses than hits, entrepreneurially speaking."

That seemed an understatement. As we bounced the mile or so up to the house, Patrick pointed out a field striated with sorry-looking vines (a failed winery), the overgrown remains of a go-kart track, and a sign welcoming visitors to an A-Mazing Maize Maze, next to a bare field.

"He's nice, Philip, although he'll no doubt regale you with his latest money-making wheeze. *His* mother—the painter Austen Willoughby's widow—is still going strong in her nineties." Patrick made a whistling noise through his teeth, "And she is something else. She was there this one time when Freddie persuaded Harry and me to row over the lake— she must have been in her eighties then—and I have never heard a telling off like it. Even Freddie couldn't smirk his way through that one. Then there's Harry's mother, Georgina. . . ."

He thought for a moment, as we swerved to avoid a particularly large pothole. "Definitely an acquired taste. You'll know very quickly

if she likes you or not. She has always approved of me, for some unknown reason, which means we will probably be sitting near her
tonight. Consider this advance warning."

"I'm sure I'll be fine," I said, as it dawned on me that, being Patrick's
plus-one, I would spend the evening being appraised and assessed.

"Well, we'll find out soon enough," Patrick said with a laugh, waving at a dark-haired woman in an apron who was marching across the
gravel. He wound down the window and shouted: "Georgina!"

She shaded her eyes to peer into the car at us.

"Patrick!" she cried, in apparent delight, at considerable volume.
"Park up here, would you, and give the keys to the chap in the hall in
case we need to shuffle the cars around to make space. I'm afraid you
won't be staying in the Green Room tonight—we were all set up for
you and then a bloody pipe burst."

She pulled a face and raised one hand melodramatically to her forehead.

"The Green Room?" I asked Patrick.

"That's the bedroom—top floor, green leaf-print wallpaper,
view of the lawn and the lake—my dad and I always get put in,
when he or I stay here. But not tonight, apparently. That's the thing
with big old country piles like this—there's always something in
need of fixing."

In illustration, he pointed at the scaffolding erected along one side of
the house, partly wrapped in white plastic tarps. More tarps shrouded
a section of the roof. Both things looked like they had been there for
some time.

Despite these signs of encroaching decay, the house was still imposing. I had done my homework: originally a smaller Georgian
manor, it had been purchased by the Willoughby family in the 1840s,
then extended and embellished in golden Bath stone in Gothic Revival
style, complete with rose windows, flying buttresses, and soaring
turrets.

Staff in white shirts and waistcoats were swarming the lawn on one
side of the building, some with meadows-full of floral arrangements in
their arms, others trays of sparkling glassware. A tower of champagne

coupes was being assembled by the entrance. Although Harry's invitation had requested white tie and promised dinner and dancing, fireworks at midnight and a hog roast at dawn, until that moment, the scale of the event hadn't really dawned on me. It was clear this would be unlike any birthday party I had ever attended.

"I thought you said the Willoughbys were tight with money," I whispered to Patrick.

"There are some things that a family like this will always pay for, and a milestone like this is one. It's no wonder they have my dad looking into selling more of Austen's paintings."

"Caroline!" I heard my name called from across the driveway, and turned to see Athena emerging from a Rolls-Royce, already dressed for dinner. I waved hello at her driver, Karl. We had met once before, when he collected Athena and me after a birthday party in London and dropped us at the Galanises' house in Holland Park. I remember being baffled at the time by how bare the place was. Only later did it dawn on me that this was probably just *one of* the family's London houses—and possibly just one of their drivers.

Athena tottered over to join us. I made some remark about turning up in style.

"You didn't offer me a lift, so what other option did I have?" she said, a little frostily.

"Athena, where exactly do you think we could have put you?" I said, gesturing to the two-seater MG. It was obvious the person she was really annoyed at was Freddie, who had not only refused to drive her here but had also told her that under no circumstances was she to introduce herself to the family as his girlfriend. Clearly, this was neither the time nor the place for me to mention I'd seen him sneaking around earlier at the Osiris clubhouse.

"And here he is," said Patrick, swiftly changing the subject. "The birthday boy."

Harry was standing on the porch, greeting people as they arrived, shaking hands, accepting gifts.

"Patrick!" he said. "Welcome." He shook Patrick's hand vigorously. "And Caroline, so glad you could make it!"

For a moment I thought he was going to shake my hand too, but instead he gave me a stiff hug. He directed us through to the hallway, where a calligraphed list on a wooden easel detailed who was allocated which bedroom. Ours was the Rose Room, on the second floor, in between Athena's and the one assigned to a Francis Gore-Wykeham-Fiennes.

"I'm going to find Freddie," Athena declared, marching off. Patrick handed his car key to a man in a waistcoat, who placed it in a dresser drawer, and then gestured for me to follow him up the stairs.

"Wait here for a second," Patrick told me when we reached our floor. "I'll drop the bags in our room and give you a little tour of the house."

As I waited for him to return, I looked over the marble balustrade at the other guests arriving, the girls with their glossy hair, the boys with their suit bags folded over their arms. When he returned, we descended and poked our heads into a succession of rooms that were clearly designed for entertaining on a grand scale—impressive rather than welcoming. The dining room, with its gleaming candelabras, put me in mind of a ghost ship; one formal living room had sofas so upright and understuffed and uncomfortable-looking it would surely have been preferable to stand.

This was the life Juliette had run away from. I could not say I blamed her.

At the end of one corridor, Patrick pointed out an ornately carved wooden door.

"That leads through to the east wing, the oldest part of the house, where Cyril had his rooms."

Above the doorframe he pointed out a sequence of hand-painted hieroglyphic symbols in gold paint. I made out an eye, a set of scales, two feathers, a different kind of eye, a hawk.

"It's also where you'll find the library and Austen's old studio. If Juliette's painting is at Longhurst, then it is likely somewhere in here."

He had opened the door just a crack when Harry's mother came marching around the corner.

"Patrick!" she said crisply, and his hand recoiled as if the brass knob was electrified. "Out of bounds tonight, I'm afraid. I did tell Philip to put a sign up."

I had thought earlier she was speaking loudly because she was so pleased to see Patrick. It turned out this—around 30 percent louder than an average person—was her normal speaking voice. Perhaps that was necessary when your dining table was ten meters long and your living room was the size of a tennis court.

"Sorry, of course," Patrick said.

He took my hand and together we beat a swift retreat back along the hall and up the stairs to our bedroom. The whole way I was thinking through what this meant, whether there was any way we might persuade Georgina to make an exception in our case, whether we might ask Harry or Philip to show us around . . .

"Here we are," said Patrick. "Hope you like chintz."

It was not hard to see how the Rose Room had gotten its name. There were roses on the curtains. The dresser was decorated with hand-painted roses. Patrick threw himself down on the rose-covered bedspread and patted it for me to join him.

"You know," he said, "we do have a little bit of time before . . ."

I was still standing, on the other side of the room.

"Patrick," I said softly.

He propped himself up on one elbow. He gave me a smile. "Yes?"

"I'm sorry, but I think there's something we need to talk about. Something you need to know about me, if we're going to be together."

"Yeah?" he said, still smiling, a little puzzled, trying to read my expression.

Was I really going to do this? Was I really going to do this now? I glanced at myself in the mirror over the mantelpiece. I gathered my resolve.

"I don't really feel like this is the right moment—at someone else's house, just before a party—but I don't think there's ever going to be a right moment. It's a lot to lay on someone, and you're probably not going to know what to say, and that's okay."

Patrick sat up fully. "Is this about your parents?"

"It is, yes. I've never told anyone the whole story, but I want to tell you because I think this thing between us means something. But if I'm wrong, if it's just a fling for you, that's okay too, but you've got to let me know now."

Patrick shook his head slightly. We both smiled a little. I felt a rush of tenderness toward him.

"God," I said. "I really don't know why I didn't wait until I'd had a drink before trying to do this . . ."

Patrick held out a hand to me. I took it. He sat me down next to him on the bed. I took a deep breath and began.

PATRICK, LONGHURST, 1991

As we walked across the lawn, Caroline held on to my arm as if her ankles depended on it, stilettos sinking into the ground with each step.

"Fuck it," she declared halfway to the tent, slipping off the offending heels and handing them to me. She scooped up the hem of her pale gold dress and walked barefoot the rest of the way.

I had never in my life seen anyone look as beautiful as Caroline did in that moment, her hair tumbling almost to her waist in the golden early evening light. Nor had I ever met anyone who had lived through so much, so young, or with the inner strength to channel all that anger and pain into trying to live the life her mother would have dreamed of for her.

I was a little awed by how much trust Caroline had placed in me, sharing her story. I understood it was a great and precious responsibility I had been given.

I was also a bit mortified, when I thought how much time I had spent moaning on to her about my father.

If anyone in the world deserved to find that painting, it was Caroline Cooper. If there really was a secret of some kind encoded in it, I could not imagine anyone more likely to unravel it.

She discreetly wriggled her feet back into her shoes as we hit harder ground. Inside, guests loitered around the tables, and we all looked for our names on the little handwritten cards at each seat, while waiters circulated with champagne and a jazz band parped and noodled away at one end of the tent. At the other end was a formal table arrangement, as at a wedding.

"My God," she whispered to me. "I feel like we've walked onto the set of some costume drama."

The funny thing was, as a child I had never found it strange, Harry living in a house like this and having his own library and lake with an island in his back garden. It was just a great place for running around. Only as a teenager did I start to reflect seriously on the peculiar dynamic between Harry's father and my father, an old friendship that was very much not a relationship of equals, that was also one of the defining relationships of Dad's professional life. Only later had I begun to wonder what it might feel like for Harry, knowing that whatever else he did with his life first, one day sooner or later he would inherit Longhurst and have to try to keep it all going.

The seating was arranged along fairly obvious lines. There were a few tables of Harry's fellow classics students plus Giles Pemberton, and four or five tables of school friends. Freddie and the Osiris boys were near the back, their long-suffering girlfriends interspersed among them, being talked over. Arno von Westernhagen, still not drinking, was holding forth on the reasons for this at top volume—he seemed to have been out cold on that rugby pitch slightly longer each time I heard the story. It was a predictable crowd, all apart from one group that seemed utterly out of place: a cluster of mathematics and computer science students from our college, none of them friends of Harry's as far as I knew, all looking as surprised to be there as I was to see them.

"What's that about, then?" I asked Harry as we filed over to the top table.

"Dad made me invite them," he explained, with mild embarrassment. "His idea being, they'll end up making all the money, so might be useful to know."

It made sense, I supposed.

To be honest, even if they spent all night daring each other to recite pi to a hundred decimal places, they were going to have more fun than anyone on our table.

Harry was in the middle with Caroline on one side and his grandmother—Granny Violet—on the other. Next to Caroline was Harry's father—I could already hear him explaining some idea he'd had about setting up an ostrich farm, detailing at length how many omelets you could make with a single egg. Georgina was next to me, and I was at the end.

At every place on every table, a little disposable camera had been set. Freddie had immediately gone around stockpiling them and was already making a nuisance of himself: earlier I had seen him step outside with one and return a moment later looking very pleased with himself and zipping back up his fly.

The third time my wine glass was topped up, I became conscious of how quickly I was drinking and resolved to pace myself. As we were all seated in a row, the only person I could comfortably have talked to was Georgina, but every time I did ask her a question, some urgent task would occur to her, and she'd scurry off to find a waiter.

On the far side of Georgina, I could hear that Caroline had finally gotten Philip off the topic of ostriches and was asking him about Juliette, trying to interest him in *Self-Portrait as Sphinx*, asking if he could think of any way that the painting might have made its way from Paris to Longhurst, if anyone had ever mentioned it.

Even from where I was sitting, I could tell she was getting nowhere.

"Good Lord, my dear," I could hear Philip saying. "I'm sure if it ever was here, someone would have thrown it away years ago. Now if it's paintings you are interested in, we have some wonderful canine portraits by Harry's grandfather Austen . . ."

On the other side of them, Harry seemed to have spent the whole meal explaining to Granny Violet who people were, repeatedly. I could just hear their conversation over the hubbub of the tent, if I strained. "Yes, it is a bit loud," I heard him agree, not for the first time.

When Philip excused himself from the table, Caroline leaned over to introduce herself to Violet. I caught her saying something in a loud clear voice about Juliette, and as she did so, she reached into her hand-bag and took out her photocopy of the photo of *Self-Portrait as Sphinx*. Violet, bobbing her head, took it and looked at it. Then she looked at it again, more closely.

And screamed.

Still screaming, halfway out of her chair now, she began trying to grab the photocopy, to snatch it from Caroline's hand, as if with the intention of ripping the thing up.

Philip came rushing back to the table and took charge, shooting Caroline a furious look, steering his mother out of the tent by her shoulders. Caroline looked mortified.

I gently took the photocopy from her, tucked it under my arm, and made my way outside after Philip and Violet. Harry's grandmother was still clearly very upset.

"Please let me explain," I kept saying, although I am not sure, even if I had been allowed to speak, I was really sober enough to do so. I did try to convey the importance of what Caroline and I had stumbled across, the historical significance of the painting's possible survival. "There must be some sort of misunderstanding," I repeated. Every time I tried to bring the photocopy out from under my arm, Violet would begin screeching again and Philip would start furiously flapping his hands at me.

Eventually, Philip, obviously very angry indeed, grasped me quite firmly by the arm and walked me across the grass to a quieter spot. We stopped in a corner of the lawn illuminated only by festoon lights in the trees. His face was close to mine in the semidarkness. His voice when he spoke was trembling with rage.

"How *dare* you, Patrick?" he barked, and I felt a finger jab me in the chest. "How *dare* you and this girl we've never met before come here and start lecturing us about Juliette? What do you know about her? What do you know about anything? Nothing, that's what."

I did try to explain why Caroline and I were so interested in Juliette, why she was so important. He cut me short.

"She was mad, did you know that? Paranoid. Delusional. They had to lock her up as a teenager, in a psychiatric hospital. For the terrible, awful things she was saying. The unhinged accusations she was making. Her father made sure she had the most expensive treatments at the best private hospital in London. And how did she thank him? By pulling a vanishing act, by running off with some married, middle-aged painter. How did she repay her family, for all their kindness and concern? She repaid them with that."

He gestured with genuine disgust at the piece of paper I was holding.

"I don't understand," I said. Never in all the years I had known Philip—even that day Harry and Freddie and I rowed over to the island—had he lost his temper like this.

"I know you don't understand," Philip said. "Well, let me explain it to you. Give me that thing."

I hesitated. He snapped his fingers. I handed it over. He held the paper up between us, turning it toward the light, and pointed at the figure in the bottom left corner of the painting, the pale, ghostly girl with the dark hair. "Do you know who that is?"

I shook my head.

"It's Lucy, Juliette's sister. Are you starting to get it now? Your girl-friend just ambushed my ninety-two-year-old mother with a painting of her dead niece."

"I'm sorry," I said. "We didn't know. I never knew . . ."

"Of course you didn't know. Because it's not something we talk about, as a family, even now. Lucy died, Patrick, when she was ten years old. She drowned in the lake, right here at Longhurst, in 1924. They were rowing to the island one summer afternoon, Lucy and her younger sister, Juliette, for a picnic, and the boat capsized. Juliette managed to swim back to shore. Lucy didn't. That beautiful girl. Everyone's darling. It was the great tragedy of the family, a sadness that engulfed everything for years. And she painted it. Juliette painted her sister, her beloved, much-missed, endlessly mourned sister. Without dignity. With mottled skin and blue lips. With floating hair. And then she put her on public display, for an audience of tittering gawkers. As if Juliette were the only person who remembered her. As if she alone spent the rest of her life trying to come to terms with her loss. As if the family had not had to deal with enough bloody scandals . . ."

He thrust the now-crumpled piece of paper back at me with a sneer of contempt. I could hear Harry's grandmother being comforted by Georgina somewhere nearby. Harry's father, shaking his head, made his way over to join them.

When I got back to the tent to find Caroline, to explain what a horrible mess we had made of everything, her chair was empty.

"The Curse of Longhurst Hall"—an extract from *The World of the Unknown: Unsolved Mysteries* (London: Usborne, 1981)

The disappearance of Jane Herries, the Missing Maid of Longhurst, was perhaps the perfect mystery for the new media age of the early 1930s. The unexplained and seemingly inexplicable vanishing of a strikingly pretty young woman from the picturesque country home of a famously wealthy and well-connected British MP, Cyril Willoughby.

The *Daily Mail* was the first paper to coin the nickname the "Missing Maid." The *Daily Mirror* put a photograph of Jane Herries on their front cover three days in a row. As if it were a case for Hercule Poirot, newspapers printed maps of Longhurst, indicating the maid's room and the last places she had been seen, itemizing the known itinerary of the final hours before she vanished.

It was Friday, September 15, 1933, when the last recorded sighting of Jane Herries occurred. Friday was her afternoon off, and after lunch in the servants' hall she went upstairs, saying she had a letter to write. She did not say to whom. That evening, when she failed to appear for dinner, several other servants realized they had not seen her for hours and decided to investigate. They went to her little attic room, and it was empty. No letter. A cold cup of tea sat on her bedside table. Her clothes and belongings were undisturbed. Nothing appeared to be missing other than Jane Herries herself.

She had not returned by the time the rest of the household began turning in, gradually, for the night. She had not returned by the next morning, when the police were first alerted.

By midday they had contacted her sister, Helen, in Bristol, who had neither heard from her nor seen her. The sisters, orphans, had no other living relatives. Nor was Jane Herries's sister aware of any other friend or acquaintance with whom she might be staying, or any reason why she might so abruptly have left Longhurst, where she had been working for several months. At no time had Jane expressed anything other than satisfaction with her post, Helen reported. As evidence of this, she presented to the police several examples—later reprinted in the press—of the weekly letters Jane would send her, written and posted every Friday, without fail.

No letter from September 15 ever arrived. Nor did any of the household—who recalled often seeing Jane Herries walking up the drive of Longhurst to deliver her weekly letter to the postbox—report her doing so on that particular Friday.

On the afternoon of Saturday, September 16, the Willoughby family—Cyril Willoughby, his wife, Diana, his daughter Juliette—joined the rest of the household in searching the grounds for Jane. The upper and lower lawns; the rose garden; the island; the woods around the lake; the summerhouse; the winter and summer stables; the meadow. They searched the house, upstairs and down. The attics. The cellars. They found no sign of her.

It is a mile walk from the house to the gates of Longhurst. From there, the nearest bus stop was a walk (along the roadside) of at least another ten minutes. The nearest train station was a fifteen-minute drive. None of the bus drivers interviewed by the police recalled picking up Jane Herries that day. No one matching her description was seen at the train station.

For a time, the assumption was that Herries had eloped with a sweetheart who had met her at a prearranged rendezvous point. However, nobody interviewed by the police knew of any such sweetheart, or had ever heard her mention one. Jane's sister described the idea as preposterous. Nor could it be explained how she could have left Longhurst undetected, or why she would have done so without a single one of her possessions.

For weeks, the newspapers reported supposed sightings of Jane Herries. Boarding a ship to New York, in Liverpool. In a restaurant with a gentleman in Bath. Reading about herself in a newspaper in a Lyons tea shop in Piccadilly.

None of these sightings was ever substantiated.

Then the rumors darkened.

A theory was advanced—her sister denied it vociferously, in multiple interviews—that there had been a secret lover, and that Jane Herries had been pregnant, and that either she or he had done something rash. The *Daily Express* published a front-page story that quoted a well-known celebrity spiritualist claiming that Herries's disappearance, like the tragic death by drowning of Cyril Willoughby's elder daughter a decade earlier, was related to an ancient curse associated with one of the items in Cyril's collection of Egyptian artifacts.

In November 1933, Cyril Willoughby announced that he was offering a £500 reward for anyone coming forward with any information about the whereabouts of his former employee, or any information about the events leading up to her disappearance. The reward money was never claimed.

Eventually, other scandals, other sensations, the gathering clouds of the coming war, displaced the Missing Maid of Longhurst from the front pages.

The mystery remains unsolved.

CHAPTER 8

CAROLINE, LONGHURST, 1991

I was standing alone and shivering outside the tent, wondering where I could hide for the rest of the night, when I heard a cough. There was a pause, then another cough, slightly louder, definitely deliberate. I turned to see one of those boys from the table of nerds to which Patrick had directed my attention with a nudge and a wry smile earlier. He held one hand aloft, like I was a skittish animal who might bolt if he got too close.

"Are you okay, Caroline? You forgot this," he said, holding up my shawl with the other hand. "It's a little cold out here. I thought you might need it."

Only when he took another step forward to hand it to me did I recognize him—it was Terry, the quiet computer science kid from the room next to Patrick's in college. Next-Door Terry, we sometimes called him. It was a bit of a surprise he knew my name, to be honest. I think the most he and I had ever spoken was to say hello to each other as we passed on the stairs, a little awkward conversation in the kitchen as we waited for the kettle to boil.

He was wearing a dinner jacket with a wide velvet collar, much too large in the shoulders and short in the sleeves.

"Thank you," I said, taking my shawl. "That's very kind."

"You're welcome. Would you like a tissue?"

I nodded, having not realized until then that my face was damp, my eye makeup presumably smudged with tears.

We stood there a moment or two in silence. It dawned on me that if Terry had heard the row from all the way over at his table, pretty much the whole tent must have too.

"There's going to be dancing in a minute, I think," he said eventually.

"I'd better pop back to the house for a moment to change my shoes, then," I smiled, pointing at my mud-caked stilettos. "If you'll excuse me . . ."

The rear of the property was a confusing collection of doors and porches, flights of stepped and layered terraces, all overlooking a large ornamental pond. I climbed a set of steps in the moonlight and found myself at the back of the house. I stopped for a second to get my bearings.

The only light visible here was coming from an open window on the ground floor, a few feet away from where I was standing. I could hear voices inside: one was that of Harry's father and the other—high, strained, still distinctly querulous—was Granny Violet.

"I should have known. I should have known not to believe your father. He said he had destroyed that awful painting years ago. He told me he had burned it."

Harry's father was trying to soothe her, or shush her, or a bit of both. Unsure what I would say if anyone caught me, I held my breath.

"Promise me," she was saying again and again. "Philip, promise me. You have to find it. You have to destroy it. It's not art. It's an abomination. She was not well when she painted it. She was not well when she allowed it to be shown. The whole thing was a deliberate attempt to cause this family—her own family, *our* family—as much hurt and harm as possible."

"Please calm down, Mummy," he begged. "Come back out to the party, have a dance with the birthday boy. He'll want to see his granny enjoy herself. I'll look for the painting in the morning and if I do find it, I'll chuck the thing on a bonfire myself."

His footsteps got closer and suddenly the window shut with a bang and the curtains were drawn.

My heart was thumping. My brain was whizzing. God, what a mess. Because of my clumsy attempts to learn more about Juliette, *Self-Portrait as Sphinx*, if it had survived the Paris fire and been brought back here, would tomorrow be found and burned. I could not let that happen.

There was only one thing to do.

I made my way over to where I could see waiters filing in and out. The kitchen door was open. With dinner finished and the bustle of cooking over, there were only a few people left in there now, clearing and stacking plates. I shrugged and gestured at the shoes in my hand.

"Going to have to admit defeat on these," I announced, a bit stagily, perhaps, as I made my way through the kitchen, up the back stairs, and up to our bedroom. Instead of fumbling for the lamp, I sat on the bed in the dark, taking a moment to gather myself. I put my hand to my chest, feeling my heart thumping. *Breathe, Caroline*, I told myself.

Suddenly, joltingly, there came a loud bang from the next-door bedroom. Something heavy thrown against the wall, perhaps. Raised voices. Athena and Freddie. It sounded like their usual argument. As usual, neither was holding back.

"What *is* this?" she was shouting, before something else landed with a thud against the wall. "What is going on with you? Why are you like this?"

There was no audible reply from Freddie. A door slammed. Swift angry steps could be heard from the corridor. A minute passed. A lighter set of footsteps followed. "Freddie? Freddie, come back!" I could hear Athena calling from the top of the stairs, her voice plaintive. I sat in the dark in my room and waited until she went downstairs too.

I swallowed down the nausea that always washed over me at the sound of fighting, a cold mouthful of spit. I told myself that Athena would be fine, that the clunk had just been her launching something at Freddie and missing. A thick-soled shoe, a hairbrush. Freddie was a prick, but not a violent one. Not all men were like my father. Not all arguments ended in a shower of punches and kicks.

I put on my flat shoes and made my way back to the door that Patrick had shown me earlier, the one that led to the east wing. When I got there I found the door still open just a crack—Patrick must not have shut it properly—and I gave it a gentle push, reasoning that if anyone saw me I could start to sway and slur, a drunk girl looking for a loo to throw up in or a place to lie down.

The door opened. I stepped through, closed it again behind me, and waited for my eyes to adjust. This part of the house had a different feel than the rest—eerier, more ornate, more oppressive. The corridors smaller, narrower, darker. Directly ahead—visible through an open doorway, drenched in moonlight—was the library, a long room, two stories high, each story lined with case after case of leather-bound books. No art in there except for one massive painting over the fireplace of a plucky Irish setter, no doubt the work of Austen Willoughby. I ran up the curved staircase, taking the steps two at a time. At the top, I pushed open a door and stumbled into the room that must have been Austen Willoughby's studio, with an enormous skylight above. Ghostly white canvas dust sheets covered what looked from their outlines like stacks of furniture and paintings, throwing monstrous shadows onto the walls. I lifted one of the sheets, tentatively. A cloud of dust rose swirling into the air.

Slowly, methodically, telling myself that nobody at the party apart from Patrick and Athena would miss me, I began sorting, item by item, through the contents of the room. It was a somewhat heart-sinking prospect. Locating anything in here was going to be no small task. The room was like a cross between the world's poshest jumble sale and the dumpster behind an auction house. There were chipped glass chandeliers, dented furniture, cracked mirrors, threadbare sofas. A box of copies of *Country Life* from the 1950s. An open black plastic bag full of fur stoles. And under every other sheet, stacked canvases, some half-finished, some blank but in ornate frames. Others, clearly deemed not of sufficient quality either to hang or sell, falling apart. The canvas sheets were heavy to lift and the jumble awkward to navigate around, especially with only the moonlight from overhead illuminating the room. I was starting to worry I might not be able to sift through it all in a single night when suddenly, there it was. A little smaller than I had been expecting, tucked at the end of a run of much larger canvases.

I was literally holding in my shaking hands Juliette Willoughby's *Self-Portrait as Sphinx*.

A bright flash of light illuminated the room. Startled, I let out a cry and stumbled backward, tripping as I did so over a group of stacked paintings that fell, domino-like, with a loud clatter. For a moment, I thought I was going to go sprawling after them.

The room was dark again. I stood there blinking, my heart thumping in my ears, trying to work out what had happened, where the flash had come from. The room was silent. As far as I could tell I was the only person in there. The door behind me was still shut. I had the painting so tightly grasped I could feel it digging into my arms.

Directly overhead a loud thump was followed a second later by a burst of green and pink across the sky. Fireworks! That was what the flash must have been. The start of the fireworks display.

Pull yourself together, Caroline, I thought.

I knew what I had to do.

Everyone would be on the back lawn watching the display. If this was going to work, it would have to be now. Small enough to be portable but still pretty unwieldy, the painting just about fit under my arm. I draped my shawl over the top, a half-hearted attempt to disguise the theft as I made my way back through the house. No. This wasn't a theft—it was a rescue. I was saving this painting. On behalf of art history. On behalf of Juliette. On behalf of my mother.

I could still hear oohs and aahs from the other side of the house as I located Patrick's car key with its red-and-gold logo fob in the drawer in the hall with all the other keys. I pocketed it. I took a deep breath. Then I made my way down the steps in front of the house, two at a time, crunching quickly across the drive over to where we had parked that afternoon. All was still and sharply shadowed in the moonlight. Patrick's car was exactly where we had left it. More fireworks popped and crackled on the other side of the house. I slipped the painting into the trunk and covered it with a picnic blanket.

PATRICK, LONGHURST, 1991

Caroline seemed simply to have vanished. She wasn't in the tent or on the front lawn. She wasn't in the rose garden or on the terrace. I even checked the women's toilets when I heard a scream—and found Freddie, disposable camera in hand, being admonished by an irate blonde for taking a photo over the top of her locked stall.

I marched off to the house to check our bedroom, but there was no sign of her there either. I peered into some of the other rooms on our corridor too, disturbing in one a couple under the duvet who screamed and threw an alarm clock at me. I checked all the rooms on the ground floor, even poking my head into the dark east wing and discreetly calling her name. Nothing.

By the time I got back to the tent, the band had started up and the dance floor was packed. Heels had been discarded, jackets were off, shirts had been sweated through already. Even Harry, unusually for him, was on the dance floor, flushed and tieless.

As I passed the bar, Ivo grabbed my arm and handed me a brimful glass of red wine, into which Douglas Burn immediately chucked a penny. The rest of Osiris then surrounded me—Toby Gough, Ivo Strang, all the boys—chanting, *"Down it. Down it."*

"Christ's sake, lads, grow up a bit, yeah?"

Eric Lam made a mock-sympathetic face. Benjy Taylor tittered. I grimaced and threw my wine back in one go. Pennying was one of the more irritating Cambridge traditions—the challenge being to drink up before the coin hit the bottom of the glass, supposedly to save the queen from drowning—and these lads never left college without a pocket full of coppers.

"Coming for a dance, old boy?" Douglas asked, clapping me on the shoulder.

"Soon. I've just got to find Caroline and check that she's okay. You haven't seen her, have you?"

He shook his head. "She can't have gotten far."

He had a point. Even if Caroline had decided to leave, she had no car. Had she tried to walk all the way to the gate and make her own way home? That was a mile's hike, then another half hour along an unlit road with no pavement to the nearest bus stop, and the next bus wouldn't be along until Monday. Might someone have given her a lift to the train station? It was possible, but she would have a long, chilly night in the waiting room ahead of her, if it was even unlocked.

I was beginning to feel increasingly worried about her.

After all the drama today, after everything Caroline had shared with me, I felt I should be with her, making sure she was okay. Instead, I had let her wander off into the night alone.

There was still no sign of her at midnight, when everyone gathered on the lawn for the fireworks. I asked around as the rockets popped overhead. Toby had not seen her. Ivo said he had no idea whom I was talking about. It was Giles Pemberton who pointed out Terry, said Caroline had been talking to him outside the marquee. To me that seemed unlikely.

I was wrong.

"Are you looking for Caroline?" Terry asked bluntly as I approached, his face illuminated in flickering shades of orange by the bonfire, around which people were toasting marshmallows.

I nodded. "Have you seen her?"

"She went back to your room, I think. She seemed pretty upset."

I did not blame her. I had warned Caroline that the Willoughbys could be touchy, but I had never anticipated anything like this. Every time I crossed paths with Philip, he gave me the same aggrieved stare, as if amazed I had the gall still to be here. Was he going to tell my father about all this? I really hoped not.

I checked our room again—on the floor by the bed were Caroline's muddy stilettos. *Thank God for that*, I thought. I'd been starting to panic that she had gotten lost in the dark and fallen in the lake.

By the time I got back downstairs, it had begun to drizzle, and guests—shivering girls wearing boyfriends' tailcoats, boys in damp shirts—were filtering into the house.

Making her way along the ground-floor corridor in my direction, peering expectantly into each room she passed, was Caroline.

I called her name and she broke into a relieved smile.

"Patrick! Where have you been?" she asked.

"Looking for you, mainly. Are you okay? Have you been hiding out in the house the whole time?"

She nodded, looked like she was about to say something, then thought better of it. She gave an exaggerated yawn. I glanced at my watch.

"Are you tired? I'm sure nobody would notice if we slipped off to bed . . ."

She shook her head.

"I'm going to turn in," she said. "But please don't feel you have to call it a night because of me."

"But I . . ."

"Patrick," she said gently, "it's your oldest friend's twenty-first. Go and find him, have a drink. Maybe if anyone is still upset, apologize to them on my behalf."

She leaned in and pressed her lips gently against my cheek. "Let's talk about all that tomorrow."

As I watched her climb the stairs, it occurred to me that I hadn't seen Harry for a while.

It being his twenty-first, the other Osiris boys had been talking big about staying up all night. Douglas and Benjy were easily wired enough to do it. Most of the others had passed out around the place already—in the main entrance hall, Ivo was on his back on the couch, snoring. Nearby, Hugo had plonked himself on an armchair by a fire-place and had his eyes closed, glass of whiskey still clutched in his hand. As I was looking around for something with which to refill my own glass, Toby sidled up to me, sniffing and rubbing his nose, and asked if I knew where Freddie was. I shook my head.

At around three a.m. coffee, hot toddies, and hog roast rolls were served from trestle tables next to the kitchen. Georgina, in a green raincoat over her pajamas, was in charge of one of the urns. Arno von Westernhagen, the only person still awake who wasn't wild-eyed or slurring, came over with a steaming mug of black coffee in his hands. "So what do you think, Lambert. Reckon you'll make it all the way through to dawn?"

"I don't think I've got it in me," I admitted. All around us, people seemed to be making the same decision, or at least to be wavering.

Arno stifled a yawn.

"I'm not sure I am going to make it myself without another pack of cigarettes. There's supposed to be a twenty-four-hour petrol station with a convenience store not too far away . . ."

He was giving me a meaningful look.

"Sorry, I've had far too much to drink tonight. I'm not driving anyone anywhere, no matter how noble the cause."

"I could borrow your car."

"Um . . ."

"I'm stone-cold sober, Patrick. I can't drink, you know that. Doctor's orders."

I made an apologetic gesture.

"Come on, Patrick. I promised Harry I would stay up, and I'm pretty sure Eric and Hugo have a bet on I won't make it. Do me a favor."

I could feel myself wavering. It did not feel like a great idea. On the other hand, Arno was sober, of that I was confident. I also knew the petrol station he was talking about—it was a straight run, left out of the drive. It was not like there would be anyone else on the road this time of night.

"Okay. Careful with her, though. Easy on the accelerator, until you get a sense of what she can do. The keys are in the hallway dresser—MG fob. Just put them back there after."

Arno was so grateful he literally hugged me.

"Don't make me regret this," were the last words I called after him.

Wearily, blearily, I made my way upstairs to our room. Caroline muttered something indistinct as I climbed into bed next to her. I slipped an arm around her waist, kissed her on the back of the neck and—with a feeling like I was actually falling—immediately passed out.

The next thing I knew, morning sun was streaming through the window and someone was hammering on the door urgently. Caroline muttered something and shifted on the mattress. I swung myself out of bed, checked I had underwear on, and crossed the room to see what was going on.

"Caroline?" Athena said, looking over my shoulder into the room.

"Yes, she's here. What's wrong, Athena?"

"Has either of you seen Freddie?"

I shook my head. "Not for hours," I said. From under the blankets, Caroline could be heard saying the same.

Athena's shoulders sank. For a moment, I thought she was about to burst into tears. I turned to see Caroline sitting up in bed, sheet clutched around her.

"Come in, babe," she called. "Is everything alright?"

I stepped out of the doorway so Athena could squeeze past me. She ran to Caroline, who was already half out of bed, and they hugged. "I'm sure he's around somewhere," said Caroline. Her voice was croaky. She rubbed Athena's shoulder, patting her arm. "We'll help you look for him."

"I've looked everywhere," said Athena. "I've been looking for hours. We had a row and he stormed off." Caroline made sympathetic noises. "I thought after he had cooled down a little he'd come back and we could talk, but he never did. Then about two hours ago I woke up and thought I would go down and maybe persuade him to get some sleep just so he wouldn't feel too terrible, but I still couldn't find him. Not in the house. Not in his room. Not in the tent. Not in the summerhouse. Not on either of the lawns. I went down to the lake, even, to see if he was watching the sunrise from the jetty. There's no sign of him anywhere."

Here she broke off to stifle a sob with the palm of her hand. As she did so, I noticed a dark smear on her forearm.

"Athena, what's that? Are you okay?"

She dabbed at it with a finger and sighed.

"I must have cut myself and not even noticed. I took a tumble coming up the steps from the lawn."

I turned to look for a towel or a cloth to offer her. When I turned back, her face had crumpled.

"Oh God," she said. "He was so angry. He was so drunk. I honestly think something awful might have happened."

Fourth Entry

Wednesday, 15th December—There was a moment, just a moment, when I thought Oskar was going to be uncomplicatedly pleased about it all. Excited and happy on my behalf that André Breton—his friend, his hero, his mentor—approved of my work. That I was going to be exhibiting alongside him, our paintings hung together.

Then I saw the expression on Oskar's face.

After Breton left, Oskar spent a long time staring at it, my *Self-Portrait as Sphinx*. Then he spent quite a long time staring at his own work. Then, without saying where he was going, he left.

He did not return for several hours. When he did, he went straight to bed without a word, and stayed there the rest of the afternoon.

Is it possible, I sometimes ask myself, that I have made a terrible mistake?

The thunderous rages. The weeklong silences. It has suddenly occurred to me who Oskar reminds me of when he behaves like this. My father.

Last night Oskar and I had the most serious fight we have ever had.

It all started when I had the audacity to ask him, as I cooked supper, if he would be home that night. This prompted him to throw his newspaper aside with a snarl and launch into a diatribe about how needy I was, always trying to smother him. He might be in, he said. He might be out, with his friends. He had not decided yet. "I was merely wondering whether I should put two bowls out for this soup," I said. He peered at the saucepan, sniffed it, pulled a face. "I ate already," he told me.

Then all evening, as I tried to paint, he kept pacing, sighing to himself, fiddling with things, standing in my light, until eventually I told him that if he wanted to go out, for God's sake he should just go out. I wasn't stopping him, I snapped. I didn't care. What I couldn't have was him moping around the place, groaning to himself. I had work to do.

Oskar did not like that. Being snapped at. Being told off.

He made some remark—as if to the air, to an unknown observer—about how full of herself she was getting, this little girl, all of a sudden. I said something about how petty and pathetic and jealous they could be, old men.

Fists clenched on the table, face taut, he stared at me. Fizzing. Fuming. For a moment, it really looked like he was thinking what it would feel like to hit me. Then he stormed out, shouting as he did so about not waiting up. On his way out, the front door slammed heavily behind him and a neighbor's baby started to cry. I felt a little bit like crying myself. Instead, I took up my brush and started to paint.

My name is Juliette Willoughby. I'm an artist. Those were the first words I had ever spoken to Oskar. They were words which, as I painted, I repeated to myself, over and over.

I was still painting when Oskar came back, four hours later.

He said nothing. I said nothing. Instead, he came up behind me and stood there, floorboards creaking underneath the heel of his boots as he gently swayed back and forth, so close I felt his breath on my neck, could smell what he had been drinking. Which would have been irritating at the best of times but was even more so because most of the time he had been away I was battling the same section of the painting, tweaking and fiddling with and then angrily starting over on that final figure I had been struggling with for weeks: Lucy. My sister, Lucy, rising from the lake, her hair sodden, her arms outstretched.

"I know," I told him, trying to preempt whatever he was about to say. "It's not right, I know that."

He gave a noncommittal *humph*. Oskar understands that this is not just a technical problem I am wrestling with. In our first weeks in Paris, after a nightmare had left me gasping, I told Oskar about my sister. About that day and how it haunted me. Every time I tried to paint Lucy, my hand, my brain, felt like it was flinching from the truth.

Both of us stood there for a long time, looking at my painting.

He rubbed the back of his neck with his hand. He rubbed the corner of his eye with the side of a knuckle. He ran his tongue thoughtfully, audibly, over the back of his teeth.

"I think," he said eventually, "I have an idea."

CHAPTER 9

CAROLINE, LONGHURST, 1991

Athena chewed on her bottom lip, oversized sunglasses hiding her reddened eyes. It was almost ten in the morning. We had knocked on every bedroom door. We had checked the summerhouse and the long-unused stable block. We wandered the gardens calling Freddie's name, peered up trees, rattled bushes. I had even walked to the end of the lawn and looked back to see if he had curled up and fallen asleep on the scaffolding. Nobody we spoke to could remember having seen him for hours—although neither did anyone apart from Athena seem at all worried about that.

The longer we searched, the more annoyed with Freddie I felt—and the more anxious I was to get away. From this house, this family. Any minute, Granny Violet might emerge and start screeching at me again. Philip Willoughby could already be sifting through Austen's studio looking for *Self-Portrait as Sphinx* to throw on last night's still-smoldering bonfire.

"Look, Athena, why don't you call Karl and get him to take you home? Or Patrick can drop you at the station and then come back for me. I promise, Freddie will turn up soon enough."

Athena was adamant she had to stay until he returned. "Something's happened, I can just feel it. It was a silly fight. But I went too far. I said things I shouldn't have. I upset him and maybe he's done something stupid," she said ruefully.

"It didn't sound so different," I said, without thinking.

"Excuse me?" she said sharply.

Oh damn, I thought, mentally kicking myself.

"Sorry, Athena. It's just that I was in my room last night, changing shoes, and, well, I could hear you two through the wall. Shouting. And—obviously I didn't catch everything and I don't know the whole story, but from the sound of it, it didn't seem that unusual for you . . ."

"So you were eavesdropping on us."

"I couldn't really help it, could I?" I said, irritated by her tone, especially after the hours I'd just spent scouring Longhurst with her. "Look, we both know he'll turn up soon enough, having spent the night in a laundry basket or a cupboard or somewhere else ridiculous enough for him to make a story out of it. And either he won't remember there was an argument or he'll claim not to remember what he said, or anything he's done, and he certainly won't apologize, and honestly, Athena, I don't know why you put up with it, I really don't. He made you beg for an invitation to come to this party, refused to give you a lift, hasn't introduced you as his girlfriend to anyone in the family, and now he's ruined the whole night with his disappearing act. Just call Karl and get him to pick you up in your dad's car and drive you back to Cambridge. Please. This doesn't need to be your problem. *Freddie* doesn't have to be your problem."

Athena said something I did not catch.

"Excuse me?"

"I said look who's an expert on relationships all of a sudden."

I decided not to rise to this.

"Look, have you eaten anything, at least?" I asked, changing the subject as I cautiously opened the trunk of Patrick's car, just enough to put my bag inside. As I did so, I could not resist checking to make sure the picnic blanket was where I had left it. I pressed it with my hand and could feel one hard corner of the painting underneath. I placed my overnight bag carefully next to it, then closed and locked the trunk again.

"It looks like they're handing out breakfast somewhere," I said, jerking my head toward Terry, Patrick's neighbor from college, who was silently standing next to a little wheely suitcase staring at us and eating a bacon sandwich, dripping ketchup onto the gravel. Seeing us look over, he raised a hand abruptly in greeting, losing several slices of bacon as a result.

"I can't possibly eat right now," Athena told me, irritated.

Something suddenly occurred to me. "Have you checked where Freddie's car is?" I asked her. "He drove himself up here, didn't he?"

"My God, you're right. The car. What if he sped off somewhere, drunk?"

"He's more likely to be asleep in the back seat with an empty wine bottle," I said, meaning to sound reassuring. Athena did not take it that way, letting out an angry little *humph* and setting off at a clip in search of Freddie's car.

"See you back in Cambridge, okay?" I shouted.

Head down, Athena ignored me. *She'll be fine once he turns up again*, I told myself. Right now I had bigger things to worry about. This was the last possible point that I could change my mind about taking the painting, and even then it would be practically impossible to return it without alerting anyone. I had tossed and turned all night in that creaky iron bed, trying to come up with a plan, waiting for Patrick to stumble back, my triumph at having found the painting, saved it from destruction, slowly curdling as a series of realizations hit. I couldn't keep the painting, couldn't sell it or donate it to any institution. I couldn't tell anyone what had happened, or how I had come into possession of it. I wasn't even sure yet how I would confess to Patrick what I had done.

Terry, having finished his breakfast, ambled over. "I don't suppose you can give me a lift?" he asked, eying the car. "I need to get back to college and everyone else I know seems to have left without me."

"I'm really sorry," I told him. "It's not my car and there really isn't room. Perhaps one of the Willoughbys could call you a taxi to the station?"

I called a further apology after him as he shuffled back toward the house.

A few minutes later, Patrick emerged from the front door and made his way down the steps juggling two coffees in white Styrofoam cups and his suit carrier. He opened the passenger door for me, and I sat down—before leaping out again immediately.

"Urgh, God, what's that?" I squealed, touching the seat. "It's soaking."

Patrick shook his head. "Fuck's sake. I told Arno he could borrow the car to go get cigarettes. What's he done?"

A frown creased his forehead. He knelt to inspect the seat more closely. After a moment, he gave it a sniff.

"Just water," he said, straightening up, obviously relieved. "Here, there's some tissues in the glove compartment we can mop it up with, and I'm pretty sure this is waterproof."

After Patrick had sponged the seat as dry as he could, he laid his suit carrier out for me to sit on. Then we drove off, turning on the gravel and speeding toward the gate.

"What was all that about, with Terry?" he asked me. I told him, still feeling a bit guilty about not being able to offer him a lift.

"I'm sure he'll be fine," said Patrick. "The person I feel sorry for is whoever had to share a bedroom with him last night."

Before I had begun regularly spending the night in Patrick's room, I thought he was joking about his neighbor's snoring. On the top floor of a nineteenth-century college building, overlooking one of the quads, Patrick's room occupied one corner of what had originally been a much larger living space, subdivided to fit in more students, with only one thin internal wall separating it from Terry's room. As a result, when Terry was in, which was always, we could hear every snore, burp, and fart, every scrinch of his bedsprings, the whir of his computer fan, and Terry tapping away in urgent bursts at his keyboard, half the night through. Patrick had once asked him what all the clattering in the small hours was about—Terry turned out to be trading on the New York Stock Exchange.

It was about midday by the time we got back to Cambridge. Most of the journey had been spent in hungover silence, both of us deep in thought. We parked in college, pulling up into a corner of my quad. There were only a couple of other cars in there for once, and nobody around. A radio blared from the windows of the college kitchen. We both climbed out of the car, unfolded ourselves, stretched, and groaned.

Several things in my back popped. Patrick yawned so widely I could hear his jaw crack.

The moment I had been silently dreading had arrived. "Patrick," I said. "There's something I need to tell you."

I beckoned him around to the back of the car. Looking a bit puzzled, he followed. I opened the trunk. I lifted my bag out and put it down on the cobbles at my feet. I flipped back a corner of the picnic blanket.

"Jesus," he said.

I returned the blanket to its place. He closed the trunk.

"Jesus," he said again. "That's *Self-Portrait as Sphinx*, isn't it?"

"Yes. I think so."

"Are you going to tell me what it's doing in the trunk of my car?" Patrick said, frowning.

"I took it," I said.

Patrick's frown deepened until his eyebrows were practically touching.

"Just wait," I said. "Before you react, wait until you've heard everything. They were going to destroy it. I overheard them, Violet and Philip, last night, at the house. I heard him promise her he would find this painting and burn it. You understand, don't you, why I can't let that happen? I didn't steal it, Patrick. I *saved* it."

I was talking too quickly, gabbling really, trying to get it all out before he had a chance to interrupt.

Patrick closed his eyes and rubbed his forehead. Then he looked around us, up at the windows. None were open. Even this late in the day, quite a few of the rooms still had their curtains drawn.

"That's not all," I said.

"Oh God. How can that *possibly* not be all?" he said, his voice cracking slightly.

"Violet said that Austen promised her years ago that he had destroyed the canvas with his own hands. I know this sounds crazy, but I think Juliette put a message in the painting, and it's something the Willoughby family are desperate to keep hidden. An awful secret."

I could see Patrick trying to process all this. "What exactly are you saying, Caroline?"

I took a deep breath.

"I don't think it was Oskar's ex-wife. I think Austen Willoughby set the fire that killed Juliette and Oskar. I think he did it to destroy that painting, but somehow it survived. And when he did manage to get his hands on it, he brought it back to Longhurst," I said, realizing how ludicrous it all sounded now that the words hung in the air between us, how many steps in the logic of this sequence were wobbly or missing.

"But why? Why not just destroy the thing, if it has a great and terrible family secret hidden in it?"

"Maybe he couldn't bring himself to destroy it. He was an artist himself, after all, and it is an undeniably extraordinary painting."

"But he *could* bring himself to murder his own niece, and her lover?"

I thought about this. "Maybe it was an accident. Maybe the fire was supposed to destroy the painting but not kill Oskar and Juliette. I don't know. But if you've got a better explanation of how it ended up at Longhurst, I'd like to hear it."

Patrick looked at me sideways and locked the trunk. "I need some time to think. I'm going for a walk."

It was only a few minutes after I had gone upstairs that I heard a light tap at the door. Dragging myself out of the armchair into which I had collapsed, I made my way over to open it.

Now listen, Patrick, I silently rehearsed. *I know this is a lot to take in . . .*

It was not Patrick at the door but two uniformed police officers, accompanied by one of the college porters.

"Caroline Cooper?"

I nodded mutely.

"Are we correct in thinking you were at Longhurst Hall last night?"

My mind was racing. What could they know, *how* could they know, about the missing painting already? I had righted everything I knocked over, placed all the canvas dust sheets back. Even if Philip Willoughby had gone looking for Juliette's painting and failed to find it, what evidence could there be that I was the one who had taken it? There was a horrible moment when it occurred to me that perhaps Patrick had turned me in. . . .

They asked if they could come in, explaining that they were trying to talk to everyone who had been at the party, that there was someone they had concerns about, someone whose location they were attempting to establish.

"You want to talk to me about Freddie Talbot," I said, trying not to sound too relieved about this.

"We want to talk to you about Freddie Talbot," one of the officers confirmed.

PATRICK, CAMBRIDGE, 1991

"He'll be enjoying this, you know," Harry said, unconvincingly, kicking his heels against the wall of the master's lodge. "It's classic Freddie. That fucker. That joker. He used to love doing this when we were kids playing hide-and-seek, freaking everyone out, hiding for so long that everyone started getting genuinely worried. He'll turn up. He'll probably come strolling in halfway through the next Osiris dinner, ask what we're all looking so surprised about, what he's missed. That will be the punch line, the look on our faces."

Eric Lam gave a half-hearted chuckle. Benjy Taylor smiled faintly. I think we were all aware that forty-eight hours after Freddie had last been seen, especially given what the police had found at Longhurst, things were starting to look very worrying indeed.

The only person who did not seem to have picked up on this was that idiot Ivo Strang, who kept making the same joke about how much money he owed Freddie for drugs and how he hoped he would never show up again. The third time he made it, just as Athena joined us, I told him quite firmly to shut up.

We had all been asked to be here to meet Freddie's mother and her husband, who had flown in from South Africa. Having arrived directly from a briefing by the police at Longhurst, they were being shown around Freddie's room while we waited outside the master's lodge. Arno von Westernhagen made it back from lectures just as we were being ushered inside, and I realized I hadn't actually seen him since he borrowed my car.

I hung back and tapped him on the shoulder as we walked single file into the wood-paneled drawing room. "I've a little bone to pick with you," I said.

"Oh yes?" he whispered, only barely turning his head, but visibly tensing up.

"What the fuck happened to my front seat?"

"The passenger seat? Oh, right, yes," he said, his shoulders dropping half an inch. "Sorry about that. I bought a big bottle of water from the service station and it leaked on the way back. If there's been any damage . . ."

He trailed off as the master—silver-haired, a world-famous economist, standing behind his desk in an olive tweed suit—cleared his throat. There weren't enough chairs for everyone, so some people had to hover awkwardly around the fireplace or by the window. No one seemed to know quite where to look or what to say. I kept trying to give Athena, who had staked a spot close to the door, an empathetic smile, but she was not making eye contact with anyone.

This must have been so much harder, more complicated, for her than for the rest of us. Caroline had tried to reach out—with notes in her cubby, phone calls, ringing her doorbell—but the response had been complete, stony silence.

"Thank you all for coming," said the master. "As you can all imagine, there are some questions that Freddie's mother would like to ask you about the events of last weekend."

It was his mother's husband, Cameron, who posed the first one. Freddie had once described Cameron to me as looking "like a tennis instructor," and I could see what he meant. Tall, slim, very tanned, somewhat younger than Freddie's mother, he actually owned a private game reserve a couple of hours outside Cape Town, where he and Arabella had been living for about the last decade.

His question was whether Freddie had been behaving oddly in the weeks running up to the party.

"I didn't notice anything," I said, mainly to break the silence. "Freddie seemed very much his usual self to me."

I was close enough to Cameron to hear him snort softly.

It was hard to know what to say, really. Caroline had already described to the police the argument she had seen Freddie having in the car a few weeks earlier. They had not seemed especially surprised by what she was saying, although they had seemed interested. What she had *not* mentioned was having seen Freddie sneaking around the Osiris clubhouse the morning of the party. I was sure that didn't matter, I told her. Harry had already discovered—and informed us all—that several very valuable items that had been in the society's possession since it was founded had gone missing at some point over the last few weeks, and it seemed pretty clear who the main suspect was.

"Has any of you ever seen Freddie use . . . drugs?" asked Arabella.

"Oh no," we all said at once, practically in unison.

She arched a plucked eyebrow. Her long blond hair—now with streaks of silver and white—was tucked up in a bun. I could not help but notice she was dressed all in black, as if for a funeral.

"What I can't understand," she said, shaking her head, "was where on earth Freddie thought he was driving to, at that time of night."

Neither could I, to be honest. The last reported sighting of Freddie at Harry's party had been around 1:00 a.m. Freddie's car had been found around midday on Sunday, halfway between Longhurst and the train station. It had skidded completely off the road and down a sharp slope into a swiftly flowing stretch of the River Ouse. The driver's door was open. The car had been abandoned.

The house and its gardens had been searched by the police, as had the woods beyond. Alarmingly, on the flagstones at one side of the house, at the foot of the scaffolding, they had found a large puddle of blood, which was later confirmed as matching Freddie's blood type. That was the point at which people had started taking things a lot more seriously. Everywhere you went in college, the past couple of days, you could hear people discussing what had happened, sharing the latest developments, exchanging theories.

One of the scenarios the police were considering, we were told, was that Freddie had climbed up the scaffolding and fallen—and then, injured and possibly concussed, had attempted to drive himself to the hospital, only to veer off the road and into the water. They were exploring the possibility that injured, and impaired by the alcohol and other intoxicants he had consumed, he had then exited his vehicle and been carried away by the current.

"If any of you know anything which would help the police with their investigation," the master interjected, "we would encourage you to inform them as soon as possible."

I tried not to look at Athena. Eric Lam stared very hard down at one of his shoes. Ivo Strang was gazing out the window. The truth was, we had all heard the rumors swirling—that the vet school was investigating a large quantity of missing tranquilizers, that Freddie was on course to fail his final year.

After an uncomfortable half hour of further interrogation, we were told we were free to leave. Athena was out of the door almost before the master had finished opening it.

Harry and I walked Arabella and Cameron to their waiting taxi. When we got to the car, Cameron paused for a moment, then turned to us.

"If you boys know anything about what's going on, you need to tell us. For Frederick's own good," he said sharply.

Harry stiffened. "I think you'll find we are all very concerned about Freddie," he said.

"*I think you'll find,*" Cameron said, in a mock-British accent. "Well, I think *you'll* find we already know you're lying about his drug use," he added. "That's not news to us—we got a letter home from his house master when he was thirteen to say Freddie was smoking pot. Did you know he was also selling drugs? Were you boys buying from him? Because some of your lot evidently were. His college friends. Your party guests. The police have told us that when they pulled Freddie's car from the river, they found a black carryall in the trunk containing a kilo of cocaine, the same of ketamine, and hundreds of Ecstasy pills."

"Bloody hell," I said. Of course I had known Freddie was dealing, but not on that scale. Harry said nothing. I looked at him. It was then I realized how angry he was.

"How dare you," he said, his pink cheeks mottled with fury. "How dare you come here and lecture me about *Frederick's* best interests. As if either of *you* has ever shown *any* interest in his best interests, or in him, before now."

Arabella flinched.

"Do you know how much it would have meant to him, if you had both invited him to stay with you over there in South Africa just one summer, one Christmas, instead of palming him off on us at Longhurst? Did it ever strike you as a funny coincidence that he was studying to be a vet, and you run a game reserve? Did you never think that all those times he got in trouble at school, and you had to engage with his existence, might have been an attempt to get your attention?"

The taxi driver, looking over his shoulder to see what was going on, asked how many of us were getting in.

Arabella climbed into the back. Cameron followed, slamming the door behind him. It took him a couple of experimental fumbles before he got the window down. He met Harry's glare steadily.

"Perhaps," he said, "if Freddie and his mother hadn't been cheated out of what should have been rightfully theirs, if Arabella's father hadn't been passed over in the order of inheritance and drunk himself to death trying to work out why, then a lot of things might have been different. But that's not something we talk about ever, is it, Harry, eh? That's not a thread anyone in your family wants to start pulling at."

Arabella leaned forward to say something and then thought better of it.

Cameron was not quite finished: "Here's something else for you both to chew on: according to what the police have told us, in the glove compartment of Freddie's car was a notebook. Full of names, phone numbers, addresses. All the people he was selling to. The people he was buying from. All of it in his own handwriting. And from what I understand it makes very interesting reading indeed."

Fifth Entry

Monday, 20th December—The idea was a simple one, Oskar assured me. Evidently the arrangements were not. It took Oskar several days to put everything in place, sneaking off at odd hours, refusing to tell me what was going on. All traces of his former sulking vanished now that he had found a way of reestablishing something of our usual dynamic: Oskar the wise and generous mentor, me the uncertain and anxious neophyte. It felt a bit like our early days in Paris all over again.

At breakfast this morning, he could barely keep a smug look off his face. Midafternoon, he disappeared on an errand, shrugging on an overcoat and marching out of our apartment, cap down over his eyes. All through dinner at Les Deux Magots I could feel his excitement brewing, his mood turning impatient, like a child with a secret. As I drank my coffee, I sensed him resisting the urge to drum his fingers on the tabletop, to start tapping a foot.

All the way up the Boulevard du Montparnasse—the pavement still slick with rain, a fine drizzle haloing the streetlamps—he stayed a step or two ahead, ignoring all inquiries about where he was leading me. A church clock was flatly striking midnight as we turned onto the rue le Verrier. It was then that our destination finally dawned on me. I hesitated. He turned and smiled, nodded once, and wordlessly reached out his gloved hand for mine. Every time we passed another person, he would force us both to slow our hurried pace briefly, to avoid attracting attention. He was, after all, someone whose name people knew, whose face sometimes appeared in the newspapers.

We passed the main entrance of the hospital without stopping. I glanced at him. He kept his eyes fixed straight ahead. *This way*, he whispered, as we navigated the tangle of alleyways. Then another tug on my hand—*This way, Jules*—his head jerking left to indicate a door I would never have noticed. Confidently he led us inside, both of us still smartly dressed from dinner, heels clicking on the parquet, our pace adjusted to the man ahead, struggling with the tall cart of clean laundry he was pushing. There was a sharp smell of disinfectant in the air.

I was gripping his hand tightly. Hospitals always make me tense. I suspect they have that effect on anyone who has been inside one and not allowed to leave.

We turned. We turned again. People passed in the other direction—a doctor and a nurse, a man in blue overalls. Despite the rush of alarm I felt each time, only the nurse gave us so much as a second look.

At the end of a long half-lit corridor a porter was waiting for us. Nobody made eye contact. "*Une heure*," was all he said, as Oskar slipped something into his palm, which he pocketed, checking his wristwatch in the same deft gesture. Then he stepped aside and opened the door next to which he had been standing. Oskar, after checking the time on his own watch too, directed me through it.

The room into which we stepped was long and windowless, cold, with a brick vaulted ceiling. At the far end was a metal gurney, a white sheet covering its occupant. I swallowed. As in a dream, as in a nightmare, I was not aware of willing myself to move and yet somehow I was making my way toward it, the echo of our footsteps the only sounds to be heard.

Oskar pulled back the sheet. On the bed was a body, naked, female. Despite myself, I shuddered.

Her eyes were closed, her hands folded neatly across her chest. Dark-haired, young, pretty, freckled, she was the kind of girl you see walking with her sweetheart in the Jardin du Luxembourg, or the sort of serious-looking maid in a starched uniform you might pass pushing her employer's pram through the Jardin des Tuileries. She could not have been much older than twenty-one.

"Was she—? Did she—?"

Oskar said he did not know. All he could tell me was that an acquaintance Pierre Gaspard, from Oskar's student days, a successful medical man we had once met for pastis, who had obviously enjoyed slumming it for the evening in a Montparnasse café with his artist friend and his friend's young female companion—had tipped him off to the presence of an unclaimed body, given him the address of the hospital, the name of a helpful night porter. Had he not thought it strange, expressed misgivings, I asked. According to Oskar, the whole thing had seemed to excite him, to remind him of the pranks they played together as students.

"They found her in the river," he said. "Pulled her out just downstream from the Pont des Arts."

Some part of me felt surprise that her hair was not still wet.

Oskar had described the old Paris Morgue on the Île de la Cité to me once, how ghoulish gawkers—or those hoping to identify lost loved ones—were permitted to enter its imposing chambers, to wander and view from behind great glass windows corpses recovered from the Seine laid on copper slabs, their pitiful damp belongings displayed beside them. Suicides, victims of boating accidents, the murdered, murderers. Men, women, children. The unclaimed. The unidentified. The unloved. I said it sounded like a final humiliation. Oskar asked me if I thought the dead cared.

I took a step closer. Her face was peaceful. No, not peaceful. Expressionless. It is just sentiment, to imagine we detect emotion on the faces of the lifeless.

I suppose you could consider this a confession.

Because there had been times, as Oskar twisted, turned, and muttered in the night, sitting up, sweat-drenched, terrified, when part of me envied him the horrors he had seen during the war, those indelible images that haunted his early work. The shattered landscapes, scattered telegraph poles. The buildings like dollhouses kicked to pieces. The horse's skull grinning up from the mud. Those uniformed bodies by the side of the road one bright morning in Belgium, wheat springing straight up out of their backs. Yes, I confess it, as I sat there in the dark soothing him, that I envied Oskar as an artist, even as my heart ached for him as a man.

Because it was not until I began painting *Self-Portrait as Sphinx* that I realized I too had seen terrible sights, lived through awful things, and began to wonder if getting them down on canvas might help to exorcize them from my own nightmares.

Because Oskar had always insisted that it is the duty of the artist to tell the truth without flinching, and I finally understood what he meant. That if I was ever going to finish my painting, this painting I had convinced myself it was my duty to complete, I had to confront the material reality of a body precisely like this one. Not a warm living body, like the ones I had sketched at the Slade, nor the cold Carrara marble statues I'd studied in Rome. Not what I imagined someone who had drowned might look like, never having been allowed to see my sister's body, to say goodbye. But this, exactly this, the bruised, mottled, heartbreaking reality.

Because I was nevertheless fully aware that what we were doing here, in this room, would horrify my father, my mother, anyone I had known growing up, including myself. It is hard to express just how distant I have felt sometimes, here in Paris, from my own past, my own past selves. The little girl at Longhurst, with her dolls, her nurse, her bubbling imagination. The bold child who declared her intention to paint at the age of seven, according to family legend. The diligent, conscientious schoolgirl, who had earnestly lobbied to be allowed to study at the Slade. The ambitious young art student I was when I first met Oskar.

Because every time I spoke to Oskar about the painting and my fears about my family's reaction, he reminded me that his father had not spoken to him for almost a year after Oskar first exhibited his painting *Crucifixion*. That there were relatives on his mother's side who were still not talking to her. That his art had been denounced by newspapers, by politicians, from the pulpit, by some of his own former instructors and colleagues as obscene, as blasphemous, as degenerate.

Because that was how some people would always greet art that told the truth, that showed things as they really were, in all their ugly complexity.

Because there had been a moment, when he pulled that sheet back, when I had been expecting the face he revealed to be another face, a face that haunts my dreams.

Because even as I was looking down at the body on that slab, a body that had been a living and breathing girl less than twenty-four hours earlier, I was already thinking how glad I was that I had my pencils, my sketchbook with me.

Because all of a sudden, I had that sort of tingling feeling I always get in the tips of my fingers when it is time to start work.

CHAPTER 10

CAROLINE, CAMBRIDGE, 1991

I prodded Patrick gently on the arm, then sat up slowly, silently, in his narrow single bed. The alarm clock read 4:00 a.m. The only sound was the throaty rumble and occasional snort of Next-Door Terry's snores through the walls.

Patrick didn't stir as I put on my coat and boots, pocketed his keys, and closed the door quietly behind me. On the nights I stayed in his room, this had become my little ritual—sneaking out to wherever Patrick had parked to examine *Self-Portrait as Sphinx*. Once or twice, when I was sure there was nobody around, I had lifted the painting out entirely, examining the back of the age-blackened canvas and what looked like a pair of thumbprints on the stretchers, where someone—most likely Juliette herself!—had moved it with paint-covered hands.

It was an extraordinary work. Complex. Intricate. Unsettling. A painting you could get lost in, that you could spend a lifetime looking at. There was always some new detail to absorb, something strange and unexpected and intriguing which seemed to possess some very precise symbolic significance, if you could just work it out. Like the golden feathered wings neatly folded on the Juliette-Sphinx's back. The wings being what made her a Greek Sphinx, like the one that pounced on travelers on the road to Thebes and asked them to solve a riddle, and if they couldn't, gobbled them up.

I felt a bit like that traveler myself.

The Juliette-Sphinx occupied a clearing, in the middle of the painting, a patch of open ground studded with boulders in a landscape overgrown with fantastically entangled vegetation—great drooping flowers, sinister coils of thorns. In the gaps in the trees, all around the painting's central figure, strange little scenes were taking place. Near the top of the painting, running down a narrow path through dark, tangled woods, was a girl with flowing auburn hair, resembling Juliette herself. What she was fleeing, whatever was pursuing her, the painting did not show. What was unmistakable was her expression: one of wild, blind terror.

Prominent in the bottom left corner stood the figure that Harry's grandmother had reacted so strongly to: Juliette's sister, Lucy, in a long white dress, soaking and translucent, with wet hair partly covering her face. Her feet were bare, in a shimmering puddle. Her arms and legs were pale and mottled. Her toenails, her fingernails, had a hint of purple to them. Knowing what I did about who this was, knowing the lengths to which Juliette had gone to get the detail right, only added to the impact. It felt like something you were not sure you should look at. It felt like something that demanded you did so regardless.

This was clearly a world in which time worked strangely. On the left of the painting it looked to be late afternoon, a storm gathering. On the right, the moon was shining and it was already night. Across the top was a pattern of dark clouds. Everywhere you looked, in every nook and cranny, were the sort of sinister flights of fancy so familiar from the doodles in Juliette's journal, every bole on every tree, every shadowed stone or wizened branch holding at least the suggestion of something else: a leering face, a pair of eyes, a beckoning finger, something scuttling and many-legged. In the bottom right was that strange hooded figure in their boat, the same boat and figure as on the fragment of ancient papyrus I had seen in the Osiris clubhouse.

I could see why it had appealed to Breton. I could also see why it had upset the family. What I could not do was make heads or tails of it.

I had hoped that when *Self-Portrait as Sphinx* was in front of me, Juliette's secrets would reveal themselves. Why she had withdrawn it from the exhibition after a single night. Why her family had been determined to destroy it. What the terrible accusations were that led to her incarceration in a mental institution. I could find none. Clearly, her sister was an important figure in the painting, but I had searched it in vain for any reference to the Missing Maid, whose disappearance must have further shadowed her childhood. Or to Oskar and his wife, who she thought was following her. Or to her father.

I was not so much disappointed by the painting—it was truly remarkable—as frustrated by it. Could it be that it contained no coherent meaning, no mysterious message to decode? Perhaps I was trying to make the wrong kind of sense out of it, and it was just a nightmarish attempt to capture on canvas the jumble of Juliette's subconscious.

Then I would remind myself of her deliberate decision to paint herself as a Sphinx with a secret. How Harry's grandmother had reacted to the discovery that the painting might still exist. How Juliette talked about the painting in her journal.

I only had one final entry left to read now, a few pages long, dated January 25, 1938.

Trying to decipher Juliette's handwriting had always been a challenge, but these four pages were so cramped and jagged as to be almost illegible. If they did not divulge anything illuminating, then that was it: the remaining pages were blank.

One full day in the library. That was all it would take to finish my transcription. First thing in the morning I would be there once again, to take my place at my usual desk by the window, my enthusiasm for the task, my consciousness of the enormous stroke of good fortune I'd had in stumbling across her journal at all, haunted always by the painful thought that within just a few weeks of writing that final entry's last full stop, Juliette would be dead.

The college chapel clock clunked five, and, realizing the library would open in just a few hours, I reluctantly covered the painting back up and closed the trunk. As I turned the corner toward the college front gate, a bright sweep of headlights momentarily blinded me. A car pulled up across the road. Its door opened and then slammed. I stood there for a moment, partially concealed by Patrick's car, hoping that nobody had seen me.

Even though the figure across the road had her back to me, I recognized that dark tumble of hair, the elegant camel coat: it was Athena, being dropped off outside her house by the same silver Rolls-Royce that had driven her to Longhurst. I couldn't imagine what she was doing at this hour—never an early riser, she only ever saw dawn if she hadn't been to bed, and given what was going on with Freddie, it hardly seemed likely she had been out partying.

For a moment, I genuinely did not know how to react.

Athena had barely said a word to me since she'd stormed off at Longhurst. She hadn't turned up for lectures, wasn't answering her phone or her door, had not replied to a single one of my messages. I felt horrible for having doubted her intuition that something had happened to Freddie, for not having acknowledged from the start the seriousness of the situation and of her feelings about it. I felt hurt and baffled by how she had been acting since.

I crossed the road, and only when I was close enough to her that ignoring me would be impossible did I make my presence known. "Athena, where have you been?" I asked, meaning tonight but also the past week, trying to sound concerned rather than accusatory.

She gave a start. Once she had established who was addressing her, she focused on fumbling for her keys in her pocket.

"London," she said, curtly, over her shoulder.

"Are you okay? Look, I'm sorry if some of what I said the other day came across wrong. You're my best friend. I'm here, please talk to me. Let me help. I've been taking lecture notes, you can have them, it's an important term and you won't want to get behind, not with just months to go before finals."

I wanted to let her know that I was sorry, that I was here for her.

"I don't know what you're doing, hanging around outside my house at five in the morning, spying on me. You've made it perfectly plain how you feel about Freddie, you literally told me I would be better off without him in my life, so there's no point pretending to be worried about him now."

"I *am* worried about Freddie. And I'm worried about you."

Of course I was. This whole situation was a nightmare for everyone, and a special kind of nightmare for Athena, but none of that changed the fact that he had treated her terribly and whether he was alive or dead, throwing everything away because of him was a mistake she would surely come to regret. Someone needed to say that to her, even if this was not the most sensitive time to say it, and if no one else was going to, then perhaps I should. Only I didn't get a chance.

Athena had her key in the lock now and turned it, stepping into her darkened hallway. She flicked a switch. She turned to face me and I thought she was about to invite me in. In that moment I was sure I detected a brief wobble of her lower lip, as if she was about to start crying. Instead, her expression hardened.

"I don't need you to worry about me, Caroline. I don't need your pity, and I don't need your sympathy. I don't need your lecture notes and I actually don't need your friendship. I just need you to leave me alone."

PATRICK, CAMBRIDGE, 1991

All around us, as if nothing had happened, the term continued. People had essays to write, lectures to attend, exams to revise for. Even though it had only been a few weeks, Freddie Talbot's disappearance had become little more than Cambridge gossip for most students—something to idly speculate about in the lunch line or library.

Although Caroline had made me promise we would take things slowly, we were now spending much more time with each other than we did apart. We worked together, we ate together, we slept together, and we panicked together over the work in progress Alice Long had asked to see before our next supervision. Our two-thousand-word samples were due on Monday afternoon, and only on Saturday did either of us really start writing, Caroline sitting at my desk with her notepad and pen, me hunched over a lined legal pad on my scratchy armchair.

By the time we finally finished on Monday morning, after two near all-nighters fueled by biscuits and tea, my spine felt like it might never unfurl. "I'll drive them over to Alice Long's house this afternoon," I told her, tucking both stapled manuscripts into my messenger bag.

"Just post them through the door, though, right? Otherwise she'll ask about our trip to Longhurst," Caroline said as we crossed the quad. "And about the painting . . ."

"The painting? You mean the *stolen* painting?" I said, only half joking. "The painting *you* stole, from the home of one of my best friends . . ."

"I didn't steal the painting, Patrick," she said once again, a little wearily this time. "I rescued it."

I doubted Harry or his parents would see things that way. Might Alice Long?

Something Caroline and I went back and forth about a lot, late at night in my room, was the rights and wrongs of what she had done— and what on earth we were supposed to do with the painting now.

Keeping the thing in the trunk of the MG was obviously not a long-term solution, but at least there it would not be discovered by a bedder when they came to clean one of our rooms or spotted by a police officer come to ask some follow-up questions about Freddie.

Returning *Self-Portrait as Sphinx* with apologies to the Willough-bys was an option Caroline had overruled out of hand. "They didn't even know it was there, until we told them," she reminded me. "If I hadn't taken it, they would have burned the thing."

It was also specifically by *burning* the painting, Caroline kept re-minding me, that Austen Willoughby had told Granny Violet he had destroyed it. A weird coincidence, didn't that seem, given how Oskar and Juliette had died?

What Caroline did not have was any explanation yet of how the painting had survived that fire, or how it had made its way to Longhurst—or how we could share our discovery with the world. And she was adamant that it was a discovery that *should* be shared.

The central practical problem was this: as far as the art world was concerned, the painting was ash, and without solid provenance, there was no way to convince anyone that what we had in our possession was Juliette's great lost work. But in order to establish it as genuine, we had to connect it to Longhurst, and in doing so identify it as stolen property, and therefore announce ourselves as its burglars.

This was a loop we had gone around time and time again, lying in bed, neither of us able to work out a solution. The only person I could think of who might be able to help was my father, but confessing we'd pinched a painting from his best friend and longest-standing client seemed unwise at best. Nor could I think of any way of explaining what had happened without telling Dad all about the argument with Philip, and how upset Granny Violet had been—and I was pretty sure I could imagine how that would go down. Fortunately, so far, for whatever reason, Philip did not seem to have said anything about it to him either.

IT WAS ABOUT FOUR in the afternoon, already getting dark, when I got to Elm Lane. Outside number 32, Alice Long's place, was a house clearance truck. I parked behind it. The back was open, and inside I could see furniture, tables and chairs, carefully stacked. The metal frame of a disassembled bed. The little two-person couch that Caroline and I had sat on in that first supervision.

The door of the house was open too. Down the front path, two men in overalls were carrying a small glass-topped table. I stepped aside on the pavement to let them pass. It was a bit odd that Alice Long was moving and had not mentioned it. What if we had just turned up for our supervision and there was someone else living there? Then it hit me.

"Everything alright, son?" asked one of the men in overalls, from the back of the truck.

"Sorry," I said, pointing to the truck, pointing at the house. "Is this . . . ? Is she . . . ?"

"House clearance," he told me. "Old girl passed away about a fortnight ago."

Just after our last supervision, I thought. I assumed no one had thought to inform the university.

"What's happening to all this stuff?" I asked.

"Going to auction, the lot of it. Ely Auction Rooms, just down the road. All profits going to some cat sanctuary, probably. Always the way."

I knew those auction rooms well, having visited them many times with my father. I made a mental note of the name of the removal company. I felt a strange impulse to ask if they were totally sure that Alice Long was dead, that they had gotten the right house. I stared up to the open doorway, the shabby front hall, the walls empty now of the pictures that had hung there. It was a poignant sight in itself. The thought that we would never get to tell her what we had discovered at Longhurst was heartbreaking.

"The milkman raised the alarm," the other man in overalls told me. "Noticed no one had taken the bottles in for a while, could see through the glass in the front door a couple of days' mail piled up. Someone called the landlord, and he let the police in. In bed, she was. Peaceful, at least."

They had positioned her desk in the back of the van and laid a thick blanket over it for protection. I stepped out of the way to let them back up the path. I could make out the silhouettes of propped-up framed pictures, armchairs, side tables.

I could hear the two men loudly discussing what they should try moving next, where it would fit in the truck, whether they would need to shuffle things around. That was when it came to me. My brilliant idea. I still do not know where it came from. Perhaps it was having witnessed similar house clearances with my father, observing at close hand his carefully honed ability to identify the one or two genuinely valuable items among a lifetime's accumulated detritus.

What I *do* know is that as soon as the idea came to me I knew immediately—without hesitation—that I was going to put it into action, and that I did not have much time. I looked up and down the empty street. It was a gloomy afternoon. I walked to the car, opened the trunk, and removed the blanket from *Self-Portrait as Sphinx*. I gave it what I very much hoped was not going to be one last look, tucked it under my arm, and walked around to the open back of the truck. Then I hopped up into the truck and lifted up the blanket with Alice Long's other pictures under it and squeezed it in alongside. I let the blanket drop. I hopped back out of the truck again. Without looking back, keeping my head down, I walked very quickly back to my car.

It was only after I had jumped back into the front seat of the MG, as I revved the engine to pull away and drive off, that it hit me I might just have made a terrible mistake. That I was going to have to drive back now and explain to Caroline what I had done and why I had done it. That I was either a bloody genius or a complete idiot.

The Final Entry

Monday, 17th January—I am a fool. For weeks, for months, I have been living in a fool's bubble, thinking solely of my art, entirely embroiled in my painting. So focused on what I was creating that I never once stopped to think about the trap I was stumbling into.

Twice more I have been back, with and without Oskar, to that hospital, forcing myself again to confront that girl on her slab, still unclaimed, to sketch her, to observe her, to make sure I was getting everything right.

To brush up on my mythology, I have been ransacking the libraries of Paris, scouring the secondhand bookshops. Wrapped up for warmth in bed at night, I have frowned and yawned over *The Book of the Dead*, Wilkinson's *Manners and Customs of the Ancient Egyptians*, Budge's *Egyptian Magic*—books whose spines I recognize from the shelves of my father's library, their content familiar from his endless uninterruptible monologues, delivered to anyone in the vicinity (a five-year-old child, a mildly scandalized curate, a gardener), about Ra and Thoth and Osiris, about the ancient Egyptian conception of the afterlife and other people's theories on the topic (which were all wrong) and his own (which were correct).

Painfully aware as I painted that this was the most complex and ambitious piece I have ever attempted and that I would only ever get one chance to get it right—and that every day brought us closer to the opening night of the exhibition.

Tonight.

All last week, Oskar and I were working on our mannequins, which artists exhibiting in the show had been asked to Surrealize. The whole week I spent listening to Oskar grunt, manhandling the thing, wrestling it this way and that. They are surprisingly heavy, mannequins. It took two of us several stops to get each one up the stairs, bumping and swearing and apologizing every time one of our puzzled neighbors stuck their head out of the door. Then we set to work, a certain competitive tension in the atmosphere. A desire to excel, to dazzle, to outdo the other artists in the show, and perhaps each other. Perhaps especially each other. Supposedly, the mannequins would be anonymous, but it was already common knowledge what Dalí had planned, what Duchamp had done. Would anyone guess which one was mine, the mannequin wrapped and wrapped again, like a mummy, like a swaddled child, the mouth criss-crossed in strips of cotton I had dyed red in the sink—badly staining the porcelain in the process?

About teatime on Saturday, just as I was standing back to admire my handiwork, I heard Oskar stamp out in his boots and the door shut behind him. *Should I?* I wondered. *Just a peek?* Oskar had hung three thin blankets on a rope across the middle of the room to prevent us from distracting each other. I crossed over and parted them. I did not immediately know how to process what I was seeing, and of course that was exactly what made Oskar a great artist, a Surrealist artist. For a moment, it felt like I was looking at a real human being, a corpse. A mutilated corpse. The sounds I had been listening to from the other side of the curtain suddenly made sense—he had been slashing the thing to pieces. Slicing at its sides. Stabbing at its chest. Right in the middle of its head was embedded the little axe we use to chop up wood for the stove. It was brutal. It was terrifying. It was brilliant.

Yesterday at the Galérie Beaux-Arts, all the artists were running around, squabbling, panicking, arranging things, overseeing the hanging of their work, bickering about the placement of their mannequins. Breton was striding around, issuing terse instructions. Other members of the organizing committee were doing the same—often in direct contradiction to the instructions Breton had just issued. Everybody looked busy, tense, preoccupied, cursing Wolfgang Paalen as he fussed over his fake pond, which covered half the floor. I had been trying not to dwell on it too much, what a huge show this would be. Two hundred and thirty-one works to hang and install before it opened, by sixty artists from fourteen countries. A phonograph recording of a woman's high-pitched hysterical laugher played on a loop at ear-splitting volume, doing little to diminish my anxiety.

It was Breton's idea—sprung on us at the very last moment—that my work and Oskar's should hang together in a little side room of their own. *Self-Portrait as Sphinx*, just finished. Oskar's *Three Figures in a Landscape*. Two pieces, painted in the same studio, meeting up like old friends, picking up an interrupted conversation, across the gallery walls. I rather liked the idea. Oskar was less keen. His vision, no doubt, had been for his great painting to occupy its own anteroom.

I had asked that the printed catalogue contain just my name and the title of the painting, with no mention of my relationship to Oskar, or the country or the city in which I lived. It had crossed my mind to ask that my name be removed from the list of exhibiting artists entirely, for the painting to be shown anonymously. It was Oskar who persuaded me I was being ridiculous. Who reminded me—his hand on my shoulder, his eyes on mine—of what I had said to him the first time we met: that I was Juliette Willoughby and I was an artist. Now was my chance to show the world, he said.

How could I resist being there on opening night, at the *vernissage*, to see the guests in their evening dress—three thousand of them, the newspapers said, the police eventually called to control the crowds—thrill and titter and shrink from the corridor of mannequins, the only light being that of the torches they had been provided at the entrance? To see how they would respond to Dalí's *Rainy Taxi*—a real taxi parked outside the gallery, occupied by mannequins, inside which it was raining. To watch them stumble around in the gloom, dust from the coal sacks hung overhead landing on their hats, as for the first time they experienced these works, like snatched glimpses of someone else's dream. To witness their reactions to my *Self-Portrait as Sphinx*.

It is not a painting I expect anyone to understand all at once.

It will take time, it will take careful attention, before the connections between the parts of the painting begin to emerge. Before you perceive that it is a single story being told. A story that is so strange, so horrifying, that it would be easier to persuade yourself that you were going mad than to accept it is really what you are seeing.

When Oskar and Breton talk of my painting, they speak of it in terms of nightmare, of private fears given public flesh, as a very personal phantasmagoria. What I don't think either of them is even close to grasping is how much of what I have painted is the literal truth.

When I entered the room there were plenty of people in there, mostly looking at Oskar's painting and talking about it, but there was one man, tall, straight-backed, with white hair and a hat in his hands, standing right in front of mine. He stood and stared at it for a long time, before he went to move on. And even before I saw his face, some quality that reminded me of my father, of the men in our family, of the way they carry themselves, gave his identity away.

I must have made some sound, a little gasp, perhaps a slight choking noise. He turned. He saw me. And from the look on Uncle Austen's face, the look of horror he gave me, I knew he had understood. The painting. What it meant. In that moment, I understood the scale of the mistake I had made, the extent of my foolishness.

The next thing I remember is running, pushing against people, stumbling through the gallery. I kept running when I got outside, despite people's stares, despite the cries after me. I did not stop running until I got to the river, panting and gasping so hard I thought I was about to choke or be sick. That was when it really hit me, what I had done.

Because it is not just a painting, *Self-Portrait of Sphinx*. Not to my family. To my family, it is a declaration of war.

CHAPTER 11

CAROLINE, CAMBRIDGE, 1991

I was not sure whether to be impressed or appalled.

It was one thing to process the news that Alice Long was dead. How ought we to grieve for a woman whom we'd met only twice but who had changed our lives irrevocably?

To absorb what Patrick had done—immediately, instinctively, unilaterally—after learning of her death was something else entirely.

"Okay," I said. "Run me through all this one more time."

"Alice Long had no relatives, or at least none she left anything to. That's what the moving guy said. From the looks of things, the house was rented and the landlord wanted it empty as soon as possible, to let it to new tenants, so everything inside was being carted off to Ely Auction Rooms when I arrived. The proceeds from the sale are going to charity, the removal guy seemed to think. They weren't doing an inventory, as far as I could see—so I slipped in our *Sphinx* alongside a load of other pictures."

"So it's just . . . gone? You just gave it away? Without even consulting me?"

Patrick shook his head. "I know the Ely Auction Rooms. I know the kind of people who attend those auctions. If it was a print of a laughing cavalier or a Wedgwood tea set, it would be snapped up for well over the estimate. If it was a painting by Austen Willoughby, it would be gone in a shot. What I can promise you is that no one in that room will want some weird painting of a cat lady with six boobs by an artist none of them has heard of. So all we need to do is wait for it to come up in the sale—in a few weeks' time, probably—and we buy it."

"With what?"

"I've got a bit of money my mother's parents left me."

"And then what?" I asked. "What happens after we buy back the painting you have just given away?"

"Then *Self-Portrait as Sphinx* has a solid paper trail. A provenance. Bought fair and square, at auction, by us—at an auction house in the very same county as the painting's last recorded location at Longhurst. It is not stolen goods, it's a sleeper legitimately bought by two lucky art-hunting students who just happened to know what they were looking at. Our supporting evidence? The journal you found in the Willoughby Bequest, the photograph we found in the Witt."

He sounded proud of himself. "Our receipt and its date will be verifiable, and the auction records will show the painting came from somebody who can't tell anyone where *she* acquired it because—"

"She's dead," I said.

Patrick did have the decency to look a little embarrassed by this. "She's dead, and we're about to rewrite art history, just like she wanted," he said.

It was his idea that we should attend the funeral, which was one of the saddest things I had ever seen. It was held on a gray Thursday afternoon, in a crematorium out on the edge of the Fens. We were the only guests in the redbrick chapel where the celebrant gave a brief talk about Alice Long's life and career before pressing a button that closed the curtains around the coffin.

Then we waited.

The Ely Auction Rooms were located in a large dusty shed on a small industrial estate. Patrick drove us there every Friday so we could scour the aisles, and when we'd finished we'd stop at the Four Horseshoes pub for lunch on the way home. Sometimes we talked about our dissertations, the new supervisors we had been assigned. Sometimes we talked about Freddie, still missing, the police having failed to find any trace of him at Longhurst or in any of the bodies of water they had dredged.

Sometimes we talked about how Harry was coping with it all. About Athena, who was still not speaking to me, who had still not responded to any of the messages I had left, the long letter I had written her. I was sorry, I kept repeating. If she needed me, when she needed me, I would be waiting. She stalked right past me in college, and on the rare occasions she turned up to a lecture she pointedly ignored any empty seats near me. Give her time, said Patrick. Give her space. The day after I put the letter through her door, I found it returned, unopened, in my cubby.

As the weeks passed, with the end of term rapidly approaching, I did start losing faith a little in Patrick's plan. There was still no sign of any of the stuff from Alice Long's house clearance at the auction rooms. I kept imagining the painting discarded in some trash bin somewhere. Patrick said we just had to be patient, although he always sounded more confident than he looked. He asked Eric Lam, a law student, what happened when someone died and left everything to charity. The gist was it all took a while—some time to apply for probate, then for an executor to distribute the assets as set out in the will. Not a complex process, unless there had been any questions surrounding the death or any challenges to the will. If things had gone smoothly, then where had Alice Long's auctionable effects gotten to? I asked. Patrick could not answer.

Then, one Friday, there it was.

Before starting our tour that day, we had skimmed as usual the cheaply photocopied catalogue for any mention of the painting we were looking for. Unhelpfully, the individual who compiled these things was not given to flowery descriptions. "Mahogany table." "Big jug." "Small jug." "Chair." We had been extremely excited one week to see "Picture: Big Cat." It had taken us an hour to find: a faded poster of a lion in a cracked frame with an asking price of £5. Today the descriptions were even more taciturn than usual: there were twenty-seven items listed only as "Medium Oil Picture" for us to look through.

"Shall we divide and conquer? We've been here an hour and we've still got about ten pictures left to tick off," I said. He looked a little put out, but nodded and then stalked off to the other end of the huge room.

It was all I could do not to squeal when I spotted it: a small collection of old cameras and lenses, piled in a battered cardboard box. I closed my eyes and mentally walked around Alice Long's cluttered living room, scanning up and down her bookcase in my head. Yes, I was sure of it—these had been on the top shelf.

Feeling suddenly lightheaded, I placed both palms on the desk next to me to steady myself, realizing that it, too, with its cracked leather top, had been in the house. Scanning the aisle, I could see that I was surrounded by remnants of the old lady's life. Lamps, umbrella stands, the very couch Patrick and I had sat on, all scattered around an unfamiliar room, all labeled with lot numbers. Things that had been chosen with care and intention, the accumulated effects of a woman who had been forgotten by everyone but us, now stripped of all context and meaning. And mixed in with all that were things that did not belong to Alice Long at all. A collection, in a basket, of dog leashes and water bowls. A stack of *Punch* annuals.

I felt a tap on the shoulder and spun around to see a very excited Patrick. Wordlessly, he grabbed me by the hand and led me to the end of the row, gesturing with a flick of his eyes to the back of a canvas that had been thoughtlessly shoved between a matching pair of threadbare armchairs. I knew it instantly from having handled it, and flung my arms around his shoulders.

"It's here," I whispered into his ear, feeling his breath hot against my cheek. "That's it!"

Patrick smiled and nodded and winked. Then he leaned in to give me a kiss, and I felt sure he must have felt the *thump-thump-thump* of my heart in my chest. Juliette Willoughby had believed—for reasons I could not fully fathom—that her family would stop at nothing to destroy this painting, take it from her, punish her for making it. For half a century it had been hidden away. Now, thanks to us, it was about to dazzle the world.

PATRICK, CAMBRIDGE, 1991

Provincial auction houses always remind me of my childhood. The smells—of dust, of varnish, of musty coats. The cases of military uniforms and memorabilia, folding screens, old records, walking sticks. The occasional stuffed crocodile.

This was what Dad and I did together on weekends, the thing I used to look forward to all week: hopping in the car and driving off somewhere "to see what we can see," as Dad put it. Only when I was older did I work out that Saturday was the one day Dad did the childcare, and that his version involved doing exactly what he was going to do anyway, but with me in tow.

He would always know a few people in a place like Ely. He would exchange nods with the owners, other dealers. My father was known to have an eye, so people always asked if there was anything in particular he was interested in. "Just browsing" was always his response.

At the viewings, if there was a painting he was interested in (but did not want to seem too interested in), he would send me to look and tell him what I thought. By the time I was about eleven, he had trained me pretty well at this—I could explain with some degree of technical precision what sort of condition something was in, whether any of his regular clients might be interested in it. Once or twice, I had pointed out a painting he had overlooked and been rewarded with a fiver.

It was not therefore unfamiliar to me, the tingling excitement you get when you know that there is a lot coming up that you think is special and that you are pretty sure only you have noticed. Getting one over on everybody else, that's part of the tingle, too. Part of the psychological gamesmanship being never to let it show when you are excited about an item, the other part being not to let your enthusiasm overwhelm your better judgment. Never falling in love with something so hard you bid more than it is worth.

It was reassuring to see that there had not been much of a turnout for today's auction. We sat on our chairs, catalogues on our laps. There could not have been more than thirty other people, all of us waiting for someone to take to the rickety lectern on its raised podium. Caroline and I were the youngest people there by far. There was no one I recognized—none of my dad's colleagues or rivals. Some of these people looked like they had only come in to be out of the rain.

Then Giles Pemberton walked in.

Caroline noticed him first, and nudged me. Just as she did so he looked over and saw us. My heart sank. Giles Pemberton, from our year, from our course, the chap from dinner who had known all about Austen Willoughby's paintings and heard us talking about Juliette's.

Oh fuck, I thought to myself.

I asked him if he was interested in anything in particular. He showed us a pair of antique hand-painted porcelain spaniels. "Aren't they just the most horrible things you have ever seen? *J'adore un petit chien moche.* They're going to look absolutely ghastly on my mantelpiece."

Caroline smiled. I said he was not wrong.

"And what are you two here for? You know, I love to come to these things. I always dream that one of these days I'll spot a misattributed masterpiece, a genuine Willoughby."

For a moment, my whole body froze. Then I realized he was talking about Austen Willoughby, the dog painter. Or was he? Was that a test, to see how I reacted? All of us—Giles and Caroline and I—were smiling. Everyone was being conspicuously amused about how funny it was to have all bumped into each other here. What a strange coincidence.

My brain was spiraling in paranoid circles. Giles had been at the party. What if he had seen Caroline take the painting? Was there any reason he could possibly have to suspect that *Self-Portrait as Sphinx* still existed, and that we had found it? If he had stumbled across the painting here at the auction house, was there any way he could have put two and two together?

Caroline was telling Giles about a pair of earrings she was interested in. Smartly, I noted she had chosen an item far down the list of lots after the porcelain dogs that Giles was here for.

On the podium the auctioneer appeared—frizzy hair, bow tie, waistcoat—and the auction itself began. I had expected to be a little nervous. The presence of Giles had sent me for a loop.

This was not the sort of auction with formal paddles you raised to make an offer, I had explained to Caroline. Here, you just nodded or shook your head. Caroline made the same joke that most people make at their first auction about hoping she did not buy anything by accident by scratching her nose. All through the early bids she kept her arms carefully folded across her chest.

Our painting was lot number 76, and so we sat and watched as everything preceding it went under the hammer, most selling at a first and only bid, easing my nerves slightly. Giles got his dogs, at a snip. He trotted off to collect them, apologizing on his way down our row. We mouthed our goodbyes.

I don't think I have ever felt so relieved to see the back of anyone. Even after he had left to collect his dogs, I kept dreading he would come back, for a forgotten umbrella, to see if he had left something under his chair.

We were ten lots now from our painting. With each one that passed I could feel my pulse quicken. Was this really going to work? Ahead of me seemed to open whole vistas of possibility—the career dreams I had so boastfully told Caroline about in the first year suddenly within reach. What a start to both of our careers this would be, what a start to our lives together. I could just picture us, on the cover of the *Cambridge Evening Post* with our discovery, being interviewed with the painting on the local news: Caroline explaining the art historical significance of this discovery, the interviewer asking us to tell the amazing story of how we had spotted it. I was already imagining how I would break the news to my father, the mixture of pride and jealousy he would feel.

"Lot seventy-six," shouted the auctioneer from the podium finally. I took a deep breath and straightened in my seat. "Who will start me at twenty-five?"

I nodded. The auctioneer acknowledged this. He looked around the room. In the corner, a man at a desk was taking offers over the telephone from remote bidders. I saw him catch the auctioneer's eye, give a nod. The auctioneer acknowledged it. Back to me.

"Fifty," I said.

Back to the man with the phone. He said something into it and waited for a response. "Seventy-five," he said.

The auctioneer turned to me again. I nodded. "That's a hundred, then," said the auctioneer.

The man with the phone said, "One hundred and twenty-five."

I felt Caroline shift in her seat next to me. Her grip on my hand tightened.

"What's happening?" she asked me. "Who is that on the phone?"

Precisely the question I was asking myself. "I guess someone who saw it and liked it," I said.

There was no reason to get paranoid, I reminded myself. There was no reason to imagine we were bidding against someone who knew what lot 76 really was. The only people we had told about the journal were Athena, Harry, and Giles at dinner, and Alice Long, of course. The only person who knew about the photograph of the painting was Alice Long. Without having seen the photograph we had seen, there was no way anyone could have identified with confidence the painting we were bidding on as Juliette Willoughby's *Self-Portrait as Sphinx*.

When the bidding hit £250, I started to get twitchy. Never had I expected anyone else to show this much interest in our painting. In the whole world, Caroline and I had, between us, £1,087.96 exactly—and that was if we both emptied our bank accounts entirely.

The painting was expected to raise one to three hundred pounds, according to the catalogue. I was hopeful that the other bidder might therefore have set three hundred as their upper limit, and made a resolution to stop there. Alas, this proved to be wishful thinking. The bidding cruised straight through and past that sum without a pause. Now bidding was advancing in fifty-pound increments. Three-fifty, four hundred, four hundred fifty pounds. It was easy to forget this was real money, a third of all the money we jointly had in the world, in fact. Five hundred. Five-fifty. Six hundred.

I had seen this before at auctions, a bidding spiral, when the competitive instinct kicked in. Was that what had happened here? Not being able to see the opposing bidder, it was hard to tell. At least the pace of the escalation had slowed a little. Now each time the price went up, the man on the telephone spent a little time conferring with his client before he gave his approving nod. A hundred quid each time we were going up now. Seven hundred. Eight hundred. Nine.

A little gasp went around the room when we hit one thousand pounds. People who had been wandering around the rest of the building had begun to gather in the doorway of the auction room to watch.

Caroline's hand was clasping mine very tightly. My stomach lurched. It seemed to take almost no time for us to reach fifteen hundred pounds. The man with the phone had begun to showboat a little now, to add little pauses before bidding with a flourish, which annoyed me, since it was not his money at stake. I kept bidding. Seventeen hundred. Eighteen. I could speak to my father, explain the situation. I was not going to let this painting go for the sake of a few hundred quid.

"Patrick," Caroline whispered, when the bidding hit two thousand. "Patrick, what are you doing?"

Now every time the price of the painting went up—and it was doing so at leaps of two hundred fifty pounds—there was a collective intake of breath.

"I'll sell the car," I told her. "I'll sell that fucking car."

By the time the bidding had reached three and a half thousand, I had mentally sold the car, maxed out a credit card I didn't have, extended my overdraft. If I needed more money I would go to my dad. Caroline was shaking her head now, which meant that every time the auctioneer turned to me and I nodded, he would glance at her and then back at me, as if to ask: "Are you sure?"

I was sure. We had to get it. Because if we did not get it, it would be my fault. This had been my stupid plan. Thanks to me, this painting, lost for decades, might be about to vanish once more, into someone's private collection, and all the castles I had been building in the air—my future, Caroline's future, our future together—were in the process of dissolving.

If I were Caroline, I did not know if I would ever be able to forgive me. That was the worst feeling of all. I was not sure I would ever be able to forgive myself.

I had often wondered what it felt like for my father to have lost that Raphael. To spend your life trying not to think about how different things could have been. To live the rest of your days with that disappointment. Clinging, as a salve, to whatever small measures of social status you could—a friendship with a Willoughby, a son in Osiris, the best table in a restaurant.

At four thousand pounds it was clear that the other bidder was not going to stop, that they would keep going until they secured the painting. I could see Caroline looking again at the catalogue, the description of the painting, the guide price, as if there might be some answers there. The auctioneer turned to me. I shook my head. It was over. It was hard to believe, after all we had been through, but we had lost our painting.

"Gone for four thousand pounds to my bidder on the phone."

PART III

THE DILEMMA

Even the most perfect reproduction of a work of art is lacking in one element: its presence in time and space, its unique existence at the place where it happens to be.

—WALTER BENJAMIN, "THE WORK OF ART IN
THE AGE OF MECHANICAL REPRODUCTION"
(1935, TRANS. HARRY ZOHN)

CHAPTER 12

CAROLINE, LONDON, 2023, ONE WEEK BEFORE HARRY'S DEATH

They pass in a heartbeat, the years.

In the Tate Modern gift shop, a dark-haired woman—she looked to be in her late twenties—was leafing through *The Surreal Life of Juliette Willoughby*. I was around her age when that book—my first and by far my most commercially successful—was published in 1998. The same year that I started my first permanent academic job, at Cambridge, that I married Patrick and he opened his gallery.

A photo of the girl I was then (young, ambitious, in love) stares out from the book's back cover. On the front, a fluorescent sticker boasts *Five Million Copies Sold Worldwide*, which is pretty extraordinary for a scholarly biography of someone who—back when I wrote it—was an almost unknown female painter. I picked up a copy and it fell open at the dedication page: *For my mother*.

A further stack of the same hardback was piled on a table beneath a poster advertising my talk tonight, a tie-in to publicize this special twenty-fifth anniversary edition, with a revised introduction my publishers requested I write, reflecting on the book's success. The truth was, I have never thought that I was responsible for it. I simply had the good luck to write about a woman artist at a point in history at which it felt like people *finally* started to care about them, an artist with a riveting life story that could be seen—depending upon the prism through which you viewed it—as a tragic romance, a family drama, a coming-of-age tale, or a parable about the ways in which female achievement is overlooked. Or all of those things at once.

Although *Self-Portrait as Sphinx* itself had disappeared after the auction, I still had Juliette's journal—a remarkable historical document in its own right—to draw upon and reflect upon. And as Alice Long had wisely suggested, once you looked for Juliette, she could be glimpsed here and there—usually called Jules (Oskar's nickname for her) or referred to as *La Rousse Anglaise*, the English Redhead, a quiet girl with little French—in the diaries and letters of her Paris circle.

Naturally enough, it was an academic press that first brought my book out, as an expensive hardback intended mostly for university libraries, to a couple of enthusiastic reviews in specialist journals and general indifference. What catapulted it straight onto the bestseller lists was the sudden reappearance of *Self-Portrait as Sphinx* in January 1998.

When a letter from the Tate landed in my college cubby requesting that I visit London and offer my academic opinion on a painting by Juliette Willoughby—the *only* painting by Juliette Willoughby—which they recently had been offered on long-term loan, my first reaction was to panic.

There was, for obvious reasons, no mention in my book of my having found *Self-Portrait as Sphinx* at Longhurst, or stolen it, or how we had lost it at auction—although privately, Patrick and I had speculated for years about who the buyer might have been, whether they knew what they had stumbled across. Instead, in the book's conclusion, I described finding Juliette's journal and the photograph in the Witt Library, proving the painting *had* survived the fire, and ending on a note of sincere hope that one day it would reappear.

The moment I set eyes on the painting again, propped up on an easel in the office of the Tate's Head of Collections, I recognized it as the one that had slipped through our fingers. Who owned it, the Tate couldn't tell me—they were communicating through lawyers to maintain anonymity, which Patrick explained was not unusual for serious collectors. Some don't want to be inundated by art dealers sharking for new clients; others worry that a high-profile loan alerts thieves to the caliber of the rest of their collection.

I was unsettled, and frustrated its owner would remain a mystery, but Patrick convinced me that overall this was good news. The painting was back, and about to go on display in one of the world's most prestigious art institutions. My status as an authority on the subject would offer all sorts of media opportunities to bring Juliette's life and work to a whole new audience.

"Frankly," said Patrick, "I think we are both extremely lucky that whoever bought it at auction did so over the phone and never got to see the people bidding against them—otherwise we both might have all sorts of awkward questions to answer, wouldn't we?"

I had to admit he was right.

Self-Portrait as Sphinx went on show at the newly opened Tate Modern to much media fanfare in 2000, newspapers worldwide covering the story, TV crews from as far afield as Japan and Argentina asking if they could interview me standing in front of it. At my publisher's request, I swiftly wrote a new chapter on this miraculous rediscovery. My book was reissued with the painting reproduced in glossy color on the front cover instead of Juliette's passport photo. This time it was reviewed everywhere, the publishers unable to reprint it fast enough to keep up with demand.

I did always mention it was Patrick who had found the photograph in the Witt, without which the painting could not have been authenticated. I did often suggest people interview him too. I was conscious that just as my career was going stratospheric, he was putting in eighteen-hour days at his gallery. It was a lot of pressure to put on a marriage.

The dark-haired woman placed my book down on the table, revealing a lanyard identifying her as Flo Burton, the events assistant I was waiting for to escort me to my talk. She did a double take, then smiled and offered her hand to shake.

"Professor Cooper? Lovely to meet you. Shall we head upstairs? We have a full house tonight," she said as she ushered me toward the escalator. "It sold out weeks ago. Members love hearing from experts, and *Self-Portrait as Sphinx* is one of the most-visited paintings here . . ."

Every seat in the gallery was taken, and—a tribute to the cross-generational appeal of Juliette's art and her story—there were teenagers next to pensioners, art students next to middle-aged couples in matching fleeces. Here and there, a past or present academic colleague or a former student. Flo clutched a piece of paper and leaned over the microphone.

"Good evening," she began. "Please join me in welcoming Professor Caroline Cooper. As well as being the world's preeminent expert on Juliette Willoughby, she was the guest curator of the exhibition *Women & Surrealism* here last year here and has written extensively on the movement in the 1920s and 1930s in Paris and beyond. We are very lucky to have her with us tonight for our lecture"—a glance at her piece of paper—"Rediscovering an Icon: The Story of *Self-Portrait as Sphinx.*"

She moved swiftly off to take a seat in the front row. Positioning myself behind the lectern, I reached into my bag for my glasses, making a self-deprecating comment about needing them these days. This got a far bigger ripple of laughter than it merited.

"Thank you, Flo. It is not every day you get invited to speak about a painting with it hanging right there on the wall behind you. Welcome, everyone."

I took a sip of water.

"If you were asked to imagine an auction house on sale day, how would it look? You're probably picturing Sotheby's or Christie's. Masterpiece after masterpiece placed with white-gloved hands next to the auctioneer's podium, collectors lifting paddles and aggressively outbidding each other in million-pound increments. Well, forget all that. Most sales in the secondary art market in the UK—that is, paintings which have been bought and sold before, rather than fresh off the artist's easel—are conducted in rather less glamorous settings. Dealing with lower-priced, lower-quality lots, provincial auction houses are in fact the backbone of the art market. But they are not often where long-lost Surrealist masterpieces turn up."

Some more generous chuckles, from two women in the back row.

"And yet when you consult the catalogue, there it is, listed in the weekly sale at the Ely Auction Rooms on November 29, 1991. Lot 76: 'Medium Oil Picture.' If we were to take the painting behind me from the wall now, you would see the label with exactly that on the back. Its owner bought it that day via phone bid for four thousand pounds— well over the estimate."

I smiled.

"It is worth considerably more than that now, of course."

Sometimes this thought did pop into my head. That Patrick and I, under different circumstances, might both be really quite rich. Millionaires many times over, surely, given the cult of personality that has grown up around Juliette. It would certainly be worth more than any of Oskar Erlich's works.

I tried to keep my face neutral as my mind flashed back to the horror of that moment in the auction room, the hammer falling, the realization of what we had lost, the absolute bloodlessness of Patrick's face.

I did not blame him. That was what I told Patrick that night, as he paced, as he rubbed his face with his hands, as he swore, as he apologized. Of course I forgave him, I promised. What would have been the point of recrimination? I could not make him feel worse than he already felt. There was still the journal, I reminded him. We still had each other. That was what mattered. I wasn't angry. But even at the time, I suspected that I could keep telling him that for the rest of our lives and he would never quite know whether to believe it.

I willed myself back wholly into the gallery, the moment. It was the official version of history I was supposed to be recounting tonight. The story not of how I had found the painting and lost it but how I had decided, once it later resurfaced, that it was the genuine article.

"There are really three ways in which you can try to authenticate an artwork. The first is to use documentary evidence to establish its provenance. With some paintings, there is a very clear paper trail leading you back to its first owner, to the time and place it was first sold, even the moment of creation. Unfortunately, with *Self-Portrait as Sphinx* that is not the case. We don't even know who the vendor was in 1991, because when the Ely auction rooms closed down a few years later, all their paperwork was lost, most likely shredded or thrown away. What we do have are Juliette's journal, passport, and pendant, which were all seemingly returned to Longhurst Hall after her death, before being bundled up with other material and donated to the University of Cambridge. So there exists proof that at least some of her personal possessions survived the Paris fire. Similarly, we have a photograph of *Self-Portrait as Sphinx* taken at Longhurst in 1961, although we don't know how it got there or what happened to it next, and the Willoughby family have always insisted they have no idea either."

In fact, Philip and Georgina Willoughby had repeatedly and brusquely refused to answer any questions about Juliette, the painting, or the journal, at all.

"The second way to authenticate a painting—or identify a misattribution or fake—is via technical inquiry. We had more to work with here. The signature on Juliette's passport matches very closely the signature on the painting."

I stepped out from behind the podium and crossed to stand directly in front of the painting, drawing a circle in the air around the bottom right corner. The audience, squinting, shifted in their seats.

"Paint analysis ascertained that the pigments used were of *exactly* the same composition as the color swatches daubed in Juliette's journal. The vibrant green you see here," I said, pointing to the robes of the hooded figure, "had traces of arsenic. And the white"—I indicated the dress of the drowned girl—"was laced with lead. Both compounds are now known to be highly poisonous but were still widely used in the 1930s. Radiocarbon dating of the wood and canvas showed them to be the correct age. And then there are the thumbprints on the back, where Juliette handled the frame with paint-covered hands. They match those left in the charcoal sketches in Juliette's journal."

I took another sip of water.

"The third and final factor on which an institution like the Tate relies is expert opinion—which is where someone like me comes in. Someone who has spent their life studying an artist and their work. Someone who is prepared to put a professional reputation they have spent years accumulating on the line. It is a big responsibility, and there can be millions of pounds at stake. But when I was asked my professional verdict on *this* painting, I did not experience a moment's doubt. The subject and the composition of the various scenes playing out across the canvas. Both fit closely with the fragmentary studies pre-served in Juliette's journal. When you take all the evidence together, there can be little reasonable doubt that the work you see behind me is the same remarkable painting that was exhibited by Juliette Willoughby at the 1938 International Surrealist Exhibition."

It was after the lecture, after the audience questions, after the book signing, when I was left to my own devices and the chairs were being packed up, that my phone rang, and I answered it, and once again my life changed forever.

It was Patrick, calling to tell me that a second *Self-Portrait as Sphinx* had been discovered.

PATRICK, DUBAI, 2023, SIX DAYS BEFORE HARRY'S DEATH

I checked my watch. I am always early for meetings with potential buyers, to ensure the stage is correctly set, to check that everything is perfectly arranged.

Dave White was late. This did not surprise me. Dave White was a very rich man indeed, with a string of supermodel girlfriends and an astronomically valuable modern art collection. I was a man with a very expensive piece of modern art to sell. What was worthy of remark was not that Dave White was late but that he was having lunch with me at all.

For years, I had been attempting to sell art to him. Contacting his offices in New York, Dubai, and London whenever we had a piece—he was a collector of Surrealist paintings from the 1920s and 1930s—that I thought might interest him. I had never yet received a single response.

Yesterday at six in the evening, Dubai time, I emailed his people to let them know I had a painting by Juliette Willoughby for sale. Fifteen minutes later Dave White called me personally to suggest we meet for lunch. I asked where he wanted to go. Without clarify-ing who would be paying, he suggested a ninety-seventh-floor sushi restaurant where a meal for two cost the same as a small car. For a moment, I thought he was joking. Then he named a time, told me to book a table, and hung up.

I resisted the urge to check my watch again. He would be here. If only to hear how I had come into possession of an impossible painting, he would be here. I forced myself to ignore the menu—more precisely, the prices on the menu—and to gaze out instead across a sea of white tablecloths through floor-to-ceiling plate glass windows at the desert in the distance.

I had gone to some effort to make a good impression. My watch was a Rolex, not fake. I was in a new Favourbrook suit. One piece of advice my father always gave me was that no one buys anything valuable from a man who looks poor or seems desperate. This being especially true when you were as poor and desperate as I was.

Dave White was almost at the table before I noticed him. He offered me a hand, I offered him mine. He glanced at my watch and a faint smirk appeared on his face. The smirk did not really fade as we sat down.

"Hello, Patrick," he said in a distinctly Brummie accent. He was wearing boardshorts, a Hawaiian shirt, and flip-flops. All around the restaurant I could see people pretending—in their bespoke suits and spotless white kanduras—not to have noticed this. In a corner, I could see two waiters discreetly conferring, probably trying to work out if they recognized him as a regular, to decide whether this man was rich or powerful enough to get away with walking in here as if he had just wandered off the beach.

One of the waiters got his phone out, perhaps attempting to google Dave—a fruitless endeavor, because even if his name had been on the booking, it would not have helped. Like all extremely rich people, Dave White takes great care to ensure that none of his personal information, even his image, ever appears online—which is somewhat ironic, given that most of his fortune was made in facial recognition tech. There are no newspaper or magazine profiles. No Rich List position in the *Sunday Times*. Just one brief mention, in a two-line paragraph of personal information on the website of Vision Corp, the company he founded and still runs.

We exchanged pleasantries. He asked about my gallery and how long I had been based in Dubai, failing to offer any explanation for his delayed arrival. Had he flown in for this occasion specially, I wondered, or just been driven from the villa he was rumored to own on the Palm? I asked if he had made any interesting art acquisitions lately—my sources had told me he already owned two Picassos, six Dalís, a handful of Kahlos, a Delvaux, and a Man Ray, plus at least a dozen Erlichs, including *Three Figures in a Landscape.*

A waiter appeared, seemingly out of nowhere. Dave ordered first—an omakase platter, a mineral water. I resisted the urge to cross-reference his order with the prices, and asked for the sea bass, the second-cheapest item on the menu. I suggested wine and, to my relief, he shook his head.

"Is it true, then?" he asked.

It was true, I said. I had in my possession, and through my gallery was offering for sale, what I believed to be an authentic painting by Juliette Willoughby.

"*Self-Portrait as Sphinx,*" he said.

"A second *Self-Portrait as Sphinx.*"

He shook his head. "That's impossible."

"We have done a full analysis and the results are compelling. The stretchers. The canvas. All dated to the 1930s. Samples of paint match the color notes in Juliette's journal. The signature is a match for the passport and there are thumbprints too. We are also speaking to the world's leading expert on Juliette—"

Dave White cleared his throat. "You don't remember me, do you, Patrick?"

I smiled, a little confused. Remember him from where? He looked like a lot of people I had met in my career, although someone this rich you'd think might stick in memory. Had we been briefly introduced at a biennale? Crossed paths at a private view?

"We were in the same college, Patrick. At Cambridge."

He named the year. He named our college. "Oh, right," I said, although I had no memory of anyone called Dave White. "I'm sure we've all changed a lot since then."

"You used to call me Terry," he said flatly. "You and your friends. People I had never met thought my name really was Terry."

"But your name isn't Terry," I said. I must have looked as baffled as I now felt.

I found myself wondering if this whole situation was some sort of setup. What had he studied? Mathematics? Computer science? Something nerdy, no doubt, given how he had made his cash. Perhaps this was the comeuppance he had dreamed of every time I swept past him on the stairs, off to some party; every time he saw me cross a quad with my beautiful girlfriend. Every time I called him Terry—for whatever fucking reason I used to do that.

"Perhaps I misheard your name when we first met?"

Dave shook his head. "I wore an orange coat, Patrick. I wore an orange raincoat that my mother bought me, and you made a joke about it, and everyone called me Terry for three years."

I let out a chuckle before I could stop myself. The orange coat. Terry's Chocolate Orange. Terry. That did ring a bell, now that I came to think of it. I wondered if the Terry's brand still even existed and, if it did, if those big orange-flavored chocolate balls in their orange foil wrappers were still a staple in kids' Christmas stockings. Dave White's face remained impassive.

"We lived on the same floor, Patrick. In college. I was literally in the room next door to yours the whole final year," he said.

"Of course!" I exclaimed, finally seeing something of the teenage Terry's pinkish, puffy face in the tanned and chiseled one in front of me. "You're Next-Door Terry!"

A smile played across his lips. Not a wholly friendly smile, but a smile nonetheless. "I was Next-Door Terry back then, yes. But we're not here to talk about old times, are we, Patrick?"

I found myself smiling too, in nervous relief. There had been a horrible moment when I thought he was just going to order a magnum of vintage Krug, tell me what a prick I had been, and walk out leaving me the bill.

"Right, yes, good idea," I said, thankful for the change of subject. "The painting was found at Longhurst, by Harry Willoughby, a direct descendant of—"

He cuts me off. "I know who Harry Willoughby is. I was at his twenty-first too."

Were you? That was my first thought. Then I remembered that table of oddballs.

Dave White asked me why I thought Harry had come to me, to the Lambert Gallery, rather than to any of the big London auction houses. The real answer was simple: Harry wanted as much money as possible, as quickly as possible. This was not the answer I gave, naturally, because selling art at this level is 1 percent expertise, 99 percent PR.

"Well, for one thing, because we're old friends, and for another, as you know, the Middle East is one of the most exciting art markets in the world, with multiple major institutions actively acquiring—the Louvre in Abu Dhabi, multiple new galleries in Saudi—not to mention some very wealthy private collectors . . ."

It never hurts to let potential buyers know they are not the only people interested in a painting.

"And you genuinely believe it's authentic?" he asked curtly. "Because I really don't see how it can be. I've done my homework. Juliette was working on *Self-Portrait as Sphinx* right up to the time she put it on display. There is no mention of any other versions of the painting in her journal. There was no *time* for her to paint any others . . ."

"And yet here we are," I said, shrugging. "As I say, we are flying out the world's leading expert to give her verdict in the next few days."

"Caroline Cooper," he said. "Your ex-wife."

"She is also my ex-wife," I conceded, a little reluctantly.

"So how are things between the two of you now?"

I mumbled something about things being perfectly amicable. They were certainly more amicable than they had been. It was five years since the divorce, after all. I was married to someone else now. From time to time, Caroline and I ran into each other at events in London, and we had always been perfectly civil. Once or twice, when I had a question about something that fell within her area of expertise, I called to get her opinion.

"And you are sure she's going to come?"

It was a reasonable question. After all, Caroline had authenticated the painting in Tate Modern and then spent a career writing and talking about it. I could hear it in her voice on the phone, her shock at what I was telling her, the steady dawning of the professional implications if this new version of the painting proved authentic. Perhaps even the faint suspicion that I might be enjoying springing all this on her.

But if Dave White was fishing for details about how the marriage had ended and why, I was not going to satisfy his curiosity. One of our strengths as a couple had always been a reluctance to air our dirty laundry. Caroline and I had both done things, said things, of which we were not proud, and had hurt each other in ways we couldn't have imagined possible. Love was never uncomplicated for Caroline, nor was that something which could be cured just by meeting the right person. The first time I proposed, she would not speak to me for a week, and then it took two more tries before she said yes. Even on our wedding day, as I was standing at the altar, part of me wondered whether she would actually show up. But there was no part of me that wondered whether she would come now.

"She'll be here," I told Dave.

She would come because when she examined the photos I had emailed her, she would see exactly the same thing I had: that this new painting was no straightforward copy of the painting in Tate Modern. Because as Caroline would recognize—even more swiftly than I had—there were two subtle but very suggestive differences between them. Two significant details which did not match up and which might shed light on the riddle she had spent decades trying to unravel.

She would come, I promised Dave, and myself.

Because if Caroline did not come, I thought as the bill for lunch landed on the table and Dave watched me pull out my wallet without reaching for his own, I was absolutely fucked.

JULIETTE, PARIS, 1938

There are some things that can never be written down.

We had to leave. Oskar and I. That was what I kept telling him. That it was not safe there. That if my uncle knew I was in Paris, then my father would know, and if my father knew where I was . . .

I was letting my nerves get the best of me. That was what Oskar kept insisting. Every time he caught me peeking around the curtain down into our courtyard, flinching at a tread on the staircase. I was not painting. I could not settle to read. Leaving the apartment, even popping around the corner to buy dinner or a little wire-wrapped bundle of firewood from the street seller, was an ordeal. As for my journal, I was far too unsettled to write in it, even if I had wanted to. The very idea of committing my thoughts to paper appalled me. Instead, the words swirled around in my brain. More than once, Oskar caught me in the kitchen muttering to myself, or had to shake me awake at night to tell me I had been babbling incoherently in my sleep.

In a moment of panic, I hid my journal and passport in the heavy-lidded cast-iron pot we used for soup, placing it on the highest shelf in the kitchen. Without my passport, my thinking went, how could my uncle force me to return to England? In that hidden journal, at least some part of my true story was preserved for others to read, some trace of my existence.

If I fell again into my family's clutches, I was certain that I would be spending the rest of my life back in an asylum. Some nights, I dreamed in horror that I was there already, being made to detail to a doctor precisely what *Self-Portrait as Sphinx* meant. One night, after the third or fourth time I had woken him up with my gasps and twitching and insistent mumbling, Oskar angrily went off with a blanket to sleep on a chair.

I had never seen him as surly and abrasive before.

He was angry that I had withdrawn my painting so abruptly from the exhibition, especially given the excitement it had generated. He was even angrier that no one had bought his painting yet.

I wanted to leave, to run. Not to England. Not Germany. Perhaps, I said, I could see a future for us in New York. Finally, reluctantly, after much nagging, Oskar went to the American embassy.

I could hear just from his boots on the stairs that the expedition had not been a success. He kicked them off at the door, their heels slamming against the wall. "Idiots," was his only comment as he threw himself down onto the bed in our room. A cloud of dust rose and settled. *"Idioten."* Both of us aware that for the classical Greeks, an idiot was simply someone who took no interest in public affairs. Like a man tasked with allocating passports, who has a number of boxes he is permitted to tick and can find no combination of them that can accommodate an applicant with a German name and a German accent, whose parents are German and whose first language is German but whose hometown is now, after the end of the last war, solidly in Polish territory.

Oskar had, aware of the line of people behind him, attempted to give a condensed history of the Kingdom of Galicia and Lodomeria, from the eighteenth century onward, believing that if he explained things clearly enough, emphatically enough, then all the bureaucratic petti-fogging could be swept to one side and some arrangement arrived at. I could imagine the sinking spirits of the desk clerk, as on and on Oskar thundered, the shuffling resentment of those waiting behind him. The response, inevitably, being: had he tried the Polish embassy?

All afternoon, I sat in our apartment and listened to the flat metallic ticking of the clock, wondering if it had always been that loud. All day long, all night long, that ticking.

Then, all of a sudden, it seemed as if Oskar and I might have a future after all.

He had been out for lunch with friends (I turned the invitation down, as he knew I would), and when he arrived back he announced before I even said hello that he had found a man who could get us passports, who could take care of all the immigration paperwork for the United States. We would both have new identities—for the journey, at least. Oskar would be French. For reasons of plausibility, because it was the only language in which I was fluent, I would remain English. He would no longer be a stateless Galician. Juliette Willoughby would have vanished from Paris without a trace.

"So this fellow is a forger?" I asked.

"A very good one," said Oskar. A lot of people in this man's line of work, explained Oskar, had trained as artists. He was known, in our circle. People had vouched for him.

"Are you sure about this?" I asked.

It was all arranged, Oskar said. He must meet the man at a certain café, with our photographs. Within three hours, he would return with our new passports. We could take the pictures ourselves, with that little Leica camera Oskar had given me for my birthday, and develop them here, in the apartment.

"We can *leave*," Oskar said. All we needed to do once we had those passports was to buy our tickets. Six hours to Le Havre. Within twenty-four, we could be in sight of the cliffs of Dover. And then? It had to be America, I told him. The new world. A new life. New York. He took my face in his hands, kissed me. Yet his smile had something a little cracked in it, like he could not quite believe all this either. As if there was a catch he had yet to spring on me. All we need now is the money, he said.

Then he told me how much money.

CHAPTER 13

CAROLINE, LONGHURST, 2023, FIVE DAYS BEFORE HARRY'S DEATH

"Hello, Harry," I said. "Thanks so much for agreeing to see me on short notice."

"Caroline!" Harry said, hesitating a moment before embracing me in an awkward hug. "Of course, of course, you're always welcome here."

We both knew that had not always been the case. For decades, as Juliette's biographer, I had been petitioning Harry's parents (through Harry, or by letter and email) for access to the house at Longhurst, feeling there were aspects of Juliette's personality, elements of *Self-Portrait as Sphinx*, that being here would help me decode. *Not a chance* was the answer I always got, via Harry, apologetically.

"Once my parents have made up their mind about something, or someone . . . ," he would regretfully begin, before trailing off. "And I can't say you made a great first impression at my twenty-first."

In the end, all it took to arrange a visit was one of the Willoughbys having something to gain financially from saying yes.

The painting itself was already in Dubai with Patrick, but I wanted to hear from Harry's own lips how and where he had found it. Nor was that all I wanted to investigate at Longhurst Hall.

"Well, Harry's in the process of selling the place," Patrick had advised. "So it may well be your last and only chance to visit before it changes hands."

I had seen the estate agent's listing online, so I knew that the house was in a bad way. What I had not been prepared for was the state Harry himself was in. He looked not only much older than I was expecting, but a lot less well. In my mind, he was forever fixed the way he had looked at university: flushed, cherubic, with buttery curls. Now his frame was angular and slight, his hair reduced to fluffy duckling tufts around the temples. He was wearing a shirt that might once have fitted but was now several sizes too big, with red corduroy trousers worn shiny at the knees and bunched at the waist with an ancient cracked leather belt.

Admittedly, it had been a long time since we last met. Harry had been at our wedding, and a few times the three of us had been out for dinner, usually somewhere stuffy and expensive, at Harry's suggestion, although somehow Patrick always picked up the bill—Harry never seemed to have the right wallet with him or the right credit card. Since then, I had caught Harry on TV too, interviewed in the lobby of the House of Commons, or sent out to defend the government's position on *Newsnight*. For a Cambridge graduate with such lofty political ambitions, his career had been surprisingly unspectacular, marred by the MP's expenses scandal and the discovery that he had claimed tens of thousands in taxpayer money for repairs at Longhurst. Shortly after the scandal broke in the newspapers, Harry announced his decision not to contest his seat at the upcoming election.

"It's freezing," he blustered, waving me in off the doorstep. "Come in out of the cold."

It was actually far colder *inside* the house, the kind of chill you get in a building in which the heat has not been turned on for a very long time.

"Can I offer you a cup of tea? Something stronger . . . ?" he asked.

I said I would take a tea. It was eleven thirty in the morning. Although from the way he was stumbling and shuffling, the sudden odd lurches a step or two sideways, I did wonder if Harry had attempted to warm himself up with a nip of something already.

He led me to a sitting room, where he had promised a fire was burning. This turned out to be an enormous hearth with a single smoldering log. There was a plastic kettle on a trolley in the corner, which he filled from a battered Evian bottle. He opened the window to grab a pint of milk from the ledge and I realized that I was standing in exactly the room where Harry's grandmother and father had been when she demanded *Self-Portrait as Sphinx* be found and burned.

"It's not the ideal setup for receiving guests. But I've accepted an offer on the house and there is a lot to pack up and clear out, so I'm living in just a few rooms. I've been sleeping in the east wing, the oldest part of the house. The walls are thicker, so it's slightly warmer."

This room remained an extraordinary space, even half empty—elaborate but injured plasterwork ceiling (chipped cherubs, denuded fruit baskets), overlapping moth-eaten rugs, and a dusty chandelier. On top of a grand piano were family photos. While he busied himself with the tea bags, I picked up a silver frame. The picture showed Harry and his parents, smiling stiffly in front of a Christmas tree.

"My mother passed away last year. I'm not sure if you heard? Father died a few years ago," Harry said, handing me a steaming mug. I pretended not to notice the way his hand quivered.

"I had no idea. I'm so sorry for your loss," I said.

"Thank you. At least they'll never know if I end up losing this place because of the inheritance tax. Millions, the taxman wants. Millions! Outrageous."

He glanced around as if to underline the absurdity of it all. I tried to look as sympathetic as I could.

"Anyway, they both lived long and full lives, so at least that's something," Harry said, and it struck me how many people associated with this house hadn't. Juliette and Lucy dying so young, Jane Herries and Freddie Talbot simply vanishing.

Occasionally, when I gave a talk on Juliette, someone at the end would ask whether I believed in the Willoughby curse. My answer was always no. Definitely not. What I *could* understand was why, faced with so much tragedy, people might feel a strange comfort in the idea that there was at least some organizing logic behind it all.

"Is that from the night of your party?" I gestured toward a photo of Harry in a lineup of fresh-faced, dressed-up young men on Longhurst's terrace. Harry nodded.

"All the members of Osiris. Ivo Strang. Benjy Taylor. Arno von Westernhagen. Eric Lam. And Freddie, of course. That's how I always picture him still: in white tie, sipping champagne. Poor Freddie. For years I think we all expected him to come sauntering back into our lives one day. That's why he has never been legally declared dead, you know, why there has never been any sort of official memorial service, because nobody in the family ever wanted to admit the obvious. And then you realize ten years have passed, twenty . . ."

I remembered Athena's tear-stained face when she told me he had vanished. Over and over I had replayed that morning, my clumsy attempts to reassure her, too distracted to apologize properly. Often in the past thirty years I had tried to imagine what more I might have done in the weeks after to stop her from pushing me away.

Harry and I both fell silent for a moment.

"Anyway," he said eventually. "That's not why you're here. Did you have anything specifically you wanted to know about the painting?"

I nodded. "Can I ask where you found it? Patrick said you were clearing out one of the bedrooms?"

Patrick's name felt a little odd in my mouth, and I realized I had been putting off saying it. Even now, I was never entirely sure how much his old friends knew about how our marriage had ended, how they would respond to seeing me, what they had heard and from whom.

It is hard to explain exactly how a partnership implodes, but I have sometimes wondered if the issue was not us but marriage itself—or at least the wedding. Because up until then, he and I had been two people who loved each other, trying every day to make each other happy. Then suddenly we were planning a Big Day and all these other people were involved, with their own expectations. For the first time, I saw how much Patrick had internalized his father's little snobberies, how much it mattered to Patrick to impress him. I'll never forget the look Patrick gave me when I suggested, in front of his dad, that we might have cava instead of champagne. The unshakable opinions Patrick suddenly seemed to hold on cutlery-related matters, whether the cheese course was served before or after dessert. Which might have been fine if he was the one doing all the organizing, but of course he wasn't. I had a book to write, and plenty of other things to do, and for me the wedding felt like admin for a job I had never applied for—especially since the only person coming from my side of the family was my grandmother, and at every stage of the planning process someone would ask me about my parents.

I hoped that after the wedding, we could get back to the way we had been, but somehow, on some level, we never seemed to. The older we got, the more different we grew, and the less either of us felt like those two people who had fallen in love with each other.

Fortunately, Harry did not seem inclined to ask anything much on the topic of my divorce at all. It was very much the painting he was focused on.

"I was clearing out the Green Room," he said. "And it was in a cupboard, along with a whole load of other paintings. Basically every time it rains this house is like a bloody colander. So over time all the good furniture, all the paintings, migrated into fewer and fewer rooms, into wardrobes and cupboards, for safety. I can show you exactly where I found it, if you like?"

As he led me upstairs and through the house, all sorts of memories seemed to rise and swirl. Some of the rooms and corridors and objects I vividly remembered. Others I had forgotten completely.

Despite it being barely midday, it was almost completely dark once we got away from the end of the house Harry was living in, all the curtains drawn, all the shutters closed. Harry stopped and opened a door. We were at once assailed with a smell of damp and mold.

"The wardrobe I found the painting in was over there," he said, pointing to a space by the fireplace, where its outline could still be seen on the faded botanical-print wallpaper.

"You recognized it at once?" I asked, before realizing with a wince how patronizing that sounded.

"Well, yes," he said, bristling ever so slightly. "It is quite a famous painting, thanks to you, Professor Cooper."

"Something I have been wondering about is why the first person you contacted was Patrick, not a big auction house or a Mayfair gallery?" I asked.

We exited the room and Harry invited me with a gesture to make my way back down the hall. "Sentimentality, I suppose. I trust Patrick, like my father trusted his father. It was also part practicality—auction houses don't work at speed, and I really need this sale to happen quickly."

"By the end of the month, Patrick said. Do you mind my asking why?"

"Not at all. Although I expect you can probably guess. That's when I'm meant to exchange contracts on this place, the point of no return. But if the painting is worth what Patrick says it is, I won't have to be the Willoughby who loses Longhurst, will I?" he said with a sigh. "I might even be able to stop the bloody place falling down around my ears . . ."

He turned to me, fixing me with a beady eye. "What do *you* reckon, by the way, about the value of the thing?"

"What a painting is worth has never been my area, I'm afraid. My part in the process is solely to reach a conclusion about whether or not it is really by Juliette," I explained. The trouble was, we already had a *Self-Portrait with Sphinx* on public display in a national institution. Any minute now I was expecting a call from Tate Modern, asking me what this all meant, or from my publisher, concerned that the painting on the cover of five million books was a fake. Which would make me something of a fake, too, I supposed. And the one thing I couldn't tell any of them—and Patrick swore he hadn't ever so much as hinted to Harry—was that a large part of my confidence in that work's authenticity had always come from the fact that I had originally stolen it myself, from this very house.

"But since *my* painting was actually found at Longhurst . . ." Harry looked at me expectantly.

I said nothing. I had no way of explaining how even one copy of the work had survived the fire in Paris, let alone two.

What prevented me from dismissing this new painting as something a desperate Harry had commissioned from a forger was that it was clear from the photos Patrick emailed me that his wasn't a straightforward copy. Forgers did not introduce their own artistic flourishes into the work they were imitating, and Harry's painting undoubtedly differed from the accepted original. The other problem was that since these were all small details we were talking about, unreadable in the murky image from the Witt Library, it was impossible to tell which of the two paintings had been photographed here in 1961.

"What I need to unpack are the differences between the works, and what that might mean," I told Harry. "Whether they might hold some clue as to which is authentic or what the relationship between them is. As far as I can see, there are two significant differences: first, in the bottom right of both paintings, there is an image of a hooded boatman, steering a vessel across dark waters to an island."

It was an image that vividly echoed the boat and robed figure in the papyrus I had seen in the Osiris society's collection of Egyptiana, that ripped fragment from which the head was missing. Which was one of those odd echoes I had spent years pondering, a strange connection between Cyril's collection of Egyptian artifacts and his daughter's lost masterpiece.

"In the version of *Self-Portrait as Sphinx* on display at Tate Modern, the boatman is just a hooded figure, faceless. In this version, he has a beak."

"A beak? Like a bird?" Harry asked.

"Like an Egyptian god," I replied.

Indeed, as far as I could see, the two differing details in the newly discovered work amplified the painting's Egyptian, mythological resonances, suggesting the possibility of the sort of symbolic reading that had always eluded me. What that might mean in terms of its authenticity, I could not yet be sure.

"So what's the second difference?" asked Harry.

"The second difference is that where in the Tate version of the painting, there is just a barren landscape in the bottom left, in yours there is something written in hieroglyphics. An eye, a set of scales, two feathers, a different kind of eye, a hawk."

Harry asked me what it meant.

"I'm afraid I don't read hieroglyphics, but a colleague has promised to take a look at it," I told him.

The phrase had looked strangely familiar, though, which was one of the reasons I was here.

We were passing the turn on the staircase, near the entrance to the east wing with the heavy oak door, the very door through which I had slipped thirty years ago to find the painting. I stopped and rested one hand on Harry's arm and pointed up at the lintel with the other. I felt a little leap in my stomach. Just as I remembered, in gilt lettering over the doorway was the same sequence of hieroglyphics: an eye, a set of scales, two feathers, a different kind of eye, and a hawk.

"Do you see?" I asked Harry.

Harry grunted, nodded, rubbed his chin. He was clearly thinking about something.

"There's something else you ought to see," he said.

WHAT HARRY WANTED TO show me involved us rowing over to the island. I did have some safety concerns about this. Not to do with the boat, which looked reasonably seaworthy. Not even because this was the lake in which Lucy had drowned. Mostly because the more time he and I spent together, the more worried I was about him. He was tuning in and out of our conversation with alarming frequency, several times asking me the exact same question twice in quick succession. On our way down to the lake, he found it hard to stick to the curving path of mossy cobbles. But I could not smell alcohol on him, nor once the old wooden boat was in the water did he struggle to steer us in the right direction, or keep his oars in sync. He leaned forward, he pulled back, and over the otherwise undisturbed water we skimmed.

On the island, all that remained of what had once been a jetty were three rotten wood stumps. We pulled the boat up onto the pebbles of a little beach and placed the oars in the hull. Harry brought a handkerchief out of his trouser pocket and dabbed his brow. The path was almost entirely overgrown. We picked our way down it, Harry in the lead, pausing occasionally to gently lift a thorny branch out of the way or kick at a clump of nettles. After a while we reached the pyramid. The tomb which, in a tragic twist of events, Cyril's beloved elder daughter, Lucy, had been the first to occupy, and in which Cyril too was later laid to rest, although his wife had insisted on being buried in the consecrated Church of England cemetery in the village instead.

Harry, out of breath, stood for a minute with his hands on his thighs. Then, with a glance back at me, he pointed up at what was carved into the entrance to the tomb: an eye, a set of scales, two feathers, a different kind of eye, and a hawk.

PATRICK, DUBAI, 2023,
FOUR DAYS BEFORE HARRY'S DEATH

Late evening has always been my favorite time in Dubai. Sitting out on our villa's terrace after dinner as the heat dies down, a gin and tonic in hand, a warm breeze rattling the date palms, a swallow occasionally dipping and diving and ruffling the surface of the swimming pool.

"Would you swap all this for a flat in Islington?" Sarah sometimes asks me.

"I wouldn't swap it for a house in Mayfair," I always reply.

The pollution. The crime. The weather. You almost forget here, opening the curtains on yet another day of sun, what rainy England is like, everyone sneezing on the tube, those November days it barely gets light at all.

It was not the weather that drew me here, though.

Sarah and I met at a dinner during Art Dubai three years ago—I spoke to the attractive Australian woman sitting next to me about the elaborate table decorations; she turned out to have designed them. We got talking. She had lived here for a decade and really sold the place to me. She was amazed—she thought I was joking—when I told her that this was my third visit and I had barely ventured beyond the art fair. I should get out into the desert, she told me. Camp under the stars. Go sailing. How long was I in town for?

I was here for a week and I ended up doing something with Sarah every day that I had never done in my life before. Scuba diving. Dune bashing. Waterskiing. She was the kind of person, she said, who believed you always had to keep trying new things. Being with her made me feel I could be that sort of person too. I was certainly sick of the man I had become, drinking too much, smoking too much, dwelling on the past.

When I was with Sarah I felt younger, and more optimistic than I had in years. It was not until my last night in Dubai that we slept together. A month later I was back again. Three weeks after that, she came to stay with me in London. It was bad timing—the boiler in my flat was acting up, the rent on my Dover Street gallery had just been hiked for the third time in as many years, and on the plane Sarah picked up (and then gave me) an absolutely stinking cold.

All the time she was there, she kept telling me how exciting the art scene was in Dubai, what a fabulous time it would be to move there. Why not get away from all this? Why not start afresh? I proposed at Heathrow Airport. She said yes immediately, eyes damp, visibly delighted I was down on one knee with an antique diamond ring next to the check-in. I was intoxicated by the joyful ease of the entire thing.

Within the year, I had sold my gallery in London and moved. To launch a new gallery. To begin a new life.

There were times when it felt like that might have been a bit hasty. As it turns out, you could get bored of sunsets. You could get tired of the beach. You could get sick of constantly having to project success, exude confidence, muster up charm. You could start to wonder whether you were actually deluding yourself, questioning if it had actually been a smart move to sell everything you owned back home to set up a new business in the UAE, a country in which you knew precisely one person. You could, in your darker moments, start to feel a creeping doubt about whether that one person was in fact the right one person for you.

"You're having a midlife crisis," was Caroline's only comment when I told her I was emigrating. I put this down to jealousy at the time. In retrospect, she may have been right.

It was a gamble, the move, the new gallery, the loans I had taken out to do both, and I was losing. Unless Harry's sale came off, unless I could persuade Caroline and she could help me persuade the world that Harry's painting was authentic, and we could find someone to buy it, I would be bankrupt in weeks. I would lose the business. I would lose this house. Nor was that the worst of it.

"Does she understand?" Sarah kept asking me, "Have you told her what happens when you go bankrupt here? She can't wish that on you, can she?"

It would not help, I said, putting pressure on Caroline, trying to influence her professional judgment. You couldn't pay most academics for their involvement in authenticating works for that very reason—they were terrified of being accused of underhanded dealings. Nevertheless, the truth was I was one painting away from bankruptcy in a country in which going bankrupt landed you in prison. Nor was skipping the country an option—I'd be handcuffed at passport control.

I was just thinking about easing myself up off my chair and heading inside for another drink when my phone rang.

Sarah glanced at it. "It's her," she said, an edge to her voice, gesturing for me to answer.

I sat upright and picked up the phone.

"Caroline! How did the trip to Longhurst go?"

"Fine. I mean, Harry looked like a sad ghost, wandering around those halls, and I have concerns about him, health-wise. But the visit was useful. Actually that's why I'm calling. This painting, the pictures you sent. You mentioned two differences between yours and the one in Tate Modern. Have you got yours there with you?"

"I'm afraid not. I'm at home. The painting is in the gallery, where it's safe," I said. Where I had invested in quite a lot of extra security measures, to ensure that it was safe, at no small cost.

"How long would it take you to drive there?"

"At this time of night? Fifteen minutes, probably."

"Patrick. There's a third difference. Between the paintings."

Twenty minutes later, I was climbing out of a cab at the Dubai International Financial Centre. The gallery was locked, of course. It was almost ten o'clock at night. I typed the code into the keypad and closed the door carefully behind me. Caroline had said she would call back in half an hour. I was standing in front of the painting when she did.

"Well?" she asked me.

"I'm not seeing it," I said.

"Look more closely at the bottom right section."

I did so.

"Jesus, you're right," I told her, a fizz of excitement gathering between my shoulder blades. "It's in the boat, isn't it. There's something lying in the boat."

"Exactly, exactly!" She sounded triumphant. "That's what I mean. A white shape. But what is it? I've been sitting here zooming in on your photos, but I can't quite make it out. Can you?"

I held up my phone and turned on its flashlight. Squinting, holding my breath, I leaned in closer, the sharp beam of light illuminating the normally invisible craquelure in the painting's varnish.

I carefully stepped to the side and held my phone up at a different angle.

"I think it's a body," I said. "A body all cross-crossed with bandages. That's what it is, the object in the boat. A mummified body."

JULIETTE, PARIS, 1938

The exhibition ended and with it our dream of escape.

Oskar's painting had not sold, nor in all these weeks had he started on anything new. I could understand that. For as long as I had known him, he had been working on *Three Figures in a Landscape*, convinced this was his masterpiece, a work that would attract derision and scorn and praise and acclaim, a work that would set the critics searching for superlatives, and buyers scrambling for their checkbooks.

Instead, it had been met with almost total silence. Barely mentioned in most of the reviews. His embarrassment—and mine—only compounded by the fact that in terms of column inches, the painting I had withdrawn from the exhibition was attracting more comment than his, which remained on display.

Embarrassment is perhaps too mild a word. By the third week of February, when the exhibition ended, the situation was excruciating. Every day Oskar would get up in the morning and grimly select one of his unfinished canvases, add a few touches, then return it dejectedly next to the others. Every afternoon he would go for long walks, or find some bar to sulk in. He was out past midnight every night. When he was home, he could hardly bear to look at me, and refused to look at *Self-Portrait as Sphinx* at all—he turned it around to face the wall, like a naughty child.

I had tried to explain to him my decision to withdraw it from public display. Still, I could not get him to understand why I was so afraid. "What can your family do, even if they find us?" he would ask mockingly. "You are not a minor. This is not England. You are here of your own free will."

It was weeks since I had been outside, and Oskar kept badgering me to leave the apartment. It was for my own good, he insisted. I was still not painting. I was barely eating. Did I really think it was possible for me, for us, to go on like this much longer? Even if my uncle was still in Paris, Oskar pointed out, how did I think he would have found out my address? Oskar reminded me that of all his artist friends, only Breton had ever been here, once, to see our paintings. It was an international exhibition in which our work had been shown, he would repeat, with fourteen countries listed in the catalogue. There was nothing in the catalogue to connect me to Paris. There was nothing in the catalogue to connect Oskar and me. As far as my uncle knew I could be in Spain, Italy, America, Japan.

Eventually, I gave in.

It felt strange to be out in the world among people again. To walk the banks of the Seine, water brightly sparkling. To feel the cold breeze on my face. I kept seeing things and thinking, *I must remember to tell Oskar about that.*

But when I got back to the apartment, Oskar was gone. And so was my painting.

The rest of the day I sat there, waiting for him to return, trying to distract myself. I started the kettle going and wandered off, confused moments later at the shrill noise coming from the stovetop and the ceiling roiling with steam. I made cups of tea and did not drink them. The light changed. The room grew dim. Dinnertime came and went. It was just before eight when his footsteps fell on the stairs, their uneven clatter making it clear how drunk Oskar was. The ancient banister complained when he put his weight on it. I could hear him muttering to himself as he fumbled his key out of his pocket and began attempting to jam it into the lock. When at last he did manage to get the door open, he came practically tumbling into the room.

When he saw me sitting there, arms folded, legs crossed, face stony, it took him a moment to readjust his focus. When he bent forward to kiss me—I did not react—I could smell the stale cigarettes on his breath. His stubble scraped my cheek.

"Before you say anything," he said, holding one hand up, reaching into the pocket of his jacket with the other. He extricated a large brown envelope, turning his pocket lining inside out in the process, and threw it on the kitchen table.

"What is that?" I said, making a point of not looking, a touch of Willoughby hauteur chilling my voice. Some people boil and hiss and pop when they are angry. I freeze. To the casual observer, perhaps even to Oskar, I might have appeared perfectly calm.

"Passports," he said, a sloppy grin spreading across his face. "Our new passports. Train tickets. Boat tickets. All in our new names. This is what you wanted, isn't it? A clean break with the past? A new start in the new world?"

Our ship was due to sail from Le Havre the following afternoon. There was a moment when the future seemed to open up brightly before the two of us. New lives. Then I asked him how he paid for all this. What had happened to my painting.

He grew furtive. I asked about my painting again and it all came tumbling out. About the gentleman—a real *gentleman*, Oskar emphasized, English, educated, a serious collector—he had bumped into at the café the other day. Who had sidled over and asked if he was Oskar

Erlich. Who had talked to him about his work. Who inquired about his *Three Figures in a Landscape* and the work displayed next to it, my painting, and why it had been withdrawn. "What could I tell him?" said Oskar. "I said no one knows except the artist herself."

I could feel my nails digging into the softness of my palms, my face growing taut. "An English gentleman?" I said. "You fucking fool."

Oskar sneered, the way he always did when women swore. And then he went that color he did when someone calls him a fool. His fists were flexing, the veins on the back of them standing up. I had never seen him so angry. I looked around for something to ward him off with, if he lost control. There was a fork on the table. There was the little knife Oskar used to scrape paint off old canvases on the corner of the sink.

"A fool, am I?" he said. "A *fucking fool?*"

As he was saying it, he reached into the inner pocket of the breast of his coat, and when his hand emerged it had another envelope in it. He threw it on the table and it landed with a thump.

"Open it," he said. "Count it."

"You stole my painting," I hissed, shaking my head. "You stole my painting and you sold it."

He told me again to open the second envelope. I refused.

"Tell me his name," I said.

"George Brown," he said in an attempt at an English accent. "His name was George Brown."

Describe him, I demanded. Oskar did so. And with every detail, my heart sank further. The long narrow face. The tidy mustache. The slicked-back blond hair with the comb marks visible. My uncle. He had been drinking all day with my uncle. He had sold my painting for an envelope of cash, to my uncle. I called him a fucking fool again, then I picked up the envelope and threw it, hard, in his face.

That was when he hit me. An open-handed slap with all his strength across my face that left my ears ringing, my jaw numb, and a taste of blood in my mouth. And he kept coming. His eyes blank with fury, he kept coming at me. He swung again and missed, knocking the rickety table across the room. I stumbled backward, up against the sink.

I raised my arms to defend myself, not really thinking about what I was holding, vaguely aware of one of my hands having closed around something on the edge of the sink. He lunged at me again, as if to seize me by the throat, and as he lunged I felt a jolt in my palm. When I looked down, I saw that it was the palette knife I had been holding, intending to wave it at him, to bring him to his senses.

But now it was embedded handle-deep in his chest, the shirt puckered around it, the blood spreading dark and sticky. And for a moment it looked like he was going to laugh, like it was absurd that I had thought this little thing was going to hurt him, like he might pluck it out and cast it across the room and then there would really be trouble.

Instead, even as he was reaching for it, even as he was formulating something to say, his knees went, and he came crashing down onto them, shouldering one of the kitchen chairs aside as he did so. Then he let out a groan. Then he fell forward, knife handle first, onto the floorboards.

CHAPTER 14

PATRICK, DUBAI, 2023,
THREE DAYS BEFORE HARRY'S DEATH

I was in the back of a taxi when my phone buzzed in my jacket pocket with a message from my assistant at the gallery: *Check your email.* Moments before, Tate Modern had issued an official statement, and she had sent it straight over. It read:

> *We have been made aware that a second version of Self-Portrait as Sphinx, the Juliette Willoughby painting which has been on loan to us since 2000, is being offered for sale as an authentic work. While we have no reasons for concern over the authenticity of the painting in Tate Modern, its owner has requested it be removed from display pending further analysis.*

So there it was. The cat was officially out of the bag. A bit earlier than I had anticipated or hoped. Still, that might be a good thing, I told myself. A load of media attention, the whiff of scandal, could actually be useful in pushing up the painting's price. Or it could scare buyers off. It was impossible to know. By far the highest-profile potential sale of my career, this was uncharted territory for me.

Just to make it all feel even less real, here I was at the Desert Palm Polo Club, very much not one of my usual haunts. Climbing out of the taxi—I could see a long line of expensive cars waiting for the valet—I gave my name at the door, took a seat at the bar, and ordered a beer. As I was waiting to be served, my phone buzzed again with new messages: someone from the art magazine *Apollo*, asking if it was true about the painting. Another from Harry saying that Giles Pemberton, now chief art critic at the *Sunday Times*, had phoned to ask him the same. And one from Caroline confirming that she had booked her flight out to see the painting in person.

Thank God for that, I thought.

Thumbing in speedy replies to each, I didn't notice one of Sarah's friends, Jerry Wilson, as he approached. A British expat of thirty years' standing, with a penchant for panama hats and striped blazers, he was always good value at a dinner party if you were in the mood for stories about the old days here.

"Patrick! Don't think I've seen you at the polo before. Know anyone playing?"

I shook my head. "Meeting an old university friend for a picnic, actually. You don't happen to know where . . . ?"

"They'll be over on the far side of the pitch," said Jerry. "Members enclosure. *Very* VIP. I'll walk you over if you like."

As we strolled, I waved hello to a few familiar faces. One of the things I hadn't anticipated before moving here was how many people I would end up sort of knowing, or would turn out to sort of know already. Friends of friends, boys from school, art world émigrés, college acquaintances, like Dave White, who would suddenly pop up at a party or be sitting at the next table in a restaurant. People like Athena Galanis, whom I was here today to meet.

It might be three decades since we had been at university together, but I had recognized Athena instantly the first time I spotted her at a private event here, last year. Sky-high heels, waist-length hair, tasteful diamonds (but lots of them). When I asked what she was doing there, my assistant informed me that she was an art advisor, a very rich woman helping very rich friends invest sensibly in the art market and pick out the perfect blue chip pieces to fill their available wall space. As she said it, I did vaguely recall that Athena had grown up in Dubai, that her father was a big deal in something here—construction, I think, although Eric Lam had always insisted it was actually much murkier than that, which might have explained at least some of Freddie's reluctance to introduce her to the family as his girlfriend.

I had spoken to Athena briefly at that event—we swapped cards and said we should get a date in the diary to meet. But we never did, until this morning, when she had suddenly decided a catch-up was overdue and called with an invitation. I suppose it was part of her job, keeping her ear to the ground. I did feel a little disloyal to Caroline accepting—given how close she and Athena had been, it always seemed to me extravagantly cruel for Athena (whatever the circumstances) to have ended their friendship so coldly, so abruptly, so finally.

Even years afterward, whenever Caroline talked about it, it was clear how hurt she still was. Well into her late twenties, she kept trying to reach out, to attempt a reconciliation. We looked for Athena on Friends Reunited when that became a thing, then on Facebook. She was not on LinkedIn or Instagram. We googled her name on a fairly regular basis, but nothing ever came up. Like Dave White, I suspected, Athena was wealthy enough that she made herself unsearchable.

Jerry and I parted ways at the gate to the VIP enclosure.

"Patrick!" Athena shouted over from where she was standing, signaling for someone to collect me.

It was an extraordinary sight. What most people probably think of, when they think of Dubai. Docile camels with Cartier-logo blankets on their backs flanked the entrance. Beyond that, a row of well-spaced Bentleys, Aston Martins and Rolls-Royces had been allowed to pull up, picnic blankets laid out beside them. At each, groups of guests lounged—women in blousy dresses and abayas, men in pastel suits and pristine kanduras—and around all of these hovered staff dispensing drinks, unpacking baskets of food.

"So glad you could make it!" She air-kissed me three times in a cloud of perfume. "Everyone, this is Patrick—a Cambridge friend of mine. In fact, we did art history together."

There were lots of faces I recognized—big-time collectors, high-end dealers, and an auctioneer from Sotheby's. Precisely the sort of people I had been attempting to cultivate ever since I had first arrived in Dubai. A white-gloved waiter offered me a champagne flute on a silver tray, another proffered a platter of caviar-topped blinis. We all made small talk about the heat, a lackluster exhibition that had just opened at the Louvre Abu Dhabi, a wonderful new Senegalese artist whose work Athena had just discovered. We all completely ignored the polo thundering alongside us, nodding occasionally for champagne top-ups. Eventually, Athena leaned over.

"So, spill the beans, Patrick. Another *Self-Portrait as Sphinx*? What is this, a publicity stunt? I can't imagine your ex-wife is too pleased about it," she said, with a sly smile—she had evidently been keeping tabs on Caroline and me over the years, too.

"It's exactly what it seems," I told her.

"It can't be," said Athena bluntly. "I've read Caroline's book. It took Juliette months to paint *Self-Portrait as Sphinx*. She only talks of a single painting in her journal, and there wasn't time for her to paint another, something that intricate, between her final diary entry and the fire."

"I'm aware of the logistics," I told her. "Nevertheless, the fact remains, the painting in my gallery is an authentic Willoughby, a genuine *Self-Portrait as Sphinx*."

Athena studied my face. "And you really think Caroline is going to torch her own reputation to acknowledge that?"

"I have absolute confidence in Caroline's professionalism, objectivity, and integrity," I said decisively.

"Always the gentleman. You haven't changed at all, have you?" Athena said with an airy laugh.

I was not quite sure how to take this, or if it was meant as a compliment.

"I'm sure Caroline would love to see you," I said. "After all these years . . ."

Most people I knew—admittedly the majority of them were middle-class, and English—would have paid this idea at least some lip service, even if they subsequently failed to follow up. Athena simply pretended I had not spoken.

"As you've probably guessed," she told me, her tone suddenly more businesslike, "the reason I invited you here is that I have several clients who would be very interested in viewing your painting. Who have asked me to gauge the sort of figure you might be looking for, if it were authenticated."

"I couldn't possibly say right now," I told her, truthfully.

As Athena well knew, that was not how private sales worked—the approach was usually much more guarded, money the last subject broached.

"Ballpark, Patrick, come on," she cajoled, suddenly switching back into her aren't-we-old-friends voice again.

"Well, I would be surprised if the vendor would consider less than thirty million."

I had suggested to Harry this might be a little ambitious for a painting that logically, technically, should not even exist. He had been insistent. The deal we shook on was that I would shoulder all the costs of restoring and marketing the painting—money I had to borrow—and would take a 30 percent commission, higher than my usual 10 on account of the level of risk. It was a gamble. If it paid off, the rewards would be extraordinary. What would happen if it did not sell, I did not like to think about as much.

"Thirty million *pounds*? The last time *Self-Portrait as Sphinx* sold on the open market—"

"The last time *Self-Portrait as Sphinx* sold was at a small provincial auction house in Ely. Before the discovery of Juliette's journal was made public. Before Caroline's book sold five million copies."

I was pleased I had managed to slip that in. I hoped it did rankle just a little with Athena that long after she and I and her clients were forgotten, Caroline's scholarship would endure.

"I'll pass the message on," said Athena, her tone once again cooler. "And I'll be in touch. It will all depend on Caroline's verdict, of course."

"Experts revise their judgment when new evidence comes to light all the time, as you know."

Under other circumstances I might have mentioned my father and his Raphael.

A waiter leaned a white-gloved hand over my shoulder to top up my champagne, and I put my palm over the top. "Actually, I'm just going to nip to the bathroom—please excuse me," I said.

I could not find the loos in the VIP zone. Having made two conspicuous circles of the area, I exited it in the direction of the toilet sign I could see near the clubhouse.

Jerry, conspicuously flushed, was swaying at the urinal.

"There you are, Patrick! Enjoying yourself?" he said. He did not wait for a response. "And was that George Galanis's daughter I saw you over there with? I should come over and say hello, perhaps."

"I actually have to leave—lots to do back at the gallery."

"Ah, shame. I knew George quite well. One of a kind he was. Tremendous energy. Wonderful polo player. Great raconteur. Always remember him with a brandy. Sort of person you imagine smoking a cigar in the bath. Who'd suddenly decide one day you were all going to fly to Paris for dinner that evening in his private jet."

I did wonder if even Freddie had fully realized the scale of the Galanis family wealth. I could imagine him rather enjoying that sort of lifestyle, had not some weird Willoughby glitch always prevented him from taking Athena seriously as a potential partner. Perhaps it was the flashiness of the family that was part of the problem—a term like *flashiness* coming with a fairly hefty helping of associated snobbery and prejudice for a family like Freddie's. I certainly knew exactly the kind of girl Freddie would have married, had he lived—blond, bland, blue-blooded. Exactly the same sort of woman, if the photographs on Facebook were anything to go by, that pretty much all the rest of the Osiris Society had settled down with.

"Of course, after George died," Jerry said, his voice dropping to a conspiratorial whisper, "from what I hear, the family found out they had rather less money than they thought."

He raised a knowing eyebrow, searching my face for a reaction before he continued. "In fact, I have heard that after his heart attack, they discovered they were completely broke. It was all just shell company within shell company within shell company. Offshore bank account after offshore bank account with nothing in it."

"That's just Dubai gossip, surely," I countered, unable to believe it. "Athena certainly doesn't look to me like she is struggling, cash-wise.

I guess she must be earning it all herself now, unless there's some rich boyfriend on the scene . . . ?"

"Never been introduced to one," Jerry said, shaking his head. "Shame, a beautiful woman like that. Still, I can see why she would want to keep it quiet, about her father. As we all know, in her line of business, and yours, it's all about appearances, isn't it?"

We were at the sinks now, and he met my eye in the mirror. "And perhaps that is even truer here than anywhere else in the world."

CAROLINE, CAMBRIDGE, 2023, THREE DAYS BEFORE HARRY'S DEATH

I knew from the knock—a precise and familiar rat-tat-tat—that it was Sam Fadel at my office door.

I had hesitated about emailing him—not least because I knew he was likely to respond to my email with a personal visit like this—but if anyone could interpret the hieroglyphics on Harry's painting and on the lintel at Longhurst and that Harry had shown me on Cyril's pyramid, it was Dr. Sam Fadel, once the curator of the Willoughby Bequest, now the Archaeology Department's Head of Archives.

"Come in," I called.

"Is now a good time?" he asked, poking his head around the door with an uncertain smile.

Not really, was the honest answer, given that it was quarter past five and all afternoon I had been fielding calls about the Tate's press release, explaining to reporters that I could not comment as I had yet to see the painting for myself, and was currently answering the last few urgent messages from students before I flew to Dubai tomorrow morning to do so.

On the other hand, Sam was doing me a favor, and he had every reason not to.

"Of course," I nodded. "Thank you so much for this."

"It's no trouble at all," he said, jabbing his glasses up his nose as he spoke, perching for a seat on one arm of an unoccupied armchair. "I have to admit I'm intrigued by the pictures you emailed. Is there any more context you can give me?"

"These hieroglyphics appear on a second version of Juliette Willoughby's *Self-Portrait as Sphinx* that has been found at Longhurst Hall. I've been asked to authenticate it. Patrick's gallery is trying to sell it."

At the mention of Patrick, his smile stiffened slightly.

"I see. And you want me to translate the phrase?"

"Yes, and perhaps offer some insight into why it meant something to Cyril Willoughby," I explained. "It was written over the door to the east wing at Longhurst, where he kept his collection. And it's carved over the entrance to his pyramid tomb. What I was wondering—"

"Is if it features in any of the materials in the Willoughby Bequest?"

"Exactly."

"I can tell you the answer to that question very easily," he said, looking pleased with himself. "It features in all of them. You see, our understanding of the collection has developed quite significantly over time. Back when I started working on the written materials in the bequest, it was assumed that Cyril had a general interest in funeral texts and coffin inscriptions. It's since become clear that in fact he spent his life collecting as many different versions as he could lay his hands on of one particular chapter of the *Book of the Dead*. Chapter sixty-four, to be precise."

"I see," I said, although I wasn't sure I did, entirely.

"Look, the thing to bear in mind when we talk about the *Book of the Dead* is that the ancient Egyptians didn't call it that, and it wasn't a book. It is a collection of writings—prayers, or spells, or instructions—on tomb walls, inside coffins, on papyri inserted between the bandages of mummies—designed to guide the soul of a deceased person through the afterlife. Then in the nineteenth century it was ordered into a vague sequence and translated by a German scholar, Karl Richard Lepsius, and given the title *Das Todtenbuch der Ägypter.*"

As he said this, something tugged at the corner of my mind—the white-bandaged body in the painting, the beaked boatman rowing it across the lake.

"Those passages were copied again and again over several thousand years, so for each chapter we have innumerable versions. Versions from a coffin which has been exposed to the elements. Versions from a tomb wall an ancient robber has gone at with a pickax. Versions where the scribe has missed something or repeated it. And that is what seems to have obsessed Cyril Willoughby. Collecting versions of chapter sixty-four, collating them. Trying, perhaps, to reconstruct an original, perfect version—or at least that's what his notes suggest," he explained.

"And that's where this hieroglyphic phrase comes from?" I asked.

"Absolutely. It's the first line in most versions: *Ga ba ka, baba ka, ka ka ra ra phee ko ko*. In Budge's Victorian translation, which is the one Cyril would have been most familiar with, it reads: 'I am Yesterday, To-Day and To-morrow, and I have the power to be born a second time.' Meaning in the afterlife, of course."

I repeated the phrase to myself, thoughtfully, wondering aloud why Juliette had chosen to incorporate it into her work.

"That's not something I can help you with, I'm afraid," said Sam. "But there is something else I noticed in the photographs of the painting you sent. I'm not sure if it's useful, but . . ."

He paused. When Sam spoke again it was with the cautious hesitancy of someone who feels themselves at the outer limits of their professional expertise.

"I must preface this by saying that I am no art historian. However, what Juliette seems to be doing with Egyptological motifs *is* interesting. By which I mean interestingly *wrong*. She has taken great care to get the hieroglyphs correct, but then look at the hooded figure in the boat."

I called the pictures up on my computer. I had spent years analyzing this image. "The figure with the Ibis beak? That's Thoth. The god of knowledge," I said, pleased to contribute something.

"And magic, yes. But that's not the right god. Thoth is not the god who carries the souls of the dead through the afterlife on his barque, his *mandjet*. That ought to be Ra, the sun god, who has a falcon's head. Completely different bird. Completely different beak. The artist knows that, just like she knows Egyptian Sphinxes don't have wings. These are deliberate mistakes, which carry some sort of significance. What I am not sure about, though, is *what*."

Welcome to my world, I thought.

"Anyway, Caroline, that's pretty much all I can tell you. But, look, if you did want to discuss it further, perhaps we could do it over dinner . . ."

"I'm sorry, Sam, I—"

"Of course. I understand. Very sensible," he mumbled, holding out a hand to shake.

"I am really sorry," I said, conscious I was repeating myself, unable to think of a kind way to say it was impossible. Because there was nothing in my life I regretted more than sleeping with Sam Fadel, and I could never let it happen again, never let even the possibility of it happening again raise its head, for both our sakes.

In retrospect, it was easy to understand how it had come about. By that stage in my marriage to Patrick, we hardly ever saw each other. By the time he got back from the gallery most evenings I'd be asleep. Three nights a week during term I was up in Cambridge, and sometimes I went for a drink with Sam, to talk about colleagues, joke about our work frustrations. He must have been able to sense I was unhappy, that Patrick and I were not getting along. He had just been through a nasty breakup himself, and he talked about how over time, relationships accumulated resentments, frustrations, flashpoints. How hard it could be sometimes to recall why you'd fallen in love in the first place. How you could reach a point when every conversation seemed freighted with the potential to turn into an argument, every comment was capable of being taken as a coded insult. It all sounded very familiar.

It was easy talking to Sam. It was something I looked forward to a lot more than I did going out with Patrick on weekends in London.

Being buttonholed by some up-and-coming young conceptual artist at a loft party in Shoreditch and harangued for hours about the pointlessness of my academic discipline. Loyally turning up to every one of Patrick's private views and having to sit there and not pull faces or wriggle through garbled speeches by the showcased artists mixing misunderstood art theory with misremembered art history. Listening at dinner parties as he and fellow dealers talked about artists and their reputations like they were brokers discussing stock prices—who was on the way up, who was on the way down. Conscious that I was probably not hiding what I thought and felt as well as I might have done. Aware that there were times Patrick found me just as irritating as I found him.

Then one day Sam kissed me.

We were in a pub, on a sofa in a corner. It was nearly closing time. We had both been drinking. I should have told him we had got our wires crossed somewhere. I should have explained that even though I thought he was kind and clever and funny and attractive, I had never thought about him like that before. That I was very flattered, but it was not something he should have done or should ever do again. That the reason Patrick's parents had divorced was his father's cheating, and he had always made it clear how impossible he would find it to stay with someone who betrayed him that way. I should have told Sam all that. I didn't. Instead, I kissed him back.

In a way, perhaps that was precisely the reason I did cheat. To break up the marriage. To bring to crisis an intolerable situation. It was only after I had told Patrick, after I had explained to him what had happened, after we had talked it over, and fought, and thrown accusations around, and cried, and come to a decision, that it dawned on me I also had to tell Sam that what had happened was a mistake, something I regretted. It was only seeing his attempts to suppress his reaction—we were in a café, it was lunchtime—I understood that he still felt very differently about things, that he had not been exaggerating when he told me how much he had always liked me, that I was watching someone's heart breaking in front of me in real time.

There was a gentle knock at my office door, and then the cleaner stuck her head around it to check if my wastepaper basket needed to be emptied. Sam used this as an excuse to hurriedly say goodbye. I switched my computer off, waiting a few minutes to make sure I would not bump into him, then left. It was time to go home. The lights were coming on around the quad as I crossed it to the porter's lodge. As I was passing, I stopped in to check my mail and grabbed a letter from my cubby.

Taking a seat at the bus stop, I had a closer look at the envelope—it was from Boots, the kind they send containing photos you've ordered online. *Here we go, I haven't had one of these for a while*, I thought. Like any female academic who does media appearances, I have on occasion been sent some weird things. Drawings. Self-published books. Helpful feedback on how I dress and how I speak and how I have failed to grasp anything about my subject.

I opened the envelope cautiously. Inside were four glossy photographs. I slid them out and inspected the first under the fluorescent glow of the bus shelter light. The photograph was dark, blurry. It took me a little while even to work out whether I was holding it the right way up. Then, all of a sudden, I understood what I was looking at, and when it had been taken. The second photograph confirmed this. It was a lot more brightly lit. I glanced at the third, the fourth. My hands were quivering. My mouth was dry. My eyes felt like they were going in and out of focus.

They were photographs of me at Longhurst, at Harry Willoughby's twenty-first birthday party. Photographs I had no memory of someone taking. Photographs I could not immediately figure out *how* someone could have taken. The bus pulled up, but I shook my head at the driver, waved him away again, uncertain whether my legs would support me if I tried to stand. I didn't understand if the bus stop's fluorescent light had suddenly started flickering above me or if the bright flashes popping in front of my eyes were because I couldn't catch my breath.

I reached into the envelope and drew out a piece of paper with the Boots store logo at the top. It read simply: "Authenticate the painting."

JULIETTE, PARIS, 1938

Oskar was dead. My beloved Oskar was dead, and I had killed him. I had taken a knife and in a moment of terror I had driven it into his chest, into his heart.

At first I could not quite bring myself to believe it. I stood there frozen, looking down at his unmoving body, and despite everything my rational mind was telling me, part of my brain remained convinced that any moment he would suddenly jump up to his feet, with a cry of pain or fury.

Someone on the other side of the courtyard was listening to their radio. Someone else was coughing. I wondered how audible our argument had been, how obvious its sudden end. Oskar and I had often rolled our eyes at that couple in the building opposite arguing—her voice getting shriller and shriller, his louder and louder, until the inevitable crash of a thrown plate, the slam of a door. The thought of that shared memory, of all the memories we had shared, stuck sharply in my throat, and silly as it might sound it was only at that moment I understood the gravity, the true horror, of what I had done, and to whom.

Part of me wanted to stick my head out the window and call for the police. Another part wanted to curl up on the floor next to Oskar, even as his blood seeped onto the floor beneath his unmoving body.

Then my eyes came to rest on the money, next to the envelope on the table with the passports in it. The next thing I knew I was standing at the sink scrubbing at my forearms, the icy water swirling pink in the basin. Then I was making my way down the stairs, passing my landlord's wife in her doorway, in her apron, the smell of her dinner hanging in the hall, responding to her greeting with a bright *bonsoir à vous*, trying to keep my face from twitching.

Then I was turning out of the front of our building, passing the café at the end of the street, busy at that time of night. I gathered my coat around me. It was a cloudless night, freezing cold, and by the time I reached the end of the street I was shaking so hard I had to hug myself to stop. Shock, I told myself; this is your body reacting to the shock of what has happened. I was very aware of the need to look normal, the need to behave normally.

I knew that every decision I made that night could change the rest of my life completely.

He was dead. He was dead and I would never forgive myself. But I could also never forgive him for what he had done. I told him that, in my head, as I walked, alternately apologizing and raging at the idiot, the poor stupid dead idiot.

Thanks to Oskar, my painting now belonged to my uncle and there was every likelihood that during the hours they spent drinking together Oskar had let slip enough information to give away where we lived. Uncle Austen might, with a policeman in tow, be hammering on the door of the apartment at that very moment, demanding I return to England with him. What a wonderful gift for my family, for my father, Oskar's death would be. Just the excuse that was needed to lock me away forever.

How clearly I remember, one of those evenings at Breton's apartment, his going around the room asking the assembled painters and poets in turn why they hated their father, and everyone giving the usual bourgeois Freudian answers. When it was my turn, I said, "I do not hate my father. My father hates me." I was not being glib. He blamed me for Lucy's loss, just as I blamed myself. But even now I could not fully bring myself to hate him. Instead, I pitied him, inasmuch as it is possible to pity someone and fear them at the same time. I pitied him for the sorrow he had suffered. I feared the monster it had made him.

Passing the window of a darkened shop, I caught a glimpse of my own reflection. The bruise on my cheek would soon bloom purple and black, but there was no outward sign of the assault yet. I had expected my reflection to greet me with flashing eyes, wild flying hair, some sort of madwoman's grimace. Instead, I looked perfectly normal, not even especially flustered. Under my arm I had a bundle of my clothes, tied up with string.

I knew where I was going. I knew what I had to do.

As I walked, I thought of the first time I had taken this route, with Oskar. As I retraced my steps, recognizing buildings I had forgotten, streets and squares I suddenly remembered, I listed all the things that would need to happen for my plan to work, and tried to block out what might happen if it did not.

CHAPTER 15

CAROLINE, DUBAI, 2023, TWO DAYS BEFORE HARRY'S DEATH

"Someone knows."

That was the first thing I said to Patrick, at the airport. There was a moment's pause before we awkwardly air-kissed, one of my bags getting sandwiched between us.

"Someone knows what?" he asked, confused. To be fair, it was probably not the opening line he had been expecting, after so long, under the circumstances.

"Take me to the gallery," I said. "Let's see this painting of yours. I'll tell you on the way there."

He picked my suitcase up with a grunt. "Jesus Christ, Caroline, what have you got in here? Bricks?"

"Books," I said. "Tools of the trade, Patrick."

With some remark about getting me a Kindle, he pointed in the direction of the airport exit. All the way here, on the plane, I had been turning it over in my mind. Those four photographs, the message that had accompanied them: *Authenticate the painting.* There was an initial instant when I had suspected Patrick or Harry of sending them, felt a rush of rage that one or both thought I could be bullied. Then I thought things through more carefully. It could not be Harry or Patrick behind this.

The first picture—I remembered that flash just before the first loud thump of fireworks—was of me in my evening dress, outlined against the white dust sheets in Austen's studio. It must have been taken through a window, from outside, at the very moment I discovered *Self-Portrait as Sphinx.* The second showed me in the process of trying to work out if I could fit it under my shawl. Presumably, amid the fizz and pop of the rockets, I missed a second flash, and the third and fourth, as I crossed the drive with the painting under my arm and stood in front of the open trunk of Patrick's car.

The fact it was his car made it unlikely he was the one trying to use these photographs to blackmail me. Likewise, if Harry knew I had stolen his family's painting, why keep it a secret until now?

The doors of the terminal silently parted, the evening air still warm outside. Patrick pointed out a battered Jeep, parked at a sloppy angle in what was clearly marked as a no parking zone. "I was sort of expecting the MG," I said.

Patrick laughed. "Not very elegant, I know. But it does mean you can just chuck whatever you need in the back—camping stuff, kite-surfing gear."

"That must be very convenient," I said with a laugh, assuming that he was joking.

Patrick looked a bit hurt.

"Sorry. I just never had you down as the outdoorsy type."

I'll say this for his new lifestyle: he looked a lot healthier than the pale, puffy Patrick I had run into a few times back in London. He was tanned. He was toned. He was slender.

Some things never changed, though. No sooner had I clicked my seat belt than we were off, Patrick pulling out with barely a glance over his shoulder into a solid stream of taxis. The main difference from being in a car with Patrick in England was that in Dubai everyone else seemed to be driving in a similar fashion.

He glanced over at me. "*Someone knows*, you said?" he asked, before suddenly swerving across three lanes of traffic so we didn't miss our exit. I told him about the photographs, the note. He looked as mystified as I had been and I could see him working through the same panicked sequence of suspicions I had done.

"This could ruin me professionally, you know that, don't you, Patrick?"

"Of course I understand what's at stake, for both of us. It's my car you're stashing your stolen goods in."

We turned off the highway. We turned again.

"This is the DIFC, the financial district. My gallery is here, as is your hotel."

On either side of us rose office buildings, black and glittering. The cars we were gliding among were shinier here too. Every so often I could feel Patrick's eyes on me, a sidelong glance, trying to read my expression. How I was reacting. Whether I was impressed. I was, despite myself, strangely touched that he cared.

There was an attendant in a booth at the entrance to the parking garage. Recognizing us, or the car, he pressed a button to raise the barrier. Patrick led me to the elevator. From it, we emerged into a shopping precinct. The Lambert Gallery occupied the bottom two floors of an office building, its windows shuttered. Patrick typed a code, and after a moment the door beeped unlocked.

"So the idea was that for tomorrow night's private view we'd recreate Dalí's *Rainy Taxi* right here outside. Just like the 1938 exhibition: a whole car, trailed with ivy, with a shark-headed mannequin chauffeur and a mannequin in evening dress in it, fixed up so it's raining inside the vehicle, snails crawling over everything. Which I think would have been even more dramatic in this climate. We managed to find an actual 1933 Rolls-Royce, the mannequins, got in contact with a guy who breeds snails, but when we looked into how many permits we'd need . . ."

He stepped into the gallery, reached into his pocket, and brought out his phone. He pressed the flashlight button and handed it to me. "My gosh, Patrick," I said.

"You'll get the idea, I think. We did our best."

It was like stepping back in time, to what I knew of that first night of the International Surrealist exhibition in Paris. From the ceiling of the gallery hung sacks, hundreds of sacks. More sacks blocked out any light from the windows. A lot of effort had gone into this. For just a moment, one strange moment, I did wonder if all this was for my benefit, some sort of weird romantic gesture.

"Oh, hold on," said Patrick. He pressed a button and a soundtrack of vintage street noise came on—a few shouted French swear words, a car horn honking, a dog insistently barking. As I stepped tentatively into the room, the phone's flashlight picked out the mannequins arranged around it, copies of the originals—by Dalí, Man Ray, Éluard, Erlich, Willoughby—each one designed to startle and unsettle the viewer. Here was one gagged and bound with a single flower on her mouth. Another was naked save a chain mail headdress.

"Are they going to let you get away with this here?" I asked him. "Not big on nudity, surely, are they?"

"I guess we'll find out tomorrow," he said. "We've got some pretty important people coming, so I can't imagine we're going to get raided. It's going to be a bit of a Cambridge reunion, too. Giles Pemberton is coming over, for the *Sunday Times*. Dave White—you might remember him better as Next-Door Terry—has been invited. Harry, of course. Oh, and I suppose I better warn you, Athena Galanis is going to be here too. She's an art consultant in Dubai now. I only found out recently. And that's not all . . ."

Patrick saw my expression and stopped himself. I had often wondered how I would react if I crossed paths with Athena one day—had imagined what I wanted to say to her, what I wanted to ask. Given everything else that was going on, this really didn't feel like the time. It had been hard enough bracing myself to see Patrick.

Flashlight in one hand, I began making my way through the darkness.

"You'll find a door at the far end of the room," Patrick told me. "Careful not to trip over anything. I hope you're not too disappointed that the sacks aren't actually dripping coal dust, but you can take authenticity too far. I can't afford the dry cleaning for everyone's sooty Dior."

I shuffled forward until my flashlight picked out the metallic glint of a door handle. There was another keypad next to the door, faintly glowing orange. Patrick typed in a code. It beeped.

"There you go. All yours. You can spend some time here first with the painting, if you'd like, then I'll drive you to the hotel, get you checked in."

Despite his best efforts to conceal it, Patrick sounded nervous. How much all this had cost him I dreaded to think, and besides that was precisely the sort of thing—like those photographs, the implications of the message that had accompanied them—I could not allow to influence my opinion. I had a responsibility to get this right. A responsibility to history, to Juliette.

I took a deep breath and reached for the door handle.

PATRICK, DUBAI, 2023, TWO DAYS BEFORE HARRY'S DEATH

"Patrick, you know I won't necessarily be able to give you an answer this evening, don't you? That there may be things I need to read up on, or think about," said Caroline, before she stepped into the room that held the painting.

I said I was sorry all this had to be so rushed. It was very much Harry who wanted it done at a breakneck pace, who was desperate . . .

"Patrick," Caroline said softly. "This is going to take a while and I am going to need to concentrate."

I said I would just be upstairs, in my office. I texted Sarah—away working on a three-day wedding she couldn't get out of, in Abu Dhabi—to say that Caroline had arrived safely, knowing that I would not get an answer immediately.

I texted Harry, to check that he was boarding his flight, letting him know about the interest the painting was generating. I started going through the mail on my desk—bill after bill after bill. I checked the time. Caroline had been in there for about ten minutes. I could have sworn it was at least an hour.

My God, those photographs. Who on earth apart from Harry and me had anything to gain from blackmail? I drank a glass of water, willing myself to calm down. Whoever had taken those photos had been in possession of them for close to three decades. Clearly, they bore Caroline and me no particular grudge, or they would have gone public with the pictures already. If her professional opinion was that this painting was genuine, there might be nothing to worry about.

What if Caroline was not convinced? The sale would still go ahead, of course. All the time, all around the world, people sold paintings over which there hung a cloud of doubt. Sometimes in the hope that the expert would change their mind, or that a later expert would be of a different opinion, or because having a painting from the school of Rubens was a lot more affordable than one from the catalogue raisonné. The difference being that the former might sell for tens of thousands, the latter for tens of millions. Tens of thousands would not even cover my expenses. The scientific analysis, the extra security, the insurance. Caroline's flights and hotel, Harry's. The private view. I was trying very hard not to think about my father and his Raphael. How much he had spent on that. How confident he had been that it would transform his life, all our lives.

After an hour and a half, Caroline finally emerged from the room with the painting in it. She cleared her throat. "Patrick?" she called. I was already halfway down the stairs when I saw her expression. My heart sank as she shook her head.

"It's impossible," she said. "There just wasn't time for her to paint two versions of the same painting. The logistics, the practicalities, the chronology make no sense."

She was right. Of course she was right. At some level perhaps I had always known she was right.

"It's impossible," she said. "But I also believe it to be genuine. That is my sincere and settled professional opinion."

"And you're willing to attest to that publicly?" I asked.

"It's the truth," she confirmed.

"And what does this mean for the painting in Tate Modern? That it's fake?"

Caroline shook her head, shrugged. "I think things are more complicated than that. The best way to explain it is this, I think. If I were forging a letter by Juliette, and I wanted to replicate a word she used in the journal, I would copy it curve for curve, exactly, maybe even trace it. So it would be an exact match. But if she herself wrote that same word again, she wouldn't get an exact match. You'd get something very similar, that was recognizably from the same hand, but with slight and almost unnoticeable variations."

"And that's what you think is going on here?" I asked.

"Well, there are also those obvious differences in the content of the painting, which we've both noticed, but at a brushstroke level, that's what I think is going on, yes. I can't explain how, but I am willing to stake my reputation on my belief that *both* these pictures were painted by Juliette Willoughby."

For a moment, I did not know how to react, how to thank her. Then I took her into my arms and hugged her. After a moment's hesitation, she hugged me back. "Patrick, there's something else," she said. We disentangled from each other, separated.

"Something else?"

"I've spotted another difference between the paintings. The strangest one yet."

"Go on, then," I said with a smile. "Show me."

We headed back into the room where the painting was hanging. She beckoned me over to it.

"Have a closer look down there in that corner," she said. "Tell me what you see."

I leaned in close. I screwed up my eyes.

"Oh my God," I said.

There it was, on the bottom right, on the island the boat was headed to, perspective rendering it easy to miss . . .

"It's a pyramid. A white pyramid on an island, just like the one at Longhurst."

"That *is* Longhurst," Caroline replied. "It's not some mythical or symbolic stretch of water that boat is crossing. It is the actual lake at Longhurst and it is Cyril's pyramid the boat is headed for."

Her eyes were bright with excitement.

"But what does that mean?" I asked her.

"The drowned sister. Juliette fleeing. The same inscription as appears over the door to the east wing and the entrance to the pyramid. What I think it means, Patrick, is that these aren't just dreams or flights of fancy. Each individual element of this version of *Self-Portrait as Sphinx* appears to refer directly to some real-life incident, something that happened, thinly disguised. What the painting is asking us to do is to fit them all together, in narrative sequence."

Her smile faltered.

"What is it?" I asked her.

"Look at the expression on her face, the Juliette in the corner, running through the woods. I have always found it so unsettling, her expression."

"She looks scared."

"She looks terrified," agreed Caroline. "Patrick, I have a strong feeling that the secret this Sphinx is telling us to piece together is something truly unspeakable."

JULIETTE, PARIS, 1938

It felt like stepping back into a dream. The familiarity of it all. The cloud of laundry steam. The smell of disinfectant. An air of enforced hush, broken only by the sound of rubber soles squeaking on the polished floor, the rattle of gurney wheels, distant doors on distant corridors swinging.

As I had been hoping, when I reached the right floor, there were wheelchairs with canvas seats and backrests at the foot of the stairs. I took one. The sound of my frantic footsteps clacking in my ears, I steadied my pace down the corridor. I was relieved to find there was no porter waiting at the door of the morgue.

When I reached it I turned the handle and stepped inside, pushing the wheelchair in front of me. I closed the heavy door gently behind me and flicked the light switch. It was an uncanny feeling, being the only living person in a room full of dead ones. It was every bit as cold as I remembered. The bright lights flickered on, out of sequence.

All along one wall there were handles, three rows of them, at knee height, at waist height, at shoulder height. On the outside, handwritten tags with names and dates—men, women, and children. I located a drawer labeled *Femme, Inconnue*—woman, unknown—just as the young woman I painted weeks before had been. The date was a week or two before—I knew from Oskar this meant her limbs would be past the point of rigid stiffness.

The drawer opened soundlessly. This woman inside was older than me, smaller and slighter, another wraith recovered from the Seine, perhaps. Her hair, tied back, was darker than mine by a shade or two. She was naked on the cold metal, and even though I knew she was dead, my brain flinched from the thought of it, chilled steel against flesh. I stepped back to allow the drawer to open fully.

Her face, absolutely white, eyes closed, was expressionless. For the second time that day I found myself apologizing to a dead person. For the second time that day, I found myself horrified at what I seemed so calmly capable of.

"I'm sorry," I said, my voice sounding cracked and echoey in the empty room. "I'm so sorry."

I tried to tell myself that if she knew the circumstances she would understand. I tried to persuade myself that the woman I was looking down upon was beyond any possible further injury or insult now.

I cracked the door open an inch and checked the corridor. No one to be seen. Then I returned to the body. Onto the end of the drawer, I dumped the bundle of clothes I had brought with me, untying the string, unrolling the dress, separating from it a pair of stockings and a cardigan, revealing in the middle of it a pair of shoes. I dragged the dress over her head. Onto her still-stiff feet I worked the shoes. Then, gritting my teeth, I took her in my arms and tumbled her off the drawer and into the wheelchair. I tried as best I could to straighten her up. I threw the blanket in which my bundle of clothes had been wrapped over her legs. I removed the label from the drawer, closed it, then pushed the wheelchair to the door and flicked the lights off once more.

I retraced my route to the entrance. The lights in the corridors were dim, some of the hallways darkened almost completely. It was well past midnight. Any second, I was expecting to run into someone and for them to spot something amiss and sound the alarm. I pictured myself wrestled to the ground by uniformed orderlies, horrified at what I had done.

I heard doors swing open up ahead and dragged the wheelchair to a sudden halt. At the end of the corridor, a white-coated doctor passed, deep in conversation with a nurse in a complicated hat. I held my breath. They did not look up. I kept as still and silent as I could, listening as their voices retreated. Only daring to breathe again when I heard them pass through another set of doors.

With every step I dreaded the next a little more, knowing I would have to bump the wheelchair up a flight of stairs, steer it out of the hospital, down along the alley.

The streets outside were dark and empty. I pulled my hat down on my forehead, my scarf up over my chin and mouth. I arranged the blanket around the body in the wheelchair. I stepped back to survey the effect. We did not have to cross any of the open, well-lit bridges, and we could avoid the main thoroughfares. With her hat pulled down, her head leaning forward, in the dark, I was confident she would pass and we could be back at the apartment in under an hour.

Then it would be time for the hard part.

CHAPTER 16

CAROLINE, DUBAI, 2023,
THE NIGHT OF HARRY'S DEATH

Surveying myself in the hotel room mirror, I smoothed my hair, then dabbed more concealer under my eyes to hide how little I had slept the night before, tossing and turning in an unfamiliar bed, freezing under air-conditioning I couldn't work out how to turn off.

Was my dress too low-key? I had wandered out of the hotel briefly that afternoon to see whether the nearby boutiques had anything more obviously glamorous, but everything was well out of my price range: Gucci. Prada. Dolce & Gabbana.

Relax, *Caroline*, I told myself. *Everyone there is going to be interested in what you have to say, not what you are wearing.*

Give me a lecture hall, give me a seminar room, even a live TV studio and I'm fine. It was events like this one that always gave me the social jitters.

The butterflies in my stomach, the sense of being rooted to the spot even though there was somewhere I absolutely *had* to be, reminded me a little of the day Patrick and I got married, of staring at myself in the bathroom mirror and telling myself that I could do this, I could make myself do this, for Patrick's sake. That love could overcome my fear of loss. That hope could overcome dread.

It did not help knowing that Athena was going to be there, that tonight would be the first time we had seen each other in thirty years.

I slipped my feet into my shoes and tucked the invitation into my clutch bag.

"Caroline Cooper!" a voice boomed from across the courtyard

outside the Lambert Gallery, where the party had gathered. It was Giles Pemberton, his face shiny above a silk cravat, his white linen jacket already showing signs of being sweated through.

I arranged my features into a smile and started toward him, scanning the other guests as I passed. For tonight's party, as expected, Patrick had assembled exactly the sort of glitzy art crowd I usually went to great lengths to avoid. Giles—famously the cattiest art critic in London— must be loving all this. I could imagine him mentally sharpening his quill already.

"Ma'am, can I offer you a glass of champagne?" a waiter asked as I passed him.

"Don't mind if I do," I heard Patrick's voice announce behind me.

How had he paid for all this? The entire eye-wateringly expensive production—the vintage Krug, the caterers, the set design, and afterward, apparently, an intimate VIP dinner. Not to mention the immaculate, bespoke suit he was sporting.

"To Juliette Willoughby," Patrick smiled, lifting his glass. Behind him, the lights in the towers of Dubai's financial district were flickering. The hulking gray arch at its heart—like a giant Lego version of the Arc de Triomphe—loomed over us.

"Has Harry not arrived yet?" I asked, suddenly aware that I hadn't seen him. Patrick's smile flickered.

"I dropped him off at the hotel this morning—he's staying at the same place you are—and I haven't heard from him since. Texted, called repeatedly, even asked the concierge to slip a note under his door. Nothing," Patrick said. "I'm just a little bit worried about him, actually."

"He didn't seem in a good way when I saw him at Longhurst," I said. Patrick nodded grimly.

"I keep meaning to have a word with him about it. Rattling around that house on his own, I wouldn't be surprised if he has been hitting the bottle a bit hard. Still, it seems a real shame, coming all this way only to miss this. On which note, do make sure to grab one of those."

Another waiter was now circulating with a tray of flashlights, offering them to intrigued guests. Someone used theirs to illuminate their face from below, to laughs.

"Join us, on a descent into the subconscious," boomed a recorded voice from a speaker adjacent to the door of the gallery, causing several guests to spill their champagne in shock.

As a line began to form to enter the gallery, with people trying to turn their flashlights on, speculating about what was about to happen, I felt a tap on the shoulder. I turned to find myself face-to-face with Athena Galanis. I was not sure how she had managed it, but she had not aged a day.

"All very impressive, no?" she said. "Patrick told me you were going to be here, but I was not quite sure whether to believe him."

"He said you would be here too. Listen, Athena, about what happened, what I said . . ."

She made a gesture with her hand as if to brush the topic off.

"Let's not talk about that now. Ancient history. It's your verdict on this painting everyone is waiting to hear. You saw that's Dave White over there?" Athena gestured with her chin in the direction of a tall, middle-aged man in what I took to be designer sunglasses and a collarless silver leather jacket, standing in the center of a circle of admiring younger people. It sounded like he was halfway through a story about himself.

"I'm not sure I ever met Dave at Cambridge," said Athena. "But he seems to remember you and Patrick very well. And these days he is a very serious art collector indeed."

I bet Patrick wishes he had given him a lift back from Longhurst now, I thought to myself.

Dave White's hair looked a lot darker than I remembered it. His chin looked stronger, also.

"Has he had . . . ?" I asked.

"*So* much work," confided Athena.

As we surveyed the line, she gave me a brief rundown of everyone else. The buyers. The advisors. Who already owned several Kahlos. Who had a villa with wall space they needed to fill. Who was actually surprisingly informed about art, despite what appearances might suggest.

"It's basically everyone who is anyone on the Dubai art-buying scene, is what you're telling me," I said.

"Dubai? More like the whole Middle East. There are people who've flown in from Qatar to be here. Bahrain. Riyadh. Jeddah."

Watching Patrick working the crowd, welcoming people, making them feel noticed, a little compliment for everyone, as happy as I had ever seen him, I could not help feeling proud. He had slogged long enough to get here, weathered enough setbacks. The disappointment of never quite achieving what everyone had predicted for him. The grind of constant precarity. The way it tells on you, year after year, having to make decisions constantly, all of them with a price tag attached, other people's livelihoods as well as your own depending on your making the right call, never quite knowing if there is even a right call to make. And now here he was, on top of his world.

And then Harry Willoughby shambled in.

He had immediately located a glass of champagne and was holding it at a slightly odd angle, as if he couldn't quite work out how to drink it.

"If you'll excuse me for a second, Athena," I said, and spotted Patrick exiting another conversation simultaneously.

He and I got to Harry at exactly the same moment. Unfortunately, so did Giles.

"Harry! Thank you so much for the invitation—I was thrilled my editor agreed to send me out here. This painting of yours is causing quite the stir."

Harry stared at him blankly. Neither of Harry's shoelaces was done up, I noticed. He was perceptibly swaying on his feet.

"Patrick, Caroline. Wonderful to see you too, of course," Giles continued. "So I was wondering if I could ask the three of you . . ."

Patrick offered an apologetic smile.

"I'm afraid we can't talk right now, Giles. We *must* have a proper catch-up and we'd love to give you an exclusive quote for the paper, but if you don't mind, we need to steal Harry for a moment now to talk through the running order of the evening."

As he was saying this, Patrick had placed his hand on the small of Harry's back. He was now steering him toward the gallery. I followed. "Harry," he said when we were out of earshot of Giles. "You could get yourself in trouble, being out and about here in a state like this. Not to mention, you could fuck up this whole thing."

Harry swayed again, to the extent I thought he might actually fall over, and glared at us balefully. His eyes were bloodshot. He looked like he had been sleeping in his dinner jacket, and his shirt was peculiarly buttoned up. He assured us in a slurring voice that *this*—the gesture itself spilled some of his champagne—was the first thing he'd had to drink all day.

"Sure," Patrick said. "Listen, Harry. We've got a little while before dinner starts. Why don't you come up to my office, gather yourself?"

We walked around the side of the building, in through the back entrance of the gallery, and into Patrick's office. Perhaps, Patrick suggested, Harry should have a nap right here on the sofa. Just a little twenty minutes to sharpen him up.

"Is everything okay, Harry?" I asked him.

"Of course," he snapped. "I'm fine. It's hot. I'm tired and I've come a long way, that's all. The question is will it all have been worth it. I can see they are enjoying the champagne, but will any of these buyers bite? Because I'm relying on this, Patrick. I'm relying on you."

"We are *both* relying on this," said Patrick. "Caroline has thrown her weight behind the work, and with the level of media attention we've received, I am pretty confident we'll secure a sale, and I am hopeful it will be swift. But nothing is ever a certainty in this business, Harry."

Patrick paused. His tone softened. "And I know that Longhurst is important to you, but it isn't *everything*," he said.

"Oh God, you don't understand," said Harry, his head dropping into his hands. "You can't possibly understand. This isn't just about Longhurst, Patrick. If we don't sell that painting tonight, I genuinely don't know what I am going to do."

PATRICK, DUBAI, 2023, THE NIGHT OF HARRY'S DEATH

"The VIPs are making their way to the dining room, Patrick," said my assistant, discreetly sticking her head around the office door. I nodded, mouthing *five minutes.*

"Harry, drink this," I said, handing him a glass of water. "And pull yourself together. There are some extremely big players out there to-night. Let's try not to scare any of them off, eh?"

Harry looked at me. He took a sip of water and grunted his assent. At least he did not obviously smell of booze. We might be able to pass this off as just posh British eccentricity. Now was the part of the eve-ning that really mattered—all the top-tier buyers who had expressed interest in one room, around one table. The last thing I wanted was for the only surviving Willoughby to ruin it. On the other hand, if he was not there it might look even odder.

Usually my approach to a big-ticket sale would be far more strategic—decide on a list of targets and work my way down it in order, showing each the painting privately, saying it was for their eyes only, nudging them to make an offer and moving on to the next if they did not. But with Harry's absurdly tight cut-off point for the sale looming, I had taken the gamble of gathering them all together and giving them a deadline for sealed offers: midnight.

There were twelve interested parties in total: two Saudis, one minor member of the Qatari royal family (advised and accompanied by Athena), a French representative from the Louvre Abu Dhabi, two Emiratis, two Russians, two Lebanese, one American, and Dave White. It was like the start of a bad joke: What do you get when you put twelve billionaires in a gallery?

Rich, I hoped. Because there were only two things I knew with confidence about people this loaded, no matter what their country of origin. One: they love to hang out at extremely exclusive events with other extremely wealthy people. Two: they are always extremely com-petitive about just how wealthy they are.

We had pulled out all the stops to make the event feel special. There was a jazz band, a bar in the corner, and eight courses with a Surrealist theme ahead of us. There was a melting clock ice sculpture, lobster served on black Bakelite telephones, baked apples with tiny marzipan bowler hats for dessert washed down with Lapsang souchong served in furry teacups (an homage to Meret Oppenheim's *Le Déjeuner en fourrure*). Caroline was to give a speech. I had originally intended to ask Harry to say a few words too, but given his current state, I had scratched the idea.

The guests were making small talk as they waited to be seated. Most seemed to know one another already, acquaintances from the international art circuit. I had agonized over the seating plan, but before anyone sat, I quietly asked my assistant to swap the name cards so Caroline and I flanked Harry. As course after course arrived, he sat there mostly in silence, breathing heavily, sweating. The few times anyone did try to engage him in conversation about the family connection to the artist, he answered briefly, vaguely. Overcompensating wildly, I did my best to ensure the conversation flowed.

Athena, sitting directly opposite, was impressive. An art advisor's role is tricky—a tightrope. The client must feel as if you're acting in their best interests, but your commission rises with the price they pay for the purchased work, so in some ways in the short term it's in *your* best interests for them to spend more. She had done her homework and was asking intelligent questions, all the while flipping back and forth from Russian to French to Arabic with casual ease—her client's English was faltering, so she was largely translating—talking confidently to Dave White about his business interests in the region, commiserating with the Russian about those pesky economic sanctions.

Of course Caroline answered all the inquiries addressed to her politely and animatedly, and spoke about Juliette beautifully. She could always bring that period in Paris to life—the context out of which this painting had emerged. She was radiant, her passion contagious. By the time dessert was served, the excitement in the room was unmistakable.

"Ladies and gentleman, if you would like to accompany me for your own, very private view . . ."

They followed me to the end of the corridor, talking among

themselves, Harry and Caroline bringing up the rear. I pushed the door open and stepped through, beckoning them all inside. The only work in the room, it hung on the far wall. One by one they approached it. Leaned in to inspect. Stood back to admire. All the while I tried to read their faces, interpret their body language. They were clearly reading one another's too. Would the person who bought this piece for the price we were hoping to reach be the envy of their peers or a laughingstock? Was it worth reminding them how many different versions of Munch's *Scream* there were in existence, each one unique? How many versions of Leonardo's *Salvator Mundi* were currently being restored in the hope that they might be accepted as the master's original, despite one having sold for $450 million to the crown prince of Saudi Arabia?

I thanked them all for coming and reminded them that offers would need to be received shortly. In my office—I indicated where it was— there was a locked box for the sealed bids, my assistant on hand beside it to answer any questions about the process I had set out thus: the two highest bidders—if there were two—would then be invited to submit their best and final. There was a palpable shift of mood in the room, scattered nods, lots of poker faces.

As the band played in the background, the small talk—now slightly more stilted—continued. Athena was deep in conversation with her client. The two Saudi collectors were engaging in an animated discussion I couldn't understand; Dave White and the American were arguing about algorithms. Not a single one of them made any sort of move toward my office.

A waiter passed by with a tray of drinks and offered me one—I shook my head, mentally adding up the cost of every martini on his tray. I stared at Harry, who appeared to be telling a story about a Labrador to an unamused Emirati, wine sloshing from his glass.

I felt a sudden ice-cold hatred run through my veins. Was Harry *trying* to fuck this up? And if so, what had all that stuff about how much was at stake been about? Then it dawned on me. He was attempting to be charming. He was actually trying to help. Half an hour ago I would have given anything for him to perk up a little, but not like this. I should have locked him in my office, told everyone he was indisposed.

If Harry loses us this sale, loses me my gallery, and lands me in jail for going spectacularly bankrupt, I thought, I am going to fucking kill him. I am literally going to fucking kill him.

As if able to tell what I was thinking, Caroline crossed the room to join me, wordlessly resting one hand gently on my arm.

"Count the people in the room, Patrick," she whispered.

I scanned, realizing there were only eleven buyers there. The representative from the Louvre Abu Dhabi was missing. Athena had noticed the same thing and in the far corner was talking quietly to her client, who was nodding. A gap in the jazz band's set exposed a silence. Dave White looked around, suddenly aware that there had been movement in the room too.

It was happening. The painting had got its claws into them.

Athena's client disappeared next, returning wordlessly. Dave White marched to my office, returning with a successful trophy hunter's precise combination of excitement and smugness. Then he walked back across the room toward me.

"Nearly best and final time, Patrick?"

I nodded, asking one of my team to politely alert everyone else in the room that if they were planning to make an offer, they should do so now. Nobody moved.

It was done.

I absented myself and took a seat behind my desk. My assistant unlocked the box, and I retrieved three pieces of paper. I unfolded the first. An offer of two million pounds from the Louvre Abu Dhabi. I swallowed hard. Had I wildly misread the room? That would only just cover expenses once Harry got his 70 percent.

The second piece of paper had Dave White's name on it. Three million. Fuck. I *had* completely misjudged the amount people were prepared to pay for this painting. My hands were shaking so much I had trouble getting the final envelope open.

Thirty-seven million pounds. I stared at the paper for a moment, then asked my assistant to confirm the figure. She nodded and smiled.

"We'll have to tell the Louvre Abu Dhabi they are out of the running,"

I said. "Please also let Dave White and Athena Galanis know—so she can translate for her client—that the bidding is set at thirty-seven million, if they would like to submit their best and final offers." I handed their two slips of paper back to her, and she left the room.

Caroline entered a moment later, waiting expectantly for me to speak first, to tell her what was happening. The truth was, I wasn't sure I was able to. She poured me a whiskey from the decanter on my desk, then one for herself, and took a seat in the armchair opposite. A few minutes later, my assistant returned with the two folded slips.

She placed both on the desk in front of me, glanced at Caroline, and left the room.

"Would you mind?" I asked Caroline. She took them, opening first one and then the other. She looked at me. I looked back at her.

"Congratulations," she said, her face breaking into the grin of a lifetime. "Sold to Dave White for forty-two million pounds."

"My God. My God, Caroline, we've done it. We need to tell Harry."

"I'm sorry, Patrick. Harry left five minutes ago. He said he really wasn't feeling well. I did offer to go with him . . ."

I briefly considered going after him myself, but Dave White, waiting outside my office, was keen that the transaction be concluded that evening. I listened as he instructed someone on the other end of a phone line to transfer the entire amount.

"As for my new painting, I'll send my driver to collect it tomorrow," he said, shaking my hand and kissing Caroline unexpectedly on the cheek as he made his way to the door. "If you'd like to spend some more time with the piece, Professor Cooper, please do call my assistant to arrange," he said, handing her a card.

And with that the party was over.

By the time I reentered the main room, most of the VIPs had left, without a goodbye. Athena congratulated me distractedly, tapping away on her phone, making a show of being disinterested. She said something noncommittal to Caroline about meeting up before she flew home. Dave and the American, when I went over, were discussing whether to have a cocktail at Zuma.

And then it was just me and Caroline. Smiling in the sudden brightness of the room as someone from the catering team circulated, collecting furry teacups. Caroline made a comment about having a nightcap at her hotel. I misheard and thought she was inviting me. "We *could* maybe grab a drink . . ." I checked the time. It was much earlier than I had imagined. I had my car. It would not take me a minute to drop her off at her hotel, I said.

The hotel bar was almost empty apart from a pianist murdering some jazz standards in a corner. We exchanged a look. Caroline shook her head.

"I do have a minibar in my room," she said. "Do you want to come up and celebrate this life-changing event with a very tiny and extremely expensive bottle of wine?"

I had texted Sarah to tell her the big news and to ask how the wedding was going. Both messages remained unread. She was in Abu Dhabi, would not be home until the next day. If I went home now, I would be driving back a rich man to an empty house.

"We should go up separately," I said.

Caroline raised an eyebrow. I shrugged.

"It's not likely to happen, but not impossible we could find ourselves in a bit of trouble. Legally, I mean. With the police. Us not being married. Me being married to someone else."

"What do you think is going to happen up there, Patrick?" she said, rolling her eyes.

"It's just how it looks. You go up first. Tell me the room number. I'll wait here and be up in five minutes. You can open the tiny wine and have a tiny drink on the balcony while you wait."

She checked her room number. We parted. She glanced back from the elevator as the doors were closing. I smiled. She smiled back. There are some people in the world who just by looking at you can make it feel like they are squeezing your heart gently in their hand. It was just a drink, I told myself. A drink on the balcony to unwind after an extraordinary day. What was the worst that could possibly happen?

JULIETTE, PARIS, 1938

The stairs were what I had most been dreading on that tense walk home, remembering how hard it had been wrestling those mannequins up five flights, knowing any sound I made at this time of night would bring the concierge out, bleary and curious in his slippers.

It was past midnight when I finally got there. The whole building was silent and dark.

I abandoned the wheelchair on the landing, for disposal later. The body, once I had it over my shoulder, was surprisingly light. They do say the desperate are capable of superhuman feats of strength sometimes.

I offered her another silent apology as we began our climb.

The slam of our front door behind me gave me such a start that I almost screamed aloud. Oskar was still lying on the floor exactly where I had left him—was I expecting him to have moved, somehow? I could not have said how long I had been away from the apartment. Two or three hours at least. Already the skin I could see on the back of his neck, on the hand emerging from the sleeve of one outflung arm, was beginning to mottle. I felt a sudden urge to sink to my knees, to beg his forgiveness. Instead, I forced myself to focus. It was only a few hours until dawn. There would be time for self-recriminations later. A lifetime, perhaps.

My first task was to arrange both of them on the bed. I did this with much effort, putting his arm around her, again apologizing. Then I removed the necklace from around my neck—the one with the *wedjat* eye pendant, one of the matching pair my sister and I had always worn—and gently fastened it around hers.

I had the other, Lucy's, in my suitcase still, to remember her by. Into that same small suitcase, I gathered my paints and brushes, camera and photographs, my journal and both passports, my real one and the forgery that had cost me and Oskar so much, one change of clothes, and all of the money, stepping over a dark puddle of blood each time I crossed the room. I set the suitcase by the door and put on my coat and shoes.

I fetched the long matches from the top of the stove and—whispering more apologies and wiping silent tears with my coat sleeve—I made my way around the room, lighting matches, scattering them. On the floor. On the bed. By Oskar's discarded canvases. By my second circuit, things were already catching. I took another bundle of matches, struck them at a single go, and forced myself to hold the flame with a quivering hand to the bottom of the curtain. Then, closing the door behind me—quietly this time, feet light on the stairs as I descended—I left.

Crossing the courtyard, I looked back to see the window already illuminated orange. Something caught, and for a moment the room glowed incredibly brightly, then a window shattered. The landlord and his wife were asleep on the ground floor, their windows dark, shutters drawn. I paused, hesitated. Then before I had a chance to change my mind, I made a fist with my hand and hammered it, four or five times against their door.

Then I ran. As fast as my feet could carry me in my shoes, into the night, carrying my little case. What surprises me now is how calm I was. How ruthlessly pragmatic I could be. What I proved to be capable of. What I have since proved capable of forgiving myself for.

Then again, ever since I was six years old, I can hardly remember a time when I did not feel like a murderess.

CHAPTER 17

CAROLINE, DUBAI, 2023, THE NIGHT OF HARRY'S DEATH

I had to admit the view from my balcony was impressive at night. The illuminated pools and fountains down below. The Burj Khalifa in the distance, its tip piercing the clouds. The oddity of looking down at the city from this high up and being able to see where the lights come to a halt, where the darkness of the desert began on one side, the sea on the other.

What are you doing here, Patrick? I thought. Meaning in this country. Meaning on this balcony, too, perhaps. With me.

It was nearly midnight, but the air was still warm on our faces. We had drunk the first bottle of champagne fast, both of us talking a lot. He pointed out other hotels, other towers, his hand once or twice brushing against my bare arm. We looked for his gallery, standing on tiptoes; he pointed out his Jumeirah villa, clearly proud of its proximity to the coastline. Every so often, he would repeat the amount the painting had sold for, in an incredulous voice.

"Will it be enough?" I asked.

He looked puzzled.

"For Harry, I mean."

"Enough to keep Longhurst? Probably. Enough to stop it crumbling?" Patrick shrugged. "Who knows? It's funny, I used to think it would be exciting and glamorous to inherit a house like that. Now I think it would be a pretty dreadful fate. Never knowing what's going to go wrong next, or how much it'll cost to fix. I'm not surprised Juliette ran away."

We watched a distant plane cross the skyline. I felt the tingle of the champagne in my veins.

"I'm sorry, Patrick, about the way things ended between us. It was a horrible thing I did to you."

He thought about this for a while. "I am sure I have plenty of things to apologize for too," he said. "I mean, I can understand why you did it, I think. I do remember what it was like, that whole period. We weren't exactly getting along."

That was an understatement. They were so many evenings that would start well enough, dinner in a restaurant, a pint at a pub by the river, and then some offhand comment would get taken the wrong way, and by the time we got home we would not have spoken for half an hour, would go to bed fuming and spend the whole night resenting every time the other person rolled over or tugged on the blankets.

We had sometimes discussed having a child, but there was no way I wanted to bring a baby into the world with someone that angry, that unhappy, that fragile. Someone obsessed, even if he wouldn't admit it, with the idea that he had failed to live up to expectations—his own, his father's, whatever they had drilled into him at school about the way his life would turn out. Patrick refusing ever to admit he found it difficult, dealing with my success, my being the star of the relationship. My resentment silently growing at pouring our savings, my book's royalties, into Patrick's failing gallery. Watching each disappointment gnaw away at him and seemingly being able to do nothing about it.

Toward the end, it was almost impossible to think of the Patrick I was married to and the Patrick I had fallen in love with as the same person at all. Now it felt like it was the old Patrick I was with, on this balcony.

This was, I knew, a dangerous feeling. He had a wife. He had a house, a business, a whole life here in Dubai, one that he had worked hard to build. I had my career, in Cambridge.

"Patrick," I said. "What are we doing?"

He took my champagne glass from my hand and put it on the table. I heard the clink as he put his own glass down too. Then I turned to him. Then he kissed me, just as I knew he would, just as I had been waiting for him to. And I can't explain how it felt, except to say that it did not just feel natural, it felt inevitable. He kissed me and in that moment it all melted away—the sadness and shame and regret. We were two twenty-one-year-olds with no idea of what was to come. I was reminded too of his gentleness, his patience, in those early days. When I pulled away. When he felt me suddenly clam up. Not at physical intimacy but—unexpectedly, uncontrollably—at any hint of emotional intimacy, domesticity. Sleeping together, that was fine. Staying overnight was a habit we slipped into. But it was months before I would let him leave a toothbrush or a change of clothes in my room, years before I introduced him to my grandmother. It can't have been easy for him, yet again and again I was amazed at the sensitivity with which he would grasp the right thing to say, the right thing to do. All the things not to say and do.

"Maybe we should go inside," he said, taking my hand.

Afterward, lying in bed, Patrick and I found ourselves talking about the past, our past, specifically our first night together. Did I remember the first thing I ever said to him? Did he remember what song was playing? I remembered his shirt. He remembered the dress I had on. How strange it was to exist in someone else's head like that, fixed forever, unchanging. I wished there was some way in which we could start it all again from that moment, live the whole thing once more and not let it go wrong, not lose sight of each other this time around.

"I think I fell in love with you that night," he said. "That very first night I met you."

"I'm pretty sure I did not fall in love with you until later," I said. "I did quite like your shirt, though."

Patrick turned to face me again, propping himself up on his elbow. His face grew serious.

"I have never stopped loving you, you know. I thought I had, until I saw you again, but . . ."

"You don't need to say things like that, Patrick. Honestly. This is nice, this was lovely, please don't feel it's necessary to say things you don't mean."

"I'm serious."

He stroked my hand.

"You should probably go," I said.

But he didn't move. For a long time he said nothing and neither did I. Eventually, reluctantly, Patrick checked the time on his phone and groaned. I asked him if he was sure he was safe to drive, and he said he thought so. He asked if I thought it was too late to knock and tell Harry the good news about the painting's sale, and we decided it was never too late to find out you were somewhere in the region of thirty million pounds better off. He knew Harry's room was on the same floor as mine because he had booked and paid for it, and that he would be passing it on his way to the elevator.

I pulled on the hotel bathrobe as Patrick got dressed and kissed him goodbye at the door. Despite everything, there was a longing in that kiss, a tenderness.

Perhaps even some kind of promise.

PATRICK, DUBAI, 2023, THE NIGHT OF HARRY'S DEATH

I was going to tell her. That was what I had promised myself on that balcony, before I kissed Caroline. I was going to tell Sarah. I would tell her what had happened and I would tell her why. There would be no attempt at concealment. I was not a man like my father, with his affairs, his assignations, his endless indiscretions. I could not be.

Room 712, Harry's room, was halfway between Caroline's and the elevator. I paused outside it, listened for sounds of life, leaned down to check under the door for lights, then knocked. No answer.

After a minute or two, I knocked again. This time I could hear a faint groan. "Who is it?" Harry croaked through the door.

"Me," I said, my voice low, urgent. "Harry, it's Patrick."

There was a thump, as if someone had just rolled heavily out of bed. A pause. Harry opened the door, just a crack, chain taut across it. "What do you want?" he said.

"Are you not going to let me in?" I asked. The door did not open wider. "How are you feeling?"

He shrugged, grunted. He looked terrible.

"Well, this might cheer you up: your painting sold tonight, Harry. For forty-two million pounds."

He nodded, mumbled something, noisily took off the chain and let the door swing open.

His room was an absolute mess. There was half-eaten room service on the bedside table, wet towels on the floor. The balcony door was open, a thin white curtain billowing inward. Every lampshade looked askew.

"Excuse all this," he said.

"Harry Willoughby, what on earth is going on? I have just told you that your money troubles are over. That thanks to the tremendous amount of work and effort I have put in, the auction tonight I organized and bankrolled, you are going back to Longhurst—which you now won't need to sell—with tens of millions in your back pocket." I placed my hands on both his shoulders and looked him straight in the eye. "I don't mean to be needy, mate, but could you at least fucking *react?*"

A thank-you would have been nice, for instance. It had been my gallery on the line as well as his house. It had been Harry who had come close to fucking the whole thing up. Still his face was sullenly blank. It was like I was telling him he had just put a winning lottery ticket in the wash. I could feel myself growing increasingly angry now.

"Harry, tell me what's wrong?"

"It's the photographs," he said.

"The photographs? What photographs?"

Then I didn't need him to answer that question, because the answer had suddenly dawned on me. If someone was sneaking about taking pictures of Caroline at his twenty-first, maybe they had something on Harry from that night too. Maybe he had received an envelope of pictures, just as she had.

"Is someone trying to blackmail you, Harry?"

Harry let out a deep sigh, and nodded. "And whoever it is, they want *serious* money."

At last it began to make sense, how strangely he had been acting. How frazzled and erratic he had seemed. Despite the mess of the rest of the room, I noted that Harry's bed had not been slept in. He looked like a man who had not slept properly for months. The question was . . .

"Harry, what on earth have they got pictures of you doing?"

There was almost a laugh in my voice as I said it, so hard was it to imagine Harry as a straitlaced twenty-one-year-old doing anything worth blackmailing him about more than thirty years later.

Harry sank onto a corner of the bed. He ran his hands over his face, through his tufts of hair. He looked up at me. He indicated with a gesture that I should find somewhere to sit down too.

Then it all came spilling out, in the way secrets will when they have been bottled up and churning around inside someone for decades. "Slow down, Harry," I kept saying. "Harry, what are you telling me?"

They had been up high on the scaffolding that night, he said, after the fireworks. He and Freddie, smoking, swigging champagne straight from the bottle. They had both been drinking enthusiastically since before dinner. Freddie kept pestering him to do a line of coke.

"*It's your twenty-first, live a little*, that sort of thing," Harry explained. "*Don't be such a boring prick.* Eventually I said yes mostly just to see the look on his face."

Freddie had chopped out the line on the wooden planks, by the light of the flashlight Harry was holding. He had passed Harry a rolled-up five-pound note, mimed what to do next. Harry had hunched to snort the line—and that was when Freddie had whipped out his camera and taken pictures. *Flash-flash-flash.*

"Of you and the coke?" I asked. Harry nodded.

"And that was the photo someone sent you? A—what—thirty-year-old picture of you with a line of coke at a party when you were twenty-one? You can't be serious—you're letting someone extort a fortune from you with *that*? You're not even an MP anymore! Who cares?"

Harry shook his head, face ashen. "There was an argument," he said. "I was furious. He kept laughing. It turned into a proper fight, like when we were kids. You know how he could be, Patrick. You must remember. I was trying to take the camera from Freddie. He kept teasing me with it, waving it above his head, talking about selling the pictures to the papers. Telling me my political career was over before it had begun. Student politician's drug shame. MP's son in cocaine scandal."

"He was just winding you up," I said.

"No. It was more than that. It was always more than that with Freddie and me because of Longhurst. Because he was bitter, resentful. Because in the normal order of things, the house should have gone to *his* grandfather, not mine. I didn't doubt for a minute he was serious about planning to sell that photograph. Not for a minute. And I knew how badly he needed money, because he was always begging to borrow it."

"What did you do?" I asked him softly.

"I was trying to grab him and his shirt got torn and he lost his temper. He punched me on the side of my head, hard. We started grappling. He got me in a headlock. I kept trying to trip him over, get him down so I could get that camera."

I asked what had happened next.

"He fell," said Harry, not looking at me. "I tried to snatch the camera again and he stumbled backward and caught his heel and he tumbled off the scaffolding. We were three stories up. He didn't even have time to scream, but I could hear the crunch as he landed. We were on the opposite side of the house to the tent, so nobody saw it but me. Or so I thought."

I did not say anything.

"I scrambled down as fast as I could, but when I got there he wasn't moving. And there was blood, so much blood, on the paving stones. I could see it spreading, thick and dark and shiny. His eyes were closed. His mouth was open. He wasn't breathing. I looked around for the camera, feeling around in the bushes behind him, but it must have been thrown from his hand."

"Jesus Christ! Your cousin was lying dead or dying on the ground and the first thing you thought to do was to look for the fucking *camera*? It didn't occur to you to call an ambulance?"

"I panicked. I was drunk, I had done a line of cocaine, and I wasn't thinking straight. And I *did* run off toward the tent to get help. Then I stopped running and started thinking. About what was going to happen to me. About the inevitable scandal. About the impact this would have on my parents, the family's reputation. He was already dead. It was an accident, but he was dead, and there was nothing I could do about it."

"I don't understand," I said, trying to get all this to fit together with what I already knew. "They never found a body. The police found the blood, but they never found his body. And his car—if he was already dead, the police's theory that he drove off drunk and drowned . . ."

Harry shook his head. "That was me," he said, barely audibly.

"What was you?"

He did not answer.

"*What* was you, Harry?"

"The car. I moved the car."

"You moved Freddie's car?"

In a way, I was even more horrified by that than I was by the revelation that Harry had killed Freddie. That had been an accident, at least according to Harry. I could imagine the panic and fear he must have felt when he realized what he had done. What I could not imagine was doing what he had done next. The coldness of it. The callousness.

"So let me get this straight, Harry. You left Freddie's body—his dead body—just lying there, you went to find his car keys, and you plowed his car into the River Ouse on purpose. So that it would look like he had driven off. So that everyone would assume what they mostly did assume, that he had driven it into the river himself and been swept away."

Harry nodded, just one nod, no eye contact.

"It makes no sense," I said. He glanced over at me. He looked angry.

"That plan makes no sense to me," I repeated. "How did you get back? His car was found a few miles from the station—it would have taken you hours to walk back to Longhurst, with the body just lying there waiting for someone to find it. There's something you're not telling me. Someone else must have helped you, driven with you, driven you back."

For a moment, Harry hesitated. Then, confirming this, he spoke.

"You remember Arno von Westernhagen?"

I nodded. Of course I remembered Arno. The last time I had seen him was at his farewell drinks perhaps twenty years ago, all the Osiris boys there, as he left for a job at Goldman Sachs in Hong Kong. Arno drunk, hugging everybody, reminiscing about the old days. Harry there too. Both of them looking pensive and somber and sad when someone—it might even have been me—proposed a toast to Freddie.

"You bastards," I said.

"It wasn't his fault. He didn't know. I told him we were playing a prank. It wasn't hard to convince him. Freddie had been winding him up all night, about Arno being sober. And of course he was the only person at the party I knew was safe to drive, because he wasn't drinking."

I was puzzled, briefly. Arno might not have been drinking, but I could also not remember him having a car at the party. In fact, I knew he had not had a car that night because . . .

"Wait a minute. He was driving *my* car, wasn't he? He was driving you around in *my* fucking car. That was why the seat was wet, wasn't it? You were soaking when you climbed out of the river. But he must have realized at that point that this was no prank, that something serious had happened. How did you persuade him to keep it quiet?"

"Because I knew his secret. I'd looked him up, his family. I was in the university library one day and I thought it would be funny to find out a bit more about them, maybe find a picture of this castle of his. It turned out there are no counts von Westernhagen, and there is no castle associated with that family name in Bavaria. It was all a fabrication. When I confronted him about it he confessed the whole thing, that it was all stuff he had concocted to make himself more popular at school which got out of hand. His father was just a perfectly normal banker, his mother a corporate lawyer."

"And that was all it took, to stop him going to the police? The threat that you would tell everyone he was not really a German count?"

Harry looked at me as if I was being very slow.

"By the time he worked out what was going on, Patrick, he was already an accessory. I told him it was an accident. I tried to convey to him everything that was at stake. Freddie was dead and there was nothing either of us could do to help him, but there were things to do to manage the fallout from his death . . ."

"Oh, Jesus Christ, the body. You are going to tell me you did something to the body too, aren't you?"

"I never got the chance. All the way to the river, all the way back, I was panicking, trying to think with Arno screaming at me, trying to work out what I was going to do. Where I was going to hide it. But when I got back the body was gone."

"Gone? What the fuck do you mean, *gone?*"

"Vanished. Disappeared. Everyone was still partying. Everyone was still over on the other side of the house. The pool of blood was still there. No Freddie."

"Someone else must have moved the body. But who?"

"That's what I don't know. That's what I have spent the last thirty years wondering. Knowing all that time that somewhere out there, there was someone who knew what had happened to Freddie, and that same person probably had the camera—which was nowhere to be seen either—and they were probably saving it all up to really fuck me over. Waiting to expose me, destroy me, anytime they felt like it. Perhaps they thought one day I'd be prime minster—*I* certainly bloody did—and then they'd really have a payday. Well, evidently they got bored waiting and decided now is the time. I received an envelope through the mail a few weeks ago, Patrick, with that photograph inside it and a demand for money. A huge amount of money."

It was the little whine in his voice as he said this that tipped me over the edge. That little whine at the unfairness of it, that Freddie had slipped, that Freddie had died, and Harry finally had to deal with the consequences of that. He had spent thirty years feeling sorry for *himself,* irritated by the position Freddie had put *him* in. Not a thought for Arno or me, or the way he had used both of us. Not a thought for Athena. *Not a thought for poor fucking Freddie.*

I have never felt rage like it. I have never despised another human being so completely as I did Harry in that instant. If I hadn't been willing myself not to, I would have literally leapt across the room and taken his throat in my hands.

"There's something else," he said.

"Something *else*?" I said, unable to swallow an incredulous laugh. "How can there *possibly* be something else?"

"I got a note under the door this evening, while I was out at the gallery with you," he told me. "A sheet of legal paper, folded in half, with a message typed on it."

"And what did this message say?"

"I'm sorry, Patrick. They want all of it."

"The money? After my commission and the expenses of the show have been deducted, that's still well over thirty million pounds, Harry. You can't possibly be suggesting you're going to just hand all that money to some . . ."

I trailed off. Harry was shaking his head. His face was solemn. "They've told me they want *all* the money, Patrick. The entire sale price of the painting. And we're going to give it to them."

JULIETTE, PARIS, 1938

The facts of the matter were simple enough, reported in the newspapers at the time. A family tragedy. A boating expedition across the lake. The two Willoughby girls, Juliette, aged six, and Lucy, ten, sneaking off unnoticed on a sunny afternoon, with a small parcel of sandwiches and cake pilfered from the kitchen, to row over to the island. What was not recorded was the fact that it was all my idea, all my fault. That I had badgered my sister, cried and stomped and sulked since breakfast, until she finally rolled her eyes and relented.

The island itself was a long, thin squiggle surrounded by reeds, one path leading from the little wooden jetty through the knee-high grass up to the pyramid that my father had built as his future mausoleum. Next to it, a little circle of stamped-down grass where we had unpacked our picnic baskets with Nanny so many times before.

We never made it. Not that afternoon, that calm, sunny afternoon.

I saw something glint in the water and then dart under the boat, and we both scrambled across to one side to lean over and see what it was. The boat tipped. We both fell. As we were falling, the boat came down on top of us.

I lived. Lucy did not.

The water was not deep, but it was cold, and neither of us were strong swimmers and we were some way from shore.

I can still taste that lake water. The feeling of being sucked down into darkness, freezing cold, the weight of my clothes growing, nobody in earshot. I remember scrabbling at the side of the upside-down boat, trying to pull myself up on it, failing, trying again, failing, trying again. In the distance, golden sunlight was falling across the still, peaceful lawn.

It was one of the gardeners who spotted me clinging desperately to the hull, threw himself into the water, and swam across. He dragged me to the shallows, my feeble kicks doing little to help, my limbs so chilled from the water I could feel nothing, desperately struggling to tell him through chattering teeth that my sister was still out there.

He pulled me up onto the bank and laid me on my side and I threw up brown water.

By the time he turned back to get Lucy, the lake's surface was still and unbroken.

He lunged in, lurching around in the water, calling her name, struggling to take his jacket off and free his arms, his shirt clinging to him as he ducked under the water again and again. I shivered violently, thinking if I was this cold how freezing poor Lucy must be. A housekeeper carried me inside, and I sat alone wrapped in a blanket on a bench in the front hall and waited for the inevitable news.

It was the only time I ever saw my mother cry.

Several times that afternoon my father asked me to explain again what had happened, whose idea it had been, how the boat had capsized. Even as a child I knew what he was really asking: who can I blame? The answer was: me. It might have been both of us who tipped the boat. But I had seen the flash in the water. I had begged Lucy for an island picnic.

My mother hugged me briefly and asked the housekeeper to put me to bed, even though it was only late afternoon. On the other side of the room my sister's bed was empty. I lay there with the light coming in still around the curtains, thinking about Lucy lying somewhere else in the house, cold and wet and alone, and I was unable to bear it, the ache in my throat sharp as daggers. A sob that would not come.

She was dead, and it was my fault. My beloved older sister. My father's obvious favorite. Everyone's favorite, really. The sister all the servants doted on. The sister who tried to take the blame for me so many times when I had done something naughty—broken something precious, torn my dress again. The sister who begged my father for months until he gave us those matching pendants—*wedjat* eyes to protect their wearer from harm—the only time he ever parted with any of his collection for anyone. The sister whose example, even when she was alive, I never seemed able to live up to. To whom I had always been compared and found wanting.

My mother had always been chilly and distant and my father eccentric, but after Lucy's death she froze completely and his behavior became increasingly bizarre.

By the time I reached the Gare du Nord, it was almost morning. It was hard to believe that life was carrying on as normal, the porters shouting, whistles blowing, a man mopping down one of the platforms and whistling tunelessly to himself. I took a seat at a table and ordered a croissant and black coffee, surprised to see that my hands were not shaking as I lifted the cup to my lips. Shock, I told myself. That is why none of this feels quite real yet. That is why it was so hard to believe that somewhere, on the other side of the city, two burned bodies were being removed from a charred apartment, the *sapeurs-pompiers* stomping around amid the ashes of my life with Oskar in their blackened boots. The landlord and his wife, watching it all. Around my neck was the pendant I found under my sister's pillow after she died—I always wondered if it might have protected her, had she worn it that day on the lake, had she not taken it off for safekeeping—with mine now resting around the neck of a dead stranger.

On the left side of my jaw, hidden by hair worn loose, was a single long bruise. The ache was steady and continuous. Every time I took a sip of coffee I had to suppress a wince as the hot liquid came into contact with the cut on the inside of my cheek. The croissant I pulled to tiny pieces and soaked in the coffee before slipping it into my mouth, and still it was painful to chew. Every time my jaw throbbed, I thought of Oskar, could see once more that look in his eyes. I had to force myself to finish the croissant. I ended up leaving most of the coffee.

It was time for my train.

As we were pulling out of the station, the sun appeared over the rooftops, setting the windows glinting. A woman and her husband belatedly found their way to my carriage and sat down. I smiled at her, looked back out the window. Did I mind if he put one of their suitcases up over my head, she asked? *Bien sûr*, I replied. I only had one small case, inside it everything I now owned in the world.

In my lap, gripped tightly in my gloved hands, was my new passport, the one with my face in it and someone else's name. No, not someone else's. That was what I had to learn to accept. My name was not Juliette Willoughby any longer, and never would be again. If this was to work, if all of this was to be worth it, I had to be the woman in that passport. A new name. A new life. That was what stretched out in front of me. To myself, not moving my lips, I practiced saying it, my new name, my only name.

Alice Long.

PART IV

THE MURDER

They thought I was a Surrealist, but I wasn't. I never painted dreams. I painted my own reality.

—FRIDA KAHLO

CHAPTER 18

PATRICK, DUBAI, TWELVE HOURS AFTER HARRY'S DEATH

A murderer. That is what they think I am. Harry Willoughby, my oldest friend, was killed last night, and the police think that I did it.

Where did I go after the party at the gallery? That is what the officer keeps asking me.

"Home," I keep telling him. "I signed the paperwork for the sale of the painting, I called and left a voice message for my wife, then I drove home."

"Straight home?" he asks.

"Straight home," I say, as confidently as I can muster. Because suddenly it has occurred to me that if I tell them where I *actually* went, or what I *actually* did, I won't be the only one in a cell.

So instead of confessing that I went back to my ex-wife's hotel room for a celebratory drink and committed adultery—which is not just frowned upon but technically illegal here in Dubai—I lie. The instant the lie leaves my lips, it hits me that if he somehow finds out I haven't told the truth, I'm going to be in even worse trouble.

When the interrogation is over, I am taken to a holding cell. The smell of it, stale and acrid, is overpowering. One large room divided by a wall of floor-to-ceiling green-painted bars. On one side of the bars there about fifteen detainees, all male. Everyone is wearing the clothes they were arrested in—laborers in blue jumpsuits, guys in hotel porter garb, an older man in a cheap suit. Several are lying on the floor with jackets over their heads. A few have managed to find an angle at which they can sleep in one of the plastic chairs. On the other side of the bars, a man in uniform sits at a desk. On the wall behind him our phones lie in numbered cubbyholes. A couple of my cellmates are up at the bars, arms outstretched, asking to use their phones, being ignored. Every so often, the guard looks up in irritation, asks one his name, grabs his phone, and hands it to him.

It is almost three hours before I am able to call Sarah.

Several times I have gone up to the bars, been ignored, and sat back down again. This time I have been standing there for twenty minutes before he acknowledges my presence, sighs, and asks my name. I tell him. He starts searching the cubbyholes in a desultory fashion, checking the plastic bags in which the phones are kept, on which our names are scribbled. I tell him mine is on the bottom row, far left. He either does not hear me or does not understand. He brings out the wrong phone several times and holds it up. I shake my head each time but try to look encouraging, praying that he won't get irritated and stop looking. Eventually, he brings over the right phone, holding up three fingers and then tapping his watch.

I have missed calls and new messages, but with the phone at just 19 percent power, I decide to ignore them. With trembling hands, I call my wife. It goes straight to voicemail. Of course it does. The sheikha's wedding Sarah is running is in the middle of the desert—no phones allowed, and no reception anyway. She won't even see I have tried to call her until sometime on the drive home tomorrow. I leave a very brief message, promising I will try to call again. I don't know what else to say.

The instant I hang up, I am surrounded by men asking if they can use my phone too, hands pressed together, imploring. "I'm sorry," I say to them, genuinely meaning it. "The battery, it's very low . . . I'm so sorry."

What happens when the thing dies, I just don't know.

At the back of my mind I can feel a storm cloud gathering, a deluge of grief that will hit when it sinks in that Harry—someone whose life has been entangled with mine for as long as I can remember—is gone. For the moment, though, I just feel numb.

I am about to hand the phone back to the guard when it occurs to me that I know a lawyer here, Tom Wilson, the husband of a friend of

Sarah's. He's not a criminal lawyer, but he must at least have some idea how the UAE's legal system works. Thankfully, I have his number saved. Tom's phone rings, keeps ringing. *Fuck*. I hang up, call again. This time, he answers.

"Patrick! Good to hear from you—"

I stop him abruptly, explain what has happened, fast, and tell him what the police have been asking me. It sounds like I've caught him at home—in the background I can hear his wife, Sumira, asking what's going on.

"Patrick's in a cell at CID, out by the airport," he tells her.

"Christ," is her non-reassuring response. "What the fuck's he done?"

"I haven't *done* anything," I say emphatically, loud enough, I hope, for her to hear too.

There is a long silence at the other end of the line. When Tom speaks, he sounds like he is considering his words very carefully.

"Patrick. There is something it is vital for you to understand. Just like the UK, the UAE's judicial system is based upon the principle that you're innocent until you are proven guilty."

"That's good news, because I *am* innocent," I say. "And as soon as they start to investigate, they'll realize that."

"In theory, yes. In practice, I am not so sure. Because I don't think they are *going* to investigate, Patrick. Not in any real way. Not if they've got a plausible culprit. Because in my experience, in this country, once someone has been charged, they almost always get convicted."

"That person being me."

"Look, let's not despair just yet," Tom says. "You may be able to convince them there has been a mistake *before* they charge you, before this goes any further."

"Oh God," I hear Sumira saying.

"'Oh God'?" I ask.

"It's nothing," said Tom. "The TV's on."

"It's on the news," Sumira says. "It's on BBC News 24."

"What is it, Tom?" I ask.

His voice sounds strained, distracted. "They're reporting that a British man has been found murdered, Patrick. At a hotel in the

DIFC. They're not naming him yet, but they are showing footage of the hotel, cordoned off. The police have confirmed they have someone in custody."

The blood in my ears is roaring. My fingers can barely grip the phone. The fact that the police have released a statement about my arrest is not good news at all. The slim chance I might still have had of persuading them they've got the wrong man has already evaporated. Tom and Sumira know that. I know that. What they do not know, what I have not yet told Tom because I cannot bring myself to say it aloud, is *why* the police are convinced I'm Harry's killer.

Because according to the officer who interrogated me, they have identified the murder weapon, the implement that was used to brutally slash his throat. It was a broken champagne glass.

A broken champagne glass with my fingerprints all over it.

CAROLINE, DUBAI, TWELVE HOURS AFTER HARRY'S DEATH

The taxi driver looks concerned as he stops outside the police station, the building's blue-tinted windows reflecting an enormous, almost empty parking lot. I open the car door and the heat instantly fogs my sunglasses.

"Are you sure this is where you want to go, madam?" he asks.

"I'm sure," I tell him. As the closest police station to the DIFC, this is the one to which everyone at the gallery seemed confident Patrick will have been taken. The best place to go for answers about what is going on.

For hours I had been hanging around at the gallery, waiting for news. The police told us nothing as they marched Patrick to the patrol car. Neither Patrick's bewildered employees nor the journalists, obviously excited by the prospect of a much bigger story than the one they'd arrived at the press conference to report, had any sense of what was actually happening. It was unclear at that stage what Patrick had even been arrested for.

One of the local journalists was the first to hear that a British man in his fifties had been found dead in his suite at the Mandarin Oriental. My hotel. I thought immediately of Harry, staying on the same floor, how terrible he had looked last night. *Please God, don't let it be him*, I silently prayed.

"Was it a heart attack?" I had asked. "A stroke?"

The journalist shook his head. "We've been ordered not to report this yet, but he was murdered." He ran a finger across his throat. "There was a lot of blood in the room."

Giles Pemberton, there at the press conference to report for the *Times*, visibly paled. Should he come with me to the police station to inquire about Patrick, he had asked. I would be fine, I told him.

I am starting to regret that decision a little now.

I ask the taxi driver to wait, not quite sure how I will get back to my hotel otherwise.

Inside the white-tiled lobby of the police station there is a water dispenser, several rows of chairs, a laminated notice in English and Arabic about the procedure for paying a traffic fine. I have been standing in front of the reception counter for several minutes before the man behind it looks up. He raises an eyebrow, which shifts his gold-badged beret up a quarter inch.

"Patrick Lambert," I say. "I am looking for Patrick Lambert."

He has me spell the name, types it noisily into the keyboard in front of him. His expression does not change. He scratches his nose. He shakes his head. "No Lambert," he says.

"Can you tell me which of the other stations Patrick Lambert is being held at? He went with the police," I say. "I saw him getting into the car—the blue lights were flashing." For some reason, I feel the need to mime this.

"You are his wife?" he asks.

"Friend," I confirm.

"Then we cannot share this information anyway, madam," he says.

"His wife, Sarah, is out of town, working. Not contactable. Please, is there anyone else here you could ask?" I plead.

It feels strange, saying her name aloud. Sarah. Patrick's wife.

All night after Patrick left I had been lying there in bed, mentally lambasting myself for what had happened, horrified at what a mistake he and I had made, swept up in nostalgia and the excitement of events like a pair of middle-aged idiots. This morning, as he introduced me to the assembled press with that dimpled smile, that discreet wink, I was forced to admit to myself that I would never feel about anyone else the way I felt about Patrick Lambert.

And now this. Now all of this.

The officer shakes his head, making it clear the matter is closed. "I cannot help you, madam."

Outside the station, I climb back into my taxi and the driver asks me where I want to go. "The hotel, I suppose," I tell him. "Mandarin Oriental, DIFC, please." I don't think there is anything to be achieved by returning to the gallery, and at any rate I need to change out of these clothes, the creased and sweltering trouser suit I have been wearing all day.

When we pull up outside the hotel, all is complete pandemonium.

Uniformed men everywhere. Multiple police cars parked out front. Guests standing around outside and in the lobby, waiting to get back into their rooms. Long lines at the front desk—people wanting to check in, to check out, find out what is going on, complain. Businessmen in suits talking loudly about missing their flights. The staff trying to mollify people, explaining that the hotel remains an active crime scene.

I take a seat in the lobby with my phone in my hand in case Patrick calls. After several hours, during which all I can think to do is obsessively check the news feeds, scouring the internet desperately for any fresh information about what is going on, we are allowed upstairs to our rooms. There is much grumbling in the elevator from other guests, some lurid speculation about what has happened. I try not to think about Harry, and remind myself it has not yet been officially confirmed it is Harry who is dead.

The elevator stops at my floor and I can see, halfway down the corridor, three policemen standing around, talking. It is Harry's room they are standing outside. As I approach them, on legs that suddenly feel reluctant to carry me, one asks my room number and directs me around the long way to get there. A few minutes after I close my door—I have just kicked off my shoes and started a cold shower running—there is a knock. A policeman. One of his colleagues is waiting at the door opposite.

"You were staying here last night?" he asks, without introducing himself. I confirm this. He asks to see my passport, which I retrieve from the safe in my closet, handing it to him. He jots down my details and asks if I saw anything or anyone suspicious, or heard any disturbance.

"I'm afraid not," I say.

He does not write anything down in his notebook. Nor does he return my passport. He is not really looking at me but over my shoulder, into my room. He asks what time I went to bed, then where I was before that. I tell him I got in around midnight, having attended an event at the Lambert Gallery. His eyes narrow.

"We will need to talk to you further, madam. Until then, you must remain in Dubai, so I will take this with me." He holds up my passport, then opens the back page for his colleague to log the details in a pink receipt book. He tears off the duplicate and hands it to me, and they both start off down the corridor.

My mobile rings. I answer it, fumbling to swipe. My heart is pounding so loudly that it feels like it must be audible over the phone line. "Caroline, thank God." Patrick's voice is very faint. I can hear other voices in the background.

"Where are you?"

"I'm in a cell, at a police station near the airport," he says, sounding exhausted. "They keep offering me things to sign. Things I can't read, in Arabic. I have a lawyer friend trying to find out where I am exactly, to get hold of someone from the British embassy."

"I can help too," I say. "I'm your alibi. You were with me last night, I'll tell them—"

The reaction from the other end of the line is immediate and sharp. "Don't tell them that, for *Christ's* sake," Patrick hisses.

At first I assume it is Sarah he is thinking of, his marriage he is concerned about. Despite everything else going on, I feel a twinge of sadness at this.

"You have to remember where we are," says Patrick, his voice insistent. "Do you not remember what I told you last night, about adultery being illegal? People have gone to prison for it. You can't provide me with an alibi. You can't help me. You can only make things worse and land yourself in trouble too."

"But did you see Harry last night? If you went to Harry's room after you left mine, you might have been the last person to see him alive."

"I can't talk about that now. Not on the phone. Caroline, I'm calling because you need to leave. Something is going on and I don't want you getting entangled in it. Get on a plane. Get out of the country. Do it now."

"I can't, Patrick." He continues talking for a second, telling me to pack and call a taxi right away, before what I have said registers.

"Patrick, the police have just taken my passport."

ALICE, LONDON, 1938

Alice Long. Alice Evelyn Maud Long. I repeated the name silently throughout the journey. As I lay on the top bunk while the ferry crossed the channel, listening to the woman below me snoring. As I lined up to disembark at Dover. I showed my passport to the man in his booth, who barely glanced at it before waving me through. For a while I shuffled along with the crowd, soaking in the English voices, eyes adjusting to English signs and advertisements, my nose picking up English scents I had forgotten: damp woolen coats, hair oil, fish and chips.

Not until I was actually standing at the train station ticket office did I realize I had no idea where to go. With Oskar at my side, the plan had been America, with England a brief stop-off. Only now did it strike me how half-formed our vision of what would happen next had been. Once in New York, had Oskar believed he would be able to normalize his visa arrangements, resume his old identity, relaunch his career? There were certainly dealers over there who admired his work. Buyers with money. Other Surrealist artists, native and imported. Were his visions of long evenings in Manhattan bars, parties at which everyone spoke French, our life in Paris reconstructed across the Atlantic? The thought of being in a city where so many of our friends and acquaintances had already assembled, where so many people knew and would recognize us, had been very appealing when Oskar and I had been planning to go there together. Now New York felt impossible, for precisely the same reason.

Los Angeles? San Francisco? I knew no one in either city. I knew nothing *about* either city. If Los Angeles or San Francisco, why not Mexico City, why not Peking, why not Casablanca? I was very aware how fortunate I was, to be faced with such choices. I had enough money, from Oskar's sale of my painting, to get me anywhere. The trouble was, it would not last forever—I would need to earn a living soon enough, and I had not exactly been brought up to do so. I did not have the skills for clerical or teaching or nursing work. I could not bear the thought of picking up a paintbrush again, not yet. I thought of the photographs I had taken in Paris of Oskar and his friends. I had those rolls of film with me. I had my camera.

The first train that arrived at the platform was going to London, which felt to me like a sign. I paid for a first-class ticket, then panicked and instead sat in second class, where I was far less likely to know anyone. I took a room in the first hotel I passed in Charing Cross. The lobby was gloomy, the elevator tiny, the bellboy sullen. The room smelled close and dusty, and when I tried to open the window, I found it painted shut. In the middle of the night, I heard footsteps in the corridor and was sure I saw the door handle turn, so I barricaded myself in with the dressing table. I put my clothes and boots on and spent the rest of the night dozing on top of the covers, fully dressed.

The following morning, I moved to a hostel for women on Gower Street. While it was marginally more salubrious, I was confident nobody I knew in England would ever come near the place. I could tell that the other women living there were puzzled by me. Who I was. What had brought me there. I did not blame them. I was wrestling with the same questions myself. At first I spoke as little as possible, conscious of my accent attracting attention, inviting curiosity. Once, I heard someone in the corridor outside my room make a joke about "her ladyship," and I was sure the object of their mockery was me. Instead of speaking I listened, to the words the women around me used, the way they said things, and practiced copying them.

I bought myself a suit, chopped off my curls so that my hair was barely long enough to tuck behind my ears, and turned my auburn dark brown with chemist-bought dye. Now that even I barely recognized the girl I kept catching sight of in shop windows, it felt safe enough for me to start traipsing up and down Fleet Street, doing the rounds of newspaper and magazine offices with my modest folder of photographs. Pictures of André Breton with his hands crossed on his chest, fingers splayed, trying to look imposing. Of Man Ray, deeply engrossed in a game of chess. Salvador Dalí and Max Ernst, pulling faces.

I developed them in the sink in my room at the hostel, a blanket draped over the curtain rail to block out the light. Every time I developed a photo of Oskar, every time his face emerged beneath my hands, I felt my heart leap up into my throat. Oskar, smiling. Oskar lying on the grass, wearing sunglasses, pretending to sleep. Oskar inspecting his own painting on the wall of our apartment. Every time one took shape before me, I felt a split second of happiness before grief took its place. Each time, I forced myself to picture the way he had looked as he came at me, his face contorted. It was an accident, I told myself. I had been terrified. I had not meant to kill him. He was the one who had struck me first.

On the third day, someone finally agreed to look at my photographs. At the *Telegraph* office, a man with gray sideburns and the sluggish air of someone who had been drinking at lunch flicked through them, making me flinch at how carelessly he shuffled each to the back. At one point, when it looked like one might fall to the floor, I almost lunged to grab it.

He looked at a long, typed list in front of him, selected a few, then excused himself and disappeared over to a bank of desks where a group of men were shouting over one another and smoking. "They're very good," he told me on his return, and passed them back. "We'll take these three. How much are you asking?"

I had absolutely no idea, and could not even see which he had selected. I made up a figure on the spot, not sure if it was too high or too low, and we shook on it.

I bought the *Telegraph* the next day and had to steady myself against a lamppost when I saw which they had used and why. It was Oskar, sitting at the little wooden table by the window in our apartment, brushes and paint arranged in front of him. It was not the picture, though, but the headline that knocked the wind out of me: "Fatal Paris Fire Kills Artist Oskar Erlich and MP's Daughter."

I had done it. The body, the necklace, the fire, my whole plan. It had actually worked.

I had succeeded in murdering us both.

CHAPTER 19

PATRICK, DUBAI, THIRTY-SIX HOURS
AFTER HARRY'S DEATH

Being in a cell with no windows and no clock does strange things to your sense of time. Overhead strip lights that are never turned off. Doors slamming, keys jangling, men shouting, crying, praying.

Dinner last night was watery curry with rice, delivered in a plastic container, with a stack of metal bowls and no cutlery. After we had finished—all silently shoveling food into our mouths with unwashed hands—a small pile of thin blankets arrived, but only enough for half of us. We tried to make ourselves comfortable for the night on the floor with spare clothing as pillows. I settled back against the wall with my head on my knees, arms wrapped around them to ward off the icy chill of the air-conditioning.

As I sat there, I tried to shake off the numbness, but still could not force my brain to process that Harry had been murdered, that somehow my fingerprints were on the broken champagne glass used to slash his throat. It felt like a nightmare, but the one thing I knew, as I shifted position again to stop my back from seizing up entirely, was that I was not asleep. Was I being set up for some reason? Harry was being blackmailed, I told the police. Maybe he had confronted the blackmailer and there had been a struggle. *That* was what they should be investigating. Did I have any evidence that such a person existed, they had asked. I was forced to admit I did not.

Breakfast is dates washed down with water from the few bottles the guard left on the floor, and I am about to take a swig when my name is called. Before they open the cell door, they make me hold my arms out and cuff me—the first time they've bothered to do so. Then I am led down a corridor with a series of small, high windows, faint daylight filtering through. The guard barks something at me and, when it becomes clear I don't understand Arabic, grabs me by the shoulder and turns me to face the wall. Another door is unlocked before I am forcibly turned back around and bodily steered through it.

This room in which I find myself is almost identical to the room in which I was first interviewed. There is a single high window, frosted reinforced glass. A table. Two chairs. On one of them is Sarah. The guard directs me to the chair opposite her. I can tell from her reaction, and the way she quickly tries to mask it, that I must look even more terrible than I feel.

I place my cuffed wrists on the table and her eyes flick to my fingernails, which still have last night's dinner caked underneath. I give her a reassuring smile. Her face hardens slightly. *She knows*, I understand from this. She knows about Caroline and me. Or at least she suspects.

"I'm so sorry, Sarah."

She does not meet my gaze. Her eyes look sore and puffy. Her lips look chewed.

"The police came to the house last night," she tells me. "They didn't leave until dawn. They were going through your office, looking through your filing, at your bank statements. They asked about your movements on the night Harry was murdered. I told them that I was working in Abu Dhabi at a wedding, no phones allowed," she says, slowly, raising her gaze to fix me with an ice-cold stare.

I nod.

"I said that you left me a message to tell me about the painting's sale and that you were about to drive home, and I am sure you did just that. I told them there was no way my husband was capable of murder. That the very idea was ludicrous."

She pauses. "That was when they told me about the CCTV footage from the hotel, Patrick. They know when you arrived there. They have you in the lobby, getting into the elevator. They have you leaving the elevator again just after three in the morning. *Three in the morning*, Patrick."

I start to speak. She stops me. "They know you're lying to them, Patrick. And they think the reason is that you murdered Harry. But *I* know why you were really there."

I let my head drop. I close my eyes. I deserve this. In some ways I deserve all of this. "Sarah. I'm so, so sorry. I never meant . . ."

I trail off. It doesn't matter what I meant or didn't mean, it matters what I did, and with whom. I have chosen the worst way possible to break my wife's heart. I have cheated on her with the most hurtful possible person I could cheat on her with.

One of the things I could never quite forgive my father for was the way that each of his affairs poisoned a whole crop of seemingly unrelated memories. "How long?" was what my mother always demanded to know, on discovering his latest illicit dalliance. Meaning which holidays, which Christmases and anniversaries have you sat and smiled through knowing you were sleeping with someone else. Meaning which of the times you said you were working late and missed school plays or bedtimes or birthdays were because you had been sleeping with someone else. Meaning how many times have you said you loved me and been sleeping with someone else. Now Sarah must be going back through all our happiest moments together, our whole life here, and wondering if the entire time I had been pining for Caroline.

"I *know* you, Patrick. You're not as hard to read as you evidently think. I always knew that the only way this would work, with us, is if we stayed in Dubai." She is choosing her words carefully. "I knew that it wasn't over with her, even if you didn't. That she was someone who still took up space in your head. So I'm not surprised. But I *am* angry, I am hurt, and I—"

Her voice catches. "It could have been nice, Patrick. Ours could have been a really lovely, happy life."

She swallows, rubs at the corner of her eye. "I have a message for you. From Tom. He is at the embassy right now. His law firm has a fixer, and they are trying to get him in here, to speak to you, but he has told me to warn you it all takes time."

"Thank you," I say, smiling weakly.

"I am not going to come here again to visit. When you get out, whenever you get out, I don't know if I'll be able to forgive you, or if I even want to. But if there is any chance of us working through this, I have to ask you something, and I need you to give me an honest answer," she says.

I nod.

"Are you still in love with her?"

What I want to say is whatever will hurt Sarah the least, something about how it is possible to stop loving someone, or to persuade yourself you have stopped, and then start again without meaning to. That to have loved the same person twice at two different points in time does not mean that everything you felt in between was invalid. I want to tell her that I know loving someone, anyone, is no excuse for the damage I have done.

"All I want is the truth, Patrick."

As I am thinking about all the many things I want to say, I see that they are all just different ways of saying the same thing. That I am still in love with Caroline Cooper. I look into Sarah's eyes and my own start to swim a little. Even though I know it means the end of my marriage, my second marriage, I nod once, giving Sarah the answer she already knows is coming.

CAROLINE, DUBAI,
THIRTY-SIX HOURS AFTER HARRY'S DEATH

It is now a full twenty-four hours since Patrick was arrested. I have left the hotel just once since yesterday afternoon, to buy painkillers for the headache lodged between my temples.

I have the unshakable feeling that if I just think about everything hard enough, an explanation will present itself. Pacing the room, raking over the past few days' events in my mind, what I can't figure out is who would want Harry dead—and who might benefit from framing

Patrick for it. Nor have I fathomed how there can be two equally authentic versions of the same painting, and how this and Harry's death might be related.

All my books and papers are on the desk in the corner of the room—my original, lovingly transcribed version of Juliette's journal, my pictures of both paintings, a copy of my biography of Juliette, feathered with sticky notes. From time to time I pick one of them up as if the answer might lie there. The sudden loud ringing of the telephone next to the bed is so unexpected it startles me.

"There is a gentleman for you at reception," a voice brightly informs me. Presuming it's the police with more questions, I reluctantly head downstairs, taking the long way around to avoid Harry's room. In the lobby, a tall man in a dark suit and mirrored sunglasses is waiting for me.

"I've been instructed to take you to the Airport Freezone, madam. Mr. White will be meeting us there," he says, before ushering me outside to a silver Rolls-Royce Phantom. So he is not a policeman. He has been sent by Dave White—someone I still can't help but think of as Terry—to fetch me, as we had previously discussed but I had subsequently forgotten, to come and spend some more time with the painting he had bought.

I suppose it should not surprise or irritate me as much as it does that Dave White plans to store it in a Freezone. Such designated districts around the world are often where billionaires stash their assets, places where business can be conducted untroubled by taxes, customs duties, or VAT. Their impenetrable chambers can hold everything from vintage cars to fine wine to watches in temperature-controlled secrecy. I do sometimes wonder what those artists in their freezing cold Paris studios would think if they could see where their work had ended up all these decades later.

The drive does not take long.

From the road, the Freezone looks like a security installation, with its barbed-wire-topped fences, its floodlights, its sequence of gates and sentry boxes, the absence of windows on the concrete buildings themselves. The driver presses a buzzer and announces our arrival, then parks outside a nondescript door. I'm led into a marble foyer and from across her desk—enormously long, like the control panel of a spaceship—a woman gestures for me to sit, and makes a brief phone call.

After a few moments, a door at the far end of the room swings open and Dave White walks out.

Patrick had told me that when they met for lunch, Dave was wearing boardshorts. At the gallery dinner, he was in an immaculately cut navy suit. Today he is in a nondescript T-shirt, jeans, and sneakers. The only thing about him that suggests his wealth is the enormous Rolex on his wrist.

"Thank you so much for coming, especially under the circumstances," he says, holding out a hand for me to shake, then leads me along the corridor of numbered doors. "I was so shocked to hear about Harry, and about Patrick," Dave says, without turning. "If there is anything I can do . . ."

He stops, and the chauffeur, who has been following discreetly behind us, overtakes us to tap in a keycode. The door slides open, and inside is a gallery-like space with a white leather sofa in the middle. Hanging around us, carefully spaced and beautifully lit, are paintings by the best-known names in twentieth-century art. I can see a Chagall, a Duchamp, a couple of Erlichs, and several Picassos. And there, on the far wall of the room: *Self-Portrait as Sphinx*.

Then I realize what is hanging next to it, and gasp. I turn to see Dave, amused by my shock, grinning.

"That's the painting from Tate Modern. The other *Self-Portrait as Sphinx*."

"The painting that is usually in Tate Modern, yes. Except that last week, given the confusion about the existence of two seemingly genuine versions of the same work—which I am quite aware is a chronological impossibility, by the way—its anonymous owner decided to withdraw it from public display pending further analysis," he says. He is now grinning very widely indeed.

"You? *You're* its anonymous owner?" I say. I had always imagined the person who outbid us for the painting in Ely to be someone older, an amateur art-lover with a little money saved up or a connoisseur who got lucky. Not some teenage nerd. Not *Terry*.

"I am. I own both these paintings. One of them I bought from Patrick Lambert for forty-two million, forty-eight hours ago. The other I bought from under his nose, for quite a lot less, in 1991."

"*You* were the telephone bidder at the auction? How?" Even as I say this, I know that we must have somehow led him to it. "Also: *Why?*"

I stumble over to the sofa as Dave pours a glass of water, places it gently onto the coffee table in front of me, and takes a seat himself.

"To be perfectly honest, I bought it to fuck with Patrick, because I hated him."

"You hated Patrick? You hardly knew Patrick."

"That was the worst of it. I hardly knew him, he hardly knew me, and still I could hear him through the wall, making fun of me."

"Dave, I'm sure you're imagining—"

"No, I'm not imagining anything. You *know* I'm not. Patrick used to joke about me all the time. About my snoring. About what I was doing in my room late at night. About me being your boyfriend. I would be in the kitchen waiting for the kettle to boil, you would come in to grab something, say hello, and the rest of the evening I could hear him teasing you about *your boyfriend Terry*. It was a running joke, that someone like you would ever consider going out with someone like me."

That did all sound vaguely familiar, now that he mentioned it.

"And that was how you knew we had the painting? That Patrick put it up for auction? You were listening through the wall?" My heart racing, I am trying to work out all the other things he might have heard.

"It would have been impossible not to eavesdrop, actually. Given the thinness of the walls. Given that it never seemed to occur to Patrick to moderate his volume, that there might be someone trying to get some studying done just a few feet away from you. I knew you were looking for a painting at Longhurst. I knew you found it and took it. I heard you fight endlessly about what to do with it. I listened when Patrick told you how he planted the painting in the back of a removal truck, and I heard him explain his whole marvelously stupid plan, and I wrote down the name of the auction house. And I just thought, what a way to pay him back. Because he was so clearly in love with you, and when his scheme backfired, I was certain you would dump him. I still can't quite believe you didn't, to be honest."

I am staring at the painting from the Tate, trying to take this all in.

"I heard him say when the sale was, what your budget was. I had some cash—from share trading. I used to dabble back then, late at night, as you know—you could probably hear me tapping away, turning years of saved-up birthday money into a nice little pot to play with."

"But if you wanted to screw Patrick over, why not crow about the painting once you'd bought it—at least to him?" I ask, astonished he could keep a secret like that for so long, resist the temptation to advertise his own cleverness.

He squirms a little under my gaze. "I wanted you to dump Patrick, not to hate me. To think he was a dick, not that I was. I *am* sorry if I hurt you in the process. I know that you've been through some . . . stuff in your life," he says, at least having the decency to look apologetic.

I feel a sudden wave of revulsion. If he had been listening through the wall all that time, he probably knew things about me that I had never told anyone apart from Patrick. Some of which my grandmother had not even told *me* until I left for Cambridge.

Such as that until my eighteenth birthday, when I reached the age of majority, my father had remained in a position of legal authority over me. That when I had gone on a school trip to France, it was his permission that had to be sought. That if I had fallen seriously ill, he would have had a say in my medical treatment. Perhaps Dave had also heard me describe the devastation I felt when my grandmother explained that a life sentence does not mean the rest of a person's life, no matter how terrible the crime they had committed. That I had to learn to live with the knowledge that someday, my father might try to find me.

I was twenty-six when he was released.

Cooper is my mother's maiden name, and Caroline is my middle name, which perhaps made me slightly trickier to track down. Still, I knew that if he put his mind to it, it would not be hard. He had done so before, after all. But years passed, and nothing. I could not fathom why this silence upset me so much, and then eventually the penny dropped:

the only circumstance in which my father would *not* try to reinsert himself into my life was if he had a new family now. And that was the most horrifying thought of all.

There is a simple reason why I tell no one about my childhood. From the snatches of my story he heard through a wall, Dave might think he knows me, but there is no way he could begin to understand all the ways in which my father's crime has shadowed my life—nor my determination not to let it define me.

Abruptly I get up and cross the room to where the paintings are hanging, to inspect first one and then the other, and to hide the tears of fury collecting at the corners of my eyes.

"What made you decide to loan your painting to the Tate?" I said, trying to smooth over the catch in my voice. "Was that just to rub Patrick's nose in it?"

Dave White frowns and shakes his head. "I did it for you, Caroline. I must admit, when I first bought *Self-Portrait as Sphinx* at that auction, I had no idea what it was. I didn't even really look at it for years—I wasn't much of an art fan back then, let alone a collector. Then I read your book. You'd done incredible research, written a brilliant biography, but as far as anyone knew Juliette's painting no longer existed, so only a few other art historians cared. Who wants to buy a book about a painter with no paintings? I felt bad, and I was in a position to do something about it."

He pauses a moment, smiling to himself. "And having the painting turn up like that did wonders for your book sales, didn't it? Of course, having *Self-Portrait as Sphinx* accepted into a national institution also increased the painting's value exponentially. And now with the publicity around there being *two* genuine, near-identical works, authenticated by the world expert, the value of both is bound to soar further . . ."

"You *wanted* me to authenticate the second painting?" I ask incredulously. I had assumed that whoever owned the original would be hoping the opposite.

"Yes. Although I'd rather not have spent quite as much on it," he concedes. "I was a little annoyed that Athena's client was so lavish in his offer. I thought I knew all of the serious Surrealist collectors, but that guy came out of nowhere."

"So it was *you*. You sent me those photos. You tried to blackmail me!" I said slowly, searching his face for a reaction.

He looked genuinely confused. "I'm sorry, I have no idea what you're talking about."

"You were the only one apart from Patrick who knew I was looking for *Self-Portrait as Sphinx* at Harry's party. You must have heard us talking about it through that wall," I say, processing it aloud. "You followed me to see whether I found it, didn't you? You were there, with my shawl, after Harry's Granny got upset. You were there the morning after, by Patrick's car. You kept tabs on me the whole time. You took those photos. I saw the flashes, but I didn't realize what they were until a set of pictures arrived in the mail last week. You made a deliberate attempt to influence my professional opinion with a threat to expose me."

He laughs. It starts as a giggle and turns into huge, shoulder-shaking guffaws. Tears roll down his face.

"My God, you have no idea how rich I actually am, do you? People as wealthy as me don't need to extort art historians. Or anyone else, for that matter. Only desperate people blackmail. I could have paid three times what I did for that painting without even blinking," he says matter-of-factly.

"This, all of this," he says, gesturing around the room, "is a hobby. A passion project. And besides, your authentication was never, strictly speaking, necessary. Do you know how I made my money, Caroline? My business is training computer systems—it's what I'd have told you I was working on at Cambridge, had you ever asked. I was based in the Vision Lab, programming neural networks to identify patterns and recognize images."

It must be clear from my face that I am not quite grasping all the connections here. Dave smiles patiently, perhaps a little patronizingly.

"I make systems that can identify faces, even when they are partly obscured—say if someone is wearing dark glasses or a burqa. For my own interest—a sort of hobby, if you will, albeit quite a lucrative one—I've also created systems that identify a particular painter's technique, flagging when the imprimatur of the artist on one work aligns exactly with another. So I know with close to one hundred percent certainty that these two paintings were undertaken by the same hand. Juliette Willoughby's."

I had heard about tech like this—although it was viewed with condescension and suspicion by the art world. What I had never heard of was the person who *invented* the tech being the collector who used it.

"I am not dismissing your expertise, Caroline, but with this AI I can do exactly the same thing faster and more objectively than any art historian."

"So why am I here, then?" I say, finding it hard to stay entirely composed. "So you can show me all the art you can afford to buy because a computer tells you to?"

He looks pained. "Of course not. It was your book that got me interested in Surrealist art in the first place. The reason I've brought you here is because I own both these paintings and you are the only person in the world who can explain *how* they are both genuine works by the same artist. Because if anyone is ever going to know why there are four differences between them and what those differences mean, it is you."

There is a moment of silence, both of us looking up at the paintings. "You spotted all four?"

"Of course. I may not have studied art history, but I do look at the paintings I own. I noticed all four of them right away. The hieroglyphics. The mummified body in the boat. The boatman's beak. The pyramid on the island. All visible in the painting I have just bought, all overpainted in the one you stole from Longhurst."

"Overpainted on *this* canvas?" I am pointing at the *Self-Portrait as Sphinx* from Tate Modern. He nods.

"Expertly done, wasn't it? With paint of *exactly* the same composition. Then a thick coat of varnish was applied to the entire thing so as to make it essentially invisible. This wasn't caught when I loaned the painting to Tate Modern twenty-five years ago, but blacklight is much more sophisticated now, so we can see that both paintings were originally *identical* in composition."

"So someone carefully concealed four significant elements in the one I found at Longhurst?" I ask

Dave nods. Something occurs to me that I suspect he has figured out already.

"The brushstrokes on the overpainting," I say. "Have you run those through your program? Did you get a match?"

He nods. "A very definitive one, from a large dataset, because the painter was extremely prolific: Austen Willoughby. What I want to know," says Dave White, "is why he did it."

It feels like a lot of synapses are firing inside my skull all at once. I could never make sense of *Self-Portrait as Sphinx* because vital pieces of the puzzle were missing, pieces that the Willoughbys wanted to hide.

"I will work it out," I said to Dave, who seems to be genuinely holding his breath in anticipation. "And then I will tell you. But I need you to help me get Patrick out of prison first."

Dave doesn't say anything for a while. Then he crosses the room to stand beside me, silently inspecting both paintings before turning to me and nodding. "Just tell me what you need."

"I need to know who Athena's client was. They were clearly serious about getting their hands on that painting. Perhaps they were angry enough, when they didn't, to pay Harry a visit."

ALICE LONG, CAMBRIDGE, 1938-1940

After the *Telegraph* printed my photographs of Oskar, someone from *Life* magazine phoned the hostel and left a message for Alice Long at the front desk. They asked if I had any other pictures of the Surrealists and if I might stop by their offices if so.

Then a week after those photos were published in *Life*, the picture editor of the *London News* contacted me, asking to meet. "I may have an assignment for you," he said after we had talked about my work for a while. "Ever been to Poplar?"

The next day I was on a train to photograph a beauty contest. Two days after that it was Enfield, for a town hall opening. And both times I must have done something right, because there was another commission, and then another, and another.

I took a room in a boardinghouse in Hackney, not a fashionable part of town, never really leaving home unless it was to work, keeping myself to myself save for the evenings I sat in companionable silence with the other boarders listening to the wireless, obsessed like everyone else with what was happening in Czechoslovakia, in Albania, then eventually in Poland.

It was only when I could afford my own place, a pokey little one-bedroom flat above a shop in Clapton, that I even began to think about painting again. But whenever I considered what I might commit to canvas, the same old apparitions popped up, scenes that haunted my dreams and spilled from my subconscious. When I looked in the mirror above the fireplace, wondering if I might try a simple self-portrait, I still saw a Sphinx staring back at me, a girl weighed down with secrets she could never share. Sometimes, I would leaf through the pages of the journal I had kept in Paris, where I had sketched those figures and creatures, or the photographs I had taken of the painting before Oskar stole and sold it. But still the box of paints that I had brought with me from France in my suitcase sat in a corner of the kitchen, untouched.

I thought about the other painters we had known, followed in the news as they scattered, fled to Mexico and Portugal. Meaning that there were even fewer places I could now go, in case one day I was walking down the street and someone saw me, a ghost from a past life.

Even though I knew I had been declared dead—I sometimes even imagined the funeral, that poor woman's remains shipped back to Longhurst, a discreet, apologetic affair in the village church—I still went to great pains to remain invisible. I built a reputation for shyness, preferring to let my photographs speak for themselves. *A. Long* was the name under which my work appeared in the papers. I only accepted commissions where I was confident I would not see anyone who knew Juliette Willoughby—nothing political, no high-society events, no gallery openings.

The possibility of crossing paths with my father was what really kept me awake at night. Fortunately, by now this prospect was fairly remote. It was well known that he rarely attended the Commons these days, spending most of his time at Longhurst, undertaking his Egyptological studies. Every now and again there would be a story in the papers, a little paragraph about how much he had paid for a single scrap of papyrus or a sarcophagus.

Then it happened. It was a bright July day, and I was traveling up to a job in Oxford. Across the tracks at Paddington, I caught sight of a tall man standing stiffly at the platform edge, a briefcase gripped tightly in his leather-gloved hands. My heart froze. It was him. He appeared to be reading one of the advertisements on my side of the tracks. If he had looked just slightly to the left, he would have seen me.

Terrified that he would feel himself the object of my attention, I turned away, walking slowly and steadily along the platform, head bowed. When I glanced back, someone was shaking his hand, perhaps congratulating him for his recent elevation to the House of Lords. I was surprised that the fear was stronger even than the last time I had seen him, a fierce revulsion at the thought that we were related, that his blood ran through my veins. More than once I asked myself if what I had done to Oskar had really been an accident, whether it was something in my bad Willoughby blood that prompted me to pick up that knife, made me capable of using it. And I reminded myself: he was not a murderer, my father; he was something far worse.

When I got home, bolting the door even though I was sure I had not been followed, I knew what I had to do. I would paint *Self-Portrait as Sphinx* once more. Oskar had sold it to my family, who had undoubtedly destroyed it. What was there stopping me, though, from painting it again? Even if I could not exhibit it, at least it would exist. An invisible victory over my family. A work that might survive me, a symbol of the truth that my father could suppress but not erase.

There was also a part of me that simply missed painting. Which relished the challenge of seeing if I could re-create my poor destroyed work in all its twisted intricacy.

I bought the canvas in the same art supply shop in Covent Garden that Uncle Austen had always taken me to as a girl (making it an early-morning in-and-out trip, to ensure I did not accidentally run into him), replacing several tubes of near-spent paint at the same time, ensuring an exact match. I found that I barely had to refer to the photographs of the original that I tacked up on the wall beside my easel. The entire story poured out of me exactly as it had the first time. I even found myself fussing and fretting over the same details: the pyramid, my father rowing the boat across the lake, his tragic cargo, the incantation in hieroglyphics from the east wing's painted lintel. All those details I had carefully arranged as a message, which would have been loud and clear to my father: I know what you did and why you did it. I am not the mad one in this family. The mad one in this family is you.

For years, everyone had conspired to ignore his growing strangeness, his steadily worsening behavior. My father had always had a temper. Once I had seen him tearing the house apart, smashing things, in search of a lost cuff link. If anyone was late to breakfast, you could see him seethe. But the rages, the screaming fits, the furies prompted by nothing and aimed at everyone, all got so much worse after Lucy died. Terrible things he would come out with, screaming them across the dinner table, accusing me of having capsized the boat deliberately, saying he wished that I had drowned instead. My mother would simply continue eating.

Every single day, always alone, he would visit the pyramid where Lucy's body lay. Every year on her birthday he would spend the whole day on the island. On the anniversary of her death, he would lock himself away in the east wing for a week.

He talked to her. We all knew it, but no one ever mentioned it. When he was alone in his study, when he was shuffling around the garden, he would conduct a muttered one-sided conversation with my dead sister. Talking to her—fondly, warmly—in a way he never spoke to the rest of us. Sometimes, late at night, in the east wing, I heard him shouting other words, foreign words, over and over. *Ga ba ka, baba ka. Ka ka ra ra phee ko ko.* When I asked my mother about this, she insisted I must have been dreaming, and forbade me from leaving my room after dark.

As I began to paint, in my cramped little Clapton flat, other vivid snapshots of my past lives presented themselves: a primly dressed little girl in the nursery, losing whole days to whimsical watercolors of plants and flowers, my beloved sister begging me to come out to play on the lawn. Eighteen-year-old me on a gloomy afternoon at the Slade, sketching a life drawing model with a stinking cold—poor girl!—a little droplet of moisture gathering on the tip of her nose.

As I set up my easel next to the window in the kitchen, I recalled Oskar's endless little practical hints in the matter of paint mixing, brush cleaning, the extreme care with which he arranged his materials before he began work. For the first time since Paris, I allowed art to take me over completely, hour after hour passing, day darkening to night, as I obsessed over a single passage. And then the spell would be broken—children shouting outside, a series of clanks from the building's ancient pipes—and I would notice it was night and I was famished.

Once I had finished, having ignored all photographic commissions for nearly three months, barely leaving my flat in that time, I knew that was it. That I was done with painting, for good this time. I had painted my masterpiece, twice. I had proven I could do it. This new *Sphinx*, both guardian and secret-keeper, I hung at the head of my bed. Then, as the phony war ended and the Blitz began, I picked up my camera once more.

CHAPTER 20

CAROLINE, DUBAI,
THIRTY-EIGHT HOURS AFTER HARRY'S DEATH

Dave's Rolls-Royce is pulling up outside my hotel when Patrick calls.

"Thank God you answered. I'm about to be charged. There's a hearing today when they'll either grant bail or transfer me to a different jail to await trial."

He is speaking fast, so fast I am having to struggle to keep up.

"Will you have a lawyer with you? A translator? Is there anything I can do?" I take a deep breath. "Listen, there's something I need to tell you. I'm in the car on the way back from—"

"I can't speak long, my phone is almost dead and once that happens, that's it," he says. "Sarah is coming to the hearing. My lawyer says the optics of that are important for the judge. I am so sorry to ask, but I didn't even know what day it was until they confirmed the hearing . . . I need someone to speak to Dad."

"Your father? Sure thing. I can call him and explain what's going on," I said, although I was puzzled why he was asking *me*.

"Jesus Christ, no. Don't tell him anything. He knows I was selling a painting for Harry, but he has no idea what's happened since. Dad doesn't read the news. He watches black-and-white films all day and tells the nurses the same three stories on repeat. I'm accused of the murder of his late best friend's son and if I'm convicted he'll never see me again. He screams the care home down when someone moves his slippers. He can't know about all this, until he absolutely has to. It would probably kill him, and I'm honestly not exaggerating."

"Tell me how I can help."

"We speak at the same time every Sunday. Dad really isn't well now. The dementia is quite advanced. He remembers things from decades ago, but he couldn't tell you what happened yesterday. He also gets extremely agitated if anything doesn't run the way he expects it to, and then he kicks off and lashes out and sometimes has to be sedated. If I'd remembered earlier, the nurses could have distracted him, but Sundays are a whole performance, getting him dressed and into his chair, setting up the iPad. He'll be sitting there right now on Zoom, waiting for me."

"Alright," I say, walking through the hotel lobby, wondering if Patrick's dad was not going to find it a bit confusing when his son's ex-wife popped up on the screen. "Send me the link."

My heart aches at the thought of Patrick, alone and scared in a prison cell and yet still so worried about upsetting a man who had never put his own son first. Their relationship had always been like this—Patrick's desperate desire to earn his father's love and approval, his obvious adulation and attempts at emulation. Quentin uncomfortably invested in Patrick's career but taking little interest in his son's personal life unless it involved a country house or a public-school friend.

I race up to the seventh floor to set up the call in the quiet of my room, logging on to find Quentin waiting. A nurse leans over the screen, fiddling with the volume, jaw clenching in irritation as he barks orders at her. "Oh look, Quentin! You have a different virtual visitor today," she says.

He shoos her out of the way, adjusts the angle of his screen, and runs a slightly shaky hand over his silver hair. I fiddle with the contrast on my laptop before realizing that it is Quentin himself who is ghostly pale. He seems to have aged two decades in the five years since I last saw him.

"Hello, Quentin. It's Caroline. Do you remember me?"

"Of course I remember you," he says defensively. "You're Patrick's wife."

"Well, I was," I say, although I am not sure this registers. The room looks cozy, comfortable. Behind him, I can see a window with a view of trees and a reproduction of Seurat's *A Sunday on La Grande Jatte*.

The nurse suggests he tell me all about what he has been up to this week. He shoos her away.

"Tell me about the painting, Sarah. I want to hear about Harry's painting." I talk him through the details of the sale as he leans in excitedly, nose almost touching the screen.

"They sold it," he is telling the nurse. "My son—he's an art dealer, you know—just sold a *very* valuable painting. Chip off the old block."

He turns his attention back to me. "For how much?"

"Forty-two million pounds," I tell him.

"I expect he'll be able to afford to come and visit you now," says the nurse to Quentin.

"Visit? He'll be able to move back. He'll be able to set up a gallery over here again. That will be the plan, won't it, Sarah? You don't want to be in that awful place forever, eh?"

"This is Caroline," the nurse corrects Quentin gently. "Caroline, not Sarah."

"Nonsense," he says, sharply. "Caroline was Patrick's first wife." He rolls his eyes conspiratorially at the screen. He claps his hands and then rubs them together.

"Tell me again," he says. "How did Harry find the painting?"

"Well," I say. "Harry found it in a wardrobe, in a bedroom at Longhurst—"

He turns to the nurse, starts to tell her at length about Longhurst, how often he stayed there, in the Green Room, describing the four-poster bed, the hand-painted wallpaper, reveling in all the details.

And I can picture it exactly, too, because I suddenly realize he is describing the room that Harry showed me, with its peeling leaf-print walls. And suddenly I remember, crystal clear, Harry's mother apologizing that Patrick couldn't stay there as usual on the night of the party because of a burst pipe.

Quentin has apparently forgotten I am there. I can see a close-up of his crotch as he gets up, then hear the scuff of slipper on carpet as he starts pacing the room. He continues to chatter away to the nurse, going on about his long friendship with Philip, and it occurs to me that Patrick told me his father had stayed at Longhurst, in the Green Room, just a few weeks before the party. That it was Quentin sending Patrick off to the Witt Library to look through the photographs there of paintings from Longhurst, among which we had found one of *Self-Portrait as Sphinx*.

One of the things I had always found unsettling about Juliette's painting is the way that all the scenes within it seem to be part of some larger, interlocked narrative. That there is a bigger story to be wrestled from it if you just look carefully enough. Yet those connections remained always tantalizingly on the cusp of reach, touchable with my mind's fingers but impossible to get a firm grip on. A closer analogy, knowing what I now did about Austen's overpainting of it, would be doing a jigsaw puzzle without knowing some of the pieces are missing.

I am getting the exact same unsettling feeling now, as I listen to Quentin.

He reminds the nurse what Patrick has sold *Self-Portrait as Sphinx* for. She comments on how amazing it is that someone found a lost masterpiece like that, just lying around the house.

"Well, it took them long enough," says Quentin.

The nurse bustles back over to the iPad and, realizing that the Zoom call is still running, fumbles with the screen to end it. I am still trying to understand what I have just heard, whether perhaps I had misheard, when, with a chuckle, as if to himself, he says it again: "It took certainly them long enough."

Then I am the only person left on the call, the only face on the screen mine, suddenly magnified, wholly bewildered. What did he mean by that? I find the number of the care home, phone the front desk. No answer. There is an email address on the website, so I fire off a message, asking the nurse to call me back urgently. I am about to flip my laptop shut when an email lands in my inbox from a protonmail.com address I don't recognize—the name a seemingly random sequence of letters.

The subject line is "As Requested: Athena's Mystery Client."

When I click through, there is no message, just ten or so attachments, all grainy CCTV captures. The man in the pictures is recognizably the man from the VIP dinner, although in none of these images is he wearing the same pristine long white tunic and headdress. Instead, he is dressed down in the same nondescript billionaire super-casual style as Dave White had been. He's slim, with a muscular build and a mop of thick, shiny dark hair. There are pictures of him at a mall, others of him outside his mega-mansion. Mainly, though, there are photos of him driving his astonishing collection of cars. Window down, elbow resting on the frame, aviator sunglasses on. Here he is in a turquoise Porsche. In this one, a gold Tesla. In another, a white BMW with the license plate R1CH. There's a Bugatti, a Lamborghini, a Ferrari . . .

I text Dave—although the email address is unrecognizable, and presumably therefore untraceable, these must have come from him. Thank you for the photographs. Can you tell me who this guy actually is?

I can do better, he replies immediately. My driver is downstairs, waiting to take you to him.

The car is ready, engine revving, outside the hotel lobby, the sly smile on the driver's face suggesting that whatever Dave is about to unveil has tickled him. "A/C okay, madam?" he asks as we pull away.

It took them long enough. As we drive, I am trying to unpack Quentin's words. Had he somehow known that the painting Patrick and I had found still existed, and that it was at Longhurst, all along? It was possible, I supposed. But why would he have kept it quiet? It was very unlike him to miss an opportunity for adulation or a quick buck.

Then another possibility occurs to me—perhaps it was the painting that Harry eventually found in the Green Room, the second *Self-Portrait as Sphinx* that Patrick just sold, which Quentin had stumbled across. That was the room he always stayed in, after all. But still the same question reared its head: If he knew it was there, why had he not claimed the credit and the commission for selling it himself?

He's a very old man, I reminded myself. A very old show-off with dementia. Perhaps he didn't know what he was saying.

After maybe half an hour, we pull off the scrubby motorway and into an oasis of frangipani and bougainvillea: the Desert Palm Polo Club.

"Here we are," Dave's chauffeur announces, pointing to the low-rise ocher clubhouse up ahead. As we pull up at the Valet Parking sign, my phone rings.

"Keep your eyes on the car in front," Dave says, without preamble.

I train my eyes on the driver's side, but instead of Athena's client, a squat, balding man in a pistachio linen suit emerges, slams the door, and places a panama hat on his head.

"That's not him," I tell Dave.

"I know. Just keep watching," he says.

The man in pistachio hands his keys to the valet attendant, and I realize that Athena's client, in a nondescript T-shirt and shorts, is the valet.

"That man was a fake buyer," says Dave. "Athena played me—deliberately pushed the bidding for *Self-Portrait as Sphinx* sky-high with a stooge."

"But why would she do that? I ask incredulously. "What on earth does she stand to gain?"

"I have no idea. But if we can work that out, I'm guessing it might lead us to Harry's murderer."

PATRICK, DUBAI,
THIRTY-EIGHT HOURS AFTER HARRY'S DEATH

Six of us are sweltering knee-to-knee in the back of a VW van. We are all in wrist and ankle cuffs, none of us in seat belts, all being thrown into each other every time we shift lanes. The van speeds the whole way, tires screeching on the turns, and I become convinced the driver is swerving deliberately to shake us up. I can all too easily imagine this resulting in a high-speed collision, all of us shackled in the back incinerated in a highway fireball.

The van skids to a halt and the back doors are thrown open. We are all bundled out, lined up, marched down concrete steps into a basement, along a corridor, and into a cell. A guard barks at us to sit down on a bench along the far wall. There is no water. No daylight. None of us has yet met an Emirati lawyer or been told exactly what the charges against us will be. We wait.

One by one, names are called. Eventually, the name called is mine.

The court is smaller and far less imposing than I was expecting. At one end of the low-ceilinged room sit two men in robes, neither looking up from his paperwork as I am led in. There is another robed man at a table in front of them. He glances over but not for long enough to catch my eye. At the other end of the room are three rows of chairs, all occupied. In the front row is Sarah, flanked by Tom and Sumira. Sarah gives me a tight smile I guess is meant to look reassuring. Tom and Sumira, understanding more about the situation, both look deeply concerned.

I am led, still cuffed, to the table and told to sit down next to a man who introduces himself, in thickly accented English, as my lawyer. He explains what the procedure today will be. In front of him are documents he has just been provided with by the prosecution, he explains.

"Where is the prosecutor?" I ask, looking around. He points toward one of the men sitting on the judge's bench. I am asked to stand and confirm my name and nationality.

It is all over in five minutes. The whole thing takes place in Arabic, and there is no translator. When I am asked a question, my lawyer offers a paraphrase of it, then does the same for my answer. I catch Harry's name. The name of the hotel. The name of my gallery. The prosecutor says something to the judge, who says something to my lawyer.

My lawyer opens the folder of documents in front of him. I turn my head away but not quickly enough. The first document in the folder is a photograph, on glossy paper, of a broken champagne flute. Its jagged edges are brown with blood; spatter marks dot the stem and base.

"This object was recovered from Harry Willoughby's hotel room," he tells me.

I feel like I am going to be sick.

Behind me I can hear chairs shifting around, their occupants trying to catch a glimpse of the pictures. The judge asks my lawyer something, then my lawyer asks me if I recognize this object. "I do not," I address the judge directly. My lawyer translates. Both the judge and the prosecutor look openly annoyed.

The judge tells my lawyer to turn to the next document. It is another photograph, a close-up of the stem, dusted and showing two partial fingerprints. The judge instructs my lawyer to turn to the next document. It is a photocopy of the piece of paper on which the police took my fingerprints when they arrested me. Next to the fingerprints is my signature. The judge asks my lawyer to ask me to identify my signature.

"That is my signature, yes," I respond, enunciating clearly, trying to appear as open and helpful as possible. I ask him to tell the judge I don't understand how my fingerprints ended up on that champagne glass. I ask him to make sure that is formally recorded. He shakes his head.

"At this stage, we just answer the questions they ask me," he says.

The next document is a frozen image from the CCTV of the elevator as I am entering it. The prosecutor discusses this image at some length. He draws our attention to the time stamp in the bottom corner of the image. It is just before midnight. I am alone in the elevator. I am standing with my hands folded in front of me, head down.

The judge instructs my lawyer to ask me to identify myself. "That's me, yes."

The last document in the file is another CCTV image. The stamp on this one is 3:17 a.m., and I am on my way back down to the hotel lobby. I'm looking distinctly disheveled—hair mussed, shirt half untucked, no tie. The judge instructs my lawyer to ask me to confirm that the man in the image is me.

I say nothing. I am incapable of saying anything. My lawyer nudges me slightly. I ignore him.

"Mr. Lambert," he says, louder this time. "Do you remember getting into that elevator?"

I do. I remember it vividly. I had just spoken to Harry and was grappling with the knowledge that my oldest friend had basically admitted to pushing his own cousin to his death off three stories of scaffolding and then had covered it up by driving his car into a river. I was trying to work out who knew all of this—who was blackmailing Harry for millions armed with that knowledge.

Understandably preoccupied, I hadn't noticed the man in dark glasses and a sport jacket getting into the elevator as I got out. A man whose face is reflected in the smoky glass of the elevator's mirror.

Suddenly I am on my feet. Shouting at the top of my voice. Jabbing with my finger at the picture in front of me. Trying to hold the picture up in my cuffed hands and show the people sitting behind me. Being barked at by the judge. Being screamed at by the prosecutor. Ignoring him. Ignoring my lawyer trying to pull me back down into my seat. Sarah is out of her chair too, unsure what is going on, unable to hear what I am trying to say, leaning forward, frowning.

The judge says something in a sharp voice, and men in khaki uniforms begin clearing the courtroom with shouts and shoves.

I am still shouting too, even if there is no real prospect of anyone hearing me in the general pandemonium, still waving the photograph as best my cuffs will allow.

The judge is reprimanding my lawyer, my lawyer is apologizing, hands clasped, on my behalf. The court stenographer has stopped typing and is just staring at me.

That man in the picture, I am trying to tell them. The other man in the elevator, I am trying to explain.

The man getting into the elevator is Freddie Talbot.

ALICE LONG, CAMBRIDGE, 1990

I should have known from the start it would be a mistake to attend that retrospective. A whole show at the Tate, the first ever dedicated to Oskar Erlich. For months, it felt like every time I opened a newspaper or listened to Radio 4, someone would be talking about his life and legacy. Juliette Willoughby was mentioned in passing, if at all: a tragic muse, a poetic footnote. If an art critic raised the subject of his temper, detailed in countless biographies, or his treatment of women—his abandoned wife, for instance—what followed was a dismissive reminder to separate art from artist, flawed character from febrile genius.

If we were to start judging great artists by their treatment of the women in their lives . . .

From time to time, I still came into town, was invited to show my work at some photographic gallery in East London, my wartime pictures or some of the things I shot for *Vogue* in the 1960s, the *Sunday Times* in the seventies. Occasionally I was invited to give a guest lecture at UCL or Kings about my career.

That day, I was in Holborn for lunch with an old friend, another photographer. We met at an Italian place, somewhere that had hardly changed in decades, an easy cab ride from King's Cross, where the Cambridge train arrived (after the war, that had seemed like a sensible place to settle, calm and quiet but close enough to London for when I had work booked). These days, there was little risk that anyone seeing Alice Long in the street would recognize Juliette Willoughby. Not with my silver hair pinned up in a neat bun. Not in these glasses, not with the walking stick and back hunched from decades carrying camera equipment up and down the country.

Every bloody bus in London seemed to have Oskar's face on the side of it. His face in a photograph I had taken, had carried in my suitcase from Paris, had sold for far too little to a newspaper. I remember carefully framing that shot so that his nose, his brow, one lock of falling hair, cast one whole side of his face in shadow. Nowhere on any of the posters was my name credited.

My friend and I talked about old times, old friends, over lunch. We hugged goodbye, promised each other not to leave it so long next time, then somehow there I was—wine from lunch still in my system— paying for my ticket to the exhibition. And then I was inside, and all around me were Oskar's paintings, some that had been in the exhibition where we met in 1936, at the New Burlington Galleries. The same physical objects, some in the same frames, as I had stood in front of that night. There were photographs of him next to them, frowning with concentration, paint in his hair.

Then there I was, too. A photograph I had never seen before— marked as on loan from the estate of Man Ray, the little description naming me as "Jules" Willoughby—that Oskar must have taken when

I was asleep, my hair flowing over the heavy bed frame, a thin sheet barely concealing the curves of my naked body. That Oskar had taken with my own bloody camera, without my permission, and given to his friend.

There was no mention of the fact that I too was an artist, just a somber few sentences identifying this as the iron bedstead in which Oskar Erlich and his young lover, a runaway heiress, had perished.

On the shelves in the gift shop were all the biographies of all the men. All the histories, all written by men. All the memoirs, by men. The influence of André Breton on Oskar's thinking was discussed, in the catalogue I angrily flicked through but did not buy. Oskar's work was compared to Dalí's. His friendship with Man Ray was detailed at length, his rivalry with Max Ernst unpacked. There was no mention of any impact I—or any of the other women working and talking about their work all around us—may have had on the men. The one picture in the catalogue of the female Surrealists—of Leonora Carrington and Leonor Fini—was one I had taken of them strolling arm in arm on the banks of the Seine. This is how we get painted out of history, I thought.

All these years, I had told myself that it did not matter, that Juliette Willoughby had been laid to rest and forgotten about. That things were better and safer for me that way. Even after I learned that my father had died—the obituary suddenly springing up from the *Times* one morning, with the strange news that it was Uncle Austen and not Uncle Osbert who had inherited Longhurst—I did not make myself known. Even though it should have been me that the house was passed down to.

I had no desire to inherit Longhurst, knowing what had happened there. I had no desire to go near the place ever again. I had a life; Alice Long had her career. I was proud of my photographs, proud of what I had achieved. I had made a name for myself, a new one. Nevertheless, there was something about that picture of me that I could not get out of my head.

Two weeks later, on a gray Thursday afternoon, a very young, very serious doctor told me it would appear from my test results that I had less than a year to live.

That was when it came to me. I might only have a year left, but I still had time to set the record straight, in all sorts of ways. It should have been up there, on the walls of the Tate, my *Self-Portrait as Sphinx*, along with the Erlichs, the Dalís, the Ernsts, the Man Rays.

I was the only person in the world who knew that the painting believed burned in Paris in 1938—or at least a version of that painting, painstakingly repainted by the artist herself—existed. In fact, it had been hanging on my bedroom wall in Cambridge for the past fifty years.

Yet if it were simply found on my bedroom wall by whoever came to clear my cottage, nobody would have a clue what on earth they were looking at. I had the only surviving photographs of the original tucked away in the now tatty suitcase I brought back from Paris. Without those, the only description of Juliette Willoughby's *Self-Portrait as Sphinx* was a single line in a 1938 exhibition catalogue, a couple of mentions in contemporary newspaper reviews.

I let the problem percolate, hoping the solution would present itself. *Coincidence multiplies when we pay attention*, Oskar had once said, probably parroting Breton. So I pottered about. Took my medicine. Attended my appointments. Supervised the occasional Cambridge student. Intermittently accepted invitations to private views, a guest lecture or two, a funeral.

Then something happened that changed everything.

It was in a window on Cork Street that I saw it, right there in a big fancy gallery. An Austen Willoughby, supposedly. An obvious forgery—at least to me. I came to a dead stop right there in the middle of the pavement. It was a greyhound in a wooded landscape, a decent enough attempt to the untrained eye, but the angle of the head was completely off—no greyhound ever held its head like that. Nor were those a greyhound's eyes. If anything, they were the eyes of a terrier. It was a painting by someone who had studied a lot of paintings of dogs, and not a lot of actual dogs.

I went inside, and I asked about the work. Humoring the old lady, they explained all about Austen Willoughby, his career, his life.

"The provenance is impeccable," I was assured by the gallerist. "This piece comes from Longhurst Hall, the artist's home. There was a complete photographic survey of the estate's art collection made by the Witt Library in 1961, in which this painting was included. It's held at the Courtauld—"

"I know where the Witt Library is," I said curtly.

I also knew that this was not an authentic work. Which meant the photographic records at the Witt had been falsified. What I wanted to know was who had falsified them. Who was bringing paintings in and out of Longhurst. Who was selling them on behalf of the family to galleries like this one.

The answer, it seemed, was a man named Quentin Lambert.

CHAPTER 21

CAROLINE, DUBAI,
FORTY-TWO HOURS AFTER HARRY'S DEATH

The drive back to my hotel from the polo club feels so fast—the city rising out of the sand like a shimmering mirage—that I barely have time to process what I've just seen. Could Harry have been embroiled in some sort of scheme with Athena? If he had, it backfired badly.

I've agreed to meet Dave at a rooftop bar next to my hotel and I arrive first, expecting a long wait—from up on the twenty-seventh floor I can see traffic snaking all the way down to the Palm, where Patrick said Dave lives. I take a seat and watch a DJ being ignored by everyone except the pouting model types in his immediate vicinity, who are self-consciously hand-waving and hair-flicking. I am so fascinated by the scene I don't notice when Dave walks in.

He plonks himself down in the seat opposite me. "Alright?"

"Jesus, how did you get here? Helicopter?"

He smiles, shrugs.

"You didn't *actually*?" I ask. He seems remarkably chipper for a man who may have just been scammed for tens of millions.

"Well, we have quite a lot to talk about," he says.

"That's definitely true. If you don't mind, can we start with how you got hold of the CCTV footage of Athena's fake buyer so quickly? I don't understand . . ."

"It's my business," he says matter-of-factly. "Well, part of it. We develop and operate extremely sophisticated surveillance technology.

My systems capture and identify people and track them as they move from place to place. Even if attempts have been made to conceal their identity. Even as their appearance changes with age."

I was poised to interject. He lifted a finger.

"I think I know what you're going to say. Like most people, the first thing that occurs to you is all the uses an authoritarian state could put this stuff to. I understand those concerns, and I share them. But don't forget all the extraordinary, positive things it can achieve. Combating child trafficking. Helping find missing persons."

"So you can search for a single face?" I ask, unsettled by the implications despite his well-rehearsed defense, unnerved by the damage this sort of tech could do in the hands of the wrong people. "So we can use your systems to search for Athena Galanis? We can see who else she has been meeting with, speaking to?"

"*Can* is a funny word, in this context. As is *we*," he says, eyebrow raised. "Because there's *can* in the sense of is it technologically possible, and there's *can* in the sense of is it legal, even in this relatively permissive jurisdiction. *We* would need to access a lot of very highly restricted data, which *we* are not cleared to access."

"But it's access that *you* have?" I ask

"Access *I* have, yes, because my company harvests and guards that data, on behalf of my clients. But it's not access I can just grant on a whim. I've already helped you out. I'm sorry not to be able to assist more, and I am very sorry for Patrick, but I'm afraid that's as far as this goes. Morally and legally, my hands are tied."

His face is regretful, apologetic. Then—it might just be a trick of the light—one side of his mouth seems to turn up a little. I narrow my eyes. He has to work a little harder to keep a straight face. "*Oh come on,*" Dave chuckles. "Do you really think I didn't run a search for Athena as soon as I realized what she'd done? I think you'll be very interested in what I came up with, actually," he says, gesturing to someone sitting at another table, who brings over a laptop.

"Is he your helicopter pilot?" I ask, half joking.

"No, I fly my own helicopter," Dave says with a straight face.

One of the unsettling things about trying to have a conversation with a very rich person, it turns out, is that you never quite know where their sense of what is absurd ends and yours begins.

"Okay," he says. "Here we go." He gestures for me to move my chair around and flips open the laptop, clicking through a series of photos of Athena going back years. Athena in a nail salon, Athena on the beach, Athena at Dubai airport. It's unsettling to watch her grow increasingly youthful as Dave rewinds time. He stops on a picture of Athena driving into a gated compound.

"It wasn't hard to find photos of her with the art-collecting valet," Dave says, showing me several of the pair talking outside the polo club. "But there are also many, many pictures of her with someone else you might recognize."

"Oh God, oh no, I knew it." I feel a sharp stab of pity for Harry, a heavy sadness that he had been desperate enough to get involved in whatever this was.

Dave looks puzzled. "I don't know what you think I'm about to say, but I'm pretty sure you're wrong."

He taps a key, and someone I haven't seen in years fills the screen. Someone *nobody* has seen in years. My brain takes a few seconds to catch up with my eyes, but it's unmistakable: the man in the picture is a middle-aged Freddie Talbot.

"I don't believe it," I say. "This is some sort of sick joke, isn't it? Something you've faked, or had your people fake. Your belated revenge for my not being nicer to you thirty years ago."

Dave turns to me, his face illuminated by the computer screen. He seems genuinely hurt by the insinuation. "Caroline, I promise you these are real—I wouldn't joke about something like that. You're stuck in a foreign country without a passport, your ex-husband is in jail accused of a murder in which your former best friend looks like she's somehow involved. I'd be a bit of a dick if I didn't try to help you, wouldn't I? And this"—he gestures to his laptop—"happens to be a way in which I am very well equipped to assist."

"Freddie died thirty years ago. The police were certain of it. The pool of blood. The abandoned car in the river. He can't have been hiding out here since he disappeared, surely?" I sound like I am trying to convince myself, and not doing a very good job of it. "He had a mother who missed him, a family who never declared him dead because they hoped he would walk back through the front door. Nobody is that cruel."

"My systems are almost one hundred percent accurate, with a decent dataset for comparison. Usually, we would scrape pictures from social media, but because Freddie is 'dead'"—Dave curls his fingers into quote marks—"he's not a big Instagrammer. There was enough to work from, though—Freddie's face was plastered all over the media for months after he disappeared."

I remember it well. You couldn't open a newspaper or turn on the TV without seeing—with a jolt—a picture of Freddie in a dinner jacket, his expression that familiar mocking half smile. Dave began to scroll through more photos: Freddie having dinner on a terrace with Athena here in the DIFC. Freddie and Athena strolling together hand in hand along a marina.

"This is Freddie in Starbucks, eighteen months ago," Dave says. He taps the trackpad. "This is him collecting his dry cleaning downtown. Three weeks earlier here he is, getting a haircut."

"How much of this stuff is there?"

"How much do you want? Here he is arriving at the Burj Al Arab in 2017. Here he is on the Palm at the start of last year. Here he is driving to Abu Dhabi in 2015."

"He's been in the UAE the whole time?" I ask.

"Since 2011 definitely. I can also tell you with absolute certainty that in those twelve years he has never flown into or out of the international airport here. But that's as far back as my data goes."

"And he's been with Athena all that time too?"

"It certainly appears so. I've got one more thing to show you," he says. "This is footage from the night that Harry died, from the hotel."

"Which you have access to how?"

"We work with quite a few of the big hotels and malls."

"And you're telling me that Freddie was at our hotel?"

"He was," Dave confirms. "Several times over an eighteen-hour period, in fact. We only have footage from the public areas, obviously, so we have him in the lobby, we have him in the gym, and we have this."

He presses play on a video, although I have to ask him to run it twice before I believe what I'm seeing. As Patrick exits the elevator on the ground floor, Freddie enters, cap pulled down low, eyes to the floor. Patrick, seemingly lost in his thoughts, barely notices there is even another person there. The time stamp at the start of the video is 3:17 a.m.

"Do you have any idea what room Harry was staying in?" Dave asks, clearly enjoying playing detective. "Presumably because of the way the camera on his corridor was angled, there is no footage of Harry Willoughby going into or out of a bedroom. There are always blind spots—it's something we are trying to correct."

"His room was a few doors down from me, on the seventh floor."

"Interesting. Well, Freddie exits the elevator on the fifth, lets himself into a room using a key card, and does not leave until nine the next morning."

"You've got to take me to them," I say. "Athena and Freddie. You must be able to find out where they live?"

"Give me until tomorrow morning," Dave promises. "And I'll have an address."

PATRICK, DUBAI, FIFTY HOURS AFTER HARRY'S DEATH

My lawyer refuses to hazard a guess at how long I'll be detained before trial. Six weeks? Six months? It is impossible to say, he tells me sternly, and my outburst will not have helped.

It is a different driver, a different van into which I am herded after the hearing—although the journey that follows is just as terrifying. Even more frightening is the realization that we are not being driven back to the police station but to prison, *real* prison, behind barbed-wire-topped walls. After we drive through them, I can hear the gates shut heavily behind us. A few seconds later, we stop again and there follows the screech of a second set of gates.

Out of the van we are herded. Into the prison we are led. Down one icy-cold air-conditioned corridor after another. Through door after door. Past cell after cell. There seem to be at least ten men in every one we pass. Sitting on bunks, sleeping or playing cards or just huddled under a blanket. The prison officer ahead of us stops every so often to explain, in Arabic, how everything works. Local inmates translate for the rest of us. We will be locked in our cells from 8:00 p.m. until 8:00 a.m. There are no washing facilities. Each shared cell has one sink and a squat toilet with a pitcher of water to flush it with. Nobody shows much interest in me when I am led into mine, except for some shifting around to show which bunks are already taken.

There is a single pay phone on the wall in the communal area, with twenty men in a line next to it. Six weeks, I think. Six months. I need to call Caroline. I need to get a phone card. The trouble is that the prison shop is open for only one hour in the morning and one hour in the afternoon, but that hour is not fixed. So everyone loiters, and when the shutter goes up, there is a scrum. After an hour of pushing and jostling, I only just make it to the front before the shutter comes down.

The line for the phone is even longer than the line for the shop.

I wait for almost three hours, aware that we will all be herded back and locked in for the night at eight. Just as I finally get to the front of the line, a buzzer goes off and the guards start shouting. It is ten minutes to eight, and those who are not back in their cells already rush off in that direction. The phone rings perhaps thirty times before Caroline answers. Just at that moment, a second buzzer goes off.

"I have seconds before I need to get back to my cell. I need to tell you something," I say quickly.

There is music playing in the background on her end. "Patrick, I can barely hear you. I'll just—"

"No, there's no time. Caroline, Freddie is alive. Freddie Talbot is alive and in Dubai. He was at the hotel the night Harry was murdered."

"I know," she says. "We're on it. Dave and I. We're going to get you out of there, I promise."

Dave White? I think, wondering if I'm hearing things. "And my dad, was he okay?"

"He was fine. But he said something strange." She is talking fast, infected by my panic. "Is there any way he might have known there was a *Self-Portrait as Sphinx* at Longhurst all along?"

A guard snatches the phone out of my hand and slams it down onto the receiver. I am the last man left in the corridor, and I practically fall over myself running back to the cell. Imitating the others, I stand by the bed, arms at my side, for the head count. The guard eyes me narrowly. The door is closed and locked, and we all fold ourselves into our beds, each of us with one thin pillow and one scratchy blanket, which reaches mid-shin.

All night, someone on the bunk below me weeps. I can hear things skittering around on the concrete floor. Lights pan across the cell at intervals: guards patrolling with their flashlights. Unable to sleep, I ponder Caroline's question, and why she asked it. It was certainly possible my father had stumbled across either version of Juliette's painting at Longhurst, in Austen's former studio or in the Green Room, but what I could not imagine was that back in 1991—without the clues and supporting evidence we had found in the Willoughby Bequest and the Witt—he would have known what he was looking at if he had.

There *was* something I had long wanted to ask him, though.

Quite often at my gallery, people tried to sell us works we were pretty sure were fakes. Picassos with dodgy paperwork. Subpar works attributed to, say, Miró, that nevertheless had excellent documentary credentials. Often I would discuss these with my father, ask his opinion. Like a lot of dealers, he was interested in the motivations and mechanics of forgery. He delighted in the details of a successful art fraud—one in the eye for the establishment, and all that. He could recount how each of the great fakers had gone about it, and how much they had made, and how they had gotten away with it. Films and books, he insisted, placed too much emphasis on the practical business of imitating a painter's style. What mattered was the provenance. The *story* of the thing. A plausible account of its journey through time.

The question that I had never quite worked up the nerve to ask him was whether he had been tempted to fake a painting himself. He had school fees to pay, blondes to woo, sports cars to buy, after all. I am sure after the Raphael episode, he would have been thrilled at the idea of getting one over on the experts.

His position as the Willoughbys' favored dealer, as they gradually sold off Longhurst's collection, must surely have put him in a very tempting position. Austen Willoughby was a forger's dream—prolific and formulaic, with a steady global market for his work. If there was a painting on photographic record in the Witt Library but no sign of it in Longhurst, and no extant record of its having been sold, how irresistible it would have been to pay someone competent to paint a replacement. Philip—always looking for new revenue streams—could well have had a hand in it.

And if you could find someone to do that, then reversing the process, taking a photograph of a forged painting—using vintage film stock, an appropriate camera—and slipping it into the Witt's Longhurst Hall file would be a fairly straightforward matter too. It had been done before: I remembered the art world being aghast when a con man was caught inserting papers into the Tate's archives corroborating the existence of fake works by the painter Ben Nicholson that he had commissioned and then sold as the real thing.

The question now floating around my head was this: If I believed my father could be complicit in faking work by Austen Willoughby, was it possible he had been involved in the forgery of a work by Austen's niece?

After breakfast—a pot of yogurt, no spoon; sweet milky tea—I join the phone line once more, determined to ask my father, who is at his most lucid in the morning, straight out. I dial the care home's number, and after a long wait, someone picks up.

"May I speak to Quentin Lambert, please?" I ask. "Usually he is awake at this time, I think?"

"Could you just hold for a second?" the woman on the line asks. I can hear an extended indistinct discussion and I am conscious of the seconds ticking away, of the men in line behind me beginning to bristle.

"Hello. Mr. Lambert?" It is a different woman's voice.

"This is Patrick Lambert, yes. Is my father there?"

"I am so sorry, Mr. Lambert," she says. "We have been trying to get in contact. I regret to tell you like this, but I am afraid your father passed away in his sleep during the night."

ALICE LONG, CAMBRIDGE, 1991

When I was eight years old, my cat disappeared. Which would have upset most children, I suppose, but I was very close to that cat. Whenever I came back from boarding school at the end of term, she was always the inhabitant of the house I looked forward to seeing most.

Being sent off like that was something of a relief, really—certainly preferable to being in that house with my mother and father, constantly feeling as if I was blunderingly trespassing on their loss. I once came running up the lawn and stopped face-to-face with my father on the steps of the terrace. For a moment, a look came across his face that I still struggle to describe: startled amazement, almost deranged joy. Then the sun passed behind a cloud and he saw that it was me and stalked off, scowling and muttering to himself.

Nor would I miss the rambling Egyptological disquisitions he would launch into, unprompted, at mealtimes, and that we would be expected to follow attentively. At dinner one night, I remember Uncle Osbert got caught pulling faces and pretending to nod off during my father's impromptu lecture on the correct ancient pronunciation of *Osiris* and it almost ended in blows. We did not see Osbert at Longhurst for a long time after that—a shame, as he had always been my favorite uncle, with his startling blue eyes, bristly blond mustache, and slightly flushed complexion. "A faint whiff of the hip flask about him always" was my mother's observation. My main memory of him was as the only adult who ever seemed to actually listen to what you were saying.

I missed Uncle Osbert, but it was Cat's disappearance that really upset me. She never had a proper name, and she was certainly not acquired as a pet for me. She was a tortoiseshell, tiny, brought in to keep the mouse population down, except that she much preferred eating scraps I stole from the kitchen and fed her by hand. She made my mother sneeze violently, and when my father crossed paths with *that creature*, as he called her, he would usually swing and try to kick her, or, if he was in an especially bad mood, threaten to drown her.

And so that summer, when I arrived home from school for the holidays and she did not slink immediately down the steps to greet me, I assumed my father had finally done what he had so often threatened to. I did ask where she was, but my mother looked at me so blankly I thought she might pretend she did not remember the animal to which I was referring at all.

"What did you do?" I asked my father.

He turned and looked at me coldly. "I have no idea what you are talking about," he said, and that got me, a little, because I had never known my father to tell an untruth before, mostly because he did not care enough what anyone else thought of him to lie.

I started searching the house, checking every corridor. I looked into every room. I peered up chimneys. I inspected behind curtains. I asked every maid when they had last seen her. A week ago, someone thought, at the far end of the lawn. Friday afternoon, someone else offered, hanging around the kitchen. It was one of the girls who worked in the scullery who said she thought she had seen my father carrying Cat in his arms, scooped up, in the direction of the island. My first thought was he had rowed her across and left her there to get her out from under his feet.

I was very strictly forbidden from going anywhere near the lake, and I had not dared to since my sister's accident. The thought of doing so now filled my heart with lead, but I had to know.

Down by the jetty was a boathouse in which three little sculls lay on their backs. I dragged the lightest down to the water and gathered my nerve to step into it. The boat wobbled and I sat abruptly down, settling the oars in their rowlocks and starting to pull. The lake was low, and at first the boat dragged slowly across the underwater foliage, oars catching. Then I was away, pulling into the bright morning sunlight, every detail of the lake bed visible through the water. I tried not to think about my poor sister. I tried not to think about that day at all.

When I reached the other side, I tied up the boat with extravagant care and then followed the narrow path up a low slope to the tree line. At the far end of the island was the pyramid. I continued on the path until I reached it. If anyone saw the boat, if anyone noticed I was missing and guessed where I was, it was almost impossible to imagine how much trouble I would be in.

"Oh, Cat," I called softly. "Psst, psst. Where are you, Cat?"

I had reached the far end of the island. No sign of Cat. At the end of the path in a glade of trees stood the pyramid. At its base, there was a door that had a bar across it with a padlock, dangling open. Never before had I seen that door unsecured. I lifted the padlock and let it drop in the grass. I found a handle, pulled the door open a crack, and squeezed inside, feeling the stone scraping against the skin of my shoulders. Steps led downward between damp-smelling walls.

There was not enough light to see the walls of the room at the bottom of the stairs, which in a way was a blessing—I kept my eyes averted from the gloomy corner in which I supposed Lucy's sarcophagus sat, swallowing the impulse to apologize to her for barging in unannounced. Somehow the cold air felt infused with her presence.

In the middle of the room there was a stone table, about three quarters of it illuminated by the trapezoid of falling light from the doorway, my own dark silhouette partially obscuring what was on it: a bundle, something small and oblong and tightly wrapped.

Bandages. That was what I thought, when eventually I gathered the courage to reach out and touch it. It was some sort of package, about the size of a cat. Something that was damp, the dampness of which had soaked through the cloth.

Then I realized what I was touching and ran.

When I was sixteen years old, one of the maids disappeared.

CHAPTER 22

CAROLINE, DUBAI,
FIFTY HOURS AFTER HARRY'S DEATH

"Double espresso, please," Dave calls to a waiter without looking up from his laptop. I glance around the hotel restaurant, wondering how many guests know that his surveillance systems are capturing them at this breakfast buffet. That if Dave decided to, he could follow them on that laptop right around the city.

Athena and Freddie's comings and goings have certainly been easy for him to track. He shows me the route Freddie takes for his daily run, the supermarket where they do their weekly shopping, Athena's preferred lunch spot—sometimes dining with Freddie, often with companions Dave recognizes as art collectors.

"That guy is from Saudi Arabia." He points to a picture on his screen of a young man. "He just bought a Klimt for eighty million, which I'd considered but my software says is fake. And she"—Dave flicks to a picture of an older blond woman—"is married to an oligarch, buys Manet mostly. I don't employ advisors like Athena because I don't need the help, but for people who *do*, it's useful that she comes from their world, speaks their language, literally and metaphorically. She's comfortable advising wealthy people, and they're comfortable listening, because she was one of them."

"*Was?*" I ask. Athena had certainly looked sleek and rich enough when I saw her at Patrick's private view.

"Well, this surveillance suggests that her money is pretty much gone. Look." Dave first pulls up a picture of Athena with designer shopping bags swinging from her wrists in front of a huge white wedding cake of a mansion, then another of her outside the same house, getting into a limousine with a well-dressed older man.

"That's her father," I say.

"Yes, that's the home they shared in Emirates Hills, and Freddie lived in too. A very nice neighborhood. *Very* different from Deira, the oldest part of Dubai and very much *not* the nicest, which is where Athena and Freddie moved recently."

From the photos, it was quite a contrast. No more mansion and Range Rover—instead, Athena is hailing taxis outside a concrete apartment block with washing flapping from the balconies.

"You found the address," I say.

Dave passes me a scrap of paper across the breakfast table.

"She should be in, although Freddie hasn't been around for a few days now," he tells me. "I could come with you, if you like."

"No. Thank you, but I'll be fine," I say, unable to imagine myself in any real danger visiting my former friend, whatever she was embroiled in. "If you're there, she'll think it's about the fake sheikh thing, and the money."

"Well, I hope that at least *you* know this isn't about the money, for me. I paid Patrick what I think the painting is worth, and I'm not sad that I did. Right now, I just want to help you unravel what the hell's going on. I'll wait for you here, as I've got a few things to do, so please at least take my driver," he says, loudly enough for his chauffeur at the next table to hear. The driver nods.

"Thank you, I'd like that," I concede, feeling grateful for Dave's concern.

"Athena should be at home now—from what we can tell, she never seems to leave the apartment before ten in the morning."

I remember how Athena felt about mornings, so this isn't a shock. I look at my watch—it's already nine.

"If anything feels off, promise me you'll leave immediately. My driver will be waiting outside the door, listening, just in case."

"What is he going to do if—"

"You'll be fine. He can't pilot a helicopter, but he has other useful skills," Dave says reassuringly.

Keeping to the speed limit is clearly not one of them. As we race up the eight-lane highway, Dubai's skyscrapers and malls pass in a blur. The farther we get from the hotel, the less imposing the buildings become, until we eventually reach street after street of chaotic corner shops, shawarma cafés, and dimly lit barbers. So numerous and similar are the grimy apartment blocks here that I don't realize we have reached Athena's until the driver pulls up and steps out to open my door for me.

"This is the place," he says, leading me over and pressing a random number on the intercom. "Delivery," he says breezily, holding the door open for me once it clicks unlocked.

We take the elevator together, but he hangs back farther down the corridor as I knock. Athena opens the door in silk pajamas, looking momentarily shocked before composing herself. "Caroline! I was hoping I'd see you before you left, but this *is* a surprise. I wasn't aware that anyone knew I'd moved—do come in."

"Thank you. We have a lot to catch up on," I remark.

She gives me an unconvincing smile, then leads me down a corridor stacked with packing boxes to a living room with a white leather sofa, a too-large TV, and very little else. She excuses herself to fetch some water for us both. While she's gone, I look out between the blinds onto the balcony, where several sets of weights, a selection of men's sneakers, and assorted sports equipment are scattered.

"He's gone," Athena says to my back, as she walks into the room.

"So Freddie *has* been living here?" I ask, meaning in Dubai, but also here, in this shabby apartment that they are clearly in the process of moving out of. She says nothing, lips pursed.

"All those years, he let his family mourn. Patrick used to meet the Osiris boys every year for a memorial. *You* pushed me away and let me feel guilty for decades that I wasn't a good enough friend. And the whole time it's been a lie? He's been *here*, with you?"

Athena sighs, places two full glasses on a coffee table. "Take a seat, Caroline. You know, it's funny. Whenever I've imagined explaining all this to anyone, it has always for some reason been you."

I lower myself onto the sagging sofa. Athena settles down cross-legged onto the floor. She takes a sip of water.

"Do you remember, a few weeks before Harry's party, you saw Freddie arguing with someone in a car? Well, it was someone Freddie owed money to."

"A drug dealer?" I ask, even though I know the answer.

She nods. "From the very start of university, Freddie had always sold drugs. His dealer encouraged him to do it so Freddie could pay for what he was using—and he was using a lot. At Harry's party, he had a car trunk full of Ecstasy pills and cocaine that he'd just driven to London to collect, to supply the Osiris boys. Look, I know you two never got on, but Freddie is a good person. He was just struggling back then, numbing himself with drink and drugs, and it got out of control."

She delivers this with such conviction, manicured hands gesticulating, that if I didn't know Freddie Talbot, I'd have bought it. Instead, the description of him as a poor, tortured soul made the bile in my stomach rise.

"But he never quite managed to sell enough to cover what he was using, or he gave too much away to his friends when he was drunk or high. The debt piled up. By his fourth year, he owed a lot of money. The interest just kept rising, and the dealer started to make threats about hurting him. *Killing* him. The only person Freddie thought might be able to come up with that sort of cash quickly, and who would care about him enough to do it, was Harry. Freddie asked him for it a few days before the party."

"But Harry spent his whole life complaining about not having any money. Why didn't Freddie just ask *you?*"

"He was too proud to tell me any of this. And anyway, he knew I had no access to that sort of money. My father was wealthy, sure. If it had been a handbag or a trip to Paris, I could have asked one of his personal assistants to buy it or book it. But clearing my boyfriend's drug debt? In cash? Impossible. Daddy countersigned any amount over five hundred pounds, and Freddie owed a *lot* more than that. He knew there were things in Longhurst that nobody would miss for months, if ever—jewelry, silverware, first editions—and Harry knew where to look for it all. He could have helped his cousin come up with the money easily, had he wanted to, but—"

"Harry said no, *obviously.*" I am astonished Freddie thought the answer might ever have been yes. "He was asking Harry to steal from his own family."

Athena snorts. "*Seriously?* It's not like that generation of Willoughbys *bought* any of the valuable things they owned, or earned any of their money for themselves. Freddie needed help, and it would have been easy for Harry to give it, but he refused. So Freddie decided that at the party, while everyone was drinking and dancing and distracted, he would go on a treasure hunt."

Exactly what I was doing, at almost exactly the same time, I realize with a flush of shame. I wonder if she knew that Freddie had also been looting the Osiris clubhouse earlier that day.

"I found him in my bedroom, hiding what he'd taken in my suitcase. I was so furious that I threw the bronze statuette he'd wrapped in my shawl so hard it bounced off the wall."

I distinctly remember the clunk it made, their raised voices, the thumping of my heart in my chest as I sat on the bed in the room next door.

"Then it all came out, what trouble he was in," she continues. "We fought, he apologized for not telling me about it all sooner. Then as we talked it through, it dawned on him that there might be a better way to get what he needed that night. If he could goad his cousin— upstanding, stuffy, future prime minister Harry—into taking a birthday line of cocaine and snatch a photo of it on one of those disposable cameras, Freddie could use it to blackmail him. But the instant that flash went off, Harry lost it. There was a scuffle. Freddie fell off the scaffolding and hit his head, hard, on the flagstones below. Knocked himself out. Split his scalp. Harry must have panicked, I suppose. He ran off, assuming Freddie was either dead or dying, presumably planning to come back and deal with the body and cover his tracks later. That was when I found Freddie."

"The blood," I say. "That morning, when you came to tell Patrick and me that you couldn't find Freddie. You had blood on your arm. You said you must have cut yourself and not noticed."

"Freddie's blood." She nods. "It was everywhere, but he didn't want me to take him to the hospital—he had so much cocaine in his system, he was concussed, ranting about being expelled from university, about his mother disowning him. I called Dad's driver—you might remember Karl—and told him to take Freddie straight to our private doctor in London. I said he was a friend who'd had a bad fall, drunk, and was too embarrassed to tell his parents. That he would be staying with us to recuperate," she explains.

"While you stayed at Longhurst and pretended to look for him, so that nobody would suspect you were involved in his disappearance. But why not just let him recover, and then both come back to Cambridge?" I ask.

"Because of what was in Freddie's car, Caroline—the car that Harry must have driven into the river to make it look like Freddie drowned. Freddie—like a fool—had written down the names and numbers and addresses of his main suppliers, the big guys, in that notebook in his glove compartment, along with all sorts of other incriminating and easy-to-decode information about what he had bought from whom and when, and knew it would lead the police straight to them. Can you imagine? He had no choice but to disappear—he needed all those people to believe that he was dead."

"Why didn't you at least tell *me* the truth?" I demand.

"Freddie and I made a pact not to tell anyone at all, but you knew me so well and could read me so easily I was worried you would work it out. So I did the only thing I could think of to stop you from suspecting—I stopped talking to you. For which I am sorry," she says, with what seems like a genuine note of regret in her voice. "Freddie stayed in one of our houses in London until I graduated, and then we left for Dubai together."

"But how did you even leave the country? Surely at the airport—"

"We flew privately," she says. "I often did, so I knew how relaxed they could be about passports. I also know there are quite a lot of people in Dubai lying low, for one reason or another."

"And he never knew? Your father?"

"Oh, once Freddie arrived, it all came out. There were rows. But Freddie won him over. And Dad was polo-mad, so it helped that Freddie was a nearly-qualified vet."

I could just imagine Freddie turning on the megawatt charm I had always been immune to but which seemed to work like magic on other people.

"Didn't Freddie ever want to come home?" I ask, trying to put myself in his shoes. I had spent most of my life wishing I could have just one more day, one more hour, with my mother—the thought of *choosing* to cut her off entirely was unimaginable.

She shakes her head. "What for? His mother was in South Africa and didn't want him. When he left England he was in debt, an addict, about to fail his degree. He could have a new start here, but the deal we made was that once he was in Dubai, he stayed in Dubai, and he stayed clean. There's no place better to do that than here, because the penalties are so harsh if you're caught."

I let this sink in—I always thought Freddie was the master manipulator, but it was Athena who had turned the situation to her advantage, getting the man she had always wanted all to herself.

"But you're clearly leaving now," I say, gesturing to the packing boxes. "What's changed?

"My dad died," she says simply.

"I'm sorry for your loss."

"Oh, so am I," she says, her voice dripping bitterness. "And it was more of a loss than we'd ever imagined, because when we came to try to make sense of his will, we discovered all he had left us was a mountain of debt. The whole thing had been a charade for years. Endless financial subterfuge. When people think you're rich, they're happy to lend you money, or extend your credit. And then when they find out you're not . . ."

"You end up here."

"Quite. This was actually our housekeeper's place at one point—a housekeeper we had to lay off because there was no longer a house to keep. It was the only thing Dad still owned outright, oddly enough. I didn't own anything at all, and I had never needed to make any real money myself. Freddie has never earned or had the capacity to. So we were broke. But Freddie has always kept an eye on what was going on back home—he had Google alerts set up, read the papers. Keeping track as over the years all the people he still owed money to, all the people he had named and incriminated in his notebook, all the people he had fled the country to escape, ended up dead or in prison for decades. We talked about it, but he still didn't want to go back, even with that threat gone. That's also how we knew that Longhurst Hall had been put up for sale."

I tried to imagine feeling so envious of an inheritance that you scoured newspapers for stories about it.

"And he wanted that money?"

"We had lived off my father for years until it all came tumbling down. Freddie wanted to do something for me, to lift us out of this horrible situation," she says defensively, gesturing around the shabby apartment. "And if Longhurst sold, he had a right to benefit from that. The house really should have passed to his grandfather and then down to him, after all."

"So he decided to get what he wanted by blackmailing Harry."

She nodded. "Freddie always held on to the pictures that he took at the party as an insurance policy. He decided to use them to demand his share. He did it anonymously—Harry had no idea his cousin was still alive. Freddie sent the photos along with a note saying he knew what had happened that night, that Harry was a murderer and had driven Freddie's car into a river to cover it up, threatening to tell the world if Harry didn't pay up."

"Then when he heard that Harry had found *Self-Portrait as Sphinx*, Freddie thought he had a right to whatever the painting sold for too," I say. Everything was starting to fit together now. "And with your phony buyer and his fake bid, you ensured that was an extraordinary amount."

"An artwork is only worth what someone will pay for it," she says with a shrug. "I didn't force Dave White to up his offer."

"But you *did* try to force me to authenticate," I say.

"Yes. Freddie took those pictures while he was on the scaffolding, waiting for Harry. He took a lot of photographs that night. When he had them developed, most were of people snogging in bushes or the Osiris boys passed out on the lawn, but a few of them came in useful," she admits.

"Had Harry figured out Freddie was the blackmailer?" I ask, remembering the haunted look in his eyes the night he died. "Because I had no idea who sent me those pictures."

"No, and the plan was that he would never find out. But when Freddie heard that his cousin was in town, he couldn't resist. He just wanted to scare Harry, demand one big payment to set us up for life." She looks down at her hands, shrugs. "But Harry's temper—"

"What a load of *absolute* rubbish." I am half shouting, unable to help myself. "You can't actually believe that? You don't accidentally slit a man's throat, using a champagne glass with someone else's fingerprints on it. I always knew Freddie was a terrible person, but I never thought *you* were an idiot."

Athena's face hardens. "Believe what you like, Caroline. I really don't care. But for the record, I've been with Freddie Talbot since I was eighteen years old. How's *your* great Cambridge love story working out for you?"

"How *dare* you." I stand up so quickly I upend the coffee table, shattering the water glasses on the tiled floor. "We might not still be together, but Patrick Lambert is the kindest, most loyal human being I've ever met, and right now, he is in prison for something Freddie did. I'll go to the police. I'll tell them what you've just told me."

She shakes her head. "They'll ignore you. Understand that I am only telling you all of this because Freddie has *already* gotten away with it. The Dubai police think they have their man, so they won't cast their net wider. That's simply not how it works here. And it wouldn't matter anyway. Freddie is in the air on a private jet with a fake passport as we speak."

"Heading where?"

"Longhurst, of course. The drug dealers he was so afraid of are all dead or banged up in prison, so that threat's disappeared. The chances of Freddie himself being charged with any offenses are slim, because who is left to give evidence? Freddie has never officially been declared dead, so with Harry gone and no other living relatives, the house will pass down to the next of kin. Freddie will get what's rightfully his— and once everything has died down, I will join him."

Although I have never hit anyone in my life before, it takes all my willpower not to slap her across her smug face.

Instead, I half run out of the apartment, slamming the door behind me.

PATRICK, DUBAI, SIXTY HOURS AFTER HARRY'S DEATH

When the guard calls my name, I assume something bad is coming. An interrogation. An admonishment. A punishment. He asks, in Arabic, if I would like to bring anything with me—a cellmate translates, and I shake my head. We seem to be heading out of the prison, not deeper into it. For a second, I allow myself to hope.

Then we stop, and I am led into a room where there are several men sitting, heads down, on a bench, all handcuffed, all looking as confused and concerned as I feel. Some seem to be in the clothes they were arrested in, instead of the prison's white tunic and trousers. Nobody makes eye contact.

The guard behind a desk calls a name, and the man at the end of the bench takes a seat in front of him, placing a blue plastic bag on the table. The guard pulls out a selection of pitiful items one by one, listing them as he goes. A belt. An ancient Nokia phone. A plastic bottle of water. When he is finished, the man is roughly escorted out the door. I slump forward, head in hands. They are taking us all to another prison. I am being digested even deeper into the system.

I can't even bear to look, but I hear more men being marched into the room and shuffling out, the rustle of plastic bags, the scratch of pencil on paper, more names called. Eventually, the guard barks my name and I take a seat in front of him. He places a clear ziplock bag in front of me, with my phone, my belt, my keys, and the clothes I arrived in.

"Goodbye, Mr. Lambert, you are free to leave," he says matter-of-factly, and directs me to a different door than the other inmates have been shoved through. Although I can just about stand, my legs can't seem to figure out how to move toward it. I am still rooted to the spot when the next name is called.

Frederick Talbot.

My mind must be playing tricks. I haven't slept in days, I've barely eaten. My brain has conjured the man walking toward me, a bundle of possessions under his arm. We lock eyes and he nods.

It *is* him. It is Freddie.

Even in handcuffs, he still has some of that old insouciance in the way he carries himself, that cocky confidence. After a little start of surprise, a wry smile spreads across his lips. As he approaches, I can feel him studying me closely. Perhaps he is assessing the ways in which I have changed over the past three decades, the past three days. Perhaps he's wondering what it feels like to be in my shoes.

"Hello, Patrick," he says. We are barely two feet from each other now, each with a guard close behind us.

"You killed him," I say. "You bastard, you killed Harry."

He does not deny it.

"He killed me first," he says.

Then a door slams somewhere and Freddie flinches, and in that moment I see the smile falter, the false bravado waver. Before I really have time to process any of this, I am being walked down the corridor and through a door, and through another, and then I am outside, blinking in sun so powerful it feels like it is literally beating down on my face. On the barbed wire along the perimeter fence, the sunlight glitters. On the tarmac, the air shimmers.

For a moment, I genuinely feel like I might fall to my knees and kiss the ground. There is a gleaming silver Rolls-Royce in the middle of the car park. Standing next to it is Caroline. I have never been so glad to see anyone in all my life. Somehow, I make it halfway to the car before my knees start to buckle. Caroline reaches me just before I topple.

Together we stagger to the car, her maneuvering me into the back seat. In my hands, I find a cold bottle of water and I drink from it greedily. From the way Caroline and the driver are looking at me, I know I must look even worse than I feel. I can see tears collecting in the corners of her eyes.

"Let's go," Caroline says. The locks of the doors automatically click, and I flinch. I see that Dave White is sitting next to the driver, and I start to think this is all a mirage.

"What is going on? I don't understand. I've just seen Freddie being processed into the prison. How did you—"

The desert is rolling past the window. For whole stretches of time, the view is so undifferentiated we hardly seem to be moving at all. Caroline and Dave share a glance, and he gives a nod.

"After we get out of this car, we can never discuss this in front of anyone else, ever again," she says. "There is what I am about to tell you, and then there is what everyone else thinks happened."

"I still don't understand, and I am not convinced you aren't a dream, but yes, fine," I say, and I want to weep when she puts her hand in mine, looks me in the eye, and confirms that she *is* here, with me.

"It was a tourist's phone," she says. "Logged into the Wi-Fi at the hotel opposite, filming the view. Their camera caught him, Freddie, climbing from one balcony to another. You recall how Freddie always loved to climb?" she says.

"How could I forget?"

"Climbing up onto *my* balcony, after I had gone to bed. Taking a glass. Your glass. The one without lipstick on it. Climbing across onto Harry's. He planned it—booked a room two floors down and checked in with a fake passport. Harry must have thought he was hallucinating when Freddie walked in through the balcony doors. Like seeing a ghost."

I try to picture it: staring at you through your own reflection in glass, someone you have assumed is dead for thirty years. A man you have always believed you murdered.

"And they shared it with the police? That's why I'm here?"

"Well, no," Dave White interjects. "Not quite. There are parts of my business that are rather less . . . publicized than others. Because CCTV cameras never have full coverage, we have developed ways to fill the blind spots. So we've been trialing, through offering free Wi-Fi for hotel guests, the ability to access self-created content. It gives us a broader range of data points, time, location, and date stamped—"

"He rifles remotely through the photos and videos on people's phones," Caroline says bluntly. "Accesses their camera rolls and pretty much anything else he can find on there and uses it to spy on them—"

"That is not *quite* right. And we never use what we harvest nefariously, or rather we don't let bad actors do so. But that *is* how we located the footage that exonerated you, searching within specific time and location parameters. And once we had that, it was easy to seed it out to social media at scale. Newspapers didn't take long to pick up on it."

"It was on the *Daily Mail* website within hours," Caroline confirms. "The police here picked Freddie up at a private airfield as he was just about to get on a private jet to the UK."

Caroline winces, and I see that I am gripping her hand so tightly my knuckles have gone white. Our eyes meet and she looks away. "They gave me my passport back," she says. "The police. I am free to leave the country."

I nod dumbly. "Of course," I say. "Of course."

"There is a flight at eight tonight."

"Right. Yes."

As the euphoria of freedom starts to wear off, it dawns on me that I have no idea what to do now, or even where I am going to go. My marriage is over, and I have no doubt whose sides our friends will be on. I am still holding Caroline's hand tight.

"My dad died," I say, a sharp pain in my throat as I realize this is the first time I've said it out loud.

"There's something I need to say about—"

We are both speaking at once. Then we both fall silent.

Caroline seems to be figuring out the best way of putting something. "I don't know why, or what was in it for him, but I think he set us up to find *Self-Portrait as Sphinx* at Harry's twenty-first," she says. "Looking back, it feels as if we were left a trail of breadcrumbs to a painting but we accidentally stumbled across the wrong one. You always stayed in the Green Room, right? Well, that was where Harry discovered the second *Self-Portrait as Sphinx*—and I think that was where your father left it for us to find."

I try to map this out in my mind. It does *sound* plausible.

"The painting *we* found in 1991," Caroline tells me, "had several key details overpainted. According to Dave's analysis, it was Austen Willoughby who did the overpainting."

"That would make sense, if that was the version in his possession," I say.

"Do you remember at Harry's party, his grandmother said Austen promised her he had destroyed it? Here's my hypothesis. Somehow in Paris, before the fire, Austen acquired *Self-Portrait as Sphinx*. Juliette's diary says he was there, at the opening night. That was why she removed it from the show. She would never have sold it to him, but maybe he stole it. Maybe he murdered Juliette and Oskar to get it, then set the fire to cover that up. And what happens next?"

"Do you know how many nights it is since I've had a decent night's sleep?" I say, scratching my head.

"For no reason anyone can explain, when Cyril passes away with two daughters dead and no heir, instead of Longhurst passing to the second-oldest brother, Osbert, he leaves it to the youngest, Austen."

"Yes, that's what happened," I say. "But why is that relevant?"

"I think when Austen got his hands on the painting in Paris, he worked out what the hidden meaning concealed in it was, and he used that knowledge to coerce Cyril into changing his will."

"Jesus, that family loves blackmail." A thought occurred to me. "What that must also mean is that the painting implicates Cyril in something."

"Exactly. Also meaning that when Austen promised his wife he had destroyed the painting, what he was destroying was evidence of how he twisted his brother's arm into leaving him the house. But for whatever reason—perhaps because he was a painter too, and understood the aesthetic value of what he had in his possession—he couldn't do it. He just painted over the bits that made its accusation legible, to those who knew what they were looking for."

We are nearly at Caroline's hotel now, and the traffic is thickening around us. I love this, I realize, being with her, watching her brain work, admiring the elegance with which her mind unpicks a problem.

"That's why I believe both those paintings must be genuine, both Juliette's," she says. "Because hidden beneath Austen's expert over-painting, both works are identical, and until now, nobody apart from her would have known that."

She is smiling, waiting for one of us to click the last part of the puzzle into place.

Dave White has turned around in his seat now to face her. He is grinning.

"You've worked it out, haven't you?" he says. "What it all means. The secret of the Sphinx."

"Maybe. The details Austen overpainted must all be vital in some way. Clearly, Cyril had concealed something in the pyramid on the island at Longhurst," she says.

"Something like . . . a body?" I suggest. "Something like, the body of the Missing Maid?"

"That would be the obvious assumption, yes."

"You think Cyril killed her—that she is the bandaged figure in the boat in the painting?" asks Dave.

"That's my theory. But that's not all. Think about the face of the boatman, his beak," she says.

"Thoth, you told me?" I say.

"Yes. God of knowledge. God of magic. And the hieroglyphics: the same phrase that appeared in the painting and over the entrance to the east wing at Longhurst. *I am Yesterday, To-Day and To-morrow, and I have the power to be born a second time.* The painting is not just telling us that Cyril killed Jane Herries and where she is buried. It's telling us *why* he killed her."

"It is?" I ask, baffled. Dave is frowning in confusion also.

"He killed her so he could try to bring her back," says Caroline. "He killed her so he could try and bring them *both* back. That's why his daughter Lucy—the bedraggled, damp girl—is so prominent in the painting. Because she's the key to the whole thing."

Then suddenly it all fits together. My initiation into Osiris, reading from Cyril's old parchment. Freddie's prank with the cat. Cyril Willoughby had founded the Osiris Society. He was not just obsessed with ancient Egypt. He was *specifically* obsessed with the idea of resurrection. No, not just the idea of resurrection. The practicalities of it. An obsession that must have taken him to even darker places when his own daughter died so young.

"Of course," she says, conspiratorially. "There is only one way of proving it. We need to confirm that Jane Herries's body is buried where the painting says it is. We have to go back to Longhurst."

The car pulls up outside Caroline's hotel. "This is your stop, I think," Dave says to her, appearing surprisingly sad at the thought of saying goodbye.

And I suppose I knew then that I was not going back to the house I had shared with Sarah, that I was never going back to that house. That this was the end of my marriage, my gallery, of whatever the last years of my life had been. That I was leaving and I would not return. There is a weight, a sadness, to that. An awareness of the hurt that has been done that cannot be undone.

Five hours later, holding hands again, Caroline and I are tilting back into the sky together. Ten hours later, we are in a car up to Longhurst.

ALICE LONG, CAMBRIDGE, 1991

Nobody saw him take her out on the lake, but I can picture how it must have happened.

I remember Jane well. How young she seemed, even to me. How shy. The way she said good morning without ever meeting your eye. Could somehow, when you passed her in the hallway, bob her head and curtsy without breaking stride. Oh, how carefully he must have picked her, his victim. Someone meek, unsure of herself. A girl who had never been taught to swim.

It would not have been hard to persuade her into the boat. He was, after all, her employer. She would have expected just to row around the island, I imagine, perhaps disembark to look at the pyramid. Even if she had intimations of danger, how could she have refused?

She had not seen what happened to the cat. She had not felt it, damp within its cocoon of bandages, and guessed how it had died, and why, and what my father had been hoping to achieve with that tiny water-logged body. Why it was so important the cat had died the same way as my sister had done.

Once they were out on the lake, Jane in that buttoned-up jacket the younger maids wore, all those skirts, how easy it must have been to give her a shove, tip her over the side of the boat. Once she was in that cold water, she would have been heavy and floundering. Did he speed things up, hold her head under? Did she even get a chance to scream? Not that it could have been heard, from the house, from the lawn, from the gardens.

My mother and I both knew he had done it. She would never have admitted it to anyone. But she knew. What I have never known is whether she understood why.

That he was trying to bring them back. That he was trying to bring them all back. The maid. The cat. My sister. That the mad old fool, with his mummies, with his hieroglyphics, had convinced himself that the ancient Egyptians really had found a way of dragging people back from the dead. He believed the reason that the descriptions of the after-life in the spells of *The Book of the Dead* are so realistic is because what is being described is actually a set of rituals to ensure your resurrection and survival in *this* life.

That was what his collecting was for. He founded the Osiris Society as a community of scholars who would work toward recovering that magic. Whether or not anyone else at Cambridge took it as seriously as my father, it's impossible to say. Perhaps he did not take it all as seriously then as he would go on to in later life. What I am sure of is that the death of my sister turned an eccentric interest into a macabre obsession. Because, he believed, if only he could establish the authen-tic, uncorrupted, original version of the correct ritual, the right way of saying those words, he could bring her back. He could row my sister back across the river of the dead and restore her to us.

Poor, sweet Jane had not run away. There had been no affair. He had drowned her and taken her body to his mausoleum and done to her exactly what he'd done to the cat and I fear many other creatures.

It was not a story you could tell and expect to be believed. My experiences in the asylum had taught me that.

That was why I painted the truth. If I hadn't, I think I really might have gone mad.

So many secrets. So many deaths. And now *I* am dying. The time has ticked on, and I have six months left, the doctors say. My lungs. My liver. My heart. All riddled. The other day I joked with my oncologist that it would be easier to list the parts of me that are *not* cancerous. Sometimes at night I wake and my sodden, gasping lungs make it feel like I am drowning.

Quentin Lambert—listed in the phone book as an expert in antiques and estate sales—was not a difficult man to find. He was one of those charming, slightly flashy types who turns up at elderly women's houses when their eyes are failing, undervalues their art and antiques, and offers to take it all off their hands. A spiv, we called them in my day. A spiv who thinks he is a gentleman. When he turned up at mine, he started sniffing around, telling me what this little Arts and Crafts chair and that little chipped Clarice Cliff vase might be worth.

I was the one who brought up Austen Willoughby. Immediately he became effusive. "Austen Willoughby?" he said with delighted pride. He had sold more of his paintings than he could count. He was a close friend of the artist's son, in fact, and had been a frequent visitor to Longhurst for decades.

"I know," I said. "Except some of the paintings you have been selling have not actually been by Austen, have they?"

All at once, his manner changed. He became defensive, started blustering about the Witt, how I could check the records there. I said I was sure the photographic records did match the paintings he had sold, probably because he had also been falsifying those records. His bluster died on his lips.

"What do you want?" he said.

All I wanted, I explained, was a little favor. Or perhaps a small series of favors.

First, I needed him to take a photograph of my *Self-Portrait as Sphinx* on whatever camera and film stock he had been using, and place it in the Witt with the other photographs from Longhurst.

He agreed without hesitation.

"Is that all?" he said.

"No," I replied.

I had already been supervising students for several years at Cambridge. This year, I just had to make sure I got the right ones, to make it clear I was only interested in students studying the Surrealist 1930s.

It is three thirty on Thursday, October 3, 1991. A red sports car has just pulled up on the road outside my house. From an upstairs window, through a gap in the curtains, I watch as the handsome young man driving gets out, scurrying swiftly around it to catch up with the pretty girl who is already making her way up the drive. They are peering up at the house, exchanging comments, perhaps trying to decide if they have been given the right address. They look young. They look eager. They look perfect.

Their names are Patrick Lambert and Caroline Cooper. One of them comes very highly recommended by her director of studies. The other is Quentin's son.

"Does he know?" I had asked Quentin suspiciously on the telephone.

"He has no idea. All I've done is suggest Surrealism as a dissertation topic. The rest is up to him."

I will send Caroline to examine the materials in the Willoughby Bequest, where I have hidden my journal, along with the pendant and passport that came back with me from Paris—enough, I think, to convince them the journal is genuine. Quentin will find a way of persuading Patrick to look through the Longhurst photographs at the Witt. Which should, with luck, lead them to my painting, carefully planted in the Green Room at Longhurst, where Quentin is staying right now and where his son will no doubt be for Harry Willoughby's twenty-first birthday in a few weeks' time.

That was Quentin's flourish. "There is a stack of paintings at the bottom of the wardrobe. If he has any suspicion this *Self-Portrait as*

Sphinx might be at Longhurst, he's bound to look through them. He wouldn't be my son if he didn't."

It will be a gift, the painting, from father to son. The kind of gift that must remain unacknowledged, unacknowledgeable. The gift of a discovery that might launch a career. Just as I shall be passing on my journal to Caroline, a journal full of my sketches and studies for the painting, a journal that tells part of the story of its creation, hoping she knows what to make of it, hoping she understands the importance of what she has been given.

I have not told Quentin who I am. Who I was. Why I am doing this, and why I am so determined it not be a Willoughby who finds this painting. Perhaps he has his suspicions, but I have him in too much of a bind for him to inquire. He knows I could ruin him, so he does what he's told.

I do wonder if I shall live to see my scheme's fruition. The final act of a long and surreal life.

Patrick Lambert rings the doorbell, stands back, frowns as if he is not quite sure whether the doorbell is working, whether there is anyone home.

As I am making my way to the door, I catch sight of myself in the mirror, of Alice Long, of Juliette Willoughby. I turn down a corner of my collar, smooth it out, brush a strand of silver hair from my forehead.

It is all about to begin.

I am about to achieve what my father spent his whole life and sent himself mad trying to do.

I am about to bring a woman back to life.

CAROLINE, ENGLAND, THE PRESENT DAY

It is a bright November afternoon and after a brief ceremony, they are re-interring the body of Jane Herries, the Missing Maid of Longhurst, in a plot next to her sister, Helen, in Arnos Vale cemetery, Bristol.

Patrick and I felt we ought to be here, really.

I was worried that there would be a lot of press in the church, but apart from one reporter from a local paper, it is just us and the few members of Herries's family who could be traced. The focus of the vicar's eulogy is her life, not her murder, the name of her murderer not mentioned. It does not need to be—the story has been endlessly reported on the news, with drone footage of the police cordon on the island, officers in hazmat suits removing items from the pyramid.

It had not been easy to persuade the police to take us seriously. I could tell that the officer who accompanied us to the island was humoring us initially, but when we arrived at the pyramid her mood perceptibly shifted. It felt undeniably eerie, overgrown. The chain on the pyramid's metal door was so rusted it looked like something from a shipwreck. The lock came away on Patrick's first tug, but the door, rusted shut, took a lot more effort to pry open. In the end, the hinges gave way entirely. Beyond was a narrow passageway, a flight of stone steps leading downward.

In single file, we made our way down them.

At the bottom of the steps there was a chamber, empty apart from two stone sarcophagi. Inscribed into the smaller one, in copper letters that had left trails of rust down the stone, were Lucy Willoughby's name and her poignant dates. The name and dates on the larger were Cyril's. I already knew not to expect to find a tomb here for Cyril's wife, Juliette's mother, who had predeceased her husband. She was buried in the local churchyard, something she had apparently insisted upon throughout her final illness and in her will.

We paced the chamber's perimeter, searching for signs of secret doors or inner chambers, but the walls were blank. There was no way Cyril could have hidden Herries's body in his own sarcophagus, as it would have been found when they buried him, and he would surely not have violated the sarcophagus containing the remains of his beloved daughter. It briefly crossed my mind that perhaps the Willoughbys were right, that this whole thing might have been a bizarre delusion on Juliette's part, her way of processing a series of horrible, senseless tragedies. Patrick looked as baffled as I felt.

"It's not here, is it? She's not here. We were wrong."

Then I thought of something. "Do you recall which pyramid this is modeled on? Which *specific* pyramid."

"Djoser, at Saqqara. The oldest of all the pyramids. That's what Cyril claimed, anyway."

"Right. And *under* the pyramid at Djoser there are catacombs—a whole elaborate system of tunnels and interconnected burial chambers. Sam Fadel told me about them."

The name was out of my mouth before I could stop myself. Patrick pointedly ignored it.

"So what you're saying is that what we're looking for might be underneath us?"

The police officer, playing along, directed her torch at the floor.

"And what exactly are we looking for, right now?" she asked.

"Something like *that*," said Patrick.

And there they were, right where the torch was now pointing: chisel marks on the stone floor where a slab had been loosened and lifted.

The police officer had a tire iron in her car, which she went back across the lake and retrieved. Even then it was tricky to find the right angle to lift the heavy slab.

The steep tunnel of damp stone that was revealed was just big enough for an adult to crawl down, the torch illuminating it to a distance of about thirty feet.

The officer insisted on going down first. Patrick followed. I waited at the entrance to the tunnel. "It flattens out after about forty feet," the police officer shouted back. "Then there is a chamber."

There was silence, then a gasp and a sharp order barked at Patrick to back up. He reluctantly did so, huffing and puffing, crawling backward up the tunnel. The police officer scrambled out after him. As I helped her to her feet, I realized she was shaking.

"What is it?" Patrick said. "Did you find the body?"

She shook her head. Her face was ashen. "Not just one body. There must be at least a dozen."

IT HAS BEEN A strange six months. Patrick's dad's funeral first, then Harry's. Freddie's trial—there was footage on the news of Athena arriving at court to support him, in her huge dark glasses, ignoring questions from the media—and his conviction. All the legal wrangling about who would inherit Longhurst, and what would happen to Harry's share of the money from the sale of the painting. Patrick's separation from Sarah. The laborious business of disentangling their financial affairs, coming to an arrangement about the house, trying to sell the gallery. Then the news in the last few weeks that she had started seeing someone else, someone a little younger than Patrick, a lot sportier. From the pictures she had shared on Instagram of them together—kite surfing, body boarding, scuba diving—they looked very well suited to each other, perhaps much better than she and Patrick had been. He had messaged to say he wished them every happiness.

As for Patrick and me, we have tried to take things in slow, tentative steps. Dates. Long dinners picking over the past, trying to work out where things went wrong last time. Serious conversations about how we can ensure it doesn't happen again.

We talk about Harry. It wasn't until his autopsy results were made public that a fresh mystery emerged. The cause of death was exactly what it had appeared to be—the severance of his carotid artery, resulting in catastrophic blood loss. What no one had expected was the level of lead in his blood. Wildly high levels of lead, which could have resulted only from months at least of ingesting the stuff somehow. Nor had the coroner been able to offer any plausible explanation for this.

The first thing that Patrick did, when he heard, was to start counting on his fingers how long it had been since Harry had moved back to Longhurst. How long since he had opened up the oldest part of the house, the east wing, and moved into Cyril's old suite of rooms.

"Do you remember how shaky, how weird and moody and odd Harry was?" he asked me. "What if this is why? Lead poisoning. It used to happen to artists all the time, from the lead in their paints. Killed Caravaggio when he was thirty-eight, but not before he murdered a man in a brawl, fell out with all his patrons, and got arrested for wandering around with a sword, probably the same sword he famously poked a hole in his own ceiling with to let more light in to paint by. Oddball behavior, just like Harry, right? Then there's Goya, and his transformation from conventional court portraitist to painter of grotesques—the theory is that lead poisoning filled his head with demons and ghouls. And Van Gogh . . ."

"I know all that, Patrick. But what has it got to do with Harry? He wasn't a painter and even if he had been, modern paints don't poison artists."

"No, but listen: What if there was lead in the pipes? That was the oldest part of the house he had moved into, and it had never been overhauled, as far as I know. Nobody else has lived in those rooms since Cyril died."

Patrick was already looking up the effects of lead poisoning on his phone. "Here you go: irritability, loss of motor control, slurred speech, headaches, tiredness. Does that not sound familiar?"

He continued reading, eyes widening. "Fits of rage. Hallucinations. Caroline, do you think that lead poisoning might partly explain Cyril's behavior too?"

Perhaps, I conceded. How many years, after all, had Cyril been rattling around in there, drinking that water, bathing in it, brooding on his grief? Was it any wonder that he grew stranger and stranger, his fixations becoming increasingly sinister and bizarre? Even now, not all of the eighteen bodies at Longhurst had been identified. Still, the police were working through old missing person reports. Searching for newspaper stories about grave robberies. Checking morgue records.

"In a way," Patrick said when he read the news that morning that Longhurst's new owner, a property developer, was planning to keep only the façade of the original building and turn the rest into luxury flats, "it's for the best that they're knocking the bloody place down."

AFTER JANE HERRIES'S INTERMENT, there is no wake, just tea and coffee in the hall next door. A member of her family approaches to thank us.

There is still, of course, one mystery left unsolved.

For six months, Dave White has been in talks with Tate Modern about the two *Self-Portraits as Sphinx*. His suggestion being that he loans both paintings to the gallery, that they hang opposite each other, the overpainted one directly facing the untouched. It is an elegant idea and one the Tate is quite taken by. The problem is, we still have no convincing explanation of how Juliette could have painted both pieces.

About once a week, Dave White messages me to ask if I have worked it out. Sometimes, lying half awake next to Patrick in the early hours of the morning, I feel like I might be on the cusp of putting it all together, but by the time I wake up fully it has always slipped away again.

It is as I am talking to one of Jane Herries's distant relatives in the hall after the service, as they are showing me pictures on their phone of her sister, Helen, in later life, and I am searching for similarities, a family resemblance, between the face of this smiling old woman and the pictures of Jane that newspapers printed in the 1930s, that something occurs to me.

Outside, from the car park, before I have even worked out the time difference in Dubai, I call Dave.

He answers straightaway. "Have you got it?"

"Maybe. Your facial recognition software—it's designed to factor in aging, isn't it? Can it also *predict* how someone's face might change, as they get older?"

"Yes, pretty accurately, as it happens."

"If I send an image to you, how long will it take to process?"

Dave says it won't take more than a couple of minutes. I google Juliette Willoughby. Her passport photo, the one I found in the Willoughby Bequest all those decades ago, comes up. I send this to Dave with the request that he age her six decades.

"You want me to make twenty-one-year-old Juliette Willoughby a very old woman? It would be more reliable if we had more images, but I'll try."

Patrick has come out of the hall to check if I am okay. I give him a thumbs-up. He goes back in again. My heart is fluttering in my chest. Years ago, in our very first supervision, Patrick said that there were two things everyone knew about Juliette Willoughby. That all her work was lost and that she died in a fire in Paris in 1938. It was now an established fact that only one of those things was true. The thought that had suddenly occurred to me was that perhaps neither was.

That perhaps Juliette had somehow survived the fire but had believed her painting destroyed. That she had painted it again. That she had somehow, perhaps with Quentin's assistance, planted it at Longhurst, along with a trail of clues—the journal in the library, the photograph in the Witt—that would one day lead someone to it and enable them to identify it when they did. Which led Patrick and me to it—except that somehow, by some quirk of fate, the painting we stumbled across there was not the repainted version but the original, the one Austen Willoughby had overpainted to conceal its message but not destroyed.

My phone buzzes in my bag. I grab it. The message is from Dave. "Any help?" it reads. Attached to the message is an image. I click on it.

"My God," I say aloud. "Oh my God."

Because I am looking at the face of Juliette Willoughby, a Juliette Willoughby who did not tragically die at the age of twenty-one but who survived to live a long, full life.

I am looking at the face of the woman who painted one of the great masterpieces of twentieth-century art, twice.

I am looking at the face of a woman who once spoke to me passionately, movingly, of the ways in which women's art is neglected and forgotten and destroyed; of what it might mean, and what it might take, to try to recover what has been lost.

I am looking at the face of a woman I once knew.

I am looking at the face of Alice Long.

ACKNOWLEDGMENTS

As ever, we have many, many people to thank. First, our daughter, who is constantly coming up with great ideas for books (all involving unicorns at the moment).

Collette would like to thank Eleanor O'Carroll, Sagar Shah, and Tania Crabbe for their forever friendship; Rob Rafalat for great plot chat; Martyn and Rachel Lauder-Lyons, Susan Henderson, Vanessa Newton, and Sam Cooper for letting us stay while we were finishing final edits. To Nads and Tanny, for being wonderful hosts.

Paul would like to thank, for their friendship and support over the years: Cara Jennings, Sarah Jackson, Julia Jordan, Louise Joy, Eric Langley, David McAllister, James Martin, Neel Mukherjee, Adrian Poole, Peter Robinson, Kevin Rowe, Claire Sargent, Oliver Seares, Katy Stewart-Moore, Tom Stewart-Moore, Jane Vlitos, John Vlitos, Irene Vlitos-Rowe, my former colleagues at the University of Surrey, and my new colleagues at the University of Greenwich.

Thank you to our first readers, who offered brilliant insight as always—Karolyn Fairs, Holly Watt, Catherine Jarvie, Cath Jeffries, and Frances Christie. And to those who read and blurbed so swiftly (and enthusiastically): Harriet Tyce, Charlotte Philby, John Marrs, Louise Candlish, Harriet Walker, Celia Walden, Lizzie Pook, Mark Edwards, Claire Douglas, Gytha Lodge, Freya Berry, Katy Hays,

Dominic Smith, and BA Shapiro. We are hugely grateful and big fans of you all.

To our super agents Emma Finn at C&W and Hillary Jacobson at CAA, and our wonderful editors Francesca Pathak and Sarah Stein—we rely on all of you for smart advice, intelligent edits, and general cheerleading. We feel very lucky to have you. To David Howe, a special thank-you for helping us master the dreaded Adobe, Saida Azizova, Kate Burton and the C&W rights team, Luke Speed, Jason Richman and Addison Duffy at UTA, and the fantastic PR, production, design, sales, and marketing teams at HarperCollins US and Pan Macmillan UK, as well the international editors and publishers whom we work with worldwide. And a special huge thank-you to Siobhan Hooper for designing our wonderful cover and Julia Karkoszka for allowing us to use her stunning photograph that features on it.

This book was a labor of love, but one in which we were offered innumerable helping hands by very generous people. Rhys Davies for your expertise on the UAE legal system, and Martin Longeran for invaluable firsthand insight into what happens when things do go wrong. Frances Christie for your art world knowledge. Lisa Redlinski at the Courtauld, thank you for a tour around the Witt Library. To Peter Paul Biro and Nicholas Eastaugh, thank you for your advice on the process of art authentication. To Chris Nichols for making sure we got the AI element right, Danny Luhde-Thompson for putting up with our endless questions about clever techy things, and Cressida Pollock for being someone we can fling almost any question at. And to Sebastian Isaac, for whom we always seem to have some odd legal query.

Juliette Willoughby may be a fictional character, but we hope this book may lead to readers reflect on the ways in which women artists have so often been undermined and overlooked, and introduce those who haven't yet encountered them to the extraordinary women of the Surrealist movement. The following works inspired and informed our novel and we hope they will inspire and inform those who wish to find out more about the themes, periods, and topics it explores.

ON WOMEN AND SURREALISM: Susan L. Aberth, *Leonora Carrington: Surrealism, Alchemy and Art* (London: Lund Humphries, 2010); Gabriel Weisz Carrington, *The Invisible Painting: My Memoir of Leonora Carrington* (Manchester: Manchester University Press, 2021); Mary Ann Caws, Rudolf Kuenzlie, and Gewn Raaberg, eds, *Surrealism and Women* (Cambridge/London: MIT Press, 1991); Whitney Chadwick, *The Militant Muse: Love, War and the Women of Surrealism* (London: Thames and Hudson, 2017); Whitney Chadwick, *Women Artists and the Surrealist Movement* (London: Thames and Hudson, 1991); Whitney Chadwick, *Women, Art and Society, Sixth Edition* (London: Thames and Hudson, 2020); Briony Fer, Davis Batchelor, Paul Wood, *Realism, Rationalism, Surrealism: Art Between the Wars* (New Haven: Yale University Press, 1993); Katy Hessel, *The Story of Art Without Men* (London: Hutchinson Heinemann, 2022); Carol Jacobi, *Out of the Cage: The Art of Isabel Rawsthorne* (London: Thames and Hudson, 2021); Honey Luard, ed., *Dreamers Awake*, int. Alyce Mahon (catalogue to the exhibition *Dreamers Awake* at White Cube Bermondsey, curated by Susanna Greeves; London: White Cube, 2017); Alyce Mahon, ed., *Dorothea Tanning* (London: Tate, 2018); Jemima Montagu, *The Surrealists: Revolutionaries in Art and Writing, 1919-35* (London: Tate, 2002); Joanna Moorhead, *The Surreal Life of Leonora Carrington* (London: Virago, 2017); Jennifer Mundy, *Surrealism: Desire Unbound* (London: Tate Publishing, 2002); Rozsika Parker and Griselda Pollock, *Old Mistresses: Women, Art and Ideology* (London: Bloomsbury, 2021); Desmond Morris, *The Lives of the Surrealists* (London: Thames and Hudson, 2018); Oliver Shell and Oliver Tostmann, eds., *Monsters and Myths: Surrealism and War in the 1930s and 1940s* (New York: Rizzoli Electa, 2018).

ON SURREALIST MEN: IAN Gibson, *The Shameful Life of Salvador Dalí* (London: Faber and Faber, 1997); Mark Polizzotti, *Revolution in the Mind: The Life of André Breton* (Boston: Black Widow Press, 2009); Robert Hughes, *The Shock of the New* (London: Thames and Hudson,

1991); Ian Turpin, *Max Ernst* (2nd edition; London: Penguin, 1993);
Man Ray, *Self Portrait* (London: Penguin, 2012 [first published 1963]).

ON COUNTRY HOUSES, THEN and now: Adrian Tinniswood, *The Long
Weekend: Life in the English Country House before the War* (London:
Vintage, 2016); Adrian Tinniswood, *Noble Ambitions: The Fall and
Rise of the Post-War Country House* (London: Jonathan Cape, 2021).

ON ANCIENT EGYPTIAN HIEROGLYPHS, papyri, and "curses": Eleanor
Harris, *Ancient Egyptian Magic* (Newburyport, MA: Weiser Books,
2015); Barry J. Kemp, *Ancient Egypt: Anatomy of a Civilization, Third
Edition* (London: Routledge, 2018); Roger Luckhurst, *The Mummy's
Curse: The True History of a Dark Fantasy* (Oxford: Oxford University
Press, 2012); Ilona Regulski, ed., *Hieroglyphs: Unlocking Ancient Egypt*
(London: British Museum Press, 2022); Evelyn Rossiter, *The Book of
the Dead: Papyri of Ani, Hunefer, Anhaï* (Fribourg: Productions Liber,
1979); E.A. Wallis Budge, *The Egyptian Book of the Dead* (London:
Penguin, 2008 [first published 1899]); Penelope Wilson, *Hieroglyphs: A
Very Short Introduction* (Oxford: Oxford University Press, 2003).

ON SPHINXES: CHRISTIANE ZIVIE-COCHE, *Sphinx: History of a Mon-
ument* (Cornell: Cornell University Press, 2002).

ON PARIS IN THE 1930s: Henri Béhar et al., *Guide du Paris Surréaliste*
(Paris: Éditions du patrimoine, 2012); Charles Douglas, *Artist Quar-
ter: Modigliani, Montmartre and Montparnasse* (London: Pallas Athene,
2023; first published 1941); Julian Jackson, *The Fall of France* (Oxford:
Oxford University Press, 1940); Mary McAuliffe, *Paris on the Brink*
(London: Rowman and Littlefield, 2018); Sue Roe, *In Montparnasse:
The Emergence of Surrealism in Paris from Duchamp to Dalí* (London:

Fig Tree, 2018); George Melly and Michael Woods, *Paris and the Sur-realists* (New York: Thames and Hudson, 1991).

ON THE ART MARKET, auctions, forgery and authenticity: Anthony M. Amore, *The Art of the Con: The Most Notorious Fakes, Frauds and Forgeries in the Art World* (New York: St Martin's Griffin, 2015); Noah Charney, *The Museum of Lost Art* (London: Phaidon, 2018); Thomas Hoving, *False Impressions: The Hunt for Big-Time Art Fakes* (New York: Touchstone, 1996); Philip Mould, *Sleepers: In Search of Lost Old Masters* (London: Fourth Estate, 1993); Philip Mould, *Sleuth* (London: Harper, 2011); Laney Salisbury and Aly Sujo, *Provenance: How a Con Man and a Forger Rewrote the History of Modern Art* (London: Penguin, 2010).

ON DUBAI: MARTIN LONERGAN, *Dubai: A Tale of Two Cities* (London: BigFoot, 2021).

WE SHOULD ALSO MENTION the following works written by Surreal-ist artists: André Breton, *Mad Love* (Lincoln: University of Nebraska Press, 1897; first published 1937); André Breton, *Manifestoes of Sur-realism*, trans. Richard Seaver and Helen R. Lane (Ann Arbor: Ann Arbor Paperbacks, 1972); (Salvador Dalí, *The Secret Life of Salvador Dalí* (New York: Dial Press, 1942); Leonora Carrington, *Down Below* (New York: NYRB Classics, 2017 [first published 1945]); Dorothea Tanning, *Birthday* (Santa Monica/San Francisco: Lapis Press, 1986); Dorothea Tanning, *Between Lives: An Artist and Her World* (New York: W. W. Norton, 2001).

ELLERY LLOYD is the pseudonym for the London-based husband-and-wife writing team of Collette Lyons and Paul Vlitos. Collette studied art history at Trinity College, Cambridge, and worked as a journalist and editor in Dubai and London. Paul is the author of two previous novels, *Welcome to the Working Week* and *Every Day Is Like Sunday*. He is Professor of Creative Writing at the University of Greenwich.